Praise for *Links*

"Witty, heartfelt, and emotionally sat?
second-chance romance! Once I picked ?

New York Times best-se??? ?n

"A second-chance romance at its finest . . . s?   ?n, sexy,
and romantic. This story is definitely on my top   ?or the year."

Sassy Book Lovers

"Simply put, *Links* will make you fall in love."

The Book Blvd

"I adored this book start to finish . . . The writing was stellar with witty
banter, clever humor, and smirk-a-minute teasing exchanges. Lisa
Becker is a comedic genius and my new favorite author."

Books & Bindings

"WOW!!! Now I remember why I love Lisa Becker's writing style and
stories so much! This is another one to add to the shelves, my friends.
You are going to fall head over heels for Charlotte and Garrett's story."

Pretty Little Book Reviews

"This book has a good dose of comedy, especially with the secondary
characters. It's funny, sweet, romantic, and will show you that people
can change when the time is right."

The Bookery Review

"If you're looking for a perfect summer read, this is one you should pick
up."

Lisa Loves Literature

"*Links* by Lisa Becker is the perfect summer read . . . light and quick."

Devilishly Delicious Book Reviews

"Becker has spun a wonderful story about second-chance romance that will have you smiling and wishing this was a series."

So Many Reads Review

"*Links* is a relatively quick and light read. I loved some of the comedic moments and the t-shirts that Charlotte wears with quirky sayings. If there was a sequel or spin-off to this book I would not hesitate to read it."

Much Loved Books

"*Links* is a fun, delightful story that I devoured on my vacation. It is the perfect getaway book that leaves you with a good feeling."

The Book Bag

"One of the best romantic chases I have read."

Donna Huber, Girl Who Reads

"A quick, light, and fun read. Seriously, this book can be devoured in one sitting. The characters and quick-wit banter make you breeze through the pages, all the while laughing and shaking your head at their antics."

Cozy Books and Coffee

"I loved this story. It's light, fun, sexy, and smart."

Two Book Pushers

"This was a feel-good read, one that had me smiling from ear to ear and one that left me with the warm and fuzzies."

The Romance Cover

"All the snark delivered with heart, all the friendship and love to spare truly made this an enjoyable read."

Satisfaction for Insatiable Readers

"If you are looking for a witty, snarky, and cute romantic comedy, then you have definitely come to the right place with *Links*."

Comfy Reading Blog

Praise for *Clutch*

"I thought the comparison to men and handbags was so genius! Becker really knows how to write to her audience, and this clever novel had me giggling throughout."

Chick Lit Plus

"LOVED. The perfect blend of sassy, smart, and stylish!"

Amazon Bestsellers Liz Fenton & Lisa Steinke

"*Clutch* is a bit like *Sex and the City* meets *Fifty Shades of Grey* sprinkled with a bit of *Bridget Jones's Diary*. It is a fun and lighthearted read and highly enjoyable."

By the Letter Book Reviews

"I loved every minute reading this book!"

Girls with Books

"Fun, witty, and sure to have you laughing and shaking your head!"

Pages Abound

"Becker always delivers a fun, feisty novel that I typically read in just two or three nights. I loved every chapter."

Marika Flatt, PR by the Book

"Do yourself a favor read *Clutch*; I promise you this story will put a smile on your face, and at times, it will melt your heart."

The Kindle Book Review

"She creates characters and stories that are realistic, engaging, and full of charisma."

Radiant Reviews

"*Clutch* was such a fun and lighthearted story. It easily kept me engaged and entertained as Caroline and Mike's opposite approach to dating is full of dramatic and hilarious twists and turns."

Jersey Girl Book Reviews

"The writing is simple yet smart and detailed . . . If you are looking for a sweet and sexy romance, then *Clutch* is for you."

"*Clutch* is a quick and entertaining read about a woman looking for her one true love. I had so much fun reading Caroline's love adventure. Never a dull moment."

"*Clutch* is a light, fluffy read which is a must-read if you're on the lookout for a cute, short chick lit to devour in one sitting!"

"Grab a bottle of Caroline's favorite wine, Chardonnay, and sit back and enjoy this fun dating tale!"

"As with the Click series, Becker writes good characters, with great, witty dialogue."

"This book is absolutely hilarious."

"I adored everything about this book—the plot, characters, humor, and witty banter. The writing style was crisp, engaging, highly enjoyable, consistently entertaining, and lushly descriptive. I think I have a girl crush . . ."

"*Clutch* is a wonderful, entertaining look at the dating world, and I can guarantee that you will start thinking about what category of bag the guys you meet would fall into after reading this book. What fun."

Also by Lisa Becker

The Click Trilogy
Click: An Online Love Story
Double Click
Right Click

Links

Clutch: A Novel

STARFISH

Jane,
ROCK
ON!
All the best,
Lisa Becker

LISA BECKER

For SJB—my rock and my rock star

One

MARIN

"Dress for the job you want." Mom always used to say that. I remember watching her get ready for work when I was a little girl. She always took great care to select classic, elegant pieces she could mix and match together for a sleek, professional look. She was a secretary for a rich investment banker at a high-end brokerage firm in our hometown of Roseville, California, outside Sacramento. Little did I know she was dressing for the job *she* really wanted—*wife* to a rich investment banker at a high-end brokerage firm.

I was nine then, and it's been fifteen years since she left me and my dad for her boss. It's also been fifteen years since I've taken much stock in anything she has to say, but "dress for the job you want" stuck with me and has served me well as I prepare for my orientation for a summer internship with Sasha V PR, the most prestigious boutique public relations firm on the West Coast. Everyone from major tech brands to television shows wants to work with Sasha's agency, which specializes in branding, media relations, social marketing, and promotion.

While Sasha runs a rather casual office, I'm dressed smartly (in black pants, a pink silk blouse, and structured grey jacket) for the job *I* want—the four-month stint at Zamon, a tech company in Seattle that Sasha's firm represents. Sasha hires four new graduates every summer and gives them a four-month position. If you survive, you either get offered a full-time job with her or one of her clients. Or, if she likes you, you can write a ticket to a job anywhere, as a recommendation from her opens doors. It's *that* prestigious and rigorous and I'm absolutely up for the challenge. Sasha seems to think so too, having recruited me right out of my master's program in communications from the University of Southern California. Not to mention I need a job. The insurance money can only take me so far.

I arrive early to the El Segundo offices, which are only an eight-minute drive from the apartment in Manhattan Beach I share with my college roommate, Grace. Our dwelling is a one-bedroom place above a larger family home located right off the strand. It's kind of small for the two of us and the rent is pretty expensive given the size, but you can't beat the location. It comes with two parking spaces, so we never have to worry about finding a spot by the beach. It's also walking distance to a fantastic dive bar with dollar beer specials on weekdays. So, there's that.

As I enter the offices, I find myself in the elevator with an attractive woman. She's my exact opposite in many ways. She's tall, thin, and leggy, where I'm lucky to break five foot five in my highest heels and have a curvy ass and thighs. She's got long blonde hair in stark contrast to my shoulder-length brown bob. A heavily made-up face with perfectly blended eye shadow, blush-covered cheekbones, and pouty, pink-coated lips stares back at me. I'm more comfortable with a quick swipe of lip gloss and a basic coat of mascara. She's wearing tight, dark-wash jeans; chunky, high-heeled boots; and a clingy, taupe-colored top, in contrast to my more conservative attire. Not to mention her clingy top sure shows off something quite different from my physique. She's got boobs—big ones. Maybe even fake ones given their size in relation to her skinny legs. Hello jealousy! Thanks to some padding from the geniuses at Victoria's Secret, I can pass for a B cup.

She looks young and when she pushes the third-floor button—despite the fact I've already pushed it and it's lit up—I figure she works for Sasha.

"Do you work at Sasha V?" I ask, as the elevator takes us up to the third floor.

"Yeah. I start a summer internship today," she says, turning to look at me. "I'm Brynn."

"Marin Collins." I hold out my hand for a shake. We make small talk while we wait for the other interns to arrive and I learn Brynn grew up in Beverly Hills and her father is a famed plastic surgeon. (Explains the boobs.) She studied communications and music at UCLA. She's smart and nice and I'm guessing we'd get along well. Too bad I'll be off to Seattle in a few days' time and won't get the chance to know her better.

We're soon joined by two guys—Rich and Pete, who both graduated with MBAs from Wharton and the University of Texas, respectively. Rich looks straight out of a Brooks Brothers catalog. I'm guessing he's a finance guy because his eyes light up when he hears the phrase *loan-to-value*, much like mine do when someone mentions tacos. Pete talks slowly with his slight southern drawl but gestures a lot with his hands and has a rather gross habit of biting his nails. He doesn't seem to have a particular niche, but I'm sure Sasha's got the perfect spot for him.

After meeting the company executives, the four of us spend the day going through human resource issues including payroll and tax forms, technology tutorials, and a review of the Sasha V Company Code of Ethics. Before I know it, it's six fifteen and we're dismissed for the day. As I'm walking out, Sasha calls me into her office.

"Take a seat, Marin." She gestures to a white leather couch. I dutifully obey. One thing I've learned about Sasha in the short time I've known her: you dutifully obey. Even at the young age of forty-two, she's already a legend in the industry. We read various case studies in grad school about projects she and her company worked on, from the launch of the first virtual reality headsets for consumer use to the passage of Proposition 22, a controversial piece of state legislation. She's savvy and shrewd and very successful. I want to be just like her.

After confirming I've had a good first day she says, "I know we spoke about this before you came on, but I wanted to confirm you are okay relocating and traveling."

"Yes," I reply, my heart racing. This is it. She's going to offer me the temp job in Seattle.

"Good. Assignments will be made tomorrow, but I hope you don't mind rain," she says with a wink.

When I get home, I tell Grace the good news and we head to our local bar for a few cheap beers.

"I'm going to miss you," Grace whines.

"I know and thank you for saving my room for me while I'm gone. But you'll have the whole apartment to yourself. Just think of all the fun you can have without sharing a bedroom for four months," I offer, raising my eyebrows up and down. Grace and I have literally shared a room since junior year of college when we moved out of the dorms into our first apartment. During that time, we've had boyfriends, which always made for some awkward encounters and tedious coordination. We've both been single for a while now and honestly that's easier.

"Ah yes. All the crazy sex I'm going to have . . . by myself," she finishes. I almost do a spit take before choking. "You okay?" She hits me between my shoulder blades.

"I'm fine." I raise my hand to ward off more pounding on my back.

"I know you think I'm joking, but I'm serious here. It's not like they're lining up on my doorstep and without my wing woman . . ." Her voice trails off.

"I'm sorry," I explain.

"You don't need to be sorry. It's only for a few months and then you'll be back, right?" Her eyes are bright and she shares a hopeful smile.

"Right," I assure her. But the truth is, I don't know what will happen. If things work out, I could stay in Seattle for good. If they don't, I'll take a job wherever I can find one. Mom always said money doesn't grow on trees. Of course she had to be right about that one.

TWO

I don't even know why I'm here and I mean that on so many levels. First off, why the fuck do I have to be in an office to meet some intern we're hiring to do promotions and marketing while we're on our summer tour? Why can't Damon just handle this crap on his own? He's the manager. That's what we pay him for, and believe me, we've made him a very rich man.

Not that I'm complaining. I've made a shit ton of money these past few years. After toiling away in crap bars and small venues, Damon landed us a small label deal, which led to opening for Maroon 5 a few years ago, which led to a three-album deal with Atlantic Records, which led to some Grammy nods and now headlining our own tour.

We're finally big enough to draw the crowds on our own. We're not big enough to garner the private charter plane to take us from venue to venue though—that's when you reach the Maroon 5 level. And that's what's next—at least Damon says so. In fact, he's even betting a big bonus from us that he can make it happen and that's why he's having us hire someone to help us raise our profile.

I don't care about reaching the next level. I'm grateful we've at least graduated from the bus tour where you sleep in those little coffin-like pods, packed in like goddamn sardines. We'll still travel by bus, but this time we're staying in hotels overnight. Until you've traversed the country in a crowded bus with a bunch of sweaty, horny guys with little privacy, women throwing their tits in your face, a steady stream of booze and drugs, and hours and hours with nothing but landscape to stare at, you won't appreciate a private hotel room and real shower.

Over these past few years, I've mellowed out on the whole scene. The constant partying and spread legs don't do it for me like they did in the beginning. I know this next statement is going to make me sound like an ungrateful bastard, but every day I question why I'm even in this band. Yeah, sure, I can play guitar and I've written a few songs attracting the attention of some prominent people in the business, but music was never my dream. That belonged to my older brother Craig. He was always the one who dreamed of being a rock star.

Growing up, both of our parents were busy as teachers at the local high school. Dad taught computer science and was pretty damn good at it . . . when he wasn't nursing a hangover. I got my love of computers from him. When he was in a good mood, I loved helping him build and program them. When he was in a shitty mood though, you'd want to be anywhere else. That's when I started to follow Craig around.

Mom was too busy to insulate us from all Dad's issues. She taught music and took extra jobs playing the organ at weddings or giving piano lessons on the side to make money to supplement what Dad spent on whiskey. Even though she had a lot on her plate, she did make sure Craig and I had an instrument in our hands by the time we could walk. We both learned piano first and then showed an aptitude for string instruments. I started with viola and within a year had mastered the guitar, cello, violin, and even the ukulele—pretty much any string instrument you can find.

Craig took to the bass guitar. He would listen to Metallica, Red Hot Chili Peppers, Led Zeppelin, and the Who for hours, watch their videos on YouTube, and had posters of John Entwistle and Flea on his walls. He was set on perfecting the craft and being a famous musician one day. To that end, when he was thirteen, he started a garage band and let me (at age nine) play along. It was the two of us, Oliver Eastland (who remains the band's keyboardist), and a hot chick named Tabitha who served as lead singer.

At the time, I had a serious case of hero worship. I would do anything to spend time with Craig and his friends. I thought they were so cool, and it was nice to be accepted, even if they did make fun of me for messing around with my computers.

After learning a few songs, we were ready to play some local gigs. Craig let his high school friend Damon join as our manager and he booked us appearances at local events like the annual Strawberry Festival near our home in Camarillo, California, midway between Los Angeles and Santa Barbara. We played more gigs and when I graduated from high school, we all moved to Hollywood to make our dreams—or I should say *their* dreams—come true. For me, it was more about spending time with the guys than the music. Don't get me wrong. It was fun, and I was good at it, but if I had my way, I would be rebuilding hard drives, coding, and getting my full computer geek on.

Craig said, though, if we'd stick together, we could make it far. We'd get away from our dad, the sleepy town where we're from, and one day kids would have posters of *our band* on their walls. Once we hit the LA club scene, Tabitha decided band life wasn't for her. We hooked up with our lead singer, Jase, and our drummer, Johnny, refined our sound, and formed what is now Kings Quarters. Fast forward to today: we just wrapped up a four-month spring tour and are ready to embark on a four-month summer tour.

Craig couldn't be more psyched to get back on the road. He gets a major rush from the crowd each night when we play. Plus, his long-time girlfriend, Phoebe, is along on tour with us. Looks like he's got everything he's ever wanted all wrapped up in a neat little bow.

If only it were that simple for me. I know I sound like a thankless prick . . . I've been blessed many times over. But it's not fulfilling me the way I want it to and I don't see any way out. How could I crush Craig's dream to pursue my own?

I'm reviewing computer code on my phone when in walks this tall blonde, who I'm guessing is our summer intern. She's attractive in an obvious, Malibu Barbie kind of way. I'm not the only one who thinks so. Jase, our lead singer, can't stop making eyes at her, and by the way she's looking back at him, it seems to be mutual. What do I care? At least someone should be getting some.

Not that I should be complaining in that area too. Once again, I sound like an asshole. There's no shortage of available and willing participants for guys like me. But after a while, the one-night stands and anonymous sex with girls who just want to bang a guy in a band . . . it gets old.

I jot down an idea for my video game—one where you choose poorly in a manager and he steals money from you—and look up to see Sasha and Damon huddled together in a corner. Sasha asks the blonde (I never even paid attention to her name) to leave and calls out for someone else to join us. Whatever. I go back to reviewing code and then there's an incredible smell of vanilla in here. Like the air freshener Phoebe sprays on the bus to kill the stench of us guys. Or like one of those scented candles you light to get everything smelling sweet and clean. I look up and, fuck me, it's a brunette wearing a brown dress that wraps around her body, showing off a curvy ass that's just begging for a squeeze.

"Marin, let me introduce you to Damon Grimes, Jase Conners, Oliver Eastland, Johnny Davidson, and the Osterhauser brothers, Brad and Craig," says Sasha, gesturing around the room to each of us.

"Nice to meet you all," the girl replies, shaking Damon's hand, as he's the only one who extended his to her. I would have gotten up, but I've sprouted a hard-on at the sight of her.

Damon gives her a good look up and down, which pisses me the hell off. I don't know a thing about this girl, yet I'm already feeling protective and possessive. Perched atop her head is a pair of tortoiseshell frames. Dear Lord. She's like all my hot geek girl fantasies come true. *Put them on,* I try to communicate telepathically. *Put them on.*

"I was hoping you could tell Damon a bit about your master's thesis," says Sasha.

"Sure." She taps a few buttons on the iPad she's holding and reaches for the glasses. *That's it. Put them on. Put them on . . . Bingo!* "My thesis centered on the impact of search engine optimization on social media metrics." She turns the screen to Damon. "I created an algorithm which enhances SEO metrics by 0.000003 percent, which may not sound like a lot but could result in millions of new impressions annually," she explains.

Fuck. She's smart. Super smart and hot. This girl is a perfect ten in my book, especially compared to the skinny blonde who was here earlier.

"She's perfect," says Damon, turning to Sasha with a big smile.

THREE

These must be the guys from Zamon. I'm guessing Damon is one of the founders and put the "-amon" in the Zamon brand name. He said I was "perfect." Inside I'm jumping up and down, but on the outside, I try to maintain a sense of calm professionalism. Things move fast in the tech space and I don't want these guys to think I'll get rattled.

I look around the room and inspect my client. They look familiar and I'm guessing it's from all the research I did on the company ahead of time. Three of the guys look like typical, hipster tech dudes, wearing faded jeans, worn-out sneakers, and t-shirts. Johnny (I think his name was) must be one of the coders. His eyes are all bloodshot and he looks like he hasn't gotten much sleep. Must be burning the midnight oil on some new app.

The last guy though, he's gotten my attention. He's cute. No, more than cute. He's pretty hot. He's kind of got a Clark Kent thing going with black-framed glasses and dark wavy hair that's begging to be tugged. Hard. *Really, Marin? You know better than to get involved with someone you work with. Don't want to end up a cliché like dear old Mom.*

"Well, Marin," Sasha says. "Let me introduce you to your new client. This is Kings Quarters. Damon is the manager and *Rolling Stone* called these gentlemen 'the next big thing.'" Kings Quarters?

"Wait. What?" I ask.

"This is your assignment. For the next four months, you will be on the final leg of the band's tour."

I'm in absolute shock. "I thought I was going to Seattle to work with Zamon." I exhale and shake my head in disbelief.

"I'm sure you can see what a tremendous opportunity this is for you, Marin," Sasha says in a firm tone.

"I just . . . you said . . . I thought . . ." I stammer out. I look around and all six of the guys are staring at me. "I . . . I can't wait," I say with a forced smile.

"Great. Amy and I will meet with you in a bit to go through all the details. In the meantime, why don't you check in with HR and make sure all your paperwork is in order?"

"Sure." I turn and walk out the door, straight to the ladies' room. I open a stall, lock the door, lower myself onto the toilet, and cry. I don't know anything about rock bands except what I've seen in movies. Someone enters the restroom and I dry my eyes with some toilet paper. When the stall door next to me opens and then closes, I slip out of my stall and walk outside. With shaky hands, I pull the cell phone from my dress pocket and dial Grace.

"Hello girlie," she begins. "What's up?" I hear her shuffling paper in the background and regret interrupting her day. She has a demanding job as an assistant to an agent at one of the world's top talent agencies.

"I'm not going to Seattle," I tell her, trying hard to keep the tears at bay.

"Yes!" she exclaims and I imagine her standing up and doing an exaggerated fist pump. "Oh, sorry. I know you wanted the

Zamon assignment but I'm happy you won't be leaving me for four months."

"I'm not going to be home either."

"Where are you going?" All of a sudden the shuffling of papers ceases as she gives me her complete attention.

"I don't know."

"You don't know? Well, did they give you an assignment yet or are you still waiting to hear? What was the reason you didn't get the Zamon job?"

"I don't know why I didn't get the Zamon job. Sasha didn't say. I did get an assignment, though. I'm going on tour with a band."

"A band?" she asks in disbelief. "What kind of band?"

"Kings Quarters."

"Holy shit!" she exclaims.

"I . . . I don't even know what to do. I don't know anything about rock bands except what I've seen in the movies," I lament.

"Oooh. Movie marathon tonight." Her fingers click-clack on her keyboard. "Okay, according to *Rolling Stone*, some of the best rock band movies of all time are"—and I can imagine her scrolling through the article—"*Almost Famous*, *That Thing You Do!*, and *The Commitments*. I'll take care of getting them for tonight."

"Grace—" I start.

"It's going to be fine, Marin. You can do anything. Listen, I have to go. Bellatrix needs me to pick up her soy-free, fat-free, sugar-free, wheat-free, nut-free . . ." 'Bellatrix' is the nickname inspired by *Harry Potter* that we gave her evil boss. Grace's voice trails off, so I interject.

"Taste-free . . ."

"Ha, yes, taste-free muffin for breakfast. At almost eight bucks apiece, they are most definitely not *free*," she adds, and it's like I can hear the dramatic eye roll.

"You're kidding me, right?"

"Nope, and she has a drawer full of candy she sneaks on the side, which makes it much more comical."

"I bet you're the one who keeps the candy drawer stocked too," I laugh.

"Exactly," she agrees. "Listen, I gotta run. Let's hash this all out tonight, okay?"

"Okay," I concede.

"Love you, girlie," she adds.

"Love you too." Grace makes everything better, whether it's dragging out my secrets so they aren't bottled up inside, inviting me into her family holidays celebrations, or making me laugh with hilarious—and oft inappropriate—changes in conversation.

I walk back into the building and up to the third floor. I make a quick stop in the ladies' room to make sure I don't have mascara running down my face, and head over to see Judy in Human Resources.

"What can I do for you, Marin?" she asks.

"Sasha asked me to come in and get set up for my assignment." I take a deep calming breath so I don't break down into tears again.

"Ah yes, Seattle bound."

"Uh, no. I've been assigned to go on tour with Kings Quarters," I correct her. Judy seems surprised at first but soon recovers.

"Well, that's a great opportunity for you."

"So I've been told," I reply with a tight smile.

"Okay, then. Let me call up some of the details for you." She types some more on her computer, taps a few keys to print, and hands me some papers. I scan through them as she explains what they mean. "So, you will be issued a laptop and cell phone, which are connected to the cloud. All photos, videos, and documents will be automatically uploaded and backed up, but please don't lose these devices."

"I will guard them with my life." I cross my fingers over my heart, eliciting a laugh from Judy.

"You can take two suitcases with you and do laundry at the hotel. Charge it to the room. In some cities, you'll share a room with another woman who is on the tour. In others, you'll be assigned your own room."

"Okay." It's hitting me that I'm going to be living out of a suitcase for four months . . . traveling from city to city . . . on a bus . . . with a rock band. Bile rises from my belly and I get that icky feeling in the back of my throat. I take a deep breath to quash the nausea.

"You'll get a fifty-dollar per diem for food and incidentals. Whatever you don't spend, you keep. The money will be deposited via direct deposit into your bank account each week." An extra fifty dollars per week? Yes please! No hotel minibar or room service for me.

"Works for me," I confirm. But what kind of incidentals am I going to need on a rock band bus tour? Groupie repellant? A gas mask to combat the skunky haze of weed? I chuckle to myself as Judy slides a two-page document over to me.

"This is a non-disclosure agreement," she explains. "Please read it over, and sign and date where noted." I look through the document which outlines I will not reveal anything I learn about the band or its members to anyone without their express permission. Any photos, videos, or content I create about them must go through proper channels before distribution. The document also outlines the repercussions if I fail to adhere to the agreement: I could be fired or sued. It all seems pretty standard, so I do as instructed and slide it back over to Judy.

"All right," I say in confirmation. "Is there anything else?"

"No, but if I can make a suggestion . . ." she says with a shy shrug.

"Of course."

"I would rethink your wardrobe if I were you." I look down at the wrap-around dress I'm wearing. It's professional and classy. Dear old Mom would be proud.

"What's wrong with what I'm wearing?" I try to keep the offense out of my voice. Judy's phone rings and she answers it.

"Yes, she's here. Okay, I'll send her over when she's done." She hangs up. "That was Amy. She wants to go over things with you when we're done here."

"I'll head over there now, unless there's more we need to cover."

"No. We're finished. Just so you know, what you're wearing is well-suited for an office or a job with a tech company. Lovely. Very professional, in fact. But you're going to be on a tour with a band. You could dress a bit more . . . casual . . . to fit in." Leave it to the HR lady to be subtle about telling me I look too conservative. Could it be I'm all wrong for this assignment?

With a sigh, I leave Judy's office and walk across the way to Amy. As I walk, I map out how I'll need to hit the mall tonight to grab a few items and hope it won't make too big a dent in my credit card.

"Marin." Amy ushers me to the empty chair next to her desk. "Looks like we'll be working together on the Kings Quarters account," she says in the typical no-nonsense tone I noticed when we first met yesterday.

"Yes," I say with a tight smile.

She explains that Damon is our main client contact and that he hired us to help elevate the band's presence during this last part of their tour, with an emphasis on traditional media and online exposure. I'll be pitching and confirming interviews, arranging for transportation, and working with radio stations on ticket giveaways and backstage passes.

"You'll work with the winners and get photos and videos of them with the band, enjoying the concert and such, and post them to social media. You need to make sure they all sign a release form, which I will email to you, and that I approve of all content before it's posted." I confirm my understanding with a head nod. "I'm sure I don't need to tell you what a great opportunity this is." Hmm. Third time in the last two hours I've been told that. Too bad I remain as unconvinced as ever.

A few hours later, I'm with the other summer interns at small brew pub near the Sasha V offices comparing notes after our first day.

"Then she told me," says Pete, putting on a high feminine voice, "'I don't need to remind you what a great opportunity this is.'"

"I got that three times today," I lament.

"Where did you think you were going?" Rich asks Pete.

"In all the time I've been talking to Sasha, it sounded like I was going to be working on a microbrew account here in El Segundo. Turns out they have me slated to leave for Seattle in two days," he explains as he brings his index finger up to his mouth and gnaws on the cuticle.

Seattle? He must have gotten the Zamon job I wanted. Lucky bastard. Although judging by his tone, he doesn't see it that way.

"I'm working on the microbrew account and I don't even like beer," Brynn mock huffs as she takes a sip of her pale ale.

"Well, I couldn't be happier," says Rich. "I'm going to be working in the development office on site at RM Real Estate," he explains with a shrug. So it looks like Rich is the only one who got the job he was hoping for.

"What about you Marin? Where are you headed?" asks Pete.

"I'm going on tour with a rock band," I state with little emotion in my voice.

"Har har," says Pete with an exaggerated but playful sneer. "Seriously, what assignment did you draw?"

"I'm serious," I tell them. My lips pull into a firm line as I try to stop myself from saying something I'll regret. To keep my loose lips from sinking any ships, I take a sip of my beer.

"She speaks the truth," chimes Brynn. "That's what I was hoping for, to go on tour with Kings Quarters."

"Kings Quarters?" says Rich, nodding his head, impressed. "No shit. That's cool."

"I'm sure for Brynn it would be, but I was hoping to go to Seattle," I say out loud before realizing I shouldn't be complaining about my new job to my new coworkers. Listening to me complain is what Grace is for.

"I don't need to remind you what a great opportunity this is," Pete repeats in the same mocking tone he used earlier. I laugh out loud and raise my bottle of beer to his for a clink.

"You got that right," I laugh.

After drinks with the interns and a quick stop at the mall to pick up a few pair of jeans, some casual tops, and a pair of taupe boots to go with anything, I return home to an empty apartment. Grace isn't home yet, which doesn't surprise me.

I plop myself down on our cozy couch and grab my laptop. Kings Quarters? I know little to nothing about them. I fire up my computer and start my search. First up is the band page from their record label. It's filled with a history of the band, a list of award nominations, and photos from various gigs.

I click on the photo link page where an album scrolls across the screen with photos of the five guys I met earlier today. The lead singer, Jase (I'm reminded via the website), is quite the front man. He is tall and well-built—as evidenced by the many shirtless shots—and covered in colorful tattoos. He must have not long ago shaved his head, because today's look was cropped closer while many of these photos show a longer blond mop.

I'm also met with a few solo photos of the drummer, Johnny. He looks much better in the pictures than he did today. I'm not certain life on the road is agreeing with him. The keyboardist, Oliver, is much shorter than the rest of the guys but brown eyes sparkle with humor.

Last but not least, there are the two brothers—Craig and Brad. Craig is a good-looking guy with dark brown hair and brown eyes. Brad, though. He's so handsome. He looks different in these photos without the glasses he was wearing at the meeting today. I like him better with the glasses. Gives him character . . . and style . . . and hotness.

Don't go there, Marin. You work for these guys now. You above anyone, know the dangers getting involved with someone at work. It's fine to ogle him from afar, but hands—and tongues—off. Tongues? Jeez, it's been entirely too long since I've been with anyone if I've let my mind go there.

FOUR

I arrive via Uber at the designated parking lot on Thursday morning. Damon is waiting for me.

"Good morning, Marin," he says. "I'm not sure what Sasha told you, but you'll be riding on the bus with the band so we can coordinate interviews and secure photos for social media posting." I wasn't clear on the logistics but am glad Damon has it all planned out.

"Okay. Just tell me where to go," I respond.

"Have you ever done anything like this before?"

"Uh, no," I reply on a laugh. Within seconds, I course correct, remembering this is my client. "I'm certain I'm up to the task, though."

"I'm sure you'll be fine." He grabs one of my bags and I take the other. I follow him over to one of four buses lined up. People bustle about, loading equipment, bags, and food.

He takes the bag from my hand and gives both suitcases to a man I assume is the bus driver and gestures to the set up. This rock band road trip is much more of a production than I had figured. I'm not sure what I expected, but it was closer to a bunch of guys crammed into a run-down bus making its way down the highway with a cloud of marijuana smoke pluming out the windows. What I find instead is a professionally run, highly organized, perfectly synchronized effort.

"There are four buses," Damon explains. "These two are for the crew." I peek inside one and it's a standard coach transport. There's a bathroom onboard, but otherwise it's basic—albeit luxury—seating. Long trailers attach to both buses, which, judging by the stuff they're hauling, house the staging and equipment for the shows.

Damon is on the move, so I continue to follow. "This bus is for the food service. If you have any specific dietary needs or food allergies, let Karine, the head chef, know."

I read about this during my rock band research last night. It's what some of the guys affectionately call the "Roach Coach." I walk onto the bus and look around what appears to be a fully operational industrial kitchen. When a band is on tour and sleeping on the bus, there is a specific transport trailing along for food preparation equipment and staff.

"Wow! This is quite an operation," I say, my eyes widening in awe. Damon looks around, and I wonder if he's trying to see things through my newbie eyes.

"This is nothing." He gestures toward the bus. "This is a modified set up for snacks on the road, feeding the crew during set up and tear down, and of course feeding the band before and after each show. When we were sleeping on the bus overnight, we had a full-scale food service team handling every meal."

"Impressive." I take a few photos and make some notes to pitch a few behind-the-scenes stories to Amy. Damon exits the bus, so I take one last glance around and follow.

He gestures for me to get on the final bus. Inside, it looks more like a private jet than a bus. Not that I've ever been on a private jet, but I've watched enough episodes about real housewives to know swanky when I see it.

Upon first boarding, I'm met with a small kitchen complete with stainless steel stovetop, microwave, refrigerator and counter-top convection oven. While compact, this is by far much nicer and more tricked out than the kitchen in my apartment.

As I walk down the narrow bus corridor, I next find a table and chairs perfect for sitting around and playing a game of cards to pass the time. At least that's how I would pass the time when I tire of Yahtzee on my phone. Somehow though, I can't imagine a bunch of rock stars playing cards.

Next to the table is a mini living room. There are two black leather couches sitting opposite one another and several black leather swivel chairs flanking either side. Along the wall is a flat-screen TV, DVD player, and fancy gaming console. Ah, now I see how they pass the time.

Farther back in the bus is a set of bunk beds, each with its own curtain. I assume a door at the back is the bathroom. I open it up and take a peek. It's only a tiny bit bigger than an airplane lavatory, and includes a shower, but looks cleaner and more modern.

"Make yourself comfortable," Damon says. "We'll be heading out in an hour and it's about a seven-hour drive to Sacramento."

So this is where I'll be hanging for the next four months. I take a deep breath and a seat on one of the swivel chairs. There's a tray table, much like on an airplane, which pulls out from the side. I fire up my laptop and start typing up some thoughts on the traveling kitchen. It's such an interesting story to tell and could be a great pitch to morning shows or a national broadcast program like 20/20.

About thirty minutes into my memo draft, there's some commotion at the front of the bus—laughter and playful bickering.

The band has arrived. The guys all take various places on the bus, a few of them waving hello. I also notice a woman on board. She's got wavy blonde hair and green eyes. She looks like a shorter version of Taylor Swift, dressed in jeans, beat-up combat boots, and a tight-fitting Kings Quarters concert t-shirt cut to reveal a taut belly and shiny navel ring. A small gem winks from the right side of her nose, and a series of small earrings and cuffs adorn her right ear. She's got minimal makeup on but what is there looks applied with precision. She looks casual and breezy and I'm guessing it's anything but effortless. She drops a green army jacket and colorful messenger bag onto one of the couches and walks over to where I'm sitting.

"You must be Marin. I'm Phoebe."

"Nice to meet you," I respond.

"I'm so glad to have another girl with me on the bus. These guys can be quite a handful," she quips. Quite a handful? I'm not sure if she means they are a rowdy bunch of guys or if her job with the band is a bit more *personal* in nature—like a professional groupie. She doesn't look like a prostitute, but what do I know? Maybe that's how it works on these tours. Maybe they bring some women along to keep the guys, uh, *entertained*. Maybe that helps them maintain their focus, so the music comes first.

As if she can read my thoughts Phoebe adds, "I handle the makeup and hair for the band."

"Oh, that's great," I reply. So, not a prostitute. Good to know. I can't help but wonder why she hangs on the bus with the band instead of with the rest of the crew, but I know it's none of my business.

"Well, I better get some work done," I tell her with a smile.

"Sure thing. Just let me know if I can help with anything."

FIVE

We've been on the road for about an hour and Marin hasn't spoken to anyone. She's hunched over her laptop with her cell phone attached to her ear. This won't do. This won't do at all. As I'm about to slide over the aisle and talk to her, Jase walks up to her with a package of Oreos.

"PR girl," he calls over to her. Marin looks up from her laptop, pushing those glasses onto the top of her head which causes her hair to pull away. She blinks her big brown eyes up at him and smiles and it's like a punch to the gut to me. There's something . . . special . . . about this girl. I haven't put my finger on it yet, but I intend to.

"Hi Jase," she breathes. I hope she's not falling for Jase's charms. He's a good-looking dude and talented too, but he's also an arrogant asshole who rarely has an empty bed. I've barely spoken ten words to Marin, but I already know she deserves better.

"Oreo?" He holds the package of cookies out to her with the plastic cover peeled back. I can tell Marin has a bit of a sweet tooth: her pupils dilate and there's a ghost of a smile on her face. Before she reaches over to take one, she catches my eye. I subtly shake my head. She grins up at him and declines. As Jase moves over to Johnny and Oliver who are sitting at the dining table toward the front of the bus, I give her a little head nod, confirming she made a good choice. I tilt my head over to where Oliver and Johnny are both taking cookies and her eyes follow mine.

"What the fuck, man!" shouts Oliver, spitting the offending cookie out of his mouth. "That's toothpaste!" He gags and reaches into the fridge to grab a drink.

"Damn right, asshole," Jase fires back with a smile. Johnny drops his cookie on the floor and backs up, his hands up in surrender mode like he's touched poison.

"Why would you ruin a cookie like that?" challenges Oliver, taking a guzzle of diet soda.

"You googly-eyed all my fruit," retorts Jase. He waves an apple with two plastic eyeballs rolling around and around. Johnny reaches over and gives Jase a high five before doubling over with laughter and slapping his thigh. Oliver shakes his head, looking pissed.

"I should have known, douchebag." He pulls his lips together in a firm line. "Since when have you ever eaten a cookie?" he adds, more to himself than anything.

"This body is a temple," replies Jase, holding his arms out and shrugging his shoulder.

"Temple of doom, maybe," fumes Oliver. While the two of them argue, Marin walks over and snaps a photo of the decorated apple before returning to her seat.

I take this as my chance to start talking to her and move over to the seat next to hers.

"You chose . . . " I pause before completing the line from one of my favorite Indiana Jones movies.

"Wisely, right?" In that moment, she becomes even sexier. Not many girls get that reference.

"Right," I confirm. I look over her shoulder and she is writing hashtags for the photo.

"Add hashtag 'save the apples'," I suggest.

"Good one. Thanks." She looks up from her phone and catches my eye with her big brown ones. This is my first chance to take a closer look. They're the color of warm chocolate with flecks of caramel near the pupils. They're the kind of eyes that say everything yet don't give anything away. I'm eager to learn about the woman behind them.

"What?" I shake my head. I haven't heard a word she's said.

"I said, are they always like this?" she asks with a laugh.

"I suppose there's no harm in lying to you now. You're stuck with us for four months. Yes, they are always like this," I confirm with a faux-grim expression.

"Great." She smiles but it doesn't quite reach her eyes.

"So you're Marin." I reach my hand out to shake hers. "I'm Brad."

She responds with a shy "hi." At least I'm assuming it's a shy one. But what do I know? Maybe this is normal for her. I hope not. I hope she's a bit friendlier and more outgoing than this. Otherwise, all the fantasies I've had about her since we met—her exuberance, her sultriness, her inhibition—will have been just that: fantasy. I'm looking to make some of them a reality.

"Nice to—"

"Yo, B.O.!" yells Craig. I turn around in my seat and look over at him.

"I know I've said it before but why are you C.O., like commanding officer, and I'm . . . B.O.?" Craig laughs while Oliver and Johnny high five.

"Yeah, you've mentioned it only twenty or thirty times before," Craig lobs back. "If you don't like it, blame Mom and Dad." Like I don't already have enough unresolved resentment brewing there.

"Whatever." I roll my eyes. "Give me a minute." I hold up a finger before turning back to Marin.

"B.O.?" she questions with a quirked eyebrow. It's the first bit of personality I've seen so far and I gotta say, I like that sass.

"Yeah, you know, for Brad Osterhauser."

"I get it," she scoffs. Whoa. Note to self: don't question Marin's intelligence.

"When we were kids, I tried to explain Brad rhymed with 'rad,' but it didn't seem to go over so well," I shrug, which elicits a laugh.

"I'm just gonna call you B," she says, nodding her head up and down and pursing her lips. She can call me anything she wants, as long as she's calling it out while she's underneath me.

"Good idea." I mirror her head nod.

She grins.

"Anyway, I wanted to say hi and that it's cool you are coming along to do promotions for us. So, welcome."

"Yeah, should be great," she says, but something about the way she says it makes me concerned she doesn't believe it.

"Alright. Well, I'll see you around," I tell her before standing up and walking back to the guys.

"What's up with the new chick?" asks Johnny.

"She's not a chick." I slap him on the back of the head. "She's a woman and she's here to do a job, asshole."

"Well, excuse me, fucker," he retorts. "She's not my type anyway. I like 'em with big tits."

"Tits? You don't talk about Phoebe with that mouth, so don't talk about Marin like that," I warn him. He holds his hands up in front of him.

"Whoa! Easy there, cowboy."

"He doesn't talk about Phoebe like that because he knows I would kick his ass," says Craig, eliciting a fist bump from Oliver.

"That's true, but they've been together for years. You laying claim to this one?" Johnny asks with a laugh.

"I am," I say with a don't-fuck-with-me-on-this look and tone.

"Fair enough," he concedes. He puts his fist out to mine and I give it a bump. I look back at Marin, her head buried in her computer.

Yeah, this one's mine.

SIX

We stop midway to Sacramento and pull off to a rest stop big enough to accommodate our four buses and trailers. I get off the bus and hop back on right away to grab a sweater. Although it's summer, there is a cool breeze and rolling fog coming off the coast.

When I exit the bus for the second time, I'm astounded the catering crew has already set up two long tables covered with nice tablecloths and topped with silver-domed chaffing dishes. The roadie crew is already lined up to the buffet and people are helping themselves to a range of cold and hot foods from salads and sub sandwiches to pesto-encrusted chicken breast and baked lasagna. I'm amazed this fine a spread could be put together this fast and so well from this kitchen on wheels.

I get in the back of the line behind Phoebe. Craig comes up behind her and puts his hand in her back jeans pocket.

"Hey babe," she says, leaning in to give him a kiss. Now I get it. Looks like Phoebe and Craig are a thing, which explains why she's on his bus. Do the other guys in the band have a "babe" on the crew they hook up with? Or are they like the proverbial sailor with a girl in every port? Who does Brad hook up with? Does he like blondes or brunettes, skinny girls or curvy ones, big breasts or long legs? I lay my plate down on the table and remove my sweater, warmth creeping up my neck. I join a group of three and we make polite introductions: Jody, the set coordinator, Harper who oversees the lighting package, and Theo, his son and apprentice. As I learn about their roles on the tour, a voice causes me to turn and do a double take. For a moment, the short brunette looks like Grace and I'm hopeful we might be friends.

"Marin, I'm Deeana." She thrusts her hand out to me. She's got a firm grip. Almost crippling. Dad always said you could tell a lot by someone's handshake. (Too bad he couldn't tell what a sleazeball cheater Mom's boss was.) "I'm the logistics manager on the tour." Ah, so she's the one keeping the trains—or in this case, buses—running on time. Judging by her grip, she's all business.

"Nice to meet you, Deeana," I respond with a professional nod.

"I'm sorry I didn't get a chance to brief you on our protocol before today. Damon didn't inform me you would be joining the tour until late yesterday morning," she explains.

"Oh," I respond, now feeling like an afterthought, or even worse, an inconvenience.

"No worries, though. We're able to accommodate you," she says, sensing my discomfort. Part of me wonders whether she is trying to spare my feelings or convince me that, even on short notice, she's got the skills to make anything work.

"I see you've met Jody. That's great, as you two will be sharing a room for the majority of the tour. We don't have a spare room available in all the tour cities." I turn to Jody who is passing looks with Theo. I'm guessing a new roomie isn't welcome news to either of them.

"I'm sure we'll get along fine," I confirm with a forced smile.

"Sure," says Jody. Her smile doesn't reach her eyes either.

*

After lunch and another four hours on the road, we arrive at the Citizen Hotel. Damon calls the band together before disembarking the bus.

"Marin, please remind everyone of the plan for tomorrow," he instructs.

"I'll be emailing you all when we get settled, but for now, please know we have an in-studio interview and acoustic performance with a radio station at eight a.m. The car service will be here at seven fifteen. We also have three print interviews we'll do by phone in the conference room from the hotel. Those start at one thirty, so you'll have a break in the morning. Again, I'll email you all the details within the hour." No one responds. They nod and walk off the bus.

"Thanks," says Brad, and gives me a small smile.

"You're welcome." As anticipated, Deeana is waiting for us when we disembark the bus with room keys and a packet of information about the hotel amenities. I'm unsure if I should wait for my luggage.

"They'll bring your bags up to your room," offers Brad, noticing my confusion.

"Oh, thanks. First day and all," I say with a shrug.

"If you have any questions about anything, let me know. You could ask Deeana, but I wouldn't. She scares me." He gives a mock shudder and I can't help but laugh.

A half hour later, Jody unlocks the door to our room. I look up from my laptop, which I've been using to confirm appointments, update Amy, and think through some additional ideas to drive more online interaction.

"Hi there," I say to her. She takes a deep breath and looks over at the two queen beds in the room. "I wasn't sure if you preferred to be closer to the bathroom or window." I figured I would let Jody have the first pick of beds. "Take whichever bed you like."

"I'll take the one by the door." She flops a faded green army bag on the bed. She opens her mouth like she's about to say something, and shuts it.

"Listen," I tell her. "I'm getting the sense you're not thrilled about having a roommate."

"That obvious, huh?" No sense in hemming and hawing. She and Theo weren't exactly subtle.

"I've been told I'm perceptive."

"Theo shares a room with Harper and ain't no way I'm doing it with his dad in the room." With his dad in the room? Is she planning on having sex while *I'm* in the room? "If you can find a way to make yourself scarce some of the time, we'll be just fine."

"I'm sure we can work it out," I tell her.

"Good." She grabs her bag and goes into the bathroom. When the shower turns on, I lower my head into my hands and exhale. This is going to be a long four months.

SEVEN

We're sitting on the bus in traffic as we make our way from Sacramento to Eugene, Oregon. My first few days on the tour were quite the education as I learned about the people and the process of putting on a live show each night. I've confirmed all our interviews for the next few days and updated all the reports for Amy. I've even sent her a few ideas for increasing the band's online presence including some ticket giveaways in key markets linked to retweets on Twitter.

The boredom must be getting to the guys too because Brad picks up his acoustic guitar and starts to strum. I notice Jase move over next to him and tap on his knee with his hand. Before I know it, Jase is singing Bon Jovi's "Livin' on a Prayer."

By the first stanza, everyone else is singing along, except Damon, who is busy on his laptop. Even the bus driver joins in. I can't help it. The music and mood are infectious. I join in too, singing with abandon. It's fun and freeing so I belt out the chorus, letting loose about being half way there and putting my faith in a prayer.

"Whoa, whoa, hold on a minute," says Jase, putting his hands up to silence everyone. "PR girl, did you ever take singing lessons?" Everyone's eyes turn to me.

"Uh, no. I wanted to take choir in middle school, but the choir teacher told me I had a terrible voice and needed to take typing instead," I say in embarrassment.

"Good. I was going to say your choir teacher needed to be fired. She was right. You're awful," he says laughing and shaking his head. Everyone looks at me, unsure how I am going to take this. I can't help but laugh out loud—a true belly laugh.

"So true, right?" I say. Everyone else laughs along. Jase looks over at Brad to start playing again and they continue singing.

"C'mon, PR girl. Belt it out," says Jase with a smile. I smile back and sing in my loudest, boldest, and most off-key voice. When the song ends, and everyone gets back to chatting and relaxing, Brad comes over to sit by me. I look up from my laptop, where I'm working.

"Hey," he says.

"Hey, B."

"I hope you aren't offended by what Jase said and did, singling you out in front of everyone." He looks over at his friend who is talking with Damon.

"Oh gosh, no. I'm fine. I kind of like it. That good-natured ribbing makes me feel . . ." I start, unsure how to describe it. "It's like I'm a part of the gang now."

"Good. Good," he responds as he pats my knee. "So, you're a terrible singer, huh?"

"Looks that way," I reply with a fake grimace. "Or, sounds that way, I should say."

"What made you want to take choir?"

"I was in eighth grade and all the cool kids were in choir. I desperately wanted to be part of the cool crowd, so I tried out for the group. As you heard, the teacher was less than enthused with my talent. I was banished to typing class, but it worked out fine. I can type more than sixty words a minute with ninety percent accuracy. Take that Mrs. Cunningham!" I add at the end.

"Attagirl," he says with a big, cheeky grin. "So why did you want to be cool?"

"Didn't you hear my story? I was in eighth grade. That's what all girls in eighth grade want," I explain to him like he's plain silly for asking.

"Well, I think you're pretty cool," he says with pursed lips and a head nod.

"Thanks, B. I think you're pretty cool too."

"I'll let you get back to your work," he says before walking back to his seat.

EIGHT

B R A D

"B.O." says Johnny, squinting his eyes at me. "Challenge."

The trip from Eugene to Boise, Idaho, is a long one. We spent a few hours working on a new song for the next album. We're still stuck on the bridge . . . the progression of chords is just not quite right. Much to Damon's dismay, we take a break. Now we're sitting around the table with Oliver's latest contribution to our bus ride entertainment.

"Accepted," I say, squinting back at him. I break eye contact and take a hundred-dollar bill from my pile and put it into the middle of the table. Johnny grabs a Benjamin and does the same.

He spins the plastic spinner on the game board, and we watch it go around in anticipation. It lands on white. Jase fishes out two white jellybeans from a pile on the table and hands them over to Johnny.

"Gentlemen," Jase says, gesturing with his hand for us to proceed. Johnny puts one of the jellybeans on the table and examines the other one, turning it over and over in his hand, inspecting it up close to his eye. He lifts his eyes to me, winks, and pops it into his mouth. His shoulders hunch forward, and a hacking and mewling sound comes from his mouth along with some spit.

Jase and Craig laugh, heads thrown back, clutching their bellies. Oliver slaps his leg over and over as Johnny continues to choke down the tiny treat.

"I'm guessing that's"—I look at the game box cover—"spoiled milk. Which makes this one coconut." I take the other white jelly bean and pop it into my mouth. My smug attitude shifts as the acrid, putrid taste of sour milk assaults my taste buds. My stomach turns, and I spit the offending candy onto the table and grab a napkin to wipe the residue off my tongue.

Johnny laughs so hard he falls out of his chair. "You should have seen your face, dude," he says, picking himself up and resuming his seat.

"Fuck, man. That is some nasty shit," I say, unable to get the taste out of my mouth. I get up and walk to the refrigerator, pulling out a beer. I pop the top and take a large gulp. Beer drips down my chin and I use the back of my hand to wipe it off. I turn back to the table and Johnny waves the two hundred dollars around.

"What can I say, man? I hate coconut." He shrugs before laughing again. I sit down at the table and my foul mood is brightened when Marin walks over. I don't even have to turn around to know she's behind me. I can smell her sweet scent of vanilla.

"What are you guys doing?" she asks on a laugh as she leans against the table we're huddled around.

"Marin!" shouts Johnny. "Break out your camera. You gotta capture this," he instructs. She pulls her cell phone out of her pocket and taps in her passcode as Johnny continues. "Oliver brought this kick-ass game called Bamboozled."

"*Bean*Boozled," Oliver corrects him. "So you have two identical looking jellybeans," he explains, holding up two yellowish candies so Marin can see them. "One is a normal flavor like buttered popcorn," he says, putting one of them forward, "and the other one is something super nasty like rotten eggs," he continues, moving the other jelly bean toward her.

"You don't know which one you're getting," she confirms.

"Exactly!" he exclaims, with a finger pointed in the air. He turns to the rest of us. "She's a smart one, this girl," he adds before turning back to Marin. She grins and nods her head. I imagine she's thinking it doesn't take a genius to figure this game out. Johnny, not being a genius himself, explains the game further.

"You spin the spinner and have to take one of the jellybeans. You don't know if you're getting a regular flavor or something puke-worthy." Marin grins harder, and from the little I know of her, it seems she's reining in the desire to tell him, "Yeah, I get it dumbass." She's way too polite to say that to his face, but it's written all over hers. At least to me it is.

"When he says 'puke-worthy,' he literally means puke-worthy," adds Craig.

"One of them is barf-flavored," chimes in Phoebe with a cringe.

Marin shudders. "That's disgusting," she comments with a pained expression.

"I know," says Oliver with a mischievous glint in his eyes. "That's the beauty of it."

"So essentially, you try to eat your jellybean with a straight face so the person who has to take the other one doesn't know if they're eating something good or something gross," I tell her.

"Yeah, it's all about the anticipation of knowing you potentially have to eat and swallow something nasty," adds Jase.

"The anticipation of swallowing something nasty?" clarifies Craig. "So we are supposed to be filled with the same amount of dread as the girls lining up to give you blow jobs?" he chuckles. Phoebe slaps him on the arm but can't help laughing either.

"Fuck you, asshat," says Jase, rolling his eyes.

"If you spit it out you lose," laughs Johnny. "Kind of like blow jobs. You need to swallow to win." Craig reaches over and gives him a high five. Jase, conceding that was pretty damn funny, pushes his knuckles out for a fist bump.

I turn and look at Marin who is recording this all on her phone, while shaking her head at our juvenile antics. What was she expecting? We're a bunch of twenty-something dudes with time to kill and money to burn.

"What are the stakes?" she asks. "I'm sure your fans want to know."

"A hundred bucks," Jase responds like it's no big deal. She whistles through her teeth. "Want in, PR girl?"

"Too rich for a hardworking stiff like me," she chuckles.

"Here," says Oliver, tossing a hundred-dollar bill on the middle of the table. Take my turn." She hands the phone to Oliver. "Spin the spinner and challenge someone," he encourages her. Marin puts her delicate fingers on the plastic spinner and gives it a flick. While it's rounding the various jelly bean colors, she looks around the table. *Don't pick me. Don't pick me.* I don't want to look like a pussy in front of her and my taste buds haven't yet recovered from the last round.

"Jase," she says with a bright smile.

"Oh, you're on, PR girl," he croons. The spinner lands on dark brown. I fish out the two jellybeans and hand them to her. My fingers brush against her hand and electricity jolts me all the way to my toes. She lets out a little exhale. Is she affected by me too or is this nervousness about the possibility of eating something that tastes like shit? I wish I knew.

"It's either chocolate pudding or dog food," I say, clarifying on the game box.

She exhales again and looks around the table. Johnny and Oliver have huge smiles plastered on their faces. Phoebe looks nervous for her. Marin swallows and puts the candy into her mouth.

I should be watching her reaction, but I'm transfixed by her perfect pink lips. My dick hardens under the table. *Lock it down, asshole.* When I look back up at her face, she's wincing, and her shoulders are shaking a bit. She swallows with a grimace. She opens her mouth and sticks out her tongue, moving it from side to side to show she indeed swallowed the candy. At least I think it's why she's doing it. I can't think much because all my blood has rushed south.

"Your turn," she says to Jase. He looks around the table with his trademark arrogant smirk and the minute he puts the jellybean in his mouth, it's clear his smugness was the same folly as mine.

"Fuck!" he shouts, spitting out the candy. "I thought that was going to be chocolate pudding," he says, wiping his hand across his mouth. The table erupts in laughter and high fives as Oliver captures it all on camera.

Marin stands up a little taller and moves her hand forward in a circular motion, like she's waiting for applause. Jase stands up and presses his hands down in front of himself.

"I bow down to you. All hail the master," he says. We all continue to laugh. Oliver hands the phone to her and she looks down to make sure it is turned off. Before she can turn around and walk away, Oliver hands her the two-hundred dollars.

"Oh, I couldn't," she says, waving the money away.

"Take it," he replies, pushing the money into her hand. "Trust me, worth every penny." She looks around, unsure what to do.

"Take it," says Phoebe. "Believe me, dealing with these guys all day, you earned it."

NINE

ME: *Lesson #1 when touring with a rock band: always knock.*

GRACE: *O!M!G! We NEED to talk, girlie. Can you chat in 10?*

ME: *Yes. Call me.*

True to her word, Grace calls me ten minutes later. "Marin!" she squeals. "I miss you so much."

"Oh, I miss you too, Grace," I say on a sigh. I'm desperate to hear her take on the crazy practical jokes that ensue on the bus. I long to taste the homemade pizza dough her mom delivers to our apartment each week. I want to share a karaoke duet to "A Whole New World" where Grace does a killer Jasmine, and no one mocks me for being tone-deaf.

"Where are you now?"

"We're in Boise and I'm backstage at the show. The band is on right now, so I slipped into the green room so we could talk for a few minutes."

"C'mon, Marin. You've got to admit it. This is pretty cool. It's ten o'clock and you're hanging out with a rock band. By contrast, I'm picking the lint out of my boss's hair dryer."

I let out a howl of laughter. Leave it to Grace to one-up me in the most hilarious way possible. I don't think she's kidding. I picture her sitting on Bellatrix's bathroom floor using tweezers to grasp balls of lint from the end of a Conair.

"You win," I reply in defeat.

"Hell yeah, I do," she says. "Now, back to the matter at hand." I can't help but let out another howl of laughter.

"It wasn't a hand, so much as a mouth," I begin.

"You have *got* to be shitting me."

"Nope," I reply, ending the word with a sharp *p* and shaking my head.

"Start from the beginning and don't leave anything out," she orders.

"Are you sitting down?"

"I am. More importantly, was he?"

"See, that's why I love you. I don't even need to tell you the story and you already know what happened."

"Don't disappoint me, Marin. I *need* the story. My life is drab compared to yours. Let me live vicariously through you," she begs.

"How do I argue with that?" I joke.

"You don't. Now spill," she says before dissolving into a fit of laughter. "I . . . said . . . spill," she manages to choke out between laughs. "I imagine . . . that might fit . . . into your story too."

"Long story short . . ." I begin, and giggle.

"Oh, Marin. We're never going to get to the good stuff if we keep laughing at all the innuendo."

"I know," I laugh. "I know. Okay," I say, shaking out my hands and letting out a loud breath. "Bottom line," I spit out before laughing again. A hand hits flesh, and I picture Grace doubled over and slapping her thigh.

"Stop. Let me catch my breath for a minute," she wheezes out. "Okay," she exhales. "Okay."

"I went to the green room to grab my phone charger and walked in on Jase getting a blow job from some random chick," I rush out.

I don't tell her that, based on the deep timber of the moans, when I first walked in I thought it was Brad. That omission in and of itself is telling. Like if I said it out loud, she'd press for more information—in true Grace style, of course—and I would be forced to vocalize that I have forbidden feelings for Brad. The jealousy had struck like a hot iron. That I wanted it to be *me* on my knees, hearing *Brad's* moans of pleasure. Feeling the swell of *him* in my mouth. The taste of *him* on my tongue.

"I—can't—even—imagine." Grace's punctuated response pulls me from my fantasy.

"I'm sure you can, you saucy minx."

"Well, that's true. I *can* imagine. But I don't think I want to."

"I think my retinas have permanent damage. You think I can get workers' comp for this trauma?"

"I'm not sure that's covered in the traditional HR benefits package," she quips. "Back to the matter at hand—or mouth, as the case may be. What happened when you walked in?"

"When I went downstairs to the green room, the door was closed. I figured the last person who left pulled it shut behind them. I heard some murmurings, which I didn't pay much attention to. Now of course, it was probably Jase giving her some encouraging 'just like thats' and 'take it deeps'."

"Who doesn't love some positive reinforcement, right?"

"Not sure she needed the boost. As I recall—which I really, really hate to do," I say with a shudder. "She was working it like a pro."

"Could have been a pro," Grace suggests.

"Could have, but I doubt it. These guys are not lacking for female companionship. It's crazy what goes on backstage and at the hotel. I mean, I walked into the room, and this girl was right in plain view, on her knees, servicing Jase."

"To her credit, the door was closed."

"Closed, but not locked," I correct her.

"Tsk-tsk, Marin." I picture Grace shaking her head and wagging her pointer finger at me in a mock scold. "If you learned anything from living with me for all these years, you still should have knocked. Remember the incident with Chad?" Cheeky Chad, as he was forever known, in homage to the muscular naked butt cheeks I accidentally saw.

"You're right," I concede with a giggle. "I take full responsibility for walking in on them."

"Okay, keep going," she eggs me on. "This is greatest thing I've heard all day. All week," she adds.

"So I walk in, see him getting his rocks off, and freeze. I was able to eke out an obligatory 'oh my God' and 'I'm so sorry.' Otherwise, I couldn't move." I'm no prude and I've seen a Tumblr feed or two that was a lot more graphic than the image of Jase getting a bcej. But it still was a shock. More than that, it created some new visuals of my forbidden crush, which I'm trying to squash right now as I recount this story to Grace.

"What did Jase do? What did the girl do?" I can hear the eagerness in her voice.

"She channeled her inner Suzette from college."

"Get out!"

"Yep. She turned toward me, his dick deep in her throat, and just kept going. Jase called out"—I lower my voice to imitate his smoky roughness—"'Jesus, PR girl.' So I apologized: 'I'm so sorry. So, so sorry.' I kept spluttering the words out, but I couldn't move."

"So a sexual, three-way standoff," she says by way of explanation. Of course Grace can take this absolutely ridiculous situation and kick it up to an even more comical level.

"I surrendered first," I admit. "Once I got over the initial shock, I raced over to my phone charger, ripped it out of the outlet, and hightailed it out of there."

"Without a parting word of encouragement?"

"What was I supposed to say? 'Feel free to go about your regularly scheduled programming'?" I wisecrack. Grace laughs out loud.

"I wish you could see me right now," she offers. "I am literally rolling on the floor laughing."

"Oh God, this confirms how much I miss you."

"Busting in on a guy getting a BJ makes you miss me?" she quips.

"No, hearing you giggle like a schoolgirl makes me miss you."

"I miss you too, girlie."

"As much as I would love to talk more, I have to get back up to the show."

"It's okay," she replies, sadness in her voice.

"I wish it wasn't so hard for us to connect. These damn schedules."

"Yeah."

"Here I took our few precious minutes and didn't once ask how you are doing."

"You're a terrible friend," she deadpans.

"I know. The worst." As much as I say it in jest, I do feel like a bad friend. Like this job and my need to find success in this unorthodox and unexpected situation is driving me to neglect the important things. "Don't give up on me."

"Never going to happen. You're stuck with me. We are going to be friends until we're old and gray. We're going to have good times, bad times, and awkward, uncomfortable times. We are going to make each other laugh, smile, throw things, and squirm. It's what friends do and it's all part of the deal. Got it?"

"Got it."

"Seriously, though. You've made my day with this story of yours. I'm going to live off the laughs for weeks at the very least."

"I love you, you know."

"Of course you do," she snorts. "I'm amazing."

"Okay, let's try to talk soon.

"Yes, and please remember to knock next time."

"Lesson learned."

Lesson learned indeed.

TEN

"He's adorable," Marin coos to Carter, one of the sound engineers, who's leaning over her shoulder. My stomach clenches seeing him so close to her. He takes the cell phone out of her hand and stares at the screen with a goofy, pride-filled grin. "Thanks for showing me," she adds.

"Thanks for asking, Marin." He tosses her a smile before boarding his bus.

"What was that all about?" I ask, sidling up to her.

"Oh, Carter was telling me last week about the baby he and his wife Emily adopted a few months ago. She just took him to get his six-month portrait and I asked to see it." She shrugs like it's no big deal.

But it is a big deal. In the short time she's been on tour, Marin has learned everyone's name, their role on the tour, where they previously worked, about their families, and more. She's even asked to ride on the bus with the crew, so she can get to know everyone better. It seems to go beyond doing her job. It's like she enjoys and appreciates people. Values them. I haven't come across someone like that on the tour before now and I'm hoping that someday she'll value me too.

We've wrapped up lunch at a restaurant in one of the sleepy towns we're passing through, and now there's a note from some stranger apologizing for hitting the bus. Damon and the bus driver have spent the last hour circling the bus, trying to figure out where the damage is. Marin is sitting in her seat and when I look over her shoulder, she's playing Yahtzee on her phone. Looks like I won't be interrupting anything important.

"Licorice?" I ask as I slide into the seat next to hers.

"Red or black?" she poses, laying her phone in her lap and scrunching up her nose like she's going to scrutinize my response.

"Does it matter?"

"Absolutely," she affirms. "Black licorice is vile. Red licorice is . . ." Her voice trails off as she thinks of the right words. ". . . a gift from the gods." I mentally give myself a high five for my excellent choice in candy.

"I'm not really a god, but feel free to worship at my feet," I say with humor as I hand her a Red Vine.

"Thanks." She laughs and tucks a piece of hair behind her ear. I don't know if it's a nervous response or a habit, but I hope it's nerves. She takes the licorice from my hand and nibbles off a bite.

"So what other likes and dislikes should I know about?"

"What do you want to know?" she challenges.

Everything.

"Hmm." I think for a minute. "Toilet paper: draped over the top of the roll or hanging down the back?"

"I don't care as long as you replace the roll," she responds right away.

"Yeah, Craig just leaves a new roll on the floor," I share. "The Beatles?" I pose, wanting to know so much more about her.

"I'm not a fan," she says with a little sneer and shrug.

"Ouch!" I respond, clutching my hand to my heart. "You wound me there, Marin." So we don't have that in common. It's okay. I'm certain there are other ways for us to connect.

"Sorry." She gives a little grimace.

"That's okay," I tell her. "We can still be friends."

"Because you get by with a little help from your friends?" She grimaces again, like she's thinking her joke isn't going to go over so well. Little does she know how attracted I am to her sharp wit.

"Touché! Okay, clowns: fun or scary?"

"Fun," she responds, like I asked an unnecessary question until it dawns on her. "You're afraid of clowns?" She tries to stifle a laugh.

"I'm not sure *afraid* adequately describes it," I confess. I don't mind her laughing at me because her smile is infectious. "Favorite band?"

"Kings Quarters, of course."

"Ha ha. You're a savvy one." I wag my finger at her. She smiles at me and bats her eyelashes. "In-N-Out fries?"

"Mediocre at best."

I want to reach out and kiss this girl. "Agreed, but they do have great shakes."

"Can't go wrong with real ice cream, right?" She holds up her palms and smirks.

"So true, so true." We sit for a silent moment while I try to think of another question. Try to think of a way to extend our time together. To learn more about her. To make her want to learn more about me. "Carrot cake? Delicious dessert or abomination?"

"Abomination, naturally. Vegetables don't belong in cake. That's not . . . well, natural."

"I agree. It's weird. I love tomatoes, but I hate tomato soup."

"I love pea soup but hate cooked peas. Isn't that funny?"

"It is," I agree. "Coffee or tea?"

"I'll take an IV drip of caffeine straight to my vein. Much more efficient way to get it into my system," she laughs. "What about you?"

"I have a lot of vices, but caffeine isn't one of them."

"Really?" she asks with a raised eyebrow. I don't want her to think I have the kind of vices associated with the typical rock star lifestyle, so I clarify.

"Oh yes. My addiction to bacon borders on the obscene."

"Well, can't blame you there," she concedes. "A healthy obsession with something even *that* bad for you doesn't qualify as a vice in my book."

"That's about the worst skeleton in my closet," I explain. "What about you? Any bones lingering in hidden places?"

"Nope," she says with a harsh *p*. "Nothing in my background to write home about."

"Speaking of home, where is that?"

"I live in Manhattan Beach with my roommate, best friend, confidante, therapist, and sister for all intents and purposes, Grace. What about you and Craig? And is it just the two of you? Or are there other Osterhauser musical prodigies running around?" she asks as I hand her another piece of licorice. I want to hear more about Grace, but by the way she deflected the question back to me, I'm not sure now's the right time to press.

"We have a place in Hollywood right now. And C.O. and I were about all my mom could handle."

"I can only imagine," she says with humor.

"Yeah, we were quite a handful," I agree with a snort, thinking about the hell we put poor Mom through. "Boyfriend?"

"No," she says, shaking her head.

"Girlfriend?"

"No." She tilts her head to the side and stares at me. "You look disappointed."

"Not to offend you or harass you sexually in any way . . ." I start.

"You don't need to hold yourself back around me. I'm sure I could handle anything you have to say."

"Well, in that case, I certainly wouldn't be opposed to thinking about you and another hot chick together." While she rolls her eyes, I have to adjust myself in my pants.

"Sorry to disappoint you," she responds with a shrug, "but I am strictly a one-man kind of woman."

"I can work with that too," I tell her. Yes, I can definitely work with the idea of her being with one guy . . . me. I'm about to ask her another question when Damon yells.

"Damn it, Oliver, we're trying to keep to a schedule here," he screams at a not at all contrite-looking Oliver, as they both stand outside the bus door.

"It was just a little joke," Oliver says, brushing him off.

"Get on the bus!" Damon points to the open door where I'm now standing.

"What's going on?" I ask, as Oliver climbs on board.

"I put the note on the bus as a joke and Damon's all bent out of shape."

"Oliver." I shake my head and watch as he takes a seat with an enigmatic grin on his face. How did *this* become my life? Meanwhile, Damon glares at me and then raises a brow as he glances at Marin by my side.

"You working on our new songs? Can't disappoint our fans." *Our fans?* There's no *our* fans. Damon is a bottom feeder. Always has been. How Craig doesn't see past his scheming and system gaming is beyond me. But if Craig and the other guys are happy, who am I to complain? I'm just along for the ride.

"Yeah, Damon. We're all good," I confirm with a fake, juicy grin. I turn to my side and inspect the charming and beautiful woman next to me. *Yeah, we're all good.* And just like that, my fake grin turns into a heartfelt smile.

ELEVEN

MARIN

We're a few weeks into the tour and I'm a few weeks in over my head with Brad. As we sit on the bus for our two-day trek from Missoula, Montana, to Bismarck, North Dakota, I'm mesmerized watching his fingers fly across his computer keyboard with the same speed and precision as they glide across the neck of his guitar. I rise from my favorite swivel chair next to him and venture to the sink to refill my water bottle. When I turn on the faucet, the handheld hose on the sink counter sprays a jet of water all over me. My shirt and face are soaked. I turn the water off with a huff and pull the hose forward to examine it. Someone—read: Oliver or Jase—has tied a rubber band around the hose, leaving it in the *on* position. I roll my eyes and grab a paper towel to wipe the water off my face.

"Sorry there, PR girl," calls Jase. The perpetrator of this hoax-gone-awry is now apparent.

"No problem," I say with a grin before turning around to scowl in private. I grab another paper towel to sop up the water on my neck and shirt. I remove the offending rubber band from the faucet and fill up my water bottle. Four years of college. Two years of grad school. One grueling thesis project. And I feel like my current job is babysitting a bunch of juvenile pranksters.

As I walk over to my seat next to Brad, I pull the wet fabric away from my skin and let it snap back, repeating the motion a few times to keep the shirt from clinging to my padded bra.

"I like this new look you've got going on," Brad says with a raised brow. I chuckle a little as I glance down at the ground and tuck a strand of hair behind my ear. I'm beyond embarrassed—and a little thrilled—although I can't imagine it's the first time he's seen a set of boobs in a wet t-shirt.

"How do you put up with the two of them and this ridiculous practical joke feud?" I ask, exasperated.

"Sometimes it's pretty funny," he admits with a shrug. "Most of the time, I ignore it. Can't complain about today though," he says, glancing down at my top.

"Yeah, right?" I roll my eyes. I'd be surprised if he wasn't disappointed with the volume on display. It's not hard to recognize a pattern in the type of women who make it backstage after a show.

"I—" he starts but isn't able to finish due to Jase's announcement to the group at large.

"Do you know what today is?"

Without turning around, Brad raises his hand.

"I know," he says.

"Yeah, of course you know, smartass," Jase retorts, sneering at Brad and shaking his head. "What about the rest of you assholes?"

"Is it the anniversary of your first blow job?" asks Oliver with a roll of the eyes. Before Jase can respond, Johnny jumps in.

"No, no, you're celebrating the STD you got rid of," he laughs. Brad reaches over and gives Johnny a high five.

"Shut up, fucker," says Jase, growing exasperated with the group.

"No, it's the date when his penile enlargement was completed," says Craig. Phoebe punches his arm, criticizing him for jumping into the fray. Brad chokes on his soda, expelling a few loud coughs while waving his hand in front of his face. Even choking, he looks damn handsome.

"You're an asshole," says Jase. He seems to have admitted defeat and is laughing along with everyone else. "It's August 8, people. Birthday of David Howell Evans." He looks for some sort of acknowledgment.

"Who?" asks Oliver.

"Who?" repeats Jase in disbelief with two raised eyebrows. "David Howell Evans." He shakes his head, his eyes bugging out because no one seems to know who the heck he's talking about.

"I know," repeats Brad, raising his hand again.

"I know you know," says Jase in mock disgust, "but does anybody else?"

"Sorry," I say with a shrug and a bit of a cringe.

"Enlighten us, B.O." Defeated, Jase gestures for Brad to educate the rest of us.

"Today's the birthday of the Edge, from U2. His real name is David Howell Evans," he clarifies. The crowd releases a collective *oh*, with some of them nodding their heads in acknowledgment.

"You a big U2 fan?" I ask Brad.

"Yeah, I am. He's one of my guitar heroes. He not only plays lead guitar and sings backup vocals, but he wrote some of their songs."

"Kind of like you," I confirm. Impressive. Talented. Special.

"Yep." Brad stands up and walks over to his guitar case, pulling out his acoustic guitar. He takes a seat and Jase comes to stand right behind him. They begin an acoustic rendition of U2's "Sunday Bloody Sunday," their voices blending in perfect harmony. As I enjoy this impromptu jam session, it occurs to me I have a job to do—documenting this experience for the band's fans. I grab my cell phone and start recording.

The band finishes to applause from the rest of us on the bus. Jase takes an exaggerated bow and tips his hand from his head forward. He high fives the rest of the guys. I manage to capture it all, attach it to an email, and send a request to Amy for her approval to share:

From: MarinC@sashavpr.com
To: AmyL@sashavpr.com
Subject: The Edge's Birthday

The band just did a fantastic impromptu jam of U2 to celebrate the Edge's birthday. I would like to post to their social media along with these hashtags: #KingsQuarters #HappyBirthday #TheEdge #U2

A few minutes later, I get an email response from Amy:

From: AmyL@sashavpr.com
To: MarinC@sashavpr.com
Subject: Re: The Edge's Birthday

Okay. Add these: #JamSession #MusicianLife #TourBusJam

I grab my laptop from my messenger bag and fire it up. Within a few minutes, I've posted the video to Twitter and Facebook, and added a photo to Instagram directing people to our website. Before I can shut my computer down, I'm already detecting a lot of likes and retweets. For all their shortcomings, the Kings Quarters guys are seriously magnetic.

TWELVE

I can't wait to crawl into bed. It's been an exhausting day. The band had two radio station interviews early this morning and a sound check at eleven thirty for tomorrow's appearance on *WCCO This Morning*. I've posted photo and blog updates to the web and social media channels; sent pitches to newspapers, magazines, online outlets, and radio stations in cities where we'll be on tour next month; fielded requests for interviews in our next two tour stops; vetted a reporter for a backstage pass for tomorrow's show; and I just now wrapped up a printout of interview prep Q&A in the hotel's business center.

It's nine thirty p.m. and we have to be at the studio tomorrow at nine. I drag my exhausted ass off the elevator and down the hall to my room. When I open the door and walk in, I'm blinded by two very round, very white butt cheeks moving up and down. It's a Cheeky Chad flashback. Damn it! Jody is *entertaining* Theo in our hotel room . . . again. Those two are like rabbits and not the cute kind. More like the nonstop battery-operated kind.

I don't even bother to expel an exaggerated cough or clear my throat to alert them to my presence. Neither of them seems to care if I'm here or not. A live peep show is not my style. Not only do I have no interest in watching other people have sex, it reminds me how long it's been since I have gotten any action. At least Grace and I—when we were dating someone—would work out some sort of early warning system. We'd also be considerate enough to not hog the room multiple days in a row. These guys don't give a shit.

"Ugh," I mumble. I put my hand in front of my eyes to shield them from Theo's very naked ass and make my way over to side of the room. I grab my headphones, computer charger, and a sweatshirt, and make a hasty retreat out the door. Judging by the nonstop grunting and mattress squeaking, I don't think they even noticed I was there.

I walk over to the hotel pool and pull a lounge chair over to an electrical outlet. I throw on my sweatshirt while my computer warms up, because the Minneapolis nights are rather chilly. In fact, it's so cold, I grab a few pool towels and wrap them around my shoulders and legs. I put my headphones on and pray the hotel's Wi-Fi signal extends out to the pool. The coverage is a bit spotty and the *Seinfeld* rerun I'm watching on my streaming app keeps cutting out. It's better than being back in my room or dealing with the hotel bar though.

My eye catches someone moving through the automatic doors and coming toward me. Because of the way the lights are situated, I can't tell who it is until the person is at the foot of my chair. I'm surprised it's Brad.

"Hey B." I can see my breath and shiver as I realize how cold it is outside.

"Marin, what are you doing out here?"

"Oh, you know, relaxing by the pool," I reply with sass.

"Ah, working on your tan, then?" he says with just enough sarcasm to elicit a laugh.

"Exactly!"

"Don't you think it's too cold for you to be out here? You're going to get sick," he warns. "Fuck, I sound like my mom, huh?" he adds with a chuckle.

"Nah. It's kind of nice." I'm not sure if my mom ever cared if I was sick.

"So what *are* you doing out here?"

"My room is . . . oh, how should I say this? *Occupied* at the moment."

"Occupied?" he repeats.

"Occupied," I wink.

"Ah," he acknowledges in recognition. "Occupied."

"Yeah, so it was either come out here and try to watch *Seinfeld* or go to my room and watch a live porn show."

"You chose out here?" he asks, shaking his head, like if the roles were reversed, he'd be watching his roommate get it on. He sits down on the bottom half of the lounge chair and leans over to view my computer screen.

"Why *Seinfeld*?"

"Before I left for college, my dad and I would watch nineties sitcoms together. We had just finished up *Friends*, which I will say was super awkward to watch with my dad because every episode is about sex." Normally I would be kicking myself for mentioning Dad. I try not to talk about him much with people I don't know. Too painful. But I don't have time to dwell on that now. Open mouth, insert foot. Why did I just bring up sex with Brad?

He poses with a smirk and asks me how I'm doing, channeling Joey from *Friends*. And that visual isn't helping my situation any. "So which *Seinfeld* episode are you watching?" he asks.

"It just started, and it keeps cutting out, but they are all going to spend the weekend in the Hamptons."

"World's ugliest baby," he chuckles.

"Uh . . ."

"That's a great episode. One of my favorites."

"I haven't seen this one yet. I've been making my way through them but I'm only on season five."

"You've never watched the series before?"

"No. It was my dad's favorite and I promised him I'd watch it. With school and work, I had been too busy, so I'm getting to it now. So far, I love it." What I don't tell him is that it's taken me a while to be ready to watch something my dad enjoyed so much without falling to pieces.

"Me too. I binged it a few months ago after exhausting everything else on Netflix," he says. "Tell you what, why don't you come hang out with me in my room and we'll watch a few episodes until your room is . . . unoccupied."

"Oh, that's nice of you, but I don't want to be a bother."

"It's no bother. I was heading up to the room to watch some TV. Anyway, if you get sick out here, who's going to make sure our lazy asses are up in time for our next interview?"

Go back to his room? I'm not sure that's a good idea, but I *am* freezing, and he does make it sound like it's no big deal to hang out for an hour or so.

"Well, if it isn't any trouble, that would be great."

"Good." He grabs my laptop. He also grabs my hand and lifts me up from the lounge chair. My skin sizzles at the contact. I'm grateful he lets go of me a moment later, otherwise I'm certain I would have begged him for more. Maybe witnessing Jody and Theo go at it has put too many dirty thoughts in my mind.

We go back to the floor where all our rooms are housed, past my shared room with Jody, until we reach a few doors down. He uses his key card to unlock the door and we step in. His room looks identical to mine except for the fact there is one king-size bed instead of two queens.

"Make yourself comfortable," he says as he puts my laptop on the bed. "Do you want something from room service?"

"No, I'm okay. Thanks." I'm not quite sure what to do. He sits down on the bed and scoots up until his back hits the headboard. "Sit down," he says, patting a space next to him.

I'm about to crawl into bed with Brad Osterhauser.

Never mind he's a rock star, he's been the object of my secret lust for the past few weeks. In my fantasies, he would pull me down and have his wicked way with me. In reality, I'm terrified he thinks something is going to happen between us. I sit down and lean against the headboard—with nervous butterflies in my belly—being sure to leave plenty of space between us. He pulls my headphones out of the jack, hits the pause button, and the episode comes on full steam.

We sit like this, the sounds of the show only punctuated by our laughter until the episode ends and the next one begins. I relax because it's obvious he was just being nice, not wanting me to freeze my ass off on a lounge chair because Jody is a vixen.

My eyelids get heavy and I scoot down on the bed to rest my head for a moment. When this episode ends, I'll go back to my room and hope Jody and Theo have gotten it out of their systems for the night.

THIRTEEN

BRAD

Having Marin here in my bed is testing my very resolve.

Never mind the fact I haven't gotten laid since before I met her in Sasha's office all those weeks ago. When she fell asleep last night, she was curled up in a little ball at the edge of the bed. I didn't have the heart to wake her. She was out cold. To be honest, I liked having her here. Little did I know, by morning she would be in the middle of the bed, both arms outstretched, legs wide, taking up *all* the space. Forcing *me* onto the edge.

Now she rolls over taking most of the hotel blanket to cover herself, except she kicks her feet out from under it. I look at her pink painted toenails—so sweet and feminine. What else on her body has a soft, pink hue? I want to roll over too and wrap my arm around her. Pull her close. But she doesn't need to learn I like her by the nudge of my hard shaft against her backside.

A few strands of her dark brown hair fall across her face, and her little pink lips pucker and part like a sleeping baby's. She's fucking adorable. I hate to wake her, but I know she needs to get up. I give her shoulder a little push and she stirs. She moans a little, and the sound is like a jolt to my dick, which has been at half-mast all night. She opens her eyes and blinks a few times. Then she sort of shudders.

"I'm so sorry," she sputters, sitting up. "I fell asleep."

"Yeah, I didn't want to wake you," I say, trying to sound as casual as possible.

"I'm so, so sorry," she repeats, pulling the blanket off and standing up.

"It's okay." I try to reassure her it's no big deal. Although I want it to be a big deal. I want it to mean something. I don't want to scare her off, though. Not when we're starting to get closer.

"What time is it?" she asks in a mild panic.

"It's six thirty. I know we have a car coming at eight and figured you would want to be up early to shower and prepare," I explain.

"Thank you," she says. She walks around the room grabbing her laptop, headphones, and computer charger. "You're very . . . thoughtful. I'm sorry again."

"It's really okay. You can crash here anytime," I offer with a small smile. What I want to say is, "Get into my bed, woman!" but I don't think that would be well-received.

"Oh, I wouldn't want to cramp your style," she jokes.

"I've got no style," I respond. "I'm all substance," I add with a smug grin.

"Ha. Well, I should get going. Thanks again." With that, she's out the door.

FOURTEEN

BRAD

We rocked Minneapolis. Man, I'm so amped right now. It's these moments when I fucking love what I do. There's no better high, except when I figure out a coding sequence I need. That's like a major head rush and I don't care if it makes me sound like a geek. I just wouldn't admit it to anyone else.

I get to the backstage green room in desperate need of a shower. I'm thankful we don't have a show tomorrow and our bus call time isn't until eleven. I can get back to the room and sleep a bit, but I look over and notice Marin. She stands out among the groupies and trashy girls who find their way backstage in hopes of scoring with a musician. Marin is classy . . . and smart . . . and I would love to have her curled up in my bed again tonight.

I stalk over to her, wiping some of the sweat from my brow. I'm not sure if it's residue from the lights and activity on stage or if I'm nervous about approaching her.

"Hey," I say.

"Great show," she replies. "You guys were awesome tonight."

"Thanks. So, are you all wrapped up here for the night?" I reach around her to grab a bottle of cold water from the craft services table.

"Yeah, I'm all done. About to hop on the bus and head back to the hotel. What about you?"

"Yeah, I'm done here too. Do you . . ." I start, my voice a bit shaky until I remember I'm a rock star for God's sake. I've never had this much anxiety or trouble getting a woman to come back to my hotel room. ". . . want to come hang out in my room again and watch TV?"

"You want me to?" she asks, her brow furrowed.

"Sure, if you want to," I shrug, trying not to let her in on the fact I desperately want to spend the rest of the night in my room with her—even if all we do is watch TV and fall asleep on top of the covers. She looks around the room, her eyes landing on a group of *friendly* girls chatting with Oliver and Jase.

"There doesn't seem to be any shortage of beautiful women who would be happy to go back to your room and do a lot more than watch TV." She raises her eyebrows up and down.

"Well, that's not really my scene." That's not entirely true, but I don't need to get into that with her right now.

"Hot women throwing themselves at you isn't your scene?" she asks with a quirk of her eyebrow. I chuckle and wipe my forehead, my hand still holding onto the water bottle.

"Oh believe me. I like pussy," I say with a confirming nod. I can't help but notice her quiet yet quick exhale.

"Considering your *likes*," she says with a sassy smile, "I highly doubt you'd be lacking in female companionship tonight." She gestures over to the group of women I noticed earlier. "C'mon," she goads me. "I've watched movies. I've seen TMZ. I'm sure it's nonstop groupies all the time."

"It may have been like that in the beginning, but tonight, I'd much rather hang out and watch a *Seinfeld* episode."

"Oh," she says in surprise. "Well, if you're sure you don't mind hanging out with me, that would be great. Jody and Theo already left and I'm pretty sure they are back in my room attacking one another."

I give a mock shudder and she chuckles.

"C'mon. Let's get to the bus before it heads out," I say, putting my hand on the small of her back to guide her out.

When we get to my room, I realize I'm starving. There was a big spread of food in the green room at the concert venue, but I was so distracted by Marin, I didn't grab anything.

"I'm going to order something from room service. You want anything?" I ask her.

"No, I'm fine." Then she exclaims, "Shoot!"

"What?"

"I don't have my computer."

"That's okay. If you know your streaming password, we can watch on my phone," I offer.

"That's perfect."

I hand her my cell phone, and pick up the desk phone and order a BLT and chocolate shake from room service.

"Hope you don't mind, but I need to grab a quick shower." She blushes, and the thought of her being aroused by me taking a shower makes me harder than stone. Better make that a *cold* shower.

"No problem. It's your room," she says. "I'm grateful you're letting me hang out here."

I grab a change of clothes and go into the bathroom. As much as I would love a scene to play out where I exit the bathroom wearing only a towel and she rips it off me and rides me hard, I'm pretty sure that would scare her off. I need to take things slow if I have any chance of getting her to come around. So, I take a quick shower, quietly rubbing one out to relieve the pressure, and change into a pair of track pants and t-shirt.

When I exit the shower, she's sitting on the bed sipping on my milkshake. She stops with the straw halfway to her lips and gives me a little shrug. I can't help but laugh.

"By all means," I say, gesturing with my hand for her to continue.

"Thanks." She bites her lip and raises her shoulders, looking guilty. I grab my sandwich, take a bite, and let out a little moan. Fuck, that tastes good. I pick up the plate, place it on the nightstand, and hop onto the bed. "So, what's on?" I ask, taking another bite.

"I hope you don't mind watching the episode I fell asleep to last night?" Her voice sounds small, like she's worried I'm going to be mad.

"Not at all."

"Thanks," she repeats. She climbs onto the bed, sitting on the far end like she did last night. She holds my cell phone at arm's length, tilting it so we can both see it.

"Here, give me that," I say, reaching for the phone. I know I could grab my laptop. But why pass up a chance to get closer to her? I grab a few pillows and place them at the foot of the bed, creating a makeshift stand. I lean back against the headboard in the middle of the bed and motion for her to come closer. "Don't worry. I won't bite. I can't imagine you taste as good as bacon." I take another bite of my sandwich, and she scoots over until she's next to me.

Heat radiates off her body. She still smells like vanilla and I have absolutely no doubt she would taste a thousand times more delicious than bacon. In fact, I would give up a lifetime of bacon to sample her sweet cream once, but that's not what tonight is about.

We watch the episode where George is figuring out all his life choices have been wrong. He commits to doing the exact opposite of every instinct he's ever had and when he does, things start to turn around. It's hilarious and Marin agrees, laughing out loud at all the appropriate times.

The next episode starts to play, and her body shifts to the side. Next, she cuddles up against my chest and her arm wraps around my waist. Her hand rests on my hip bone. It's not one of those V-shapes women talk about. I'm not *that* built, but I am lean and toned. Her thumb brushes back and forth all feathery and I go hard, fantasizing those soft fingers are stroking farther south where I'm aching. I'm quite certain my dick stood to attention and bumped her arm.

I don't want to scare her off with my hard-on, but I also don't want her to stop touching me. I move slightly from side to side and she lets out a little moan. She moves her arm and hand up to my shoulder and continues with those little motions back and forth. Even though I'm wearing a t-shirt, it's like her touch is burning my skin. Jesus. I sound like a fucking romance novel. What the hell is this girl doing to me? Her hand stills but I've gone from floppy and laughing to full hard-on and horny in about ten seconds. Is she as affected by me as I am by her? I put my hand on her wrist and it feels limp. I check her pulse and it's calm compared to my riotous one. She's not feeling lustful.

She's sleeping.

FIFTEEN

With the sound of an alarm clock, a body shifts from under me before I feel the weight back underneath my head. It must be morning and I'm guessing that noise was a wake-up alarm. It hits me I've fallen asleep in Brad's bed . . . again. This is bad. Very bad, but I can't for the life of me move. He smells so good. Not like the hotel soap. He must bring his own body wash. I would camp out here and breathe him in all morning if I could because he smells clean and crisp. Like the beach.

Before I know it, I snort, thinking about the *Seinfeld* episode I watched last week where Kramer's cologne invention got stolen by Calvin Klein.

"What's so funny?" he asks, his early morning voice rough with sleep, making him sound even sexier than he already is.

"Thinking about *Seinfeld*," I say, lifting my head.

"Mmm. That show is funny." He scrubs his hand over his jaw.

"Looks like I'm making a habit of falling asleep in your bed," I say, looking at the clock. I have more than an hour before we're scheduled to depart on the bus. I get up and smooth out my clothes.

"You're welcome in my bed anytime." It's hard not to miss the innuendo there and the thought of being with him—like really *being* with him—starts my heart pounding harder.

"I . . ." I sputter, and he flashes me a slow, lazy smile. "I should get going," I say. If I don't leave now, any attempt to resist him will be futile.

As I head back to my own room, it hits me how homesick I've become. I've been working nonstop. Constantly moving from one locale to the next, always surrounded by people but feeling friendless . . . it's taking its toll. I miss Grace. I miss my friends. I miss my apartment. I miss the comfort of familiarity. That's what this little obsession with Brad is all about. Just missing some comfort, because that's all it can be about.

SIXTEEN

BRAD

"Open up, asswipe!" Jase yells. I was exiting a much-needed shower, rinsing off after our show so I'm not a sweaty mess, when the pounding began. I open my hotel room door to see Oliver standing in Jase's doorway offering him a wide smile. Oh boy. I sigh. Trouble's brewing.

"Oh, hey there, Jase. What's up?" Oliver says. Jase is fuming, shaking his head back and forth, panting out his nose.

"What did you do to my shower?" Jase demands.

"Your shower?" asks Oliver with fake innocence. "I didn't do anything to your shower."

"My shower isn't working," says Jase, "and I know you had something to do with it."

"On my brother's life, I didn't do anything to your shower," says Oliver with a shrug.

"Hey guys, what's the problem?" I ask. "I'd like to get some sleep." As I move past the door jamb of my room, I see that Jase is holding a bar of soap in his hand, waving it around while he accuses Oliver of doing something to his shower.

"I tried taking a shower and it won't work," he fumes. "I know this asshole did something."

"What do you mean it won't work?" I ask, trying to clarify what the issue is.

"It—" he starts, still agitated.

"Calm down," I tell him. "Just tell me what happened."

"Okay," he says, taking a breath. "I got in the shower and got wet but I couldn't get the soap to work."

"The soap wouldn't work?" I ask, confusion written all over my face. I glance over at Oliver who is grinning like the Cheshire Cat.

"Yeah, it won't lather up. He did something," Jase says, pointing to Oliver.

"Oliver . . ." I say. I lower my head and tilt it to the side to let him know I'm disappointed in him.

"I *might* have used some of Phoebe's clear nail polish to paint his soap," Oliver concedes. Jase lunges toward him.

"God damn it, Oliver!" he yells.

"Shh. Calm down," I say, pulling Jase away while Oliver laughs.

"You're an asshole," says Jase, pointing his finger at Oliver.

"C'mon." I guide Jase to my room, walk inside, and hand him a fresh bar of soap from my bathroom.

"How did he even get it in there?" Jase ponders aloud. He's calmer now as he takes the soap, his voice filled with less anger and more wonder. "Thanks man," he says, patting me on the back before walking back toward his room where a half-naked blonde, wrapped only in a hotel towel, waits in the doorway. I reach out and grab his arm, stopping him. I lean into the bathroom again and hand him the complimentary hotel shampoo and conditioner too.

"Just in case," I say.

"Good thinking, man. Thanks for having my back," he replies before going back to his room, shaking his head in disgust the entire way.

The two of them are exhausting. How did Oliver manage to swap out Jase's hotel soap?

I've finished brushing my teeth when there's a faint rap at my door. I open it to find Marin, who has returned from the show and changed into a pair of sweat pants and a tank top. She's pulled her hair into a messy bun on top of her head and I can't help but look at her neck. I want to put my mouth on it.

"Thanks for letting me crash here . . . again," she says, as I step aside and make way for her to come in. "I feel like I'm always putting you out, and maybe you'd rather be here with someone who will *put out*," she says with a sassy wink. I let out a low growling laugh. She's so fucking funny and clever.

"No problem. Sorry Jody and Theo keep commandeering your room," I respond, when in actuality, I'm thrilled she's been chased out again by those two horndogs. I need to remind myself to buy them a round of beers next time we're hanging out at the hotel bar.

Honestly, I feel like Marin is a skittish dog or cat I don't want to spook. I need to take things slow and steady, getting a few steps closer each time, because one way or another, I've got to find a way to make her mine.

She grabs one of the pillows, fluffs it up, and lays it down on the bed. Next, she pulls the comforter and sheet from the corner where they are tucked into the mattress. She settles herself onto the bed, curling up at the edge, and pulls the blanket over her, making sure her feet are exposed. I lie down in the middle of the king bed and pull the comforter up over me.

"Marin, you don't have to stay all the way over there," I tell her, pulling the blanket up on her side and patting the space next to me with my other hand. "By tomorrow morning you'll be spread out in the middle of the bed or curled up to my side. Might as well get comfortable now."

She chuckles. "This isn't weird for you?" she asks, scrunching up her nose as she slides over and nestles into me.

"I never complain about having a beautiful woman next to me in bed," I say with a snort.

"Yeah but we aren't like that," she says, lifting her head off my chest. I already miss the feel of her against me.

"I don't mind. Does it bother you?"

"No. That's one thing I miss about having a boyfriend. The cuddling at night." She readjusts herself on my chest and wraps her arm around my waist.

"Do you miss regular sex?" I ask, putting my arm around her back.

"Regular?" She lifts up to look at me with a quirked brow and confused expression. "Like normal guy-on-top stuff?"

"Well, yes," I chuckle, "but what I meant was regularly *recurring* sex."

"Oh. Definitely. It's been a while since I've been with anyone." She curls back up and gives a little laugh.

"I could help you out with that, you know?" I offer, trying to lace my voice with humor in case my suggestion offends her.

"I won't get involved with anyone I work with. It's a rule I have," she says firmly.

"Why's that? Doesn't it seem natural you would meet someone at work considering it's where you spend most of your time?" I run my hand up and down her back.

"I just don't," she says with the same firm voice, her body stiffening next to mine. I'm thinking there is a story there—that perhaps she got burned by an office romance before. "That shouldn't stop you though. I imagine you get your fair share. This has got to be cramping your style," she adds.

"I miss regular sex," I say. It's hard (no pun intended) to have this intense want for a girl who doesn't seem to want me back. I'm a guy for God's sake. Sex is kind of what we're all about. Now's not the time to push her though. "I miss irregular sex too," I joke, seeking to lighten the mood.

"Irregular sex?" She laughs, lifting up off my chest and leaning on her elbow to look at me.

"You know what I mean," I say, raising my eyebrows up and down at her.

"I'm not sure that I do," she says with a faux grimace.

"What's the kinkiest thing you've ever done?" Not sure if I can handle the answer in my state of perpetual horniness, but I ask anyway.

"What?" she asks, shocked. "I am not having this conversation with you." She shakes her head, still perched onto her elbow, and looks down at me in disbelief.

"Why not?"

"It's totally unprofessional," she replies, affronted.

"You in my bed, in my arms, isn't?" I retort. Her body sags next to me.

"You're right," she says in a quiet voice. She exhales a shaky breath and pulls away. "I should go." She bites her lip and shakes her head, her eyes getting glassy with moisture. Crap! I'm making her cry.

"Don't be ridiculous Marin," I respond, resting my hand on her arm and guiding her back toward me. "I know this is nothing more than the necessity of needing a place to sleep. We need you well rested to keep us on track."

"You're sure?" she questions. The concern she's doing something wrong is written all over her face. I know her job is important to her. I also know this is a very unorthodox situation, but I am just trying to help her. No. That's not true. I like her a lot and am willing to do this platonic friend thing while I figure out my next move or wait for her to realize we could have something great between us.

"Of course. Now, c'mon. Just tell me," I implore her.

"Tell you what?"

"Your kinkiest secrets."

"No way," she taps my chest with her hand. "You tell me."

"Oh, you'd like that wouldn't you? Get me to spill all my secrets while you keep yours safely tucked away. I see how it is." I'm glad we're back to our playful banter.

"I have no secrets," she says with a shrug.

"Somehow I find that hard to believe," I respond with skepticism. I can tell there's a lot lurking under the surface—

things she doesn't want me to know and things holding her back from giving us a chance. Or maybe she's not interested in me.

I don't mean to sound like an arrogant ass, but why wouldn't she like me? I'm a pretty nice guy. I make a nice living. I'm not hideous to look at. She could do a lot worse. So she's either keeping me out on purpose or she's not into me. Either way, I'm not going to press. Not tonight anyway.

"I'm sure you have your fair share of good tabloid fodder stories," she tells me, and I sense she's deflecting the attention away from herself.

"I'm no saint, but I'm no Jase," I laugh.

She pauses, then concedes. "I can see that. Seriously though, I don't need to stay here. I know guys have, uh, needs and I would find it hard to believe you'd have any trouble finding a willing participant."

"I'll take that as a compliment, but it's nice to come back here at the end of the day and feel companionship and not have anyone want anything from me. Know what I mean?"

"I do," she confirms with a solemn nod. "I notice how some of those girls act. I figured—"

"That I would bang anyone who comes along?" I huff. I normally wouldn't let a comment like that get to me. I have indulged in my fair share of one-night stands. But for some reason, having Marin think so little of me pisses me off.

"No. No, I didn't mean it like that." Does she think I'm a manwhore? "I thought you would want to enjoy one of the obvious perks of your job."

"Perks of my job?" I snort. Judging by her reaction, she knows she's digging herself into a hole.

"Oh God, this is coming out all wrong." She tips her forehead to her hand. "Maybe I should go."

Don't go.

"I'm giving you a hard time, Marin. Come lie down. I like having you here with me. I miss having someone to put my arms around." It's the truth. Little does she know how very much I like putting my arms around *her*.

"I kind of need that right now," she admits, lying on my chest. "It's lonely being out on the road like this." She lifts up to look at me.

"Always alone but never by yourself."

"Exactly." She exhales through her nose before lying back down on my chest.

"I kind of need it too. So why don't we be what each other needs right now?"

"If you're sure?" She lifts up again, looking at me with her warm, sad eyes.

"I'm more than sure." She's exactly what I need and want. She draws small circles with her fingers at my waist while my arm strokes her back. Within a few moments her fingers stop and her breathing becomes even and calm. She's asleep and falls asleep with ease. I, on the other hand, have a raging hard-on. Sleep seems nowhere in sight for me. So I stroke her hair and inhale her vanilla scent. I'll take a nap this afternoon after our sound check.

I manage a few hours of sleep here and there but awaken when I feel Marin stir. She's spread-eagle across the bed and of course my mind (and dick) goes straight to all the things I want to do to her while she's unfolded like this. I look over at the alarm clock and we have another hour before we need to be up.

"We have another hour," I tell her. She lifts up off the bed.

"I can go back to my room so you can have the bed to yourself," she yawns.

"No, stay. If you're still sleeping, I know I'm not running late," I say with a grin. I pull her back down to the bed and over to me. She rests her head on my chest. I've got to take a piss, but don't want to move away from her so I stroke her hair. She lets out a little moan and pushes her head and tits deeper into my chest.

"Are you drooling on me?" I ask with a laugh.

"Mmm hmm," she sighs.

"Sexy," I say with another laugh.

"Mmm hmm," she lightly snorts. I lie there, listening to her breathe, touching her hair. I feel like a wack job stalker, but I can't help myself. When the alarm sounds an hour later, she's still curled up onto me.

"Morning again," she whispers, lifting up to look at me. I give her a sleepy smile and yawn.

"Still tired?"

She rolls over onto her side and props herself up on her elbow. Her hair sticks up on the side that had been against my chest and I'm tempted to lean over and smooth it down.

"I couldn't sleep over all the snoring," I tell her.

"I don't snore," she huffs. I love this side of her, all defiant and feisty.

"Yeah, you do," I egg her on. "You make these little grunting noises." She's horrified. It's written all over her face, so I push further. "It's cute," I shrug. "Endearing," I add with a smug nod.

"I don't snore," she repeats. Her tone is serious. She sits up, placing her hand on her hip. "In all the years I've slept with Grace, she's never said anything to that effect."

"You sleep with Grace, huh?" I say, raising my eyebrows up and down. She responds with a disapproving stare, her head titled to the side.

"We've shared a room for years."

"You and Grace sleeping together. Now there's an image I can work with." I roll my eyes up toward the ceiling and grin from ear to ear.

"You're such a pervert," she laughs, shaking her head.

"Yep, and proud of it," I acknowledge. "So, tell me about Grace."

"What do you want to know?"

"You know, likes and dislikes, measurements, sexual predilections," I suggest.

"Oh my God. You are terrible," she says with humor.

"What can I say?" I shrug.

"Well . . ." she starts. "Sorry for . . ."

"What?"

"Invading your space again," she says, crinkling up her nose.

"It's no problem," I tell her, but what I want to say is she can invade my space anytime, preferably with no clothes on.

SEVENTEEN

MARIN

"Mail call!" shouts Deeana as she boards the bus. She hands a few envelopes to Damon and a padded envelope to Jase.

"Mail? For me?" he questions.

"Looks so," she says before turning around and getting off the bus. The guys keep a watchful eye on Jase who tears open the package and pulls out a CD-sized sleeve and handwritten note.

"A friend who works for Paramount sent me a copy of the new Jason Statham movie," says Jase, pulling out a disc.

"Yes!" Craig calls out, pumping his fist. He gets up from a chair at the small dining table, bumping Phoebe as he does. "Oh, sorry babe," he says with a laugh.

"That's okay," she replies, waving her hand. "Go." She tilts her head, and he leans over and kisses her on the lips with a loud *smack*.

"You're the best," he tells her as he races to a spot on the couch in front of the flat screen, plopping down right next to me, where I'm working on my laptop. I pick up the computer and—without a word—walk over to the dining table, giving the guys some space. I'm imaging a smile crossing Craig's lips as I go. I'll plan to grab a few candids of them watching the screener.

All the guys—minus Damon, of course, who is glued to his cell phone—gather onto the couches. They're packed in like sardines, sitting a lot closer to each other than they usually like to sit. Space is limited though, and they all appear eager for a good car chase and shootout. Brad scoots over on the couch pushing Craig even farther into Johnny. Craig glares at him and I stifle a laugh. Then Brad pats the space next to himself.

"Want to watch with us?" he asks with a hopeful smile.

"Thanks for the offer but I have work to do." Do I want to sit and watch a movie with Brad? Of course I do. I want nothing more than to be with him. Laugh with him. Cuddle with him. Couple with him. But I've got a job to do and no amount of tuggable hair, witty banter, or musical genius is going to get in the way.

Craig and Johnny push themselves back over toward Brad with such force he almost falls off the couch. He leans over and punches Craig in the arm and looks back at me with a shrug and a smile.

Jase loads the DVD and sits down on the couch next to Oliver, who is pursing his lips together like he's trying to suppress a laugh. I have a feeling sparks are going to fly, so I lean against the wall of the bus to catch the action.

Jase takes out the remote, holds it up toward the game console, and presses his thumb to a button. The screen comes to life and the credits roll. A moment later, the movie freezes. Jase grabs the remote again and hits a few buttons bringing the movie back to life. Again, the screen freezes.

"What the hell?" he mumbles. He stands up and ejects the disc, inspecting it for scratches. Not seeing anything unusual, he pops it back into the player and sits down, aiming the remote at the console again. The movie starts from the beginning.

A dead body is lying on a gurney in what appears to be a crude morgue when Jason Statham pops up from under a sheet and destroys three bad guys with a scalpel. As he's about to escape the room and encounter a few armed guards, the console returns to gameplay mode.

Jase shakes his head in frustration. He hits his remote and the movie resumes. It switches over to gameplay a moment later. Jase resumes the movie. Back and forth. Back and forth. Jase grows more and more agitated while Oliver sits by, grinning. Brad, Johnny, and Craig are holding back their laughter.

"Damn it," Jase mutters. Brad can't hold it back any longer and laughs out loud. "What?" Jase snaps.

"Dude," Brad says, and he can't even get any more words out because he's laughing so hard.

"Oliver!" Jase shouts, turning to the keyboardist next to him. Oliver pulls a different remote out of his pocket and holds it up. Craig and Johnny are also in full laughing mode now too. "Asshole," Jase gripes. He reaches out for Oliver to hand the second remote over. "Can we watch the movie now?" he asks, irritated.

"Sure," says Oliver who lets out a few snorts. I manage to get a few photos of the guys laughing to post another time with some hashtags about general fun and antics. I also snap a few of the movie experience and send them to Amy for approval along with some accolades for the film. *Is promoting these juvenile antics what I went to graduate school for?* I think the end of the tour can't get here soon enough, until I hear Brad laugh and my heart clenches.

EIGHTEEN

With a rare day off tomorrow, Jase has financially incentivized—*bribery* is such a dirty word—hotel security to give us after-hours access to the hotel's rooftop pool and invited the entire crew to join us, plus a whole host of women who were hanging around backstage and outside the venue. He's also managed to get the bar opened and taken care of the tab, so the alcohol is flowing. The sound system is cranked up too, and pop music tunes flood our ears.

Craig and Phoebe are sitting in the hot tub whispering to each other while Oliver and Johnny each hoist a scantily clad woman on their shoulders in the pool for a round of chicken. Jase is holding court in a cabana while three different topless women vie for his attention. It's a carnival of fake tits, wet bodies, and tequila shots. A few months ago, I'd be smack in the middle of it all. But, now?

I look to my left and spy Jody and Theo sitting on the steps at the shallow end of the pool, hands roaming across one another like no one else is around. No wonder Marin is always hanging out in my room. Who wants to see that?

Speaking of Marin, she's not here yet. She said she would come down for a little while. I guess the summer heat and humidity is wearing down her professionalism, as I can't imagine she would be hanging out in a bathing suit with her clients under normal circumstances. So remind me to thank whoever scheduled this tour during a heat wave. I'm itching to see how Marin fills out a bikini.

I nonchalantly glance at the pool gate every few minutes to see if she's here. At least I hope I'm being casual about it. I don't want the guys giving me a hard time about my growing feelings for Marin. Oh, who am I kidding? The guys aren't paying one iota of attention to me right now. My breath catches as she approaches.

I don't miss her tucking her hair behind her ear as she opens the gate and looks around. She's wearing a terry cloth hotel robe, which has got to be hot as Hades right now. Her eyes widen as she takes in the debauchery around her. I have no doubt she won't be posting *anything* to do with this scene on social media.

She licks her lips and then bites down on the lower one as she scans the pool. When her eyes settle on me sitting off to the side in a lounge chair, she visibly exhales. I grin at her and she waves in response. I tilt my head to the side in a few rapid bursts, calling her over. She looks around again and walks over to me. I stand and pull an empty lounge chair over to me and place a fresh pool towel across it so she can sit down.

"Thanks," she says as she lowers herself to the chair. She kicks off a pair of flip-flops, leans back, and adjusts the recline bar on the lounger so she's sitting up and watching everything unfold before her.

"So . . ." I start.

"So," she cringes.

"Do I even need to ask what you think of . . ." I gesture around the pool. "This?"

"It's like a scene from a movie," she says, shaking her head in disgust. "One of those raunchy spring break comedies that people seem to like," she sneers.

"And what are you? The nice girl who joins the fun to lose her virginity?" I joke.

"Oh, I'm no virgin," she sasses back and now all I'm thinking about is sex with not-a-virgin Marin. Her writhing underneath me. Her raking her nails down my back. Her screaming out my name. I clear my throat and, as she looks away, adjust the growing wood in my swim trunks.

"Really?"

"I may not flash my boobs at rock stars or wear revealing clothes, but I'm not a prude."

"Hmm. I think I might need some evidence to support that assertion. Perhaps some hands-on proof." She lets out a huff and rolls her eyes. "Why are you being so defensive?" I joke.

"I'm not," she replies in indignation. I challenge her with a look. Marin has a chip on her shoulder when it comes to some of the women we encounter in this line of work. I don't know whether that should piss me off or make me damn proud of her.

"See the blonde there with the fake tits sitting on Johnny's shoulder? How do you know she's not a nuclear physicist? And the brunette that looks about ready to give Jase a blow job? Maybe she works with homeless inner-city veterans." I say, and Marin raises a questioning eyebrow.

"Seriously?" she retorts.

I bust out laughing. "Listen, Marin. We all respect you and know you are a professional woman with an important job to do but it's okay to have a little fun. No one is going to judge you for having a drink with us or think less of you for swimming topless. In fact, some of us might even think more of you." I toss a wink at her. I can sense when she lets her guard down by the way her shoulders relax and she exhales. "C'mon. Take a shot. That's an order."

"Okay," she concedes. "One shot. But my top stays on," she adds, pointing a finger at me. I'm not surprised at the addendum but will admit to being disappointed. "I could use a stiff drink." Stiff? Why did she have to bring up the word *stiff*? We get to the bar and I place both hands on the counter when I feel a spray of water cover us. Johnny has hopped out of the pool and, like a wet dog, shakes the water off his body and hair. Marin rolls her eyes and laughs.

"What will the lady have?" I ask, turning to her.

"Patrón. Make it a double," she requests of the bartender.

"I'll have the same," I add.

"Make it three," chimes Johnny, who has now wrapped his wet arms around Marin's and my shoulders. "I *love* you guys," Johnny slurs as the bartender lines up our shots.

Marin reaches for the salt shaker and lifts her arm to her mouth. I'm mesmerized as I watch her lick her wrist, pour on some salt, and lick it again. With all the blood in my body rushing south, I'm on the brink of passing out.

"Yeah, Marin!" screams Johnny as she knocks back the shot of tequila and slides a lime wedge between her teeth. "You're one of us now," he howls, tossing his head back with a maniacal laugh.

I swallow hard watching her cringe at the sour taste. She then looks at me, and like a stalker, I stare at her with my jaw hanging open rather than downing my own drink. I clear my throat, tilt my head back, and let the strong liquid burn my throat. Maybe it's my imagination but it looks like she's staring at my Adam's apple as the shot slides down. She licks her lips and then turns away. Johnny shoots the tequila, slams the glass on the counter, lets out a loud wail, and jumps into the pool, splashing water everywhere.

Back in our lounge chairs, Marin closes her eyes and rolls her neck from side to side as the tequila relaxes her a bit. She gives a little sigh and then looks at me and grins.

"Aren't you warm in that hotel robe?" I toss out.

"Yes." She loosens the belt and peels it off her shoulders. I'm rooted to the spot, eyes glued to all the creamy flesh she's revealing. Okay, so it's not a bikini as I had hoped, but one of those suits that looks like a tank top. It's black and simple with a deep V and ties around the neck, molding to her tits and showing a hint of her belly. My mouth goes dry.

"Better?" I eke out.

"Mmm. Much," she says with a giggle. She takes a deep breath which only causes her breasts to push out farther. She's killing me. It's going to be a slow, tortuous death. But the end is certainly near. I'm pulled away from my near-death experience when the music stops pumping and Jase shouts.

"Belly flop contest! Winner gets a thousand dollars!" The girls whoop and holler, going over to where Jase is indicating for people to line up. Hell, I think even the bartender wants to come over and take a chance at a grand. Marin purses her lips and shakes her head.

"You in?" I ask on a laugh. She scowls at me in response. "Didn't think so."

"Don't let that stop you," she says, making a sweeping gesture with her hand for me to go ahead.

"Nah. My dignity's not for sale."

"Good to know." We watch as some half-naked women and the rest of the band and crew jump into the pool in an attempt to make the biggest, loudest, and messiest splash. The winner ends up being Harper, the lighting guy, who manages to soak everyone in the near vicinity. The crowd returns to its regularly scheduled programming of making out, groping, and sloshing around.

It's ninety-five degrees at two in the morning and I need to cool off. A dip is in order.

"Let's get wet," I tell Marin as I turn to face her. The sexual innuendo hangs between us, the humidity stifling the flow of air. She clears her throat.

"I'm okay. But go ahead."

"C'mon. You've got to be hot." Again, I've made something ordinary sound like a come-on.

"I'm okay," she breathes out again. I watch a bead of sweat slide down between her breasts. I've got to get my head out of my ass.

"Uh-uh," I say, shaking my head. "You said you were going to lighten up." I stand up and reach my hand out to her. She slaps it away playfully.

"Really. I'm okay, B. Go enjoy the pool with your friends."

"Don't make me throw you in."

"You wouldn't dare," she huffs. I was kidding, but because of her snippy tone, there's nothing more I want to do right now than toss her in the pool.

"Don't tempt me, Marin," I warn.

"Don't threaten me, Brad," she explodes.

"Challenge accepted," I retort in annoyance. I reach down and with little effort, lift her up into my arms. She kicks her legs.

"B! Put me down!"

"Oh, I'll put you down, alright." She continues to squirm in my arms, now using her hands to try and push off against my chest. Feeling her tight up against me, her skin brushing against mine, I want to bury my nose in her neck, take in her sweet vanilla scent, and touch her everywhere. I'm getting carried away here. I let up on my grip a little bit and pull back to look at her. She's panting and that pink-hued tongue peeks out to lick her lips. There's some sort of electric connection between us right now. Could be all the alcohol. I'm about to lower her down to the ground, and if I'm being honest with myself, lean in for a kiss, when Johnny starts to shout.

"Yeah, B.O., throw her in!" I look around and everyone is now staring at us. I'm certain Marin recognizes it too, as she stiffens in my arms. She lets out what I'm interpreting is a panicked exhale. This can't be the kind of attention she wants.

"B," she starts with fear in her voice. But is she afraid I'm going to throw her in or afraid that everyone can sense the unbelievable chemistry between us? I think it's the latter.

"Do it! Do it! Do it!" Johnny starts to chant with the others joining in the chorus.

"It's okay, Marin," I assure her.

"Do it! Do it!" the crowd continues.

"B," she exhales, tilting her head to the side and giving me a mock glare. "Don't."

"What to do? What to do?" I say feigning uncertainty, as if I'm struggling with my decision.

"B," she pleads. In reality, the choice is clear. I lean back and toss Marin into the air. She lands in the pool with a splash. I jump in right after and come up for air to find her half coughing, half laughing as she pushes her hair off her face and neck.

"You jerk!" she laughs and slugs me in the arm. I put a hand on her waist and help steady her. I look in her eyes and give her a little grin. I'm trying to communicate so much to her without saying a word. I want her to know how much I like her and want to be with her. But I also want her to know I'm not going to push her or do anything to make her uncomfortable or compromise her job.

"Had to be done," I shrug. She gives me a little smile and I'm not sure what to make of it.

"Now that I've cooled off, I'm going to head back to my room," she says and swims toward the pool steps. I watch her curvy, round bottom lift up from the water, and I swallow hard. She walks over to the lounger and wraps her towel around her body. She leans down and grabs the hotel robe, laying it across her arm. I watch as she walks to the pool gate, opens it, and walks through. She turns around to find me staring at her. She gives a tight smile and a wave. I wave back and watch as she travels up the walkway to her room. I turn around and Craig's watching me. He gives me a little head nod and I return it.

Before I can get out of the water and head up to my room, a blonde walks toward me in a tiny bikini, wraps her arms around my waist, and presses herself against my back. I turn around to her big green eyes staring at me, her front teeth pressing into her plump bottom lip. She raises up an arm, reaches behind her neck, and unties her top. It drops down to show perky, round breasts.

I scrub my hand over my jaw. Not because I'm tempted to enjoy this gorgeous woman who's offering herself up to me. It's because I'm not tempted at all. There's only one woman I want and that's Marin.

nineteen

It's five p.m. and I'm lying in the hotel bed watching the *Friends* episode where Chandler pees on Monica's leg after she gets stung by a jellyfish. If I'm being honest with myself, I don't have too many friends who would do that for me. Grace would. Of course she would. And I would do the same for her. I tried calling her but got voice mail.

> ME: *I would pee on you if you got stung by a jellyfish. Just sayin'.*

An hour later, my phone pings with her response.

> GRACE: *Good to know. What about hiding a body? Can I count on you for that?*

> ME: *Why? Have you murdered Bellatrix?*

GRACE: *Only in my fantasies. Will try calling later. XOXO, girlie!*

Fantasies. That word seems applicable right now. I stretch my arms above my head and let out a healthy yawn. Despite coming back to my room at three a.m., I tossed and turned all night. I couldn't get the image of that girl in the green and white polka dot bikini wrapping her arms around Brad. Normally I don't care if girls want to throw themselves at a guy. It's not my style but I won't begrudge anyone else the right to be as forward as they want. But this is Brad we're talking about. He's different than the other guys. At least I want him to be different. Judging by the way he looked down at her while she lowered her top, I'm not so sure he really is different.

I feel like a total stalker for having watched them through the bushes after I left the pool. I wanted one more glimpse of him with his shirt off before I went to bed. One little sneak peek to fuel my nightly fantasies. Jody thinks I've been the one to cramp her style but having a roommate has been hard on me too. I've definitely taken advantage of the time when I have my own hotel room by putting my pocket vibrator to work. As if he can read my mind, my phone chirps with a text.

BRAD: *Everyone's just waking up and going to a brew pub for dinner. Want to come?*

ME: *Really? More drinking?*

BRAD: *Best hangover cure? More alcohol. LOL*

ME: *Thanks but I think I'll just get room service and catch up on some work.*

I want to say yes. But I'm not certain I can face him and the guys tonight. Do they know that I've been crashing in his room—in his bed—when my horndog of a roommate is in heat? Do they know my feelings for Brad have gone beyond a harmless crush to full-blown admiration? Are they aware of how many lines I've circumvented and why there's a major one I can't cross? I need to keep a bit of distance, at least when the other guys are around.

BRAD: You work too much. It's your day off.

BRAD: Come with us. Phoebe says she doesn't want to be the only girl.

What about the girl in the green polka dot bikini? Will she be there?

ME: Sorry to disappoint Phoebe, but I'm going to pass. Have fun.

Have fun? If I'm being honest, I don't want him to have fun. I want him to be as miserable as I am. I want him to be paralyzed with desire to the point where he doesn't even blink an eye when another girl walks by. I drop my shoulders and exhale, considering how selfish I sound. Brad deserves someone special and fun and sweet. I just don't want it to be the girl in the polka dot bikini.

BRAD: Okay. See you tomorrow.

TWENTY

"You need a place to crash tonight?" We just rolled into Omaha, Nebraska, and it's a little shy of two a.m. What should have been a one- to two-hour bus ride turned into a twelve-hour nightmare due to a major truck overturn on the highway. Everyone is tired and irritable—except for Jody and Theo, who look horny.

"Probably. That a problem?" I ask on a yawn.

"Not at all. Just knock when you're ready," Brad responds.

I drop my bags off to my room and Jody and Theo watch, waiting as I grab some pajamas and throw some toiletries into a bag. Do they wonder where I go almost every night? Do they even care?

"Have fun you two," I say on my way out the door. They both smile and wave before what I imagine is a mad dash to remove their clothes and get down to it.

I walk down the hall, feeling a bit self-conscious, hoping no one comes out of their room and notices me slinking into Brad's. Not that anything is going on between us. He's just a good friend doing me a favor. I don't need people talking, though. After that *moment* at the pool, I'm paranoid that everyone thinks we're sleeping together.

I knock on the door and he moves to the side as he opens it, giving me room to come in. I glance around and notice he has two doubles instead of his normal queen- or king-size bed. Looks like I won't be putting him out too much tonight.

After a quick change into some yoga pants and a tank top, and a good scrubbing of my face and brush of my teeth, I leave the bathroom to find Brad stretched out on the side of one bed, with the covers pulled back on the other side. It looks like an invitation for me to join him.

"I'll sleep in this one," I explain, gesturing to the empty bed in the room.

"Actually," he says, scrubbing his hand over his jaw, which now has a light stubble on it. "I've kind of gotten used to having you next to me in bed," he shrugs.

"Oh," I say with a grin. I glance down at the ground and tuck some hair behind my ear. I'm not sure how to respond. If I'm being honest, I've enjoyed being tucked into his side at night too. It's comforting and comfortable. I climb in next to him, kicking my feet to dislodge the sheet tucked into the mattress, and drift off.

I had slipped into an easy sleep when I'm awoken by a loud clap of thunder followed by the sound of rain pouring down in heavy sheets against the windows of the Sheraton. I roll over and look at the digital clock on the nightstand, which reads 4:24 a.m. Based on the weather, it looks like the band won't be doing an outside concert performance this morning on the *Big Party* radio show. Because I'm a professional and damn good at my job, we have a contingency plan in place. They will appear for an in-studio interview later in the morning.

I reach over and grab my cell phone. I call up a group text to the band, Phoebe (who was scheduled to come with us to prep the guys for their appearance), and Damon.

ME: *Rain! Our backup plan is in play. The car will pick us up at nine for an in-studio interview only. No performance.*

Next, I create an email to the car service we are using and type out a quick message to them:

From: MarinC@sashavpr.com
To: Jeff@UnitedCoachTransport.com
Subject: Change for morning pickup at Sheraton

Given the rain, we won't need the car here until 8:45 a.m. for a 9:00 a.m. departure. Please disregard the original 5:45 a.m. pickup. If there are questions, please call me.

I'm composing a new email when Brad mumbles from the other side of the bed.

"Marin. What are you doing?"

"It's raining. I'm letting everyone know about the change to our morning plans. I figured you would all be happy to wake up to my text telling you that you can sleep a few more hours, rather than getting out of bed to see for yourself it's raining," I explain. I feel him shift over closer to me.

"Are you done with the updating?"

"I was going to email Sasha and Amy to let them know of the change." Brad takes my phone out of my hands and places it on the nightstand by rolling me onto my side and reaching across me. I can feel him hard against my backside, his strong arm across my torso, and my nipples tingle. After depositing my phone onto the table, he scoots over even farther so he is right behind me and wraps his arm around me.

"Go to sleep, Marin." I disentangle myself from his arm. "What now?" he huffs in annoyance.

"I need to reset the alarm." I reset the hotel alarm clock for 7:45 and also reset the backup alarm on my phone. After I place the phone back down, I can feel Brad's arm tighten around me.

"Go to sleep, Marin," he repeats. I lie there . . . very still. "Turn off your mind, Marin. Just relax," he says.

"I am relaxed."

"You're not. I can feel how stiff your body is. My guess is you're running through today's to-do list in your mind." He's right, of course. Now with his warm breath tickling my ear and his arm tightening around me, my mind thinks and panics about other things. "You're doing a great job, Marin. Everyone thinks so. It's okay to relax."

"Okay." I try not to read too much into the compliment or what it means to have him aroused and spooning me in his bed. I try to do what he says. I try to turn my mind off and relax. Despite all the thoughts marathoning through my mind, exhaustion takes over. Before I know it, my body melts into the mattress, into him, and I fall asleep.

TWENTY-ONE

M A R I N

I get up from the chair and sway back and forth, gripping onto the arm to steady myself. This earache is beyond painful and I'm starting to feel hot and woozy. It's been bothering me for the past week and I should have addressed the pain sooner. I've just been so busy.

The guys wrapped up an interview with the CBS affiliate in Topeka, Kansas, and now we have a break until the sound check at the concert venue tonight. I was planning to head back to the hotel and confirm the two newspaper interviews we have late tomorrow, go through the photos from this morning's interview session, and write up several social media posts for Amy's approval. Thankfully today's a light day and we don't have anything pressing for tonight. All I can think about, though, is sleep. I take a few deep, steadying breaths and walk over to Damon who is huddled in a hushed conversation with Jase.

"Damon," I say. He turns to look at me.

"What do you need, Marin?" he asks, annoyed.

"I'm going to run an errand or two. I'll make my way back to the hotel on my own."

"Okay." He dismisses me by turning away and continuing his conversation. I pull out my cell phone and search the nearest urgent care facility, which appears to be about three miles from the radio station. Next, I use a car service app to arrange for a ride to take me there.

The wait on the curb is excruciating, as the ache in my ear increases. It feels like a sword being thrust into my eardrum over and over again. My lip quivers and tears fall as I'm unable to handle the intense pain. I thank the Uber gods when the Toyota Corolla arrives within a few minutes and it is a fast ride to the doctor's office. Because it's early in the morning, the office is empty. Within an hour, I'm being examined by the doctor.

Turns out, I've got a 103-degree fever and a severe ear infection. The doctor says with strong antibiotics and some rest, I should be fine in a day or two. She writes out a prescription for me and leaves. It takes all my energy to get up and catch another car back to the hotel.

I'm standing at the concierge desk waiting to ask for the hotel's assistance in finding a local pharmacy to deliver my medicine when Brad walks by.

"Hey, Marin. Where have you been?"

"I had to take care of something," I breathe out. He inspects me more closely and is undoubtedly appalled at my ghastly appearance. I can feel sweat pouring out of every pore.

"Jesus, are you okay?" he asks with concern. He guides me over to a chair in the lobby. "You look awful."

"Thanks," I reply with a weak smile.

"I'm going to get a doctor." He stands up to walk to the concierge desk, but I grab onto his arm.

"I just came from urgent care. I have a bad ear infection and need some antibiotics."

"Well, then let's get you up to your room." He lifts me from the seat.

"I need to talk with the concierge and find a pharmacy that delivers," I say, falling back in exhaustion on the seat.

"I'll take care of it. Give the prescription to me." I'm too tired and in too much pain to argue with him. I reach into my purse and hand him the script. "Give me your room key too." I hand it over and he helps me up. I don't recall much about the elevator ride to my room, only my head hitting the pillow.

TWENTY-TWO

BRAD

I'm getting more and more pissed. I've put Marin into bed in her hotel room and am on my way to a local pharmacy to get her prescription filled. What the hell was she thinking going to urgent care all alone? She could barely stand up. The way she was sweating, you could tell she had a high fever. I feel terrible for her.

It's not surprising she's not feeling well. She's always tired and works so damn much. She is with us every show at night and with us for all our interviews in the morning. Where we can go to sleep in the afternoon or take some time to rest, she's always on her laptop or cell phone planning and attending to details for our tour. Her work ethic astounds me. Now, she needs medicine and rest and I can do something about both of them. I walk into the pharmacy and up to the prescription drop-off window.

"I was hoping to get this prescription filled quickly, Jazmin" I say, reading the name tag of the young woman working behind the counter. I flash her a smile, hoping I can charm my way to a quick turnaround.

"I'm happy to help you," she says with a flirtatious smile. "I'll need the patient's insurance card and date of birth." Shit! I don't know Marin's birthday and I didn't think to get her insurance card.

"I don't have either of those things," I shrug. "Can I get the prescription filled and pay cash?"

"You can, but it will be more money," she explains. "For an antibiotic like this, a prescription co-pay is usually ten to thirty dollars. If you pay cash," she starts, using her fancy painted nails on the pharmacy keyboard, "you're looking at 129 dollars."

"That's fine," I say. "I'll pay cash."

"Okay." She returns her fingers to the keyboard and processes Marin's order.

"How long will it take to fill?"

"Give us fifteen to twenty minutes," she says.

Before I walk away, I turn back around and ask, "She has a pretty high fever and is sweating a lot. Is there anything else I should do?" She refers me to the pharmacist who recommends an over-the-counter pain reliever to supplement the antibiotics.

While I wait, I browse the aisles and pick up a bottle of Advil and a small stuffed alien with enormous googly eyes wearing a tiny t-shirt that reads "EYE hope you feel better." It reminds me of the googly-eyed apples from Marin's first day on the bus, which makes me smile.

After paying for the medicine and catching a car back to the hotel, I get to her room to find her in the exact same position as I left her an hour ago. I open a bottle of water from the mini fridge and take one of her antibiotics and two pain relievers out for her.

"Marin," I whisper, sitting on the edge of the bed and brushing my hand over her head. "Marin," I repeat, a little louder. She's dead to the world. I push her shoulder with a bit more force now and jostle her awake. "C'mon, Marin. I need you to wake up and take your medicine."

She opens heavy-lidded eyes and rasps, "B."

"Hey, there," I whisper. "I need you to take these pills." I hand her the medicine and the water bottle. She tries to sit up but is so weak. I wrap my arm around her and lift her up. She opens her mouth and sticks out her tongue. I can't stop staring at her pretty pink lips and thinking about better uses for them and her tongue. What the hell is wrong with me? She's sick. Like really sick. Clearly, *I'm* the one who's sick. She swallows the pills and I help her back onto the pillow.

"B," she whispers.

"Yeah. I'm right here."

"I'm all sweaty. I need to get out of these sweaty clothes."

"Of course you do. Where are some clean things?" She points to the middle drawer of a hotel dresser across from her bed. I open it and pull out a pair of yoga pants and a Kings Quarters t-shirt.

"You have excellent taste," I quip. She tries laughing, but it comes across weak and pathetic. "I'll step into the bathroom and give you some privacy."

"No," she whines, reaching out her hand to grasp my arm. "I need you to help me." *Gulp!* Marin wants me to help her out of her sweaty work clothes. I scrunch up my face and rub my fingertips on my forehead.

"You can't manage on your own?"

"No," she says on a moan. "I *need* your help."

I blow out a shaky breath. "Okay." I cringe in discomfort from this awkward scenario as I pull the blanket off of her and look at her. She's wearing a pair of black work pants, black socks, and a blue shirt. So yeah, I've fantasized a couple (hundred) times about removing Marin's clothes. I've wanted a closer look . . . and feel . . . and taste . . . since the first time we met, but only when Marin was an active and oh-so-willing participant. This isn't sitting right with me. Reluctantly, I remove her socks and she sighs in relief.

"Keep going," she encourages me. I lift the shirt to uncover her belly, careful not to touch her skin, enough so I can see the button on her pants.

"I'm going to turn around and let you take your pants off," I advise.

"B, help me, please." She blows out an irritated puff. Even dead tired and in pain, she's still got some sass in her. I concentrate on undoing the button without touching her and then look away, trying not see anything. I drag the pants over her hips and down her legs. I look back at her with the yoga pants in hand, but she waves me off. "No pants. I'm too hot. Just help me replace my top." She lifts her arms over her head.

"Uh," I mumble, hesitating.

"Seriously, B," she scoffs. "It's not like you've never seen a woman without her top on." That's true. It won't be the first time I've seen a set of tits. I've even signed a few pairs with a Sharpie. But this is different . . . This is *Marin*. I lift the shirt up, figuring she's wearing a bra underneath, but she's not. Shit! I tried not to see anything. I did. But I managed to catch a quick glance of dusty pink nipples in tight buds before I scrunched my eyes tight.

"Uh, Marin. You're not wearing a bra," I exhale.

"I know. I don't need one with that shirt," she explains. "Is this making you uncomfortable? I need your help. Either close your eyes and accidentally cop a feel or open them and help me cover up." She's laughing at me now. So I open one eye, put the fresh shirt over her head, pull her arms through, and yank the shirt down over her chest.

"Thank you. I know that must have been a real hardship," she mocks.

"Hardy har har," I reply with a smirk. She closes her eyes and inhales through her nose and out through her mouth, taking in and expelling a big lungful of oxygen. I untuck the sheet from the foot of the bed like I've watched Marin do before. I cover her with the sheet but lift it up over her tiny feet, which are sporting light blue polish today. It doesn't matter how arctic the hotel room is, she's always pushing her feet out from under the covers.

Hours pass, and Marin hasn't stirred. A few times, I pressed a cold compress to her forehead, but other than that, I stretched out on the other bed in the room and worked on my video game with the TV playing some sort of cop procedural marathon in the background.

When Jody came by after handling her work for the day, I told her Marin was sick and gave her my room key for the night. Knowing what Marin has shared with me about Jody and Theo's nightlife, I need to make sure housekeeping changes my sheets before we swap back.

When it's apparent Marin is going to need at least another dose or two of the antibiotic to be remotely functional, I pick up the phone and text Damon.

> ME: *Bumped into Marin earlier and she's pretty sick. Doctor put her on heavy-duty antibiotics. She needs to sleep for the rest of the day and likely tomorrow. Can you work it out with Sasha?*

> DAMON: *No problem. Hope she feels better.*

> ME: *Thanks. I know she's going to be worried about work shit, so let me know when you got it covered with Sasha.*

I was tempted to add, "And don't dock her pay." I wouldn't put it past Damon to do something shitty like that. Ten minutes later, my phone buzzes again.

> DAMON: *All squared away. Amy and Brynn have it covered, and I can take photos tonight and tomorrow.*

> ME: *Thanks, man.*

I'm worried Marin has been sleeping for hours. Not that it surprises me. She's been pretty sick. But she's still curled up into a little ball on the side of the bed where she started out six hours ago. Based on what I know from our past nights together, by now she should have sprawled out—arms and legs in every direction.

It's now midnight and time for her next dose. I go over to her and wake her, keeping my voice calm so as not to startle her.

"Hey there," I say. "Time for your medicine."

She rolls back and groans. I help her sit up and she swallows her pill and a dose of pain reliever. I lay her back down and she's out. While she'll be due for her next dose at six in the morning, it's best to let her sleep. I set my alarm for eight thirty just in case, crawl into the other bed, and go to sleep.

*

Marin stirs when the alarm clock reads eight in the morning. I climb out of bed to check on her. "Hey." I lay a gentle hand on her forehead and brush some sweaty hair away from her skin. She feels clammy but she's no longer burning up. Even though the fever broke, she's still got a thin sheen of sweat covering her face. She pulls back the covers a bit to try and sit up, and I notice a few sweat stains under her arms and around the collar. She gives a small moan and lies back down. "Hey," I repeat. "Don't try to get up."

"What time is it?" she asks, lifting up to look at the digital clock on the hotel nightstand.

"It's eight."

"Eight? In the morning?" Her voice is panicked. "I've got to get up," she says, trying to pull the covers away.

"What you need to do is rest," I tell her, "and take your next dose of antibiotic."

"But I have work—"

I cut her off before she can finish. "You don't have any work to do today. Damon already talked with Sasha and explained the situation to her. Someone from the office is handling whatever needs to get done and Damon will handle everything at the show tonight."

"It's okay. I can work," she says, and she pulls the blanket off and tries to shift her legs over the side of the bed. She gets winded and slumps forward a bit.

"It's not okay and you're not okay. You're sick and you need to take care of yourself and let me help you."

"Have you been here the whole time?"

"I have. You looked pretty bad when you came back from urgent care," I start and before I can stop myself, I add, "and so help me, Marin, if you go to urgent care alone again, I'm going to be pissed. Really pissed." I'm shaking my head now and getting angrier and angrier at the thought of her sitting by herself, half passed out in a waiting room.

"Thank you," she says in a quiet, near apologetic voice.

"You're welcome," I respond. Her apparent embarrassment about acting so foolishly calms me down. "I got your antibiotic prescription filled and helped you change your clothes, because you had sweated completely through them." She nods and pulls the covers down enough to see she's got some wet marks around her collar and under her arms.

"Oh my God. I'm all sweaty again."

"You had a pretty high fever." I put my hand up to her forehead and her big, round eyes are my undoing. "Your fever broke and you're okay now."

"Thanks," she says with a small smile. I can't help but stare into her eyes. I'm so entranced by her and I wonder if she's looking at me with similar thoughts in her mind. I break the spell, realizing she needs to take her medicine. "It's time for you to take another dose," I get up from the side of her bed and return with some water and a pill. She takes it without argument.

"How are you feeling? Better?" I ask.

"Much," she says. "I think I—"

"Don't even think about working," I warn her. "Not gonna happen today."

"No. I was going to say I think I could use a shower."

"Oh, okay," I reply. "Do you, uh, need some help?" I pray she says no. Just helping her change her clothes last night was enough awkwardness to last a lifetime.

"No thanks. I can manage."

I move off of the bed and she's slow to rise. I help her walk into the bathroom and when she closes the door, I stand outside of it, taking in a deep breath. I knock and I'm sure I've startled her because she sounds panicked.

"What?" she calls out. "I mean, um, what's up?" she says through the door, and I can tell she's trying to act casual.

"I'm going to order you something to eat. The doctor said the medicine is better when you've eaten and I'm sure having something in your stomach will help improve your energy."

"That would be great. Thank you."

"Anything in particular you want? If I recall, you like chocolate shakes," I say, remembering the look on her face when I caught her red-handed sipping on my shake after she told me she didn't want anything from room service.

"I do like chocolate shakes," she says with another little laugh. "But since it's early in the morning, maybe something a little lighter?"

"You got it. Take a shower and your food will be here after you're done."

"You're not leaving, are you?"

"I'll head back to my room. Give you some privacy. Just need to let Jody know I need my room back since I swapped with her."

"Stay. Have something to eat with me. Please."

"Uh, sure." I call room service and order a plate of scrambled eggs (for protein) and some wheat toast for her and a bowl of oatmeal and plate of bacon for me, along with a pot of coffee. I take out my phone and thumb through my emails, answering a few while I wait for her.

About fifteen minutes later, steam billows from the doorway as Marin emerges from the bathroom in only a towel. Her wet hair is slicked back, and beads of water dot her narrow shoulders and fall down her back. I get a quick hard-on, looking at all that creamy naked skin and imagining myself licking all the water off with my tongue. Yeah, I'm a total asshole. She's sick and all I can think of is maintaining enough self-control I don't jump her and hump her.

She looks over at me with wide, embarrassed eyes before grabbing some clothes and going back into the bathroom. She emerges again a few minutes later, dressed in a pair of black sweat pants and a black tank top that fits tight across her chest. She runs a hand through her wet hair and walks over to the bed and sits down.

"How you are feeling?"

"Much better," she says with a sigh. "Tired, though." She leans her head back and closes her eyes. "Taking a shower wiped me out, but it sure feels good to clean up."

"I'm glad you're feeling better. I think another good night's sleep will help."

"It's only nine in the morning," she says with a laugh. "Surely I can't sleep all day."

"You can, and you should." Before she can respond, room service arrives with our breakfast. She manages to get a few bites down while I inhale six slices of bacon and two cups of coffee. I'm about to tuck her back into bed when she stands up.

"Seriously," she says. "I'm feeling better. I should check my emails," she adds as she looks around for her phone.

"No way." I stand up and walk over to her bed. I help her sit down and then sit next to her. "You are on bed rest until tomorrow at the very least." I take the phone off the nightstand where it's charging and unplug it, moving it to an outlet across the room.

"Listen, B. I appreciate your help. I truly do," she begins, getting out of bed and reaching toward her phone, "but my job is really important to me and I don't want Sasha to think I'm not able to keep up the pace." Her mouth is writing checks her body can't cash, because she sways and sits back down.

"Marin, it's not gonna happen. Sasha knows what a superstar you are. We all do. You are accomplished and smart and work so hard to make a bunch of losers like us look good, but you need to rest."

She lets out a loud exhale. "Okay." I'm not sure if she's giving in because she believes me—that everyone knows getting sick has nothing to do with her work ethic—or because she's plain exhausted. Either way, I'll take it. I'm just worried about her.

"Thank you," she whispers before falling back to sleep.

I text Jody and let her know I need to get back into my room to shower and grab some stuff for the day. I leave Marin a note telling her I'm heading to my room and will be back in an hour. After getting cleaned up, I return to Marin's room to find her still asleep exactly as I had left her.

I spend the next few hours hanging out in her room, coding on my video game and eating the lunch I also got from room service—a turkey sandwich and chocolate shake. Marin has continued to sleep through it all. At two in the afternoon, I gently wake her, as it's time for her next dose.

She takes the pill but won't accept anything to eat. She falls back on the pillow and is out like a light again. It's time for me to head out to the concert hall where we have our show tonight. We've got a sound check scheduled and I think another interview. I leave her a note again and let her know I've got to take care of stuff for the show. I leave her phone plugged in on the nightstand so she can reach it to call for help if she needs it. I also leave the room service menu in case she wakes up hungry.

As much as I would love to cancel tonight and stay here to make sure she has everything she needs, I can't let Craig down. I consider talking with the concierge about getting somebody from the hotel—a caregiver of some sort—to stay here with her and wake her to take her medicine, but I change my mind. I think Marin would freak out if a stranger were in her room. Plus, I have a better idea.

TWENTY-THREE

MARIN

I slowly wake, stretching out my arms and legs. I feel a bit disoriented and have to look around to determine where I am. Oh yeah, I'm in bed and have been all day because of a damn ear infection. Can something like this derail my career? Damon must think I'm a total slacker. He's never warmed to me and this will give him ammunition to think even less of me. Damn it!

I look over at the clock and it's a little after 4:00. On the nightstand, I find my phone, a room service menu, a note from Brad letting me know he had to get to the show, and a little "Get Well" stuffed toy.

Brad. How do I even begin to process this all? He went to get my prescription and has sat vigil by my bedside these past twenty-four-plus hours. He also changed me out of my sweat-soaked clothes. Oh God. I groan at the thought. What must he think of me? What do I want him to think of me? What is happening between us? Is this how it happened for Mom? How did I let this happen when I'm supposed to be focusing on work?

Shit! Work. I grab my cell phone and start scrolling through the dozens upon dozens of missed emails. I scan the senders and subjects until I land on one from Sasha titled, "Sick." I click it open and sit up in the bed. It reads:

From: Sasha@sashavpr.com
To: MarinC@sashavpr.com
Subject: Sick

Marin: You should have told me how sick you were. You're no good to us in the hospital. Please take the next day off and rest. If you need more time to recuperate, let Damon know. Damon has the promotion winners handled and Brynn and Amy will handle any media needs. Feel better!

I click over to the sent messages and there are at least fifteen media inquiries that have been opened and responded to. I sigh in relief. Nothing's fallen through the cracks and Sasha seems genuinely concerned about me. Maybe it is okay to lie in bed and rest up.

I turn on the TV and scroll through the guide until I find *Mean Girls* on TBS. I settle into bed and grab the room service menu because now I'm hungry. I enjoy the movie and a big bowl of creamy macaroni and cheese, letting the comfort food nourish my body and spirit. Around eight thirty, after watching another film—*Can't Hardly Wait*—I feel tired and close my eyes. I know, based on Brad's note, my next dose of medicine is at ten, so I set my alarm. Before the alarm rings, my phone buzzes. I look at the caller ID and it's Brad. Shouldn't he be at the concert right now?

"What's wrong? Don't you have a show right now?" I ask, worried. It's almost impossible to hear him on the other end, the noise is so loud.

"Marin?" he calls into the phone. I can imagine him standing wherever he is, pushing a finger into his ear.

"I'm here. Where are you?"

"Okay, everyone. I've got Marin on the phone, but I can't hear her very well. I need you all to settle down." His voice fades a bit, like he's pulled it away from his mouth. The background noise has softened, although there are a few whoops and hollers. "Marin, you there?"

"Yeah?" I say with skepticism. "What's going on?"

"Well, we're at the show right now," he starts and there's a bit of an echo, almost as if it's feedback from him talking into the phone and the mic at the same time.

"What?" I exclaim. He's calling me during the show?

"Yeah. We're at the show and I was telling everyone here how sick you are," he explains, "and you're due for your next dose of medicine at ten, so we thought we would call."

"Wha...aa?" I stammer out.

"Okay everyone, say hi to Marin," he says before forty thousand people shout hello to me. "You're on speakerphone, if you want to say hi back," he adds.

"Hi everyone," I laugh.

"Anyway, we wanted to make sure you take your meds," he says.

"Thanks everyone," I say back, shaking my head and trying to comprehend what an amazing guy Brad is that he would not only think of me during his show but take time out of performing to make sure I'm okay.

"Alright. One last thing," he continues before the entire stadium shouts "Feel better Marin!" He hangs up the phone. Once I'm no longer talking with him, my phone buzzes—the alarm I had set earlier to remind myself to take my antibiotic. I like Brad's way much better.

TWENTY-FOUR

BRAD

I pass the little kitchenette on the bus as I make my way back from the bathroom to my spot next to Marin. I spy a Krispy Kreme donut box on the counter and can't resist. I flip open the lid and the entire carton is filled with broccoli. There's a note on the inside cover:

Happy eating, asshole.

I'm guessing this is a Jase special and payback for Oliver changing all the autocorrect settings on Jase's cell phone to something dirty and pervy. Jase's mom wasn't thrilled when he referred to lasagna as "vagina" and her EpiPen as an "epic penis."

I look over at Marin and she's got much better color in her face. I'm not sure why that's important, but they always say that on TV shows so it must be a good sign. She's not sweating, and she seems to have more energy too. I think she's close to being one hundred percent.

Phoebe sits down next to us. "I'm so glad you are feeling better, Marin," she says, laying a hand on Marin's shoulder.

"Thank you. Me too," Marin responds with a smile. I warm thinking of the two of them becoming friends.

"I got to say, I'm a little disappointed you didn't let us know you weren't feeling well. We certainly could've been there to help you."

"I know," Marin says, glancing down at her lap where her hands are now folded together. "I feel really silly for not speaking up sooner. Maybe if I had, it wouldn't have gotten so bad," she admits. Damn straight.

"We're like a family. We take care of each other," Phoebe responds, looking Marin in the eye. "Just know if there's anything you need, you can always count on us, and especially me," she adds.

"Thanks Phoebe. That means a lot to me," Marin replies. Phoebe pats her leg and walks back over to Craig.

"What's the look for?" I ask her.

"What look?"

"I don't know. That's why I'm asking. You look like you're happy and sad at the same time."

"I have a strange ache in my heart," she explains. "It's so nice to feel like you've found a true friend and it makes me miss Grace so much. I can't wait to see her."

"I'm glad you have Grace . . . and Phoebe. You have me too, you know?"

"Thanks," she says with a grin. The bus pulls over at a local gas station to fill up and Marin gets out. She returns a few minutes later and resumes her seat next to me. Now she has a plastic bag from the convenience store in her lap and she pulls out a handwritten letter on hotel stationery from her purse.

"Listen," she begins. "I, um, wanted to thank you again for being so sweet to me these past two days." Her eyes shine with sincerity as she places her hand over mine.

"I'm glad you're feeling better," I say with a shrug and a smile, my dick twitching at the skin-to-skin contact. What I want to say is that she scared the shit out of me and I want to be there to make her feel better every day. That I can't stop thinking about her. That she's the most amazing girl I've ever met. That when she puts on her glasses, I feel like a teenager about to come in his pants. I don't because I know that will scare the shit out of her.

"So, I hope you enjoy this little thank you gift, bearing in mind my limited access to adequate resources," she says, placing her purse underneath the seat in front of her and putting her hand in the plastic bag, no doubt searching for something. "I wanted to take five," she starts, pulling out a Take5 candy bar and handing it to me, "to say thank you for being a real . . ." Her voice trails off as her hand fishes around the plastic bag further. She pulls out a roll of Life Savers and hands them to me. "For being a real lifesaver," she says with a knowing wink.

I can't help but chuckle at her cleverness. I'm about to say something when she continues, glancing down at the paper in her hand.

"Don't think I'm a nerd," and she hands me a package of Nerds candies, "but this is all I could find at the Circle K and I didn't want this opportunity to slip through my butterfingers," she says, tilting her head to the side and giving me a cheeky grin. I take the box of Nerds and Butterfinger bar and place them in my lap. Seeing the bag is not yet empty, I stay silent, eager for more.

"I have mounds of appreciation for you," she says, handing a chocolate and coconut Mounds candy bar over to me. She giggles when I shudder to indicate I'm not a fan of coconut. "I feel like an . . ." she continues, searching the bag and pulling out a bright red Airheads wrapper, "airhead for not saying something earlier about being sick."

I nod my head. "You should be. Don't do it again," I say, pointing a finger at her.

"I won't."

"Good." I place my hand over hers.

"I'm not done yet," she says, pulling her hand away from mine. Is she uncomfortable with the contact? "The sleep and medicine were good and plenty," she nods, handing over the telltale pink Good & Plenty box of candy-coated licorice. "Now, I feel like a hundred grand," she says, sitting up a bit taller. She hands over a 100 Grand bar, which is one of my favorites. I clutch it to my heart and roll my eyes heavenward with a sigh.

"It Mentos"—both of us cringe a bit at the awful pun—"a lot to me that you took such good care of me. I'll appreciate it now and later," she continues. She pulls out a roll of Mentos and a bright pink pack of watermelon-flavored Now and Laters. I haven't seen those candies in a long time and now I'm thinking back to Halloween as a kid. My mouth waters as I think about sucking on one of those never-ending treats. Marin's sweet voice pulls me from the Now and Laters to the here and now.

"I scored," she says, pulling out a Skor bar from the bag, "having a friend like you." In a matter of seconds, I've lost my appetite. I don't want to be her *friend*. I want to be so much more. I take the candy from her with a tight smile. Yes, I need to figure out a way to break through the friend barrier with her. "I hope this thank you makes you snicker," she says, pulling a king-sized Snickers bar from her bag. I'll be sure to pass it along to Craig. It's his favorite.

"Thank you," I say. "That was incredible." I mean it. She is so smart and clever and funny.

"Oh, there's one more," she says with a mischievous smile. "Don't eat all this at once or you'll get chunky," she says in mock warning, handing me a Chunky bar. I'd never heard of it, but one look and it appears to be a big slab of chocolate with peanuts and raisins. Again, I'm blown away by her. Her humor drives me wild and my hearty laugh ensures she knows it.

She hands me the bag and starts to put all the candy bars—that are sitting in my lap—inside. Her hand brushes against my upper thigh and it takes all my fortitude to not spring a boner right there. I casually brush her hand away, fearful if she accidentally touches me again, I won't be able to fight the intense sexual attraction I have for her.

"I've got this," I say, scooping everything into the bag. "Can I offer you anything?" I open the bag and show her what's inside.

"No thanks," she laughs. "I'm good."

"Okay then," I say, tying the handles of the bag into a loose knot and placing it under the seat in front of me. "I'm going to save this until after lunch. Plus, I need to heed your advice or risk losing my girlish figure." She laughs before growing somber.

"Seriously. Thank you," she says, looking me square in the eye.

"Seriously. You're welcome."

TWENTY-FIVE

MARIN

It's close to one thirty when we arrive back at the hotel after the show. I'm exhausted and nothing other than falling asleep in Brad's bed, in his arms, sounds better. Gah! I've grown attached to him. Too attached. These growing feelings can only end badly, I fear. Yet I'm helpless to stop them. I slink down the hallway after changing in my room. As I'm about to knock on his door, the one across the hall swings open.

"Get out of here!" screams Craig as he shoves some woman out of his hotel room. She's gripping his shirt, almost ripping the sleeve off the arm. "Call security," he calls into the room. I press myself up against the wall.

"I love you Craig," the woman whines. "I know you love me too." Phoebe comes out of the room, shaken. She's running her hands up and down her arms, unshed tears filling her eyes.

"What's going on?" shouts Brad, opening the door at the commotion. The woman turns and lunges toward Brad but is unable to escape Craig's tight grasp on her arms.

"Tell him, Brad. Tell him we are meant to be together," the woman implores.

"What the hell?" Brad takes a subtle step back. By this time, other people on the tour, including Deeana and Damon, have come to check out the disruption.

"You know we're destined to be together," she cries, sinking down to the ground. "You know you love me." Craig, seeing security coming down the corridor, let's go of the woman and rushes to Phoebe's side. He pulls her close to him and kisses the top of her head. Phoebe swallows hard and pushes away from him, turning back into the room. The two security guards lift the girl off the floor and haul her away.

"Why are you doing this Craig?" she pleads, now starting to sob. "Why? I love you."

"I found her hiding in my shower," explains Craig to the security guard, who nods and drags the woman away while she continues to question why Craig doesn't love her back. Craig turns to Deeana.

"I don't want this shit happening again," he says, pointing to her. "Someone's head's gonna roll," he adds, shaking his head.

"You okay?" asks Brad, walking over to him and placing a consoling hand on his shoulder.

"Yeah. I'm fine," Craig exhales. "Phoebe's pretty shaken up, though. Damn it," he mutters. Brad gives his shoulder a squeeze and walks back to his doorway.

"Alright everyone. Show's over," says Damon, ushering everyone back to their rooms. "We've got a 10:00 a.m. roll out tomorrow so go get some sleep." The lookie-loos go back to their rooms. "Deeana and I will handle this," he says, lowering his head to make eye contact with Craig, who is still staring at the ground and muttering to himself. "Hey, look at me," Damon says. Craig lifts his head up. "Deeana and I got this. Go take care of Phoebe."

Damon stalks to Deeana, who pulls her shoulders back and raises a pointer finger in the air.

"Damon—" she starts.

"This is a monumental fuckup," Damon hisses, raking his fingers through his hair. Looking back at the now-closed hotel door he continues, "If Phoebe pulls him from the tour, you'll never work in this business again." He storms off before Deeana can respond. I feel Brad's hand on the small of my back.

"You okay?" he asks.

"Uh, yeah." I turn to look at him and he ushers me into his room. I'm certainly better off than Deeana. Or Phoebe.

"I'm sorry you had to see that." He scowls toward Damon and guides me to sit down on the bed. By the way he's acting, and the way I'm feeling, I'm pretty sure I'm in some state of shock. "Can I get you anything?"

"No, I'm fine." I put on a brave grin. "Does that happen a lot?" He runs his hand over his stubbled jaw and stands up, pacing the room.

"It's happened a few times."

"Oh."

"You tired?" he asks.

"Exhausted," I say, my shoulders sagging forward.

"C'mon." He helps me stand up and guides me to lie down on the bed to where he's pulled the covers back. I lie down, and he sidles up behind me. He wraps his arm around me and whispers, "Good night, Marin."

"Good night," I whisper back.

When I wake in the morning, his firm body is still pressed against mine as he spoons me from behind. His arm is underneath my head and wrapped around my jaw and my fingers grip his bicep. Without thinking much about it, I rub my fingers across his skin and notice how soft it is. Other than that, I don't move. I don't want to break the spell. I want to lie here in his arms and imagine we are two different people.

We are a normal couple sleeping in on a Sunday morning. We are not two people who work together, my interest in him forbidden by ethics, morals, family history. I want to imagine he's a normal guy. Not some rock star with a crazy lifestyle and a future filled with groupies and disturbed fans and the inevitable jealousy from women throwing themselves at him all the time.

Later that morning on the bus, I sit down next to Phoebe, unsure if I will be a welcome intrusion. "How are you doing?" I recall how sweet she was to me when I was sick, and I want to reciprocate.

"I'm okay," she says, nodding her head, trying to convince herself more than me. "I wish I could say that's never happened before, but unfortunately it's not the first time I've found a strange woman in Craig's hotel room." I raise a quirked brow. "Don't get me wrong," she adds. "I trust him one hundred percent. I just don't trust other women," she snorts.

"How do you do it? How do you put up with"—I gesture around the bus—"all this?"

"I love them. All of them," she says with a shrug, like it's a simple explanation. "To me, it's worth dealing with all this other stuff if I get to have Craig." She pats my knee and walks over to Craig, squeezing Brad's shoulder on her way.

TWENTY-SIX

MARIN

The hotel air conditioner kicks on, the hum rousing me from sleep and reminding me I'm sprawled out in Brad's hotel bed. The noise must wake him too, because I feel his body cover mine and his warm breath tickle my neck.

"I can't deny myself anymore, Marin," he says, his fingers in my hair, gripping my head and pulling it to the side exposing more of my neck to him.

"Ahh," is all that comes out in frantic little spurts as Brad lifts my tank top over my head. His lips wrap tight around my nipple and he sucks with the right amount of pressure and moisture. My body heats all over and my panties are wet. Just when I think I could come from this exquisite, sensual torture alone, he moves his talented mouth down my body, peppering my belly and hips with tender, moist kisses.

"Your skin tastes so good," he pants in between kisses, his erection pressing into my thigh. My hips move of their own accord, seeking contact, friction, and relief when I feel his fingers inside my panties.

"I've waited for this for so long. Too long," he groans as his fingers push past any barriers and explore my wet heat. My hips buck off the bed when his finger touches my most sensitive spot.

"Oh, B," I moan. "Me too." I encourage him.

"Fuck, Marin. You're so wet," he groans.

"You made me that way," I pant as he strokes me from the inside, hitting that spot destined to obliterate all sense of normalcy.

"I can feel you gripping my finger so tight," he says, sucking my earlobe into his mouth. The sensation brings goose bumps to my skin.

"Oh God, B," I say between quick exhales. "That feels so good."

"I'm going to make you come so hard," he says before adding a second finger and pumping them in and out of me. My hips come up off the bed, searching for more intensity before everything goes blank. There's nothing but pleasure coursing through me and I release a strangled cry as I convulse.

I wake with a shudder, the tingling ripples of my orgasm still coursing through me. My breathing is ragged, and I've got a thin sheen of sweat covering my body. Brad is fast asleep, but grows a bit restless, rolling over and readjusting his pillow, unaware I've had the most arousing and intense sex dream—about *him*—of my life.

I glance over to the clock—it reads 3:02 a.m. I slip out of bed and go into the bathroom. Reflecting back to me in the mirror are flushed cheeks and woozy eyes—a haze of postcoital bliss.

I splash some cold water on my face and contemplate going back to my room. Jody and Theo are probably asleep. Come to think of it, they may be going at it. *Come* to think of it, I chuckle to myself. That's what I did.

Oh my God.

It hits me.

I had a full on, mind-blowing sex dream about Brad, along with a real-life orgasm. Was I talking aloud? What if he heard me? What if he had woken up? Would it be that good in real life?

Would his body feel as good as I imagine? Would it make mine feel as good as I imagined?

I feel flushed again, my body humming in anticipation of what Brad could do to me. What we could do together. I'm building already, my nipples aching and my center throbbing. I let out a loud exhale before opening the door a smidge to check on Brad, still blissfully unaware at how supercharged my libido is right now.

Although I'm guessing he would be more blissful if he knew I was in his bathroom right now, fantasizing about touching him. I lock the door and slide my hand into my panties. Then I turn on the bathroom fan to mute the sound of my labored breath and muffled moans as I stroke and tease, build and climb. The tightening low in my belly warns my orgasm is fast approaching. I want to draw it out, prolong the intensity because the thought of him is making me feel so good.

At the same time, I strum faster, working to grasp that sweet relief because I know Brad is a few feet away and could wake any moment. The last thing I want is to be discovered touching myself in his bathroom.

I pinch my nipple hard and bite down on my lip, imagining Brad taking me in this hotel shower, and then I let go, playing greedily with myself while the tremors rock my body.

I let my breathing settle, wash my hands, and splash more cold water on my face. I tiptoe out of the bathroom to find Brad in the same position as before. I crawl back under the covers relieved he's none the wiser. I fall back asleep with a smile on my face but an ache in my heart.

TWENTY-SEVEN

BRAD

If it's Tuesday, we must be in Dallas, Texas. The tour is flying by, or maybe it's time with Marin making things go so quickly. This is our last stop before a much-needed break in the schedule. The band will fly home while the crew takes the buses back to LA, and then we'll all get a few more days off.

I swing by Marin's room to see what time we need to be ready for our interview with the local morning show tomorrow. I already know the car will be here at five thirty a.m. I also know I could text her if I needed the information. But honestly, I'll take any excuse to spend time with her. I knock on the door.

"Did you forget your key aga—" she says as she opens it up. I'm guessing she thought Jody had come back to the room. She stands there, shocked, so I take the opportunity to give her a quick once over. Holy . . . She looks so hot. She's wearing a tight black tank top and a little pair of cotton boy shorts. Yes, I know what the underwear style is called because, as a teenager, I jacked off to the Victoria's Secret catalog I stole from my neighbor's mailbox. Damn if I don't feel the urge to run to the bathroom with a bottle of lotion in hand to take care of this boner that popped up upon seeing her shapely legs and curvy ass in those tight little black panties.

"You're not Jody," she says with a chuckle.

"Uh-uh" is all I can utter as I stare at her. That's a feat considering all the blood in my body has flown to my pants.

"Give me a sec," she says, an unmistakable blush rushing across her face. She closes the door and I pull my sweatshirt over my head and fold it over my arms in front of me to hide the huge erection she's sure not to miss. She returns a moment later wearing a white terry cloth hotel robe. All I want to do is back her into her room, pull open the belt, and feast on her.

"Sorry about that," she says.

"Hey, no problem," I say, trying to brush off the fact she's in her underwear.

"So, what's up?"

"Uh . . . I came by to see what time we had to be ready tomorrow," I manage to spit out.

"The car arrives at five thirty, so you need to roll out of bed before then. We'll do hair and makeup at the studio, and no one aside from me and the guys will see that mess of hair you have first thing in the morning," she says, smiling. I like her knowing how messy my hair is after a good night's sleep. I like it a lot.

"You don't need to crash in my room tonight?" I ask with a hopeful grin.

"No, but thank you. Jody is spending the night in Theo's room for a change, so you can have the bed to yourself."

"Yeah, you really do take up so much space."

"Excuse me," she says, affronted, cocking her hand on her hip. "Is that some kind of comment about the size of my ass? It's not my fault craft services always has freshly baked chocolate chip cookies on the table."

"Not at all," I say, putting my two hands up in front of me in surrender mode, my sweatshirt dangling from my arm. "I meant you start out the night curled up in a ball and end up in the morning all spread out in the middle," I explain.

"Yeah, my dad says I sleep like a starfish," she laughs.

"A starfish?" I repeat, my brow crinkled in confusion.

"Yeah, I'm a bunch of limbs all sprawled out in different directions, taking up all the space," she says with a good-natured shrug.

"That's great. Well, happy to let you crash at my place anytime," I say, and I mean it. I wish she would crash into me wearing those sexy-as-hell boy shorts. If she's a starfish, then I'm a greedy octopus. I want to wrap my arms and legs around her. I'm normally not a cuddler. I'm normally not like this, but there's something about this girl.

"Thanks. I really appreciate it," she says. She shifts from one foot to the other and glances down at the floor. "Well, we should get to bed," she says. "Early morning and all."

"Yeah. We should get to bed," I say, wishing Jody and Theo were hooking up in her room tonight so she would join me in mine. We both stand there, staring at each other. She breaks the silence first.

"Okay then. I'll see you bright and early tomorrow," she says with a small smile.

"Yeah. See you tomorrow. Good night, starfish."

She smiles, glances down at the ground once more and closes the door.

TWENTY-EIGHT

MARIN

I'm sitting in my hotel room, sending email confirmations to some radio stations scheduled to interview Kings Quarters while we are in Las Vegas in a few weeks. My cell phone rings and from the caller ID I can see it's someone from Sasha V.

"This is Marin," I say in my most professional voice.

"Marin, it's Sasha and Amy," says Amy in a clipped tone. Sasha and Amy are calling me. I hope everything is okay. Butterflies start up in my stomach.

"Hi. What can I do for you?" I ask, trying to keep my voice even.

"As you know, Oliver's brother is getting married soon and the band is taking a week and a half off before the last month of the tour," Sasha continues. I did notice a break on the tour schedule and was excited at the prospect of heading home, sleeping in my own bed, and catching up with Grace.

"Yes, I did see that on the schedule."

"Well, Amy had a great idea. She thinks we should follow each of the five band members around for a day and chronicle what they do on their time off," explains Sasha.

"That's a great idea," I offer. It *is* a great idea and I regret not coming up with it myself. As she's talking, it hits me: I thought I was getting a nine-day vacation. I should have known better.

As if she can read my thoughts, Sasha adds, "I know you figured you were going to get some time off, and you will. Even if you spend a day with each of the guys, you'll still have four days to recharge your batteries."

"It's no problem," I say with conviction. As disappointed as I am, I don't want to give them any reason to doubt my commitment to this post or my future with the company.

"We've already talked with Damon about the idea and he'll chat with the guys to ensure you have access to each of them during the break," explains Amy. "Just work directly with him."

"Okay. Will do," I reply.

"We'll talk soon, Marin," says Sasha before she hangs up. I sit there disappointed. Looks like I have some coordination to do.

TWENTY-NINE

BRAD

These past few weeks with Marin have been torture. I've either spent the night with a painful erection as she lies in my arms in my bed, her sweet smell of vanilla filling my nose. Or, on the nights when she's in her own room, I've jerked myself raw to the thought of her. I've even resorted to paying the housekeeping staff not to change the sheets, so her scent lingers when she's not here. If the guys knew any of this, they would mock me to death.

I've been good about keeping this all to myself—I've kept both my emotions close to the vest and my own hand close to my shaft, but last night, I kissed her. I wasn't thinking. We were in the bed, lights out, talking about why Dumbledore didn't destroy the Elder Wand in *Harry Potter* when he had the chance. I argued Dumbledore thought the wand would die with him. He had arranged for Snape to kill him and therefore technically wasn't defeated which would mean the wand's power died with him. Of course, things changed when Draco Malfoy disarmed Dumbledore and disrupted the plan, unknowingly becoming the wand's master.

Marin thought Dumbledore wanted Voldemort to get the wand from Snape, not realizing he couldn't use it because Snape had never been its master and therefore, even though Voldemort killed Snape, couldn't be the wand's real master.

It was a playful yet heated debate about which we agreed to disagree. Realizing we had to be up early in the morning, I leaned over and kissed her before saying good night. I rolled over to my side in the other direction and . . . cringed.

Not that the kiss was bad. On the contrary. It set me on fire. Her lips were soft yet firm with a faint hint of her minty toothpaste. I wanted so much more. I was hoping she did too.

Judging by the way her body stiffened up and she held her breath, I figured I was wrong—that this was all one-sided and I had been imagining what was happening between us. In other words, I seriously fucked up. I spent the next hour lying still thinking of how I was going to fix this. As much as I wanted all of Marin, I was willing to take whatever little she was willing to give.

This morning, though, she traced my lips with her finger while she thought I was sleeping. Her finger. Brushing across my skin like a whisper. It took all my strength not to roll on top of her and pound her into the mattress. I let her have the moment though, and when she snuck out of my room a few minutes later, I continued to feign sleep and let her leave unnoticed. I've got to be careful about my next move so I don't scare her off.

THIRTY

"Hey girlie," says Grace, chipper as always. I've grown accustomed to our chats and gossip sessions. This tour has been a total killjoy where our friendship is concerned, and I feel thrilled I managed to catch her on the phone now.

"Hey there," I say, an ache in my chest because I miss her so much. "What's going on?"

"Oh, you know, at the pet store buying Bellatrix's dog, Cujo, his custom-made organic dog food," she laughs, taking it all in stride.

"I don't know how you put up with as much crap at work as you do," I say with admiration. "I would have cracked a long time ago."

"Yeah, well, we just finished recasting a few pilots, so she's been on an unusually hideous tear, but whatcha gonna do, right?"

"Bellatrix is so lucky to have you. So is Cujo. That dog eats better than most people. You're such a dynamo."

"Aww, go on," she says, sounding embarrassed. "No, really, go on," she commands, encouraging me to continue talking. She always makes me laugh like that.

"So, what's going on with you? Where are you now?"

"We're in Dallas and I'm exhausted. I've never worked this much in my life. In fact . . ." I start, about to tell her I was pretty sick for a while.

"Listen, brat," she says with a laugh. "You haven't had to do laundry, cook a meal, grocery shop, wash a dish, or do anything else domestic in weeks. Plus, you are hanging out with hot rocks stars, and you're complaining because you've got a lot of work to do?"

"Ugh. If I have one more glass of freshly squeezed orange juice for breakfast . . ." I start in mock despair. Despite the fact she can't see me, I'm holding my hand up to my forehead, pained.

"You really are a brat," she whines. I bust out laughing.

"Yes, I know. I shouldn't be complaining when I know you work as hard as I do and aren't enjoying the perks of maid service, free food, and laundry."

"Exactly. So there's got to be something else. What gives?" She knows me too well.

"A few weeks ago I got pretty sick." I take her silence on the other end as shock and want to assure her there is nothing to worry about. "I'm fine now."

"What happened?"

"I got run-down with all the long hours and contracted a bad ear infection. I finished up my course of antibiotics and now I'm feeling back to normal."

"Ay yi yi," she says. "That doesn't sound fun."

"It wasn't. You weren't there to make me ramen noodles."

"I am a whiz with boiling the water," she quips.

"I miss you."

"I miss you too. Is it lonely out there on the road or are you making friends?"

"It's not too bad. I'm honestly pretty busy with work. When I do have free time, it's on the bus rides and back at the hotel at night. The makeup artist, Phoebe, is sweet, and I've been hanging out with Brad, one of the guys in the band. In fact, he was the one who helped me when I was sick. He took care of me, went to the pharmacy to get my medicine, and even called Sasha to let her know I needed some time to rest."

"Which one is Brad again?"

"He's the lead guitarist. He's got dark wavy hair that he spikes up sometimes, and big brown eyes. When he's not in front of the camera or crowds, he wears these sort of Clark Kent glasses. He's not at all what I expected. Not that I had given it much thought. They sprung this job on me at the last minute. He's so nice and sweet and smart and oh, he's so talented. He can pick up practically *any* instrument and just start playing it. Did you know he wrote the band's song 'Honestly'? It was nominated for a Grammy last year."

"You like him," she says.

"Brad?"

"Yes. You like him."

"Well, yeah, sure I like him. He's a really good guy. I don't know what I would have done if he hadn't helped me out. I'd probably still be sweating like a pig in a hotel room in Topeka," I say with a chuckle.

"No, you *like him* like him," she responds in a sassy tone.

"Don't be ridiculous. I don't *like him* like him."

"You talk about him like he's the Second Coming."

"I do not," I scoff, shaking my head. "I *like* like my job and I want to keep it."

"C'mon, Marin. It's me. We could go around and around with me trying to convince you that you like him and you giving denials. You and I both know at the end of the day, I will be right, you will be wrong. You will admit I am right, I will gloat, and we will have the truth. So let's cut out all the middle steps and get down to it. What are you gonna do about this?"

With a resigned sigh, I reply, "There's nothing to do about this. It's a little crush, but it won't go anywhere."

"Do you think this crush is one-sided?"

"Uh . . . no," I say quietly, knowing the barrage of probing questions is about to begin.

"Really? What makes you say that? Has something happened?" I can picture her getting more excited and animated as her words come out in a rush.

"He kissed me."

"What? When? Where?" Now I'm picturing her jumping out of her skin.

"Two nights ago . . . in his hotel room," I whisper, like saying it out loud makes it even scarier.

"You were in his hotel room?" It's the same suggestive tone she used when she'd ask if I would be leaving a sock on the door to let her know our room was to be occupied for the night.

"Yes. We've kind of been sleeping together for a few weeks."

"Whoa, whoa, whoa. Back it up. You've been *sleeping together* for a few weeks and you think he likes you because he *kissed* you? I am so confused. Start from the beginning," she says, so I do. I tell her everything from Jody and Theo to playing games to falling asleep in Brad's bed.

"Two nights ago, after we were discussing *Harry Potter*, he turned to me and laid a soft and gentle kiss on my lips before rolling over and going to sleep."

"Wow" is all she can say. The fact I've rendered Grace mostly speechless is saying something. We sit there on the phone in silence while I let all this sink in for her until she's speaks up. "So what happened in the two days since the kiss?"

"Nothing. He's acting like it never happened, and I certainly haven't said anything."

"You've been sleeping in his room?"

"Not the past two nights. Jody and her man spent the last two nights in his room, so I had my room to myself. Now we are about to have a bit of a break. So I don't really know what is going on."

"What do you want to happen?"

"Things need to go back to the way they were," I say.

"Meaning what?" She sounds as confused about things as I am.

"Meaning I want to be his friend and hang out with him. He's really awesome. Very talented and very smart. You know he's like a computer programming genius, and the way he plays the guitar? It really isn't fair."

"An embarrassment of riches, huh?"

"Exactly. He's pretty much perfect."

"Sexy?" she asks with a sigh.

"Oh yeah," I respond with a sigh of my own.

"Sounds to me like he's the kind of guy you want as more than a friend." She makes it sound so simple.

"In another life, perhaps, but in this one, I need this job. I like this job. I'm good at it. I won't do anything to mess that up."

"Well, it sounds like we've got lots more analysis to do . . . over beers," she laughs. "I'm so excited you are coming home tomorrow!"

"Me too. I should warn you, I have some work to do, which is why I called. I originally thought I was getting a bit of a vacation and I know you took a few days off to hang with me. Turns out I need to spend a day with each of the band members, chronicling what they do on their time off. But I'll be able to sleep in my own bed and have dinner with you every night, and we'll still have a few days together."

"Awesome. When do you get in?"

"I think we're scheduled to get in around three."

"I won't be home until at least seven thirty so let yourself in and feel free to clean the bathroom if you're bored."

"Ha. I don't think I'll ever be that bored, but I'll definitely keep it in mind."

"Suit yourself," she says with a laugh.

"Okay, see you tomorrow."

"'Night, my friend. Don't worry about all this stuff. It'll all work it."

THIRTY-ONE

It feels incredible to be home. I plop my bags down in the entryway to our apartment and go to the fridge for a cold drink. There's a six-pack of my favorite microbrew inside along with a sticky note:

Drink me!

I also notice a handwritten note on the kitchen counter.

YAY! You're home! I've missed you sooooo much. Get started without me. Chips and salsa in the cupboard and beer in the fridge. I want you nice and drunk when I get home so we can delve into your rock star problem with abandon. Did I mention I'm so excited you are home?! Love you, girlie!
XOXO

God how I've missed her. I grab a bottle of beer from the cardboard holder and open the drawer for a bottle opener.

Everything is exactly where I left it and it feels like comfort and home. I forgo the chips and salsa. Not only have I put on a few pounds out on the road, but I figure the food would only slow down the effects of the alcohol. Knowing Grace, the great inquisition will be on. Honestly, I wouldn't want it any other way.

A few bottles of beer and two loads of laundry later, the door to our apartment opens. It's a small place but has been perfect for the two of us. In this moment, with Grace's big personality, it feels crowded in here. She's jumps up and down and tackles me onto the sofa. My dad once gave me a Charles Schulz book called *Happiness is a Warm Puppy*. To me, happiness is Grace.

"I'm so happy to see you!" she shouts. Before I can protest, she's crushing me. Then she jumps back up and heads into the kitchen. She opens the refrigerator and grabs herself a beer. "You've had three beers," she says, counting the empty slots in the cardboard holder. "Right where I want you." She comes back into our tiny living room and plops herself down on the couch next to me. She reaches over and plants a big, wet kiss on my cheek. "I missed you!"

I missed Grace too. My warm, sweet puppy. "Me too," I say, throwing my arm around her and pulling her in close. "You hungry?"

"Nah. I ate at the office," she says with a shrug. "If you are, I can make you something here with the meager fixings in the fridge or we can go out and grab something or call something in."

"I'm fine," I say. "I want to sit here on my couch, in my apartment, with my best friend, and be."

"Well, that's all fine and good, but we need to talk," she says, sitting up and turning her body to the side, pulling her leg up and bending it under her other one.

"Okay," I say, concerned something is wrong.

"Now this is important." She takes on a very solemn demeanor and tone. I stiffen a bit, unsure what has got Grace in an unusually serious mood. "You like this boy and he clearly likes you."

I sag in relief.

"Oh," I say with a sigh. "I thought something was really wrong," I continue, shaking my head.

"Something *is* really wrong," she says in a serious tone. "Listen to me, Marin. I haven't heard you this excited about a guy since . . . well, never. If he's really as amazing as you say he is, you need to see where this thing can go."

"Right," I scoff. "There's nowhere for it to go, Grace. Think about it. I have a temporary assignment with a company in LA for a few more weeks where my hope is to get transferred to a tech company in Seattle. Brad's a musician who tours the country playing in a band. We have no future."

"So have a present," she offers with a good-natured shrug and a sassy tilt of her head.

"To what end? Sex?"

"You can't tell me you haven't thought about sex with him," she says, wiggling her eyebrows up and down. "I did an online search and the guy is yummy."

I take a deep breath and expel it sharply through my mouth.

"He is pretty sexy," I say, closing my eyes and letting my mind wander for a moment.

"See?" she says in a tone that lets me know she will always think she knows best. "Why not have a little fun?"

"I'm not hooking up with someone I work with. If I learned anything from dear old Mom, that's lesson number one."

"I get it, but your situations are totally different."

"It's not different to me," I say in a strong voice. "Now, unless you have something else serious you want to talk to me about, I'm ready to visit with you, the housewives, and any other mindless reality TV people who happen to be on the DVR."

Realizing the conversation has been shut down, Grace bounces off the couch, grabs the chips and salsa, and returns.

"Enough about me. Tell me something good about you. I want to hear all about *your* love life," I tell her.

"Well," she says. "I might have met someone."

"What? You've been holding out on me. Details. I need details," I say, bouncing on the couch, imitating her joyousness.

"His name is Trevor. He works in the mail room at the agency. I don't think it's anything serious."

"Why isn't it serious?"

"Well, first of all, he went to UCLA," she sneers with disgust.

"Oh, the horror. The horror." I shiver and grimace, mocking her.

"I know, right?" she agrees, playing along.

"Just because we went to USC doesn't mean you can't get serious with a Bruins fan," I chastise her.

"Second, he's like three years younger than me."

"So what? That's nothing."

"It's a lot. I'm old enough to be his dad's trophy wife. It's weird."

"His dad's trophy wife?"

"I don't know," she shrugs and rolls her eyes "But three years is a lot. That's like . . . eight percent or something." Eight percent? She cracks me up.

"I never pegged you for a cougar, but I like it," I say with a quick nod of the head.

"I'm serious," she moans. "He's the same age as Justin Bieber," she sneers. I bust out laughing.

"As long as he *isn't* Justin Bieber, I think you're okay," I manage to choke out between chuckles. Grace giggles too and before I know it, we are both rolling with laughter.

"Okay, enough boy talk," she says. "Let's see what the housewives have been up to." She grabs the remote and clicks through the shows saved on the DVR until she comes across a new episode we plan to watch, mock, and dissect. It's the perfect end to the day.

THIRTY-TWO

MARIN

I arrive at ten p.m. at the La Luna theater as instructed by Jase. I look around but don't spot him, so I get in the line at the entrance. There are a host of people dressed in trendy clothes ahead of me, all waiting to get into this small music venue. I check a few messages on my cell phone and text Grace I can't wait to get home and back onto the couch with her and some chips and salsa.

"Marin, Marin!" I hear a shout above the crowd's chatter. Jase is flanked by two security guards, who are trying to hold back some people that have discovered the lead singer of Kings Quarters is here. "Marin! What are you doing?" This is the first time he's ever called me by my name. It's weird.

"I'm here to meet you," I say with a shrug.

"Why are you waiting in line?" he sneers, like standing next to these ordinary people—who frankly look much hipper and more beautiful than your average Joe and Jane—is insulting.

"Oh, I didn't know," I say, hunching my shoulders forward and lowering my head. He grabs my hand and pulls me out of line. He puts his arm around my shoulder and we walk right between the velvet ropes into the theater. He guides me over to another velvet rope that sits astride a private booth to the left of the stage. It's not your ordinary booth with a static bench seat around a table. Instead, the table is surrounded by a red velvet barrier, with metal and red velvet chairs around it.

Two additional body guards—even bigger and more menacing than the first two, if that's even possible—stand on either side, their eyes roaming around the theater as they assess the crowd for potential threats.

Jase pulls a chair out for me and I lower myself onto it, all the while surveying the scene in front of me. The red velvet of the seats matches the red carpeting and red draped walls. With the lights dimmed, there's a sultry, sexy vibe going on in the club. It's a buzz of people talking and drinking yet it reeks of fakery. I give Jase a tight smile.

"So, what's the plan for tonight?" I ask.

"I'm here to hang out and enjoy time with some friends," Jase says, looking over at a woman talking with the bodyguard, a woman I recognize as a Victoria's Secret model. Not that I've been a regular at Victoria's Secret lately. No one remotely appropriate has seemed interested in my skivvies. The woman glances back at Jase, lowering her face and looking up at him with her false eyelashes fluttering. Gag! This is so not my scene.

"Sounds great," I say. "Let me know if I can photograph you with anyone."

"Yeah, yeah, sure," he says before standing up and walking over to the model in question. He takes her hand, lifts it to his mouth, and plants a small kiss on it. She quirks an eyebrow at him and grins. I spend the next forty-five minutes watching these two flirt with one another in the booth while some other people I'm neither introduced to nor interested in meeting sit and drink from the bottles of alcohol chilling in buckets in the center of the table.

Meanwhile, a band called the Morning Jacket performs on stage. They have a Kings of Leon-type sound. They're good. Really good. Too bad the audience isn't paying all that much attention.

The band finishes its last song to a smattering of applause. I feel sorry for them. It's got to be hard to perform like that and not have the crowd behind you. Even during my limited time with the band, I've learned how important live feedback can be.

A man wearing faded blue jeans and a blue crushed velvet jacket approaches and whispers in Jase's ear. The two exchange words and Jase nods with a smile. He leans over to me.

"Fire up your camera," he says before rising and walking to the back of the theater. I look to the stage and watch as another band takes its place, setting up instruments and adjusting the mic stands.

The man in the velvet jacket stands front and center on the stage, taking the microphone off the stand and holding it up to his mouth.

"Hey everyone. I've got awesome news to share," he says. The crowd doesn't take notice. While some guys come out on stage with guitars and a set of drum sticks, he continues to talk. "I know you're going to want to hear this." He points a finger in the air and circles it around. The theater lights flicker and the crowd settles down to quiet murmurs as people look around to see what's going on.

"Welcome to the La Luna," he continues. "Hope you enjoyed the Morning Jacket." He pauses to let the smattering of applause die down. "We've got a special treat tonight," he continues. "Put your hands together for the Stills with a special lead vocal performance by Jase Conners of Kings Quarters." Now the crowd applauds, whistles, and catcalls with abandon.

Jase strides out onto the stage, oozing confidence and charisma. He looks like the quintessential rock star and the crowd loves him—almost as much as he seems to love himself. He puts his hand up to shield his eyes from the light and looks over in my direction. He's not looking at me, though. He's looking at the hot model he was eye-fucking earlier.

"This song is for someone special," he says, before turning back to the band and whispering something to them. The guitarist and drummer nod. I grab my cell phone and open the video app. I walk toward the stage and hit *record* as the guitarist and drummer begin the intro.

The melody sounds familiar but it's not until Jase starts to sing that I recognize the song as the Willie Nelson classic, "Always on My Mind." Of course the band has sped up the tempo and with Jase's sexy voice, it sounds much less twangy and much more seductive.

I look back over at supermodel, who has an enigmatic grin on her face as Jase croons and sways on stage. Not wanting to invade his privacy, I keep the camera trained on him and the band. A few times, I pan the crowd at large, but don't focus on anyone specific.

When the song ends, the crowd applauds with sheer enthusiasm. Jase takes a small bow, turns back toward the band, and bows again. Humble Jase is not a sight I'm used to, but I like it. Jase performs a few more songs with the Stills before returning to the booth. I record them all and plan to send them to Amy for review and approval.

"Listen, I hate to seem antisocial," I explain to Jase, pulling him away from the supermodel's attention. "Unless you feel like there's something else tonight worth capturing, I'm going to take off. I have Oliver's brother's wedding tomorrow and need to handle a few things."

"Yeah, sure," he replies. He stands up and leans over, giving me a hug and a small peck on the cheek. "Thanks for coming tonight." This is the most attention Jase has ever given to me and I'm not sure what to make of it. I know it's nothing sexual. It's quite apparent he only has eyes for the supermodel—at least for tonight. Honestly, I don't feel like pondering the possibilities. I'm tired and I've got a long day tomorrow.

THIRTY-THREE

BRAD

It's only been a few days since I saw Marin, but I miss her like crazy. Who knew in only a few weeks I would be whipped by a girl who doesn't even want to be with me. Well, that's not entirely accurate. I think Marin *does* want to be with me. I think I affect her as much as she does me. No woman traces her fingers across a guy's lips when she thinks he's asleep unless she has some feelings for him. She's just so worried about how it will impact her job.

I don't think anyone would give a shit. Craig and Phoebe have been together for years. While it's not public knowledge, Damon, the crew, and the rest of us guys are all very aware. They share a hotel room on tour for God's sake.

Marin—my Marin—is so scared though. I need to find a way to break through her walls and show her we could be amazing together. That I'm worth taking a chance on.

This little break from the tour, where she needs to report on what I do in my free time, is the perfect opportunity. I'm not sure how she'll respond, but I'll tell her today at Oliver's brother's wedding. Marin will be there to follow Oliver for the day and post to our social media accounts about his role as the best man.

I arrive at the hotel ballroom and it looks like an explosion of cotton candy, all decorated in different shades of pink. I know Oliver's brother Jeff had nothing to do with this. It must all be his girlfriend—soon-to-be wife—Allison. No way would Jeff ever pick something so girly. I can't fault the guy, though. Right now, I'd give Marin anything she wanted and I'm not even sleeping with her.

I walk around and say hello to a few of Oliver's relatives and some of the other guests I know. Next, I head to the bar and grab a beer. I take a swig, turn, and there *she* is, across the room, talking with Jeff and Oliver. Marin's wearing a dark purple dress that ties around her neck and fits tight across her tits. The skirt is airy and light and floats around her legs. She turns away from me, revealing her back is all exposed. Damn, she's not wearing a bra. I sprout a boner and have to adjust myself in my suit pants before I walk over to them.

"So remember, no photos of the bride," says Oliver. "She doesn't want pictures of her in her dress to leak before her family and friends see her walk down the aisle."

"I got it," confirms Marin. "Just photos of you and your brother together doing typical groom and best-man stuff."

"Marin," I say, and she turns to look at me, giving me a soft smile.

"Well, look at you." She gives me a good look-over. "You clean up nice," she adds with a bite of her lower lip.

"You look beautiful as always," I say, leaning in to give her a small kiss on the cheek and placing my hand on the small of her naked back. I linger for a moment, inhaling her vanilla scent. Her breath catches as my nose brushes against her jaw. Oh yeah, I'm having an effect on her.

"I didn't know you were going to be here," she offers with a shaky breath. I glance over to Oliver, who is looking back and forth between us.

"I'll let you guys talk," he says. "Marin, I'll see you in the groom's dressing room in fifteen."

"Okay, I'll be there," she responds. She turns to me and grins.

"All of us guys have known Oliver's brother for years. We're like family."

"That's great. I'm sure Jeff and Allison will love having you here." She glances down at the ground and I follow her eyes to a pair of black strappy shoes that would look amazing draped over my shoulders.

"So, I wanted to fill you in on my plans for later in the week," I start, trying to keep my focus off how much I want to strip her naked right now.

"Yes, tell me where to meet you and what the plan is for the day. I'm sure all your fans are eager to learn how you spend your time off."

"I'm going camping overnight in Ojai," I state in a matter-of-fact tone.

"Overnight?" she asks with wide eyes. "I . . ."

"Yeah. Have you ever been camping before?"

"Once, when I was a kid, I think. I don't remember it well," she explains.

"Well, Ojai, California, is one of the most beautiful places on Earth. You'll love it," I say, wanting to convince her she'll have a good time.

"I don't think that's a good idea," she says quietly.

"What? Going camping with me?"

"Overnight," she says, nodding her head.

"It's not like we haven't spent nights together before, Marin," I scoff mildly. "Anyway, your job is to chronicle what I'm doing on my time off and that's what I'm doing," I say with a shrug. She gives a resigned sigh. As much as I hate pulling the work card, I know with as dedicated as she is, she won't deny a request to do her job.

"You're right," she says with a tight smile. "So, how do you want to do this?"

How do I want to do this? I want to crawl into a tent and bury myself in you for twenty-four hours. Fast. Slow. Deep. Me on top. You on Top. Forward and backward. That's how I want to do it. But I know I can't tell her that.

"I'll pick you up at your place on Wednesday at eight thirty. We'll drive up, spend the night, and I'll have you back by late afternoon on Thursday."

"Okay," she responds. "Is there anything I need to bring?"

"Just the stuff you'll need for yourself. I'll take care of the food and the tent and stuff."

"Sounds like a plan. Well," she says, looking down at her feet again, "I guess I should get to the groom's dressing room."

"Yeah. Save a dance for me later."

She doesn't respond, but instead offers me a small grin and little wave. I watch her walk away, her dress swaying back and forth, my fingers itching to roam across her skin.

After the wedding ceremony, the party is in full swing. I sit down on one of the chairs covered in fabric and a big pink bow and sip another beer. I look around the ballroom and watch all the people talking and dancing, keeping an eye out for Marin the entire time. I spot her over at the chocolate fountain, talking with Phoebe.

She takes a little wooden stick and attaches a piece of pineapple. I watch as she dunks it into the fountain, drenching it in chocolate. She lifts it up to her mouth and a drop of chocolate falls onto her lower lip. Daaaaaamn! What I wouldn't give to march right up to her and lick that drop of chocolate off. I squirm in my seat and try to calm down. If I don't stop watching her, I'm going to have to go rub one out in the bathroom.

"Hey B.O.," says Craig, who has interrupted my thoughts and sits down next to me. He follows my sight line to where I'm watching his girlfriend and Marin. "You better not be looking at my girl with that boner," he says without humor in his voice.

"Screw you." I tilt my head and give him a sneer. If anything can stifle an erection, it's Craig.

"She's pretty great," he says, gesturing with his head to Marin.

"Yeah, she is," I reply with a tight smile.

"You tapping that?"

"You're an asshole."

"I take that as a no."

"What the hell did you come over here for?" I ask him in frustration.

"Seriously. It's pretty obvious you like Marin. What's going on with you two?"

"Nothing's going on. I like her. A lot," I say and give him a look warning him not to make any snide comments about me being pussy-whipped. He puts his hands up in front of him.

"I'm not judging. I'm so damn in love with my girl, I'm going to ask her to marry me."

"It's about time," I reply, rolling my eyes. He punches me in the arm. "All joking aside, C.O., that's awesome. We all love Phoebe and she loves you back."

"Hell yeah, she does," he says with pride. "Back to Marin. She's really smart, no?"

"She's amazing. So smart and so funny."

"She's cute," he adds, inspecting her appearance.

"Yeah, she is," I concur, staring at her from across the room. "But when she puts on those glasses, man . . . she's so goddamn sexy."

"You always were a sucker for a girl in glasses," he says with a light laugh.

"Don't I know it," I agree, shaking my head.

"Well, we only have a few weeks left on the road. Then we'll be in LA for at least four months while Damon gets things sorted out with the European tour," he offers, suggesting I'll have time to work my magic on Marin. All I can think is how four months at home isn't going to be enough for me. The thought of touring Europe makes my stomach tighten.

"Yeah. About that . . ." I start.

"What? Europe?"

"Yeah."

"It's going to be epic, man. It's what we've always dreamed of. Aren't you psyched?"

What I want to say is, "No, man, I'm not psyched. I'm most definitely not psyched." This isn't my dream. It never has been. The thought of another six to ten months on the road sounds like a fucking nightmare. How can I do that to him, though? How can I keep him from what he loves when I know how much he's done for me?

"Yeah. Psyched," I respond with fake enthusiasm.

"Anyway, I think you should go for it with Marin. Does she feel the same way?"

"I think she does but is afraid it's going to impact her job."

"I can see that," he starts. "Not it hurting her job, of course. I mean I can see where she takes her work seriously and has worked hard to get where she is."

"I know. That's where I'm conflicted. I don't want to mess anything up for her, but I also know she and I could be something amazing." Before we can discuss it further, Johnny stumbles over and plops down on a chair next to me.

"What up, bitches?" he says with a laugh.

"Not much, man." I pat his leg and stand up. "If you'll excuse me, someone owes me a dance." I walk away and make a beeline to Marin. She's still over at the chocolate fountain, laughing with Phoebe.

"How's it going ladies?" I ask, putting my arm around Phoebe and giving her a kiss on the top of her head, letting my hand linger on his girl while I look over at Craig. He flips me the bird and I laugh. I let go of Phoebe, take the empty plate out of Marin's hand, and say, "Can I collect on that dance now?"

"Sure," she says, giving me a little smile. She turns to Phoebe. "Excuse us." Again, I put my hand on the small of her back and guide her to the dance floor. The DJ is playing Eric Clapton's "Wonderful Tonight."

I pull Marin into my arms and stroke her bare back. Her skin is so soft I can't help but run my fingers up and down. Her breath catches and I can feel her nipples harden into sharp points against my chest. I'm sure Jeff would be pissed at me if I untied the top of Marin's dress, let it fall forward, and feasted on her tits. Yeah, that would probably be frowned upon.

It shouldn't come as a surprise I've sprung one hell of an erection right now. I try to keep my crotch away from Marin so she can't feel the wood I'm sporting. I try to think of some boner killers—things to reverse a hard-on in a heartbeat. Hangovers. My Aunt Karen's holiday fruit cake. Baby seals getting clubbed. The hair that accumulates at the bottom of the shower. Yeah. That's getting the job done.

Next, I focus on the song, realizing my time with Marin in my arms is coming to an end. I push my mouth toward her ear and whisper the lyrics, telling her how wonderful she is tonight.

When the song ends, she pulls back and looks into my eyes. I swear to God she looks like she wants me to kiss her. I'm tempted. So tempted. I know I need to bide my time, though. This isn't the right time or place.

I lean in again and whisper in her ear, "Thanks for the dance." I give her a chaste kiss on the cheek and pull away.

"I should be going," she says on an exhale. "I've finished up my work for the night." With that, she walks away. As she does, I call out after her.

"See you Wednesday, Marin." She turns around, gives me a small smile and waves.

THIRTY-FOUR

It's my afternoon with Brad's brother Craig, the bassist for the band. At first, he told me he was planning to spend the day with his girlfriend, Phoebe. Correction: he said he planned to spend the day *naked* with his girlfriend, Phoebe. While I'm sure his fans would be eager to hear all about his sexual prowess, I'm not interested in a porn show. I feel like I've been getting enough of that from Jody and Theo.

Lucky for me, Phoebe and I discussed some ideas over pedicures on the bus before the tour break and decided on Craig visiting some kids at Los Angeles Children's Hospital. She confided in me that her younger brother died of leukemia when he was only three and she was five, so this is an important cause for her.

What Phoebe wants, Craig is helpless to resist giving to her. He's completely smitten. The two have been dating since high school. After they graduated, Craig and the band built a name for themselves, playing bars, festivals, and clubs, while Phoebe attended the MVA Beauty Institute, graduating with honors in both makeup and hair artistry.

Having seen what happens in the entertainment world over the course of her studies, she's fiercely protective of her privacy and has made it well known to me and everyone else around us that her relationship with Craig is not to become public knowledge. There are very few photos of them together online and all of them show her working with him in a professional capacity. Being a career-focused woman myself and wanting to be valued and find success in my field, I understand and respect that.

While Craig grumbled a little bit about having to do volunteer work on his day off, Phoebe promised him she would make it worth his while. I meet Craig at the children's hospital and record footage of him outside talking about why this is an important cause to him. He cites the death of a dear friend's brother at a young age.

Because this visit wasn't publicized, we walk through the large lobby and up to the children's cancer wing unnoticed. Once we arrive on the floor, we are met by the head of the hospital's public relations team along with two security guards. She knew we were coming and understands the parameters of our visit—Craig will visit with patients for two hours but no photos are to be taken and released by the hospital or us. Instead, I will post the video we shot along with a note about how, out of respect for the privacy and dignity of individual patients, Craig won't be posting any photos or other videos from today.

Realistically, we know photos—lots of photos—of him visiting with patients will hit online. Patients and their parents will share them on social media. That's great press for him and the band without us looking like we're taking advantage of sick kids. I plan to set up an alert to track all the coverage, so I can report back to Sasha and Amy how this idea has helped with PR.

For now, I follow Craig from room to room and watch with glee as kids from ages four to eighteen are shocked and uplifted by both his visit and his gifts of concert t-shirts and teddy bears, which I had brought along. After a few hours of small talk, impromptu lyric battles, and lots of photos, it's time for Craig and me to depart. He walks me down to the parking garage, making sure I get to my car.

"This was actually a lot better than I thought it was going to be, but don't tell Phoebe," he adds with a wink.

"Your secret is safe with me," I chuckle. "All kidding aside, you brought a lot of joy to people today. Thank you."

"Thanks for arranging it all. Now if you don't mind, I've got some naked time planned with my girl." As he's walking away, he turns back to me as I'm about to lower myself into my driver's seat. "Oh, have fun camping with B.O."

I freeze.

"You know about that?" I have a hard time keeping the worry or fear from my voice.

"Yeah. He mentioned he was going to Ojai for the night and you were tagging along to take photos and shit."

"Oh," I say, unsure what else to add. Perhaps I shouldn't read too much into this. Of course Brad told Craig where he was going. They're brothers and they live together. That makes perfect sense. "Well, I'll see you back on the bus," I add before climbing into my car and driving home.

THIRTY-FIVE

MARIN

The next day, I show up at Johnny's house at noon as he requested. He was vague about what he had planned for the day, but I'm hoping it involves hanging out on the sand. It's a gorgeous summer day and it would be a shame to let it go to waste.

His place is a charming cottage on a small side street adjacent to the Venice Beach strand, which is known for its pedestrian-only walkway featuring artists, panhandlers, outrageous street performers, and psychics. It's also home to small independent shops, restaurants, and bookstores. It's funky, weird, and unique.

I approach his door and notice a bunch of flower pots with shriveled up dead plants in them along with an array of takeout menus and real estate flyers littering the porch. I guess he doesn't have anyone to water his plants or take in his mail while he's on tour.

I ring the doorbell, but there is no answer. Huh. Maybe he went for a walk on the beach. I step back and look around. I don't see him anywhere nearby, so I knock this time. Still no answer so I knock louder. Deciding no one is home, I turn to walk away when someone answers the door. He's a tall, lanky guy with dirty blond hair falling into his eyes. His skin looks weathered from being out in the California sun.

"Yeah?"

"Hi. I'm Marin. I have an appointment with Johnny," I explain.

"Cool. Come on in." He moves to the side so I can enter. The smell assaults me first. I can't quite place what it is, but I'm getting hints of stale beans, skunk, and beer. As I move into the place, I also notice all the window curtains are drawn and the only light comes from the oversized TV and a small floor lamp.

This is definitely the apartment of a dude. There is a brown leather couch and a black reclining armchair with drink holders on the side. It looks like the type of chair he sits in for hours at a time, nursing a beer while he watches sports on TV.

I'm guessing that's exactly what he is doing now. It is noon and it looks as though Johnny has been sitting here for hours. I wouldn't be surprised if he had fallen asleep in this chair last night. His hair is disheveled, his clothes are wrinkled, and he has some Cheetos crumbs caught in his unkempt beard and trailing down his shirt. There are empty chips bags, pizza boxes, cans of beer, and other assorted food trash items littered around the chair and table. His bloodshot eyes barely connect with mine.

"Oh hey, Marin. What's up?" he asks, surprised I'm here.

"Uh, I'm here to spend the day with you and chronicle what you do on your time off, so your fans can feel more connected to you," I explain, bugging my eyes out and tilting my head, hoping he doesn't miss the gesture that should serve as a "Hey dummy, remember?"

"Cool."

"Yeah, cool." I turn away from him to roll my eyes and grimace at the stench. "Do you mind if I open the window?" It's not a question but a statement, and I don't wait for him to respond. Rather, I walk over to one of the windows, draw back the curtain, and open it up. I can feel the breeze from the ocean, and the smell of the salt air is already a huge improvement over the current conditions.

Johnny looks rather displeased but if I'm being honest, I don't care. I think the fresh air will do him some good and perhaps encourage him to get his ass up off that chair.

"So, what fun things do you have planned for us today?" I ask, turning back to him.

"You're looking at it," he says with a laugh. Lanky Blond Guy walks over and gives Johnny a sloppy high five.

"And you are . . . ?" I ask with fake politeness.

"Name's Jackson, but my friends call me Crazy J."

"Crazy J," I repeat. "Great to meet you. I don't mean to be rude, but I have some work to do today with Johnny."

"Don't worry, sweet lady."

"Marin. My friends call me Marin," I explain, not wanting, as one would imagine, to be called *sweet lady*.

"Don't worry, Marin. I won't get in the way."

"Yeah, he's cool," adds Johnny.

"Sure," I say with a smile plastered on my face. "So, what's the plan for today? As I mentioned, the Kings Quarters fans are excited to see what their favorite band is doing during a few days off. It's a beautiful day outside. Perhaps a walk on the beach? Or some paddleboarding? I've heard that's really fun."

"Nah," says Johnny. "I don't feel like going out today."

"Okay." I try to think of something compelling we could do here in this disgusting apartment that wouldn't turn his fans off. I look around and notice a gaming system. "You play video games?" I ask hoping to find something we can use as a foundation for photos.

"Dude." He holds his hands out in a way that suggests I'm an idiot for asking such a stupid question.

"Great. Why don't we fire up a game and we'll get some photos of you playing your favorites? You can tell me what you like about them and some tips you have for being more successful."

"Sweet lady is smart," says Jackson, nodding his head, impressed with my suggestion.

"Ah, ah, ah," I scold with a teasing tone. "My friends call me Marin," I remind him. "Crazy J," I add, hoping to endear myself to him for the short time we'll be together and ensure he will stop calling me *sweet lady*.

"Yeah, Marin," he says, nodding again.

"So, Johnny, why don't you go freshen up in the bathroom and I'll straighten up around here." With a huff, Johnny rises from his place on the recliner, leaving behind a strong imprint from where his derrière has likely not moved for hours, maybe even a day.

As he occupies himself in the bathroom, I find a plastic convenience store bag on the ground and start loading in some of the trash lying around his place, using my fingertips to grab items from the floor and tables and place them in the bag while I cringe in disgust. I'm thankful scents can't be transmitted via Instagram. Yuck!

Johnny and Crazy J emerge from the bathroom amidst a plume of smoke. From the funky, skunky smell, it's not from smoking a cigarette. He's high and the mellow feeling is making his eyes glaze over. I turn away from him, let out a defeated exhale, and pin a smile on my face before turning back around.

"Johnny, what would you think about putting on a different shirt? The one you have on is . . . lovely," I start, trying hard not to vomit in my mouth. "But I think a different color"—and something clean—"would be better for the photos I need to take."

"Uh, okay, if you think so," he says with a loopy smile.

"I do. Would you like me to pick something out for you?"

"Yeah, knock yourself out." He plops himself back down on his reclining chair. Thank goodness it's not covered in crispy orange chip shavings and crumbs any longer. In his bedroom, there's a pile of clothes atop his dresser. I'm not certain if any of them are clean or not, but anything has got to be better than the stained and wrinkled shirt he has on now. I grab something suitable and bring it out to him.

"This one will look great on camera," I say, handing it to him.

"Ooooh," laughs Crazy J. "Look who's a supermodel."

"Shut it, asswipe," says Johnny. With a groan of displeasure, he takes the clothing from my hands and before I can turn away, he's whipped off his shirt right in front of me. I resist shuddering and instead look away, taking a few calming breaths. I wait a minute or two and am pleased he's covered up his inappropriate nudity and looks somewhat decent in the replacement shirt.

"So, what game do you like to play the most?" I ask. Over the course of an hour, Johnny and Crazy J play an alien shooter game where they get killed more than half the time because they are so baked. I manage to squeeze three tips for playing the game from Johnny and Crazy J and snap a few photos. Crazy J tends to photobomb. I'm not sure the rest of the band, Damon, Sasha, and Amy want this wack job associated with the band, so I surreptitiously grab a few photos when he's not looking and also do a little creative editing. My job complete, I make a beeline for the door.

"Thanks for letting me hang out for the afternoon," I call out. "It's been real."

"See ya," Johnny shouts, raising his hand in the air, but not bothering to pause the game or even turn around to look at me.

"Bye sweet lady," calls out Crazy J.

I roll my eyes and laugh.

It's four thirty as Grace and I sit in the outside patio of one of our favorite little beach cafés, enjoying the summer sunshine. I'm thrilled she chose to keep today as one of her vacation days. Despite the late afternoon hour, according to Grace, it's never a bad time for pancakes.

Grace admires the bevy of surfers walking past us with their tanned, toned torsos and long board shorts. I fill her in on my afternoon with Johnny. I don't mention my suspicions that he has a major drug problem. I've signed an NDA and as much as I would love to have someone to talk with about my concerns for him, I know it wouldn't be appropriate. She cringes, laughs, mocks, and makes the whole ridiculous thing a funny memory and no longer the nightmare it was at the time.

"So, who's next?" She tunnels a mouthful of buttermilk pancakes into her mouth.

"Brad," I reply and look out at the ocean to avoid her eyes.

"Really?" she says with a raised brow. "And what, pray tell, does *Brad* have planned for you?" she asks. I ignore her sassy tone.

"I'm going up to Ojai with him tomorrow for the night." Grace doesn't miss the fact I'm biting my lip and looking uncomfortable. A slow grin crosses her face.

"Just the two of you?" she raises her eyebrows.

"Yeah," I say with a nod. "He wants to spend his day off camping, and I need to chronicle what he does and post photos to the various social media accounts."

"So, sexy rock star Brad, who you've been sleeping with and who you've kissed, wants to take you away, alone, on an overnight camping trip, and you're still trying to convince yourself this is just about work."

"This *is* work, Grace. You of all people know I can't and won't get involved with someone I work with," I say, doing my best to shut down the direction of this conversation.

"As I've said before, I don't think you can compare this situation to your mom. It's not like you're married or even have a boyfriend. You are a beautiful, single woman who happens to be the object of desire of sexy rock star Brad."

"Ugh," I respond, shaking my head. "It's not like that and it's not going to be like that."

"Okay, if that's what you want."

What I want? What I want is for Brad and me to have met under different circumstances and have a different trajectory for our futures. I don't want the job I need to be tied to the guy I'm trying to resist.

"It's what it is," I say resigned.

"Okay, well, don't do anything I wouldn't do. Wait. That makes no sense," she says, shaking her head. "Do what I would do."

"And what is that?" I already know the answer.

"I would have steamy sex with sexy rock star Brad and not feel one iota of guilt about it."

I shake my head, laughing as Grace takes another bite of her food.

THIRTY-SIX

B R A D

I pull up to Marin's beach apartment, excited to get her away from the tour and the guys. I'm hoping when it's just the two of us she'll admit to the amazing chemistry we have. Before I can walk the stairs to her apartment, she comes down wearing a pair of denim shorts, a tight red t-shirt, and hiking boots. It's simple. It's sexy. It's perfect. She gives me a small wave and I walk over to grab her bag from her.

"Morning," I say.

"Good morning," she returns.

"Is this everything?" I eye the small duffel bag she's got.

"Yep."

"Okay, let's head out," I say, noticing the awkwardness between us. I open the passenger door to my big ass SUV. It's one of three cars I own. When our song "Firefly" got used in a Toyota commercial last year, we not only made a shitload of money but each of us got a car out of the deal. It's a beast but I only use it for camping trips.

Realizing she's too short to climb in on her own, I wrap a hand around her waist and hoist her in. She smells like sweet vanilla, as always. I'm already congratulating myself on this brilliant plan to get closer to her. It's working already.

After helping her in, I shut the door and walk around to the trunk to load her bag in. I circle around to the driver's side, climb in, and we set out on our way. Marin takes her tablet out of her purse and turns it on. She lowers her glasses to her eyes, and I have to take a deep breath to avoid crashing the car before we've even gotten onto the freeway.

"So, tell me why you chose to go camping on your day off?" she asks. She's in full on work mode right now and I play along. If this is what I need to do to get her comfortable, it's worth it.

"I've always loved camping," I start. "We used to go on trips when I was a kid. It was one of the only times when my family life felt . . . normal." I shrug.

"Did you and Craig have a difficult childhood?" she asks with genuine concern, putting the tablet down in her lap.

"You could say that."

"What was it like?"

"My dad was—is—a functional alcoholic," I state with little emotion in my voice. I'm judging by Marin's gasp, she didn't expect to hear that.

"I'm so sorry," she says, reaching over to place her hand on my arm. I look away from the road to find concern etched on her face.

"It's okay," I reply, shaking my head at her. "I've had a long time to get used to it and thankfully had Craig who insulated me from a lot of the crap that went down."

"Did he ever get violent?" she asks with a shaky voice.

"No, not physically. He was more of an emotional abuser."

"That's still awful," she exhales.

"Now, I love to go camping alone and get away from everything. It helps me clear my head."

"What's keeping your head so cluttered?"

"Stuff," I shrug. "What about your family?"

"Oh no, we're not done with you yet," she replies, waving her pointer finger at me. "What was your mom's role in all this?"

"My mom is great, and she tried to keep the family together. She's a music teacher and is the reason Craig and I have music running through our blood. Before we could walk or talk, we had an instrument in our hands. I know she tried her best to deal with Dad and make a happy home for us. For the most part it was. I don't blame her at all. She had her hands full with work and side jobs, and Dad, and us two boys who didn't want to focus on school. At the end of the day, though, it was Craig who protected me. He not only took the brunt of Dad's abuse, but he pulled me into his music dream, so we could have an escape from all the stuff going on at home."

"You're lucky to have him."

"Yeah, I am," I acknowledge with a nod.

"You said it was *his* music dream. Does that mean it wasn't yours?" Of course she picked up on that. My Marin. So smart and perceptive.

"Can I confess something to you? You know, off the record?" I ask, turning my head away from the road to look at her again.

"Of course, B," she replies with a serious expression. "You can tell me anything." She tilts her head to the side and gives a small reassuring nod. I inhale and let the air out in a slow gust, like I'm gathering the courage to tell her.

"I never wanted to be in a band," I tell her, keeping my eyes on the road. I turn back to look at her and her eyes are wide in surprise. "Not what you expected to hear, huh?" I say on a cross between a chuckle and a huff.

"No. Not what I thought you were going to say," she replies. "I guess I'm surprised because you're so good at it and you seem to love being on stage. I've never met anyone who knows how to play so many instruments."

"Thanks." I look over at her while we continue down the freeway. "Don't get me wrong. I like it. But it's not my dream. It was always Craig's."

"So what is your dream?"

"If I wasn't in the band, I would be a video game developer," I tell her and it's the first time I've ever said the words out loud to anyone else. A lump forms in my throat and my palms get sweaty. "You're not going to post that, right?"

"Of course not," she replies right away. "I would never post or share anything you didn't want me to," she explains. "Tell me more about the video games."

"Dad is a computer science teacher and all my good memories of him are working on computers. We'd build them and code them. It was amazing. As the drinking got worse though, it wasn't good for me to be around him so much. So I started doing stuff on my own when I had free time. Between school and the band, there hadn't been that much. Now that we're on the road, I try to spend my free time on gaming."

"Is that why you always have your head buried in your laptop?" she poses.

"Yeah. I've been working on a new game that's a combo of *Guitar Hero* and *Forge of Empires* where you get to create your own rock band from the ground up and have to prove your mettle to make it a success."

"Wow! That sounds *really* cool."

"Thanks."

"How far along are you?"

"I'm still in the early stages. I've got an overall outline, some storyboarding done, and some of the initial coding."

"Does Craig know?"

"Hell no," I scoff. "No one knows . . . except you."

"Oh, um, well, thank you for confiding in me," she shrugs. "So, this is what you want more than anything, to create video games?"

"Honestly, right now," I say, turning to look at her, "more than anything, I want a chance with you." She lets out a little exhale. She bites down on her lower lip and knots her fingers in her lap.

"I'm flattered, B. Really, I am," she begins. "It would be futile to deny there's an attraction here." I'm thanking God I haven't been misreading cues. She *is* attracted to me, hopefully as much as I'm into her. "But it's not a good idea because we work together."

"Lots of people on the tour are together and it doesn't affect anything," I explain, glancing at her while we transition onto the 101 freeway. "Look at Craig and Phoebe, or Jody and Theo."

"It isn't a good idea, B."

"Let me ask you something. If we had met under different circumstances, would you feel differently?"

"That's not a fair question because we didn't meet under different circumstances. We met under *these* circumstances, and under *these* circumstances, it won't work."

"Humor me, Marin. If you aren't into me, that's cool. You aren't going to hurt my feelings. I just want to know if I would have had a chance with you had things been different."

"So if you were a regular guy and we met at a bar or something, would I give you my number?"

"Yeah. I'm a regular guy and I ask for your number. What do you say?"

"I would have said yes. Happy?"

"Not how I would describe it, but yeah, thanks for telling me."

"I'm sorry, B. I've worked hard to get this job and I need it to open doors for me. For my future."

"I get it," I tell her before deciding to change the subject. I don't want to push her too far. For right now, I'm okay knowing she's attracted to me and that, under different circumstances, I'd have a shot with her. I've got the rest of the day to convince her to give us a try. "So, what do you think of the job so far?"

"It's been a good experience so far. I'm enjoying the opportunity to work with media and social media."

"Marin, this isn't a job interview. I'm not going to tell anyone what you tell me. For God's sake, I told you my biggest secret."

She chuckles to herself. "I shouldn't be telling you this, but I was hoping to be assigned to a tech job in Seattle. That's why I thought Sasha had hired me," she confesses.

"First, I like you telling me things you shouldn't," I offer, raising an eyebrow at her. She laughs and shakes her head. "Second, I kind of figured this wasn't your first choice. You appeared kind of shocked that day in Sasha's office."

"Yes, not my finest moment. I'd like to think I recovered okay though," she adds.

"You did, and you're doing a great job."

"That's nice of you to say. Not that your opinion isn't appreciated or important, but I wish I was getting a better vibe from Damon on my progress so far."

"He's not the warm and fuzzy type, but believe me, if you weren't pulling your weight, you'd be hearing about it. Damon doesn't spend money unless he thinks it will yield twice its return. He fired one of the catering staff because she threw out some food instead of saving it for leftovers. Went on and on about how she was costing the tour with her thoughtless waste."

"Jeez," she cringes.

"He has us hold monthly band meetings at his condo, so he can write off his mortgage as a business expense." Marin's face scrunches up in disgust. "Yeah, he's *that* guy. No one games the system like Damon." Her eyes widen in surprise but she's otherwise stoic. "So, what are your impressions of the band—aside from the lead guitarist being mega-talented and exceedingly handsome?"

"Yes, well, all of that is of course true," she smirks.

"So. The band?"

"I shouldn't say."

"Say it. C'mon. We've already gone well past what we *should* be telling each other."

"I think Johnny has a drug problem."

"He does," I confirm with a solemn nod. "Craig and I have talked about it with Damon and he said he's trying to get him help."

"I'm not sure it's working. I spent one of his days off with him and he was pretty strung out."

"I'll talk to Craig about it when we get back. Thanks for telling me."

"I really admire your friendship with Craig. It's evident how much you two care about each other."

"Yeah, he's the best. He's the most important person in my life and I would do anything for him."

"You already are, aren't you?"

"What do you mean?"

"Well, you're sticking it out with the band to help him fulfill his dream, even though it isn't yours." Damn it if she didn't hit the nail on the head. What am I supposed to do, though? I take a deep breath and I can sense she thinks she's upset me.

"You didn't say anything wrong, Marin," I say, keeping my eyes fixed on the road.

"Are you sure?" she asks. "I kind of feel like I overstepped my bounds."

"No, it's cool." She looks at me with skepticism. "No, it's fine," I say, giving her a genuine smile. For some reason, talking with her about this is easier than I thought it would be.

After many more miles traveled over the course of conversations about everything from favorite movies (mine: *Godfather*; hers: *Love Actually*) to biggest fears (mine: clowns; hers: failure), we arrive in Ojai. It's pretty quiet here over the summer because of the daytime heat. Reservations aren't allowed, but I know one of the park rangers. A couple of comped tickets to a show in Santa Barbara two years ago and he's like my best friend. He's cordoned off a secluded campground for us so there's little chance we'll be bothered by anyone else.

As I unload items from the trunk, Marin helps carry them over to the campground clearing, setting them down as I direct her. I notice she didn't bring her own sleeping bag. Good thing I considered that possibility.

Marin offers to help me set up the tent, but I brush her off. It's an easy-to-assemble four-person tent with linked, collapsible poles. I've been out here many times on my own and can set this sucker up without any assistance. While I anchor it to the ground, Marin snaps a few photos she'll upload when we're back. Next, I set up the camping stove and hook up the gas tank.

"Boy, this is a lot of work for one night," she says in surprise.

"It is, but it's absolutely worth it," I assure her. "There's nothing better than hot dogs over an open flame or pancakes from an outdoor griddle."

"Mmm. Sounds good. I'm getting hungry."

"Feel free to open up that small cooler—the blue one—and grab anything you want." I've stocked it full of cold drinks, cut fruit, granola bars, and other snacks. There are also some cold beers in there and a bottle of wine in case Marin wants some. I watch as she nibbles on trail mix and strawberries. She holds her hand out to me and offers a few bites here and there. I take them with appreciation, having worked up quite an appetite myself. Once the campsite is set up, I grab waters and a few sandwiches I had made and put them in my backpack.

"C'mon, let's go for a hike." I reach a hand out to her where she's sitting in a low riding camp chair and pull her up. We start walking and I take in a deep breath of air. Everything is so still and quiet. The only sound is our breath and our feet crunching on the ground beneath us as we climb and trek farther.

"This is so beautiful. Thank you for bringing me here."

"Thanks for coming with me." I look back at her, an ache building in my chest. We get to a clearing and look out over the Topatopa Mountains. She's standing at the edge of the trees and I can see the sincere awe in her eyes. I'm not surprised. Nature is pretty damn impressive, and this is one of my favorite places on the planet.

I move in so I'm standing pressed up against her back. She turns her body to look at me and I can't hold back any longer. I cup her jaw in my hand and rub my finger over her cheek. Her body stiffens.

"I really want to kiss you, Marin. But I won't do anything to make you uncomfortable."

"I know. And it's one of the things I admire about you," She cups my jaw and rubs my bottom lip.

"Do you want this? I need to hear the words from you."

"Yes," she whispers. I pull her into me and place a soft kiss on her lips. She runs her hand into my hair, which spurs me on. I dip my tongue into her mouth and her tongue matches mine swirl for swirl, movement for movement.

It's slow and steady but full of heat. I'm about to take the kiss deeper when she pulls away, eyes trained on mine.

"This is a bad idea," she pants.

"Probably," I agree, my breathing ragged, "but I want you, Marin. I don't want there to be any doubt. I want to be buried in you. Deep and hard until we're both sweaty and breathless."

"Now there's another tent popping up beside the one we'll be sleeping in," she jokes, looking down at my shorts. I'm guessing it's an effort to diffuse all the sexual tension dripping between us.

I swallow hard, my erection growing more and more painful. I dip my head back down to her. She wraps her hands around my neck and tugs me toward her, pushing her face, her mouth, her lips, her tongue closer to me. I wrap my arms around her more tightly. I know I'm being greedy, but I can't help it. I know she can feel all eight inches of me pressed against her thigh. Without warning, she's pulls away.

"We should get a picture of you by these rocks," she says with a shaky breath.

"What?" I respond in complete confusion.

"A picture of you," she repeats. A picture with my obvious hard-on.

"What the hell are you talking about?" I ask, adjusting myself in my shorts. She walks over to a grouping of rocks and pats them with her hand.

"Yes, this is a good spot."

"What are you doing Marin?" I walk to her and put my hand on her shoulder.

"My job," she says emphatically. "We'll need a picture of you for Instagram on your day off." She moves away from me and makes room for me to sit on the rocks, so she can snap some photos. And I know she's not a hundred percent ready to take a chance on us. Yet.

THIRTY-SEVEN

MARIN

If ever I've had to endure temptation before, it was truly nothing compared to this moment. Seeing Brad so comfortable, so masterful at this camping thing, is beyond sexy. It's all I can do not to launch myself at him. The sun has gone down, and it's gotten quite chilly. We both change into long pants and sweatshirts before huddling around the campfire he built.

"So, what now?" I ask. "What do you do when the sun goes down? Work on your video game?"

"No. This is my time to be unplugged," he explains. "I come up here to play and write."

"Music?"

"Yeah, music." He stands up and strides over to an acoustic guitar case resting next to a camping chair. He removes the instrument from the case and comes to sit next to me. He strums a few times and adjusts the little nobs at the top. For someone working with a rock band, I should learn the real terms for the instruments and their parts.

I stop thinking about work when he plays the Eric Clapton song from Oliver's wedding. It's sweet and slow and so beautiful. His voice is clear and soulful, and the way his fingers move along the strings makes my heart ache. There's so much depth to him.

"Huh?" I ask, and he chuckles.

"You zoned out there for a second," he says. "I asked if you had any requests."

"Oh." I tuck a strand of hair behind my ear. "Yes, I want to hear something you wrote." He looks down at his fingers and strums the guitar, evoking a beautiful melody.

"That was wonderful," I tell him when he's finished.

"I wrote it this week. I don't have the lyrics yet, but it's the start of something."

"I like it," I confirm.

"You know what I like?" he asks, looking into my eyes.

Me. You like me. Please don't say it. I don't think I can bear to hear it again. I don't think I can resist.

"B," I whisper in a plea.

"S'mores," he responds, looking away. "Can't go camping without s'mores."

I sigh in relief. "Of course," I agree. "They're a must." I watch him walk over to a cooler where he pulls out a Hershey's bar. We sit in comfortable silence, toasting marshmallows and eating sweet treats.

When he offers me seconds, I put my hand up. "No thanks. I'm good."

"Suit yourself," he says with a mischievous smile before devouring a second s'more.

"So, what next?"

"When I've eaten two s'mores and sung myself out, I go to bed."

"To bed," I say on a swallow. Bed. With Brad. Not sure why this is making me so nervous, but it is.

"Do we need to put out the fire?"

"Yeah. It's not safe to have it going all night. We'll be warm in our sleeping bags and tent."

"Okay, well, if you give me the sleeping bags, I can roll them out for us," I offer.

"Mine is right there," he says pointing to a navy blue roll. "I'm not sure where you put yours."

"Where I put my what?"

"Your sleeping bag," he replies and turns his back to me, throwing dirt on the fire.

"I didn't bring one," I say in a panic. "You told me you would bring the camping stuff."

"No," he corrects me in a gentle tone. "I told you I would bring the tent and food. I told *you* to bring all your stuff."

"I didn't think 'my stuff' meant a sleeping bag," I confirm in agitation.

"Hey," he says, coming over to calm me down. He places his arms on my shoulders. "It's okay. My sleeping bag is made for two people. You're not going to freeze." Share a sleeping bag with him? I'm not worried about being cold. My lustful thoughts about him are heating my body up well beyond its core temperature. I don't think I could bear to be that close to him—yet again—and not let my libido take over.

"I . . ." I'm not even sure what to say.

"C'mon." He takes the sleeping bag into the tent and squats down to roll it out. It's got a navy blue quilted exterior and the inside looks like a blue plaid flannel. It looks so warm and cozy, especially now the fire is out, and the cool mountain night air is hitting me straight on.

Not knowing what else to do, I pull off my boots and grab a pair of yoga pants from my bag. I'm about to walk outside to put them on, when Brad spots me.

"It's better to wear less clothes," he advises. "Body heat and all."

"What?" I squeak.

"You want to wear as little as possible in a sleeping bag. They're specially designed to use your body heat to help keep you warm. With the two of us, we'll be sure not to get cold." He turns away and starts to remove his pants and shirt. I'm frozen—rooted to the spot. He turns back around in nothing but a pair of blue Calvin Klein boxer briefs. He starts to shiver, using his hands to rub up and down his arms. He drops to the ground and climbs into the sleeping bag . . . the sleeping bag he expects me to crawl into—half naked—and fall asleep pressed up next to him.

It's not like I haven't been plastered against his body before. Despite my initial efforts to stay on my side of the bed when I've been crashing in his hotel room, it wasn't long before I wound up sprawled in the middle, a limb or two draped over him. On more than a few occasions, I've found myself lying on his chest, with his arms around me. I've tried convincing myself that was . . . practical. This feels different. This feels . . . intimate. Of course, that's ridiculous. It's all been intimate and I'm the queen of denial. Unsure of what to do, but starting to feel very cold, I turn away from him.

"Close your eyes."

"Okay," he agrees. I look back and he indeed has his eyes closed. I remove my jeans and sweatshirt, leaving me in a pair of boy shorts and a t-shirt. I fold my clothes and put them on top of my bag and lie down next to Brad in the sleeping bag.

"Can I open my eyes now?"

"Yes." He looks at me and smiles. I give him a shy smile back. He reaches over to turn down the lantern, leaving a little bit of light. He pulls the top of the sleeping bag over us, using the inside zipper to zip the bag up.

I can already feel the heat from his legs and chest against my body. It's perfection and testing my very resolve. I take in a breath and move an inch or two to the left, adjusting to the uneven ground, when I feel my leg brush against his.

"This was a bad idea," he says, as he scrubs his hand over his face.

"Or was it?" I bite my lip and stare into his eyes. I'm powerless to resist him. No, I'm not powerless. I'm powerful. I want him and I'm tired of denying myself.

THIRTY-EIGHT

BRAD

"Marin," I groan. "Clearly this was a set up to get you alone and try to seduce you. My intentions have been less than honorable."

"I know. I've known."

"This wasn't fair of me. Let me go get you—"

"You're a good guy. One of the best." She brushes her thumb across my lower lip.

"I . . . I want to do things to you. Things that would make you blush."

"That's so hot," she pants.

"I want to sink into you and stay there forever. I want to run my tongue all over your body and taste your come on my mouth. I want to take you slow and deep and I want to pound you from behind. I want everything," I confess, leaving her with no doubt of my intentions.

"I want that too. But I can only give you tonight."

"I'll take it." In desperation, I crash my lips down to hers. I take my time exploring her mouth with my lips and tongue. She tastes like minty toothpaste and smells like vanilla and I can't get enough of it. I'm afraid if I stop kissing her, the spell will break and she'll come to her senses. I lift myself up over her onto my elbows and use my hands to stroke her jaw, her cheek, her hair. Her hands are roaming up my arms and over my back, setting my skin on fire. I pull her top off while she removes her panties. Damn it if I can't stop kissing her. It's making me giddy and dizzy all at once. I feel her hand reach for my shaft, and I pull it away.

"What?" she asks in quiet shock. "What's wrong?"

"Nothing," I reply, lifting her hand to mine and kissing her knuckles. "But if you touch me there right now, this is going to be over way too fast."

"Oh," she giggles.

"If I only get one night," I say, looking deep into her eyes and grazing her cheeks with my thumbs, "I want to make it last." I kiss her neck and she arches her back and tilts her head back. I'm spurred on by the little moans of pleasure erupting from her.

I lower myself to her tits which are the perfect size for me. I've never been one for big breasts, and definitely not big fake ones. I take Marin's nipple into my mouth and suck with a little pressure. I'm loving her reaction. I pop it from my mouth and lavish it with attention from my tongue. She squirms underneath me, unable to stay still.

"Yes, B," she moans as she raises her arms over her head and pushes her tits up toward my mouth. I can't get enough of her and thank God tonight I'm going to get my fill. I lower myself farther, peppering her stomach and her hip bone with kisses. She knows where I'm heading next. I sink down, flinging the top of the sleeping bag off of us as I go. I don't think either of us are very cold anymore.

I swipe my tongue across her most sensitive place and she cries out. I love how her body responds to me. She reaches her arms out and grasps at the sleeping bag.

"God, B. It's too much," she calls out, but I don't relent.

"You taste so good, Marin."

She moans and starts to scoot away, but I hold her hips.

"Do you want me to stop?" *Please don't tell me to stop.* It's all I've been able to think about for weeks and already it's better than I imagined.

"God no," she says. "Don't you dare stop."

I chuckle and resume feasting on her sweet and tangy juices.

"Damn, Marin. Do you know how many times I've jacked myself off at the thought of how you taste?" Does she know how I feel hollow when she walks out of a room? How jealous I get when she shares her laugh with someone else? How desperately I want to show her that I'm worthy of someone as smart and hardworking as she is?

"Me too. I've thought about this so many times," she pants. Within seconds she comes on my face, moaning and writhing beneath me. I crawl up her body, leaving a trail of wet kisses along her torso as she shivers.

"I think I could get addicted to this."

"Me too," she confesses.

I lean over to my jeans on the tent floor and grab a condom out of the pocket. I yank off my boxer briefs, put the condom on my aching cock—which feels ready to explode—and position myself over her. When I enter her, it's like heaven. Her body feels so wet and tight.

"I've wanted you since that first day in Sasha's office," I grunt. "You were so hot, and then you put those glasses on and I thought I was gonna come right there in my pants."

"I wanted you too. I wanted to run my fingers through your hair," she whimpers.

"By all means, go ahead," I reply as I continue to relish the feel of her body's snug fit around mine. She does—tugging the strands hard while squeezing her muscles, pulling me in even deeper.

Without warning, she rolls so she is straddling me. Now she's riding me like a goddamn rodeo champ and I love that she takes what she wants. I place my hands around her waist to keep a steady rhythm and drive my hips forward. Her body is buzzing and she's dripping around my stiff cock. Her thighs clasp my sides, gripping me with her muscles. She matches me thrust for thrust, roll for roll. I reach down and use my fingers to stroke her, and she comes apart above me.

With her back arched, she pulses around me and calls out "Oh, B. Oh." I guide her off of me and roll over so I'm beside and then behind her. She's leaning forward on her elbows, her lush ass in the air. I pull her hair to the side and kiss her neck before I push back into her.

She screams out. "I don't think I can go again."

"You can," I assure her and push and pull. She moans in delight.

"Oh God, B. That feels so good," she groans.

"Come for me, Marin. One more time."

"Oh God." She cries out and I can feel the orgasm rip through her. She's pulsing around my cock, milking me for everything I have, and I finally spill my load right there. She falls forward, flat onto the sleeping bag. I lean forward, being sure not to put all my body weight on her and pepper her neck in light kisses.

"Fuck, that was hot," I pant.

"Hmm," is all she can muster in response.

"I'll be right back," I whisper and exit the tent, still naked, to throw away the condom in a dumpster a few campsites away. It's pitch-black out and there's no one around to see me. When I come back, she's still lying in the same spot, spent. I lie down next to her and run my fingers up and down her back.

She turns to her side, so she can run her hand across my jaw, her fingers tracing my lips, like she's memorizing my face. Like this really is a one-night thing. Like she won't be lying next to me naked in bed ever again. Like she'll be able to walk away.

But I know there are more stanzas in our song.

"Let's get some sleep," I say. I lean over her a bit to access the top of the sleeping bag. I cover the two of us up and zip it closed. She rolls over and rests her head on my chest. My heart aches at the thought of her. "Good night, Marin," I whisper, kissing the top of her head.

"Mmm. Good night, B," she murmurs in response.

I fall asleep, blissful, after all this time, knowing I've got Marin where I want her.

THIRTY-NINE

MARIN

"Wake up. I have a surprise for you," Brad whispers in my ear, his warm breath tickling me. Nothing in my life has ever felt so right and so wrong at the same time.

"Yeah, you already surprised me with that in the middle of the night. I'm not falling for that again," I murmur back.

"That's not the surprise, but that sounds good too." He brushes his nose along my neck and chuckles as he leans in farther to kiss my earlobe, giving it a little lick as he does.

"It's still dark out. What time is it anyway?"

"It's five thirty. C'mon. You have to see the amazing sunrise." When he kisses my bare shoulder, I am wide awake and eager for the kind of surprise he gave me last night over and over again. I push back against him.

"Someone seems happy to be next to me this morning," I murmur.

"You can feel that, huh?" He nuzzles my ear again.

"Hard to miss," I snort.

"That's how I felt that first night you fell asleep in my bed. And the next morning. And every night and morning since then. And about three or four times every afternoon too." I can feel him growing even harder against my backside.

"Hmm. You should probably see a doctor about that," I offer with sass.

"I need to see someone, but it's not the doctor," he groans. "As much as it's killing me right now to say this, we need to get out of this sleeping bag." He pulls away and, as I look over my shoulder, he scrubs one hand over his stubbled jaw as he lets out a loud and pained exhale.

We both crawl out from underneath the sleeping bag. He stands before me naked and his body is a sight to behold. He's not covered in hulking muscles, but he's toned. He's very much on the lean side and I like it. His eyes roll up and down my body. You'd think I'd be embarrassed standing before this man naked, considering the junk in my trunk and the bit of a muffin top that's developed since joining the tour, but I'm not.

"Jesus," he says on an exhale. "You are so beautiful." He looks at me like he looks at bacon, so I know it's sincere.

"Keep looking at me like that and we won't get to the sunrise," I say. When he leans forward to kiss me, I put my hand up in front of my face. "Let me brush my teeth first and have a few sips of coffee. Then you can have your wicked way with me." He chuckles as he leans down and grabs some of our clothes, handing mine to me.

We dress in silence and brush our teeth. Outside the tent, Brad puts on a pot of water. Before I know it, his portable stove has warmed it up and he drops in a few single-serving coffee packets for a hot, steaming mug of freshly brewed coffee.

"Mmm," I moan as I take a sip. Brad hands me a flashlight. He carries another flashlight and a blanket in one hand and links our fingers together with the other.

"Come on," he says. "Let me show you what makes this place so amazing in the morning." We hike a short distance, Brad holding my hand the entire time. He walks ahead of me and I follow along, my hand held tight in his. When we get to a small clearing, he puts down the blanket. We sit down, and he puts his arm around me, pulling me into him. We sit in a comfortable, companionable silence waiting for the light show. It doesn't disappoint. The sun rises over the mountains in a majestic display of bright color.

"Which do you like better—the sunrise or the sunset?" he asks.

"I like the sunset better," I respond. "The colors, the streaks of light in the sky, the sun moving between the clouds—I think it's beautiful. What about you?"

"I've always preferred the sunrise. Something about the start of a new day. New possibilities. Beginnings." With that, he brushes his big hand against my jaw and I can feel his callused fingers, rough from playing the guitar for years, scratching against my cheek. He kisses me so softly and gently, and I melt into him.

"Let's go back to the campsite. I want to show you that surprise again from last night," he says.

We get back to the tent and he takes care in removing my clothing, trailing his fingers across my skin and letting them linger in spots that make me gasp. He imprints kisses along my neck, shoulder, and chest, and as he does, I use my fingers to touch his neck, shoulders, and torso, like I'm reading Braille and mapping his skin gives me all the answers and information I need.

Back inside the tent, we remove our clothes and lie down side by side. He threads his fingers through my hair. He grabs my thigh and wraps it around his. It doesn't take much for him to enter me. I'm already slick with moisture from his arousing, drugging, gentle kisses.

I want nothing more than for him to pound into me. I want it harder and faster and deeper, but he keeps this sensually slow pace, gently rocking into me, while he continues to murmur in my ear how beautiful I am and how good it feels. It is the most amazing kind of agony. The buildup to my orgasm is tortuous. And then like a waterfall, I go over the edge and it thunders on and on with chaotic crashes, until I'm a messy, shivering heap.

Tears leak from my eyes as he continues to wring every last ounce of pleasure from me before succumbing to his own release with a shudder and a quiet moan.

I fall back onto the ground, the sleeping bag rumpled beneath me. I'm sweaty and panting yet decidedly calm. This wasn't like the night before. That was frenetic. Passionate. Forbidden. This morning was more . . . intense. If that's even the right word to describe it. Lying next to Brad, being so close to him and looking into his eyes as he gently took my body to places it had never really been before stirred up some emotions I'm not entirely sure I am ready address.

I lean over and lay my head on his chest and absentmindedly run my fingers across his skin. A moment later, I open my eyes. We had both fallen asleep with me sprawled across his body. If it hadn't been for the heat—from both the summer sun and his body—I probably would have slept longer. As soon as I stir, he runs his hand up and down my back.

"Sorry," I mumble. "I kind of took over the space here."

"You never have to apologize for having your naked body pressed up against me, babe."

I lift my head and grin at him. He looks so sexy, with a bit of stubble on his jaw and his hair sticking up in all directions. I lie back down on his chest and sigh.

"We should probably head back," I suggest, my voice tinged with sadness. "I promised to spend the day with Grace before I have to leave for the road again."

"Ah, Grace, the roommate extraordinaire."

"She's the very best person I know," I say in complete honesty.

"Yeah. By the way you talk about her, she must be something pretty special."

"She is." I lift my sticky body off his and we dress in silence.

We pack up all the camping equipment and Brad double- and triple-checks to make sure all fire has been extinguished and we haven't forgotten anything. The ride back to LA is filled with classic rock tunes, which Brad sings with precision and in perfect pitch. We talk more about politics, preferred brands of candy, religion, and our favorite *Seinfeld* episodes. Every once in a while, I'll catch him stealing a glance at me, or touching my knee or squeezing my hand.

We pass a sign along the freeway indicating we're now entering Los Angeles. That's when fear and doubt and immense sadness creep in. This is it. This is the end of the greatest day and night in my life. As if he can sense my shifting mood, Brad grabs my hand and lifts it to his mouth, placing a gentle kiss on my knuckles. All I can do is give him a shy smile. I'm afraid if I open my mouth, I'll beg him to quit the band, run away with me, and spend all our days making love in a tent in the middle of the mountains.

FORTY

After our long drive, we pull up to Marin's place. I hop out of the truck, open the back, and pull out her duffel bag, placing it on the sidewalk.

"Well, looky here," I say. "What's this?" I ask in an exaggerated tone. "An extra sleeping bag. Huh?" I plaster a dumbfounded expression on my face. Marin slaps my arm.

"You jerk!" she exclaims, laughing.

"What's so funny?" A short brunette has bounded down the stairs onto the sidewalk.

"Nothing, Grace," says Marin, shaking her head and giving me a mock disapproving look. Marin wraps the little dark-haired bundle of energy into a hug.

"Yay! You're back," Grace says with a genuine smile. She turns to me. "You must be Brad. I'm Grace. The best friend." She reaches out her hand to shake mine. I pull the beanie off of my head, wipe my hand on the front of my jeans, and shake Grace's. "I'm sure she's told you all about me," Grace says with a wink.

Grace is exactly as Marin had described her. Her brown ponytail bobs up and down and she hops with enthusiasm from one foot to the other. Her energy is infectious, and I understand why Marin enjoys being around her.

"She has mentioned you," I respond. Marin spent a lot of time talking about the special relationship she has with Grace. "She thinks you hung the moon. I guess you are sisters from another mister," I say with a laugh. From my peripheral vision, I notice Marin cringe. I must have said something wrong. "What did I say?" I ask, trepidation in my voice. Before Marin can respond, Grace pipes up.

"Oh, she doesn't like that expression."

"What? Sisters from another mister?" I ask.

"Yeah, that's the one," says Grace, pointing her finger at me.

"I already have a sister from another mister," Marin explains with a sneer.

"That's sort of a sore topic for her," adds Grace.

"Oh, I'm sorry," I say, turning to Marin. "I didn't mean to upset you." I reach out to grab her hand, but she steps out of my reach. I don't mistake the subtle shift in her behavior. She can't wait to get away from me.

"You guys must be exhausted after your long drive. Let's get you and your bag inside," Grace says.

I bend down and pick up Marin's duffel bag. She reaches her hand out for me to hand it to her. Like I would even consider letting her carry her own bag. Before I can protest, Grace loops her arm through mine and guides me up the stairs.

"Oh, I'm sure Brad has things to do—" Marin starts but Grace interrupts her.

"Don't be rude, Marin," she scolds in a good-natured way. "The boy just spent hours in the car. I'm sure he would at least like to use the restroom and have a cold glass of water," she explains as we continue up the steep staircase toward their place.

"Oh, that would be great. I am a bit parched." I look back at Marin who is trailing behind us, her eyes open wide in disbelief.

Upon walking through the door of their apartment, I take a look at the surroundings. The kitchen is small, with light wood cabinets, white Formica countertops and white appliances. It reminds me of the house I grew up in and is a far contrast to the chef's kitchen in our Hollywood Hills rental with dark granite counters and six-burner cooktop.

The living room is also small and feels even smaller with the overstuffed couch taking up the lion's share of the space. It looks so inviting. Like you could curl up on it with a soft blanket and watch Netflix all day—which is exactly what I want to do with Marin at the first opportunity.

I look out the window, notice the ocean view, and feel a sense of calm. I could dig living by the beach. Maybe I can convince Craig to move.

I continue to look around the room and find that it's accented with other pieces of cozy furniture, neutral-colored pillows, and beach-themed trinkets like seashells. A smattering of celebrity magazines like *Star* and *Us Weekly* litter the coffee table. Next to them is a wooden bowl filled with colorful sea glass. Atop the pile is a sea star. I pick it up and finger the arms. I turn around and Marin is staring at me. Grace is in the kitchen getting me a glass of water. From the other room, I can still hear her talking about a time she went camping as a little girl.

"A starfish," I say to Marin. She gives me a tight smile, takes the starfish from my hand, and puts it back in the bowl. Grace returns and hands me the glass of water. After thanking her, I finish it in three large gulps.

"Well . . ." Marin starts, as if she's trying to usher me out.

"It's time for beer," Grace finishes with a smile. "You're joining us, of course, Brad—right?" she asks, turning to me. Marin whips her head around to Grace. It's not hard to guess Grace wants me to come along and Marin is itching for me to leave, but hell if I'm ready to walk away from her. Before Marin can say anything, I respond.

"I'd love to join you, but only if I can treat."

"Of course you're paying, rock star," says Grace with a laugh. She gives me a look like I'm the silliest thing ever, and once again she links her arm through mine and guides me out the door.

I put on my glasses and pull on my beanie. I don't want to be recognized as a rock star today. I want Marin to see me as a regular guy, a guy who's totally fallen for her.

Over a pitcher of beer and a midafternoon snack, I ask Grace about her job and learn that, as an assistant to a talent agent, she handles a range of activities from talent booking and scheduling to grabbing dry cleaning and fetching coffee.

"The most *interesting* part of my job is what we call rolling calls," she explains.

"*Interesting?* What's a rolling call?" I ask.

"I spend most of my day chatting it up with her clients and keeping them occupied on the phone while they wait to talk with her."

"So you stall them so they don't realize they aren't the most important person in her Rolodex?" I clarify.

"Precisely," she responds with a laugh. "You're more than a pretty face, aren't you, rock star?" I take that as a compliment and hope Marin agrees that there's more to me that she wants to explore and enough depth to sustain her interest.

"I try," I shrug in jest. "So you spend most of your day on the phone, huh?" She opens her purse and pulls out two cell phones, a phone charger, and a backup battery pack.

"Indeed. God forbid I miss a call on my day off," she jokes.

"Holy shit," I laugh. "You carry that around with you all the time?"

"All the time," she says with a big, faux-happy grin.

"Even though Grace took today as a vacation day so we can spend time together, she's still at Bellatrix's mercy," shares Marin.

"You never know when someone has an *emergency,*" Grace says, using air quotes.

"Oh, and her boss has *emergencies* all the time," Marin adds, shaking her head.

"I'm surprised she hasn't called yet with some insane request, like ordering her a case of the salad dressing she had at dinner last night," she says laughing and rolling her eyes.

"Grace's boss is less Ari Gold from *Entourage* and more Miranda Priestly from *The Devil Wears Prada*, if you know what I mean," explains Marin.

"I've got my Man Card proudly displayed in my wallet," I respond, holding my hands out to the side as I shake my head. "I have no idea what you're talking about." Grace and Marin laugh.

"Her boss doesn't yell and scream and get irrational on her," Marin explains. "She assumes Grace always knows *exactly* what she's talking about and makes outrageous requests and demands."

"Outrageous requests and demands," I repeat back, intrigued. "What's the craziest thing she's asked you to do?" I say on a laugh, crinkling my brow. Being on tour with a band for months and interacting with egotistical rock stars, I've heard my fair share.

"Hmm. That's a tough one. Giving bubble baths to her dog—which she carries around in her purse and treats better than most of the office staff—is my least favorite," she says with a sneer and a nod of the head.

"Grace is highly allergic to dogs and has had to endure weekly allergy shots since she got hired," Marin elaborates.

"Damn," I reply. "That's dedication." Marin excuses herself to use the restroom and I take it as an opportunity to speak candidly with Grace, who I'm certain is well aware of everything transpiring between me and Marin.

"Aren't you going to warn me you'll kill me if I hurt her?" I ask, taking a sip of my beer.

"I always tell her to look for a man who will ruin her lipstick and not her mascara," she responds. I love Grace's sassy sense of humor.

"Are you afraid I'm going to be the wrong kind of guy?"

"Nah," she says, pushing her hand forward. "You seem like a decent guy and she needs to be pulled out of her comfort zone for a bit," she explains. "Honestly, if anything, I'm afraid she'll hurt you."

"I've been warned," I chuckle in response, "and I'm not going anywhere." Grace raises her glass and mock salutes with it as Marin returns. After a few beers and some chicken fingers with a kick-ass barbeque sauce, the check arrives. Grace hands it to me.

"We're paying back student loans," she offers with a grin and exaggerated bat of her eyelashes.

"Both of you, huh?" I ask.

"At least I make a salary," Grace offers with a shrug. "Marin here is working for peanuts."

"My internship with Sasha comes with a small stipend, which doesn't cover much. And now that I have a job, I have student loan payments. I know every dollar I took out will probably cost me three dollars to pay back when I include the interest."

"That sucks," I say. "I know what it's like to not have a lot and luckily, I'm now in a position to not worry about money. What's that expression? 'I've been rich and poor. Rich is better.'"

"Ain't that the truth," says Grace as I pull some money from my billfold and take care of the check.

"So, do you have any plans for your two days off before we head down to San Diego?" I ask as we walk back to their apartment. I'm hoping Marin's got a light load so we can spend some more time together.

"Grace here and I have big plans," she starts.

"Really?" I ask. "What are you going to do?"

"All the big important things like laundry and reality TV and cupcakes," she says, wrapping her arm around Grace's neck and pulling her in for a hug.

"Ah," I acknowledge. "Sounds like you've got things prioritized well."

"What about you, Brad?" asks Grace, who has pulled out of Marin's embrace and is now walking with her arm linked in mine.

"I don't have any plans other than hanging out." I'd love nothing more than to watch Marin fold laundry (including her sexy boy shorts), comment on crap TV, and lick chocolate frosting off her lips. But I get the sense I'm not welcome.

"I'm sure you'll enjoy having some down time," says Marin as we keep heading up the few blocks along the beach walkway to their place.

When we arrive, Grace lets go of my arm and wraps her short arms around me. "Thanks for the beers and great company," she says. "It was awesome meeting you and I hope it won't be the last we see of each other." She gives me a quick wink and walks over to Marin. She squeezes Marin's arm and walks up the stairs to their apartment.

Marin and I stand on the sidewalk, staring at each other. "Well," she starts, and I think we're both unsure what to say. "I guess I'll see you on Saturday," she finishes, reaching out to shake my hand. What the hell? After all we've shared, she thinks a fucking handshake is going to do.

"Really, Marin?" I say, tilting my head to the side and giving her a disapproving look. Seeming contrite, but still unsure of the appropriate response, she leans forward and gives me a hug. I wrap my arms around her and inhale. She smells like vanilla, campfire smoke, beer, and sex. I'm sure I smell the same—except for the vanilla of course. Maybe she doesn't like it, but I'm turned on as hell. She tries to pull away, but I keep her tight against me. When I relent, she places a chaste kiss on my check.

"Thank you for a . . ." she starts but her voice trails off.

"Thank *you*," I say. She sighs.

"It was . . . wonderful. As amazing as it was"—she casts her eyes downward—"we both know one night is all it can ever be. At least we got it out of our system," she says with a shrug. What the hell is she talking about?

"Out of my system?" I ask in disbelief. "You're in my system. Like the blood flowing through my body." Can't she tell how pained I am?

"It will be a great memory," she offers. "You're such a special guy, but now I need to get back to focusing on work," she says shaking her head, trying to convince herself more than me this is the right thing to do. "Good-bye B," she says, and it seems so simple for her. "See you Saturday."

With that, she walks back to her apartment. I stand on the sidewalk, stunned she could walk away like that. Doesn't she feel this too? Doesn't she know what we have doesn't come along every day? I mean, I get it. Her job is important to her. She's smart and driven. But she's also funny, clever, and kind. I don't want to mess anything up for her, but damn it, she's all I think about.

FORTY-ONE

"Not a word, Grace," I say in warning, as I walk into our shared bedroom. She takes a few hesitant steps inside, watching my reaction, before making her way in and sitting down on the bed beside me.

"How about a hug?"

The floodgates open and the tears fall. Grace holds me and rubs my back in little circles while I sob, soothing me. "Shh," she murmurs. "It's okay." After a few minutes, my tears subside. "Do you want to talk about it?"

"I slept with him," I blurt out.

"Well, I figured that. One look at you and it was painfully obvious you two had done the deed," she says matter-of-factly. "Not that I even have to ask, but how was it?"

"Amazing. Perfect," I whisper.

"I knew it." she sneers. "So jealous."

"His body is lean and firm and he totally knows what he's doing," I say, blowing out a puff of air and trying not to get turned on thinking about our incredible night together.

"Of course he does. He's a rock star. I know *you're* a good lay because I had to listen to Dan Daniels shout it over and over during the two years you dated. Never mind I had to hear *you* shout 'Dan Daniels' over and over too," she says in mock horror. "I'm not sure why you had to say his full name. 'Dan Daniels! Dan Daniels!'" she yells, feigning an orgasm.

"It was alliterative. I couldn't help myself." I dissolve into giggles.

"Seriously, though, you've cast quite a spell over your rock star. The boy is smitten."

"It's mutual. It is so mutual, Grace. He's . . . amazing . . . in so many ways. It's not just the music, either. He's smart and creative, and there's this passion in him for his work. And despite how busy he is or how much people feed his ego, he calls his mom every Sunday without fail. It's admirable and sweet. And beyond sexy."

"Well, I guess you're going to have to make some tough choices," she offers.

"This was a complication I wasn't expecting," I huff. "When the tech position fell through, I figured I would pay my dues with the rock band and then move on to bigger and better." I don't add that working with the band after my internship ends (even with all the juvenile jokes, backstage shenanigans, and insane hours) is sounding more and more appealing, just so I can stay with Brad.

"Brad seems pretty big. No pun intended," she winks.

"You're shameless, you know that?" I chuckle.

"I do. So, what are you going to do?" she asks. "I always say: go with your gut. What does your gut say?"

I shrug, tears welling. "My gut always wants tacos," I pout. The entire bed shakes with Grace's infectious laughter and before long, I'm cackling too.

"Well, before you get a taco tattooed on your ass, try to remember your job is how you make money. But your *life*, that's how and with whom you choose to live."

I stare at Grace, nodding my head in slow motion. She pulls me back into an embrace. As much as I know she's right, I also know that no job means no money and no money is not an option. So I let the tears fall as I think of the lucky girl Brad will meet next and how she gets to keep Brad for herself.

FORTY-TWO

"Whatever you're doing isn't working," I tell Damon. Craig is by my side and we're having a frank conversation with our manager about Johnny. Damon looks over at our drummer, who is playing cards with Oliver.

"He looks fine to me," Damon shrugs. "Do you have something concrete?" As pissed as I am at Marin right now, I don't want to betray her confidence. I know it wasn't easy for her to share her impressions with me. She probably figured it wasn't her place and maybe even feared it would come back to bite her in the ass. But I'm glad she confided in me. It was the right thing to do and her putting people above work is one of the many reasons I'm drawn to her.

"Maybe we need an intervention," I toss out. Damon smirks. and I think he's about to brush me off when Craig interjects.

"Listen. He's been showing up and doing his job, but if B.O. thinks something's going on here, I trust his instincts."

"Yeah, of course," agrees Damon. "I will talk with him. Tonight when we get in."

"Maybe we could have one of the security guards keep an extra eye on him, on the down low of course," I suggest.

"Sure," agrees Damon. "I'll handle it."

Feeling satisfied that Damon will address our concerns, I sit down. Without Marin to help me pass the time, the bus ride down to San Diego drags. No cell phone Yahtzee. No *Seinfeld* reruns. No travel Scrabble. No fun chats or debates. Nothing. It's like life has gone back to the way it was before she joined the tour and I fucking hate it.

She's in the back of the bus, working on her laptop and cell phone. She walks over to talk with the guys, who are huddled at a table near her, playing poker. She says something and they nod their heads before she walks toward me.

"So, you're talking to me now." I can't keep the hurt out of my voice.

"B," she says with a frown.

"What's up?" I try to put on a smile.

"I wanted to let you know we have an interview with 91X at the radio station tomorrow at eight thirty. Phoebe will do your hair at seven thirty and there's a car coming to the hotel at eight."

"Okay. I'll be ready."

"Okay." She turns on her sexy boots and walks back to her laptop. I'm about to put my earbuds in when Oliver pipes up.

"Yo, Oliver here. Who *is* this?" he asks into the phone in annoyance. His brows crinkle up and he pulls the phone away from his ear. I can hear a guttural "rrrrrrr-ghghghghgh!" He hangs up and lets out a little huff. A few minutes later, his cell rings again. Oliver looks at the caller ID but judging by his scrunched face, he doesn't recognize the number.

"Hello?" he asks. He listens for a minute and hangs up. Before he can put the phone on the table, it rings again. "The fuck?" he mumbles. This time, he puts the call on speakerphone. What comes out silences us all.

"Grrrrrllhhhhhrrr!"

We exchange curious glances with one another.

"So, did I win?" asks the disembodied voice on the other end of the line.

"Win what?" asks Oliver. His tone is less annoyed now and more amused.

"The Chewbacca growl contest."

"Contest?" Oliver questions.

"Yeah, there was an online ad. Win five hundred dollars by giving the best Chewbacca yell," the guy explains.

"Ah, yes. The contest," confirms Oliver. "No," he says in a sympathetic tone. "No, you didn't win. Good luck next time," he adds before hanging up with a laugh. Oliver puts the phone on the table and looks up at Jase, who is smirking.

Before Oliver can say anything, his phone rings again. Instead of answering it, he turns off the ringer. Oliver turns to Jase and tips an imaginary hat to him. Jase tips his imaginary hat in return. Although the ringer is silenced, the phone lights up on the table. Oliver looks down at it and back up at Jase with a tight smile.

"Looks like I need to change my number," he says.

"Looks so," Jase shrugs.

A month ago, this hilarious practical joke would have had me rolling. Now, it doesn't shake me from this funk. On some level, I fear their pranks are escalating and one of them is going to shave off the other's eyebrows, or do some serious damage. Even more, it's a time waster and I'm sick of wasting time. I've got things I want to accomplish. Video game-related things. And the tour is just killing time.

After a short drive, we arrive at the hotel and Marin exits the bus, giving me only a tight smile. I check into my room and take a shower, trying to wash off my foul mood. After dinner with the guys, I head back to my room instead of joining them in the hotel bar for beers. That holds little appeal for me right now. Instead, I text Marin. I don't know how she'll respond, but I've got to try.

ME: *Hey. What are you doing?*

MARIN: *Just hanging out in my room.*

ME: *Alone?*

MARIN: *No. Cal's here.*

Cal? Who the hell is Cal?

ME: *Cal?*

MARIN: *You know. The roadie with the big beer gut and dead tooth. He's so my type.*

Ah, Cal. Of course I know him. He's been with us since the beginning. I didn't realize Marin knew who he was. Oh, who the hell am I kidding? She knew everyone's name by the first day—from bus drivers to the catering staff. She chatted with everyone breezily and made everyone feel like their job was important. She's amazing like that.

ME: *If you're trying to make me jealous, it's working.*

MARIN: *I knew you had a thing for Cal! You guys would make a cute couple.*

Uh, that would be a resounding no. Don't get me wrong. My favorite cousin is gay and I was best man at his wedding last year. If I *was* into dudes though, Cal wouldn't be my type. And I'd like to think I would attract someone rather hot. But I'm only into Marin.

ME: *The only person I'm interested in coupling with is you. Come to my room?*

I sit and wait for her reply. The silence is killing me. I'm not even seeing the "dot, dot, dot" come up on the screen to show she's typing.

ME: *Please. (Pathetic to see a grown man beg, isn't it?)*

Yeah, I'm begging.

MARIN: *We talked about this, B. Not a good idea.*

ME: *Pretty please. (Even more pathetic!)*

MARIN: *What happened over the weekend was . . . amazing–*

Hell yeah, it was amazing. Best sex of my life. Not to brag, but as noted, I've had my share of sex. More than that, we really connected, and not just on a physical level.

MARIN: *–but we both know it was just one night.*

ME: *Just to talk.*

ME: *And hang out.*

ME: *And make out.*

MARIN: *B!*

ME: *Okay. I won't try anything.*

ME: *Just come hang out with me.*

ME: *I miss you.*

Again, she doesn't respond right away. After a few moments of silence, save for the rat-tat-tat of my beating heart, she types a response.

MARIN: *I miss hanging out with you too.*

Of course, she does. We're great together.

MARIN: *It's better if we just keep things professional from now on.*

ME: *Okay.*

Not okay! No way is that okay. A minute later I type out another response.

ME: *No. It's not okay. We need to talk.*

MARIN: *I'm not coming to your room.*

ME: *Fine. I'll come to yours.*

MARIN: *Jody is here now so not a good idea.*

ME: *Meet me by the pool in 5.*

FORTY-THREE

"Hey," Brad says, gesturing to the top of the lounge chair for me to sit down. He lowers himself onto the bottom half. Rather than climb into the same chair as him, I pull a different chair over. He scrubs his hand over his face and lets out a loud exhale.

"B . . ."

"No. Don't say anything yet, Marin. Hear me out." I nod and purse my lips. He runs his hand through his dark, spiky hair. Hair that, only a few days ago, I could feel brushing against the tender skin of my thighs. "This is bullshit, Marin," he says, sounding pained.

"I . . ."

"No. Let me finish. This is bullshit. This," he says, gesturing back and forth between us, "doesn't happen every day. It sure as hell hasn't happened to me before."

"You're my boss," I whisper, feeling the pain and guilt of knowing I'm repeating Mom's pattern.

"I'm not your boss," he scoffs. "You work for Sasha."

"Who works for you," I insist.

"Sasha works for Damon."

"Who works for you," I retort.

"Jesus, Marin. You've got to be kidding me."

"I'm sorry, B. I am, but we agreed one night was all we would share."

"You're willing to walk away from something this . . . this special?" He grabs my hand, drawing little circles across my wrist with his fingers. But I'm not *willing* to walk away. I *have to* walk away.

"What do you think is going to happen? We're going to get married and live the rock star life happily ever after? Be real, B. In a few more weeks, the tour will be over. You'll go back to your life in Hollywood and I'll get a tech job in San Francisco or Seattle. We'll go our separate ways and have some wonderful memories."

"I didn't think about what comes next. I was enjoying what we have now. Can't we do that?" he begs.

"That's not a good idea, B. We shouldn't have let things get this far. It was a mis—" Before I can finish, he interjects.

"Don't say it was a mistake. Don't you dare say that," he fires back, dropping my hand before turning his back to me and running his fingers through his hair. My tongue darts out and licks my lower lip as I shake my head.

"It *was* a mistake," I begin, and he turns around and looks at me in anger. "My feelings aren't a mistake but acting on them was. I'm sorry," I say, getting up off the lounge chair and rushing back to my room.

*

We're backstage after another amazing show and a thin sheen of sweat covers Brad's brow and the collar of his gray t-shirt. He looks delicious and lickable.

I'm not the only one who thinks so. Two women are flirting with him, tossing their bleached blonde hair back and pushing out their big breasts. Since I've been on tour, I've noticed he's never taken an interest in the groupies who hang out after a show. That seems to be more of Jase's M.O. I guess Brad is channeling his inner Jase tonight because he can't tear himself away from their flirtatious death grip on his arm. He leans over and whispers something in one of their ears and Miss Fake Tits tilts back, pushing her boobs up even higher, and laughs. I've never been prone to violence but right now I'm having murderous thoughts.

Those thoughts betray me as Brad looks over and can sense my fury. For a second, it looks as though he's contrite—like he knows how wrong and betraying it is to be openly flirting with these groupies—but then he wraps his arm around the waist of one of them, pulls her close, and buries his face in her neck. Tears threaten, and I race down the stairs into the main dressing room.

As the tears fall, I wrap my arms around myself and let the reality of the situation wash over me. He's moved on and he's definitely gone down market. Before I can further internalize his betrayal, I feel Brad's hand on my shoulder.

"What are you doing here?" I ask, using the back of my hand to wipe my nose.

"Why are you crying?" His tone is soft and concerned. He puts his hand on my jaw and wipes some errant tears away.

"What do you care?" I spit out.

"Of course I care, Marin," he scoffs. "If anything, you're the one who doesn't care about us."

"Is that what you think?" I ask in disbelief, pushing away from him.

"That's what you've shown me and what you've said and what you've done. What else am I supposed to think?"

"You don't think I want us to be together? You don't think you affect me? Of course you do."

He stalks toward me, and I back up against a table covered in hairstyling products.

"Then let's be together," he says, likes it's so simple.

"We've been through this, B," I say, my eyes welling with tears again.

"Yeah, I know," he huffs, scrubbing his hand over his now stubbled jaw. "You've made yourself perfectly clear." He shakes his head, turns, and walks away. As he exits the doorway, I find Phoebe standing there. She puts her arms around me and lets me sob.

"Do you want to talk about it, honey?" she asks. Of course I want to talk about it.

"No," I respond.

"Okay," she says and continues to let me be sad. It's times like this I feel most homesick, when I miss having Grace by my side.

FORTY-FOUR

BRAD

Jesus, I'm an asshole!

FORTY-FIVE

M A R I N

I get up from my laptop (where I'm analyzing the metrics on social media engagement for one of the band's accounts) to use the bus bathroom. The guys are sitting on the couches enjoying a round of beers, while Phoebe sits next to Craig and strokes his hair and neck. He leans over and gives her a sweet kiss. The two of them are cute together. Could a relationship with someone you work with—on the road like this—work out? It seems to be working for them.

"Okay," says Jase. "You're up, Craig." Craig strokes his chin, his eyes intense, as if he's deep in thought.

"Alright," he begins. "I've never been ice skating. I can run five miles in under forty-five minutes. I can hold my breath underwater for two minutes."

"What are you guys doing?" I ask.

"We're playing Two Truths and a Lie," says Oliver.

"What's that?" I respond.

"You give the group three statements—two true and one a lie," he explains. "People guess which is the lie and if they get it wrong, they drink."

"Oh, so you're being super productive with your time," I confirm, nodding.

"It's important we *really* know each other well," Oliver smirks, justifying this time waster.

"Yeah, the success of the band is based on trust and communication," laughs Johnny.

"And beer," Craig chimes in. Phoebe laughs and kisses his temple.

"Come play with us," Oliver says. "Let us get to know you better."

"Oh, I don't think that would be appropriate," I respond. Little do they know—or perhaps they do—I've gotten to know one of them intimately.

"Sit, PR girl," says Jase. "That's an order." He scoots over and pats the empty space next to him. I consider whether this is a good or bad idea, and after a beat, lower myself to the seat and steal a glance at Brad. He won't even make eye contact with me.

"You're up," says Oliver.

"You tell us two things about yourself that are true and one thing that isn't," says Johnny, ignoring the fact that Oliver explained it to me less than two minutes ago.

"I got it," I confirm, trying to avoid my rising irritation. "Okay," I say, thinking. "I'm color-blind. I went to high school with actress Brie Larson—"

"Oh, she's hot," says Jase. "I hope that's true and you still know her."

"She's an Oscar winner," adds Phoebe.

"She is?" asks Johnny.

"Yeah, for *The Room*," Phoebe responds.

"Never heard of it," says Johnny.

"That's because it doesn't have any nudity in it," Phoebe lobs at him.

"Can we let Marin finish her turn?" huffs Jase. "Go ahead, Marin. You said you're color-blind and went to high school with the hot Oscar winner. What else?"

"I've never seen *Star Wars*," I say.

"You mean the original?" Brad asks.

"No. I mean I haven't seen any of the six movies."

"There are technically eight *Star Wars* movies, although some may argue that point," he considers. "Unless, of course, you count things like spin-offs, such as *Solo* or the upcoming Boba Fett movie, or one-offs like the *Star Wars Holiday Special* or the Ewok *Caravan of Courage*, in which case there are many more."

"You're such a dork," Jase snorts, shaking his head.

"In that case," I pipe up, not wanting an argument to start. Tempers have been short these past few days and I know Brad is not in the best of moods. "I haven't seen any *Star Wars* movie. So, what's true and what's the lie?" I challenge.

"Gotta be the *Star Wars* one," says Johnny. "She didn't even know how many movies there were."

"She was very specific about the actress she went to school with," Oliver notes, pondering my statements.

"Be specific when you lie. Con artists always say that in the movies," notes Craig.

I scrunch up my shoulders, tilt my head to the side, and bat my eyelashes.

"I say the *Star Wars* one," says Johnny.

"I have to agree," chimes Oliver.

"I'm going with the high school friend," says Craig. "That's too specific. What about you B.O.?"

"I'm going with color-blind," he says, staring at me.

"Jase?" asks Craig.

"*Star Wars*," he scoffs, like Craig asked an idiotic question. Craig turns to me. In fact, all the guys' eyes shift to me.

"Well?" he says.

"I'm color-blind," I say.

"You scammed us," says Oliver.

I toss out a quote about fear of loss being a path to the Dark Side in my best Yoda voice.

"That's telling," mutters Brad before getting up and walking to the bathroom.

"You're color-blind?" asks Phoebe, "But your outfits are always so well put together."

"I'm not sure that has anything to do with it," I respond, not focusing my attention on the guys. Instead I process how Brad stood up and walked away.

"So, you know Brie Larson, huh?" says Jase. "Can you put in a good word for me?" I turn to Jase, shake my head, and laugh.

"Double or nothing," says Oliver. "We already know everything about each other. We need some fresh meat."

"Yeah, Marin," says Phoebe. "Go again."

"Uh, okay," I say, glancing back to see if Brad is returning. "I came in second in a pie eating contest—" I begin when I notice Brad walking toward us. He passes and grabs a black-and-white composition notebook from his backpack before walking to the back to the bus and climbing into one of the bunk beds, leaving the curtain open. A look passes between Oliver and Craig before Craig shrugs. He leans over to Phoebe and kisses her cheek.

"Go on," says Johnny, leaning forward with his hand in his palm, like I'm the most interesting person in the room.

"I know how to juggle," I say with a quirked eyebrow. "Or, I sewed my own prom dress."

"Damn!" says Oliver, shaking his hand out in front of him. "You got skills."

"Impressive, PR girl," adds Jase. After the guys learn I cannot in fact juggle and give me mad props for being a finalist at ten years old in a pie eating contest at the Placer County Fair, I determine I've given them enough personal details for today. I excuse myself and email Amy.

From: MarinC@sashavpr.com
To: AmyL@sashavpr.com

Subject: Social Media Engagement Concept for Approval

Amy,

The guys were playing a drinking game called Two Truths and a Lie earlier on the bus, where you make three personal statements, two of which are true and one is a lie, hence the name of the game. Others have to guess which statement is the lie. I thought this would be a fun way to engage with fans. We could post videos on the website where people could vote on which statement is the lie. We would cross-promote through our social media channels. Winner would receive concert swag. Thoughts?

From: AmyL@sashavpr.com
To: MarinC@sashavpr.com
Subject: Re: Social Media Engagement Concept for Approval

I like it. Put together some video samples and send them to me for approval.

From: MarinC@sashavpr.com
To: AmyL@sashavpr.com
Subject: Re: Social Media Engagement Concept for Approval

Will do. Thanks.

FORTY-SIX

"Godda uthafucka!" screams Jase as he slams the bathroom door behind him and charges up the bus aisle. He grabs Oliver by his shirt collar and lifts him off the couch, tightening his hand around his neck. Oliver gasps and coughs. Jase rears his arm back to strike. Brad and Craig jump out of their seats and pull Jase away. Jase continues to lunge forward but Craig holds him back. Meanwhile, Oliver wheezes and smooths out his shirt.

"What the hell is going on?" exhales an exasperated Damon. He turns and shakes his head at me. Like I would be filming and sharing this? He doesn't have much confidence in my judgment if he felt the need to warn me off. "You two are like children," he huffs, shaking his head again.

"Di ahole puh umthin in uy ooth ase," splutters Jase, jerking his shoulder out of Craig's hold.

"What?" says Damon.

"Di ahole," Jase repeats, pointing at Oliver, "puh umthin in uy ooth ase," he says again, emphasizing each syllable to make it easier to understand. I look over at Oliver who is pursing his lips trying to hold back a laugh.

"What did you do, Oliver?" Damon demands.

"Why do you assume *I* did something?" asks Oliver, with an innocent look. I can't help but roll my eyes.

"What the fuck, Oliver?" Brad says, shaking his head.

"It was a harmless prank," he responds with a laugh. "Don't have to get all bent out of shape."

"What did you do?" Brad repeats in frustration.

"I put some Orajel in his toothpaste," he says with little tremors in his shoulders as he chuckles.

Damon is fuming. "Damn it, Oliver. This shit has got to stop."

"C'mon. It's funny," Oliver laughs.

"Dude," exhales Craig. "He's the lead singer. You can't go fucking with his mouth."

"I fucked his mouth," Oliver repeats, laughing out loud now.

"It's not funny, Oliver," Brad tells him.

"Damn right, it's not funny. Thank God we don't have a show tonight or this could cost us a lot of money," says Damon. He puts his hand out and Oliver reaches into his pocket to produce a small tube of gel for numbing tooth and gum problems. "How long does this shit last?" Damon fumes, turning the tube over to read the instructions.

"He should be fine in an hour or two," says Oliver, like it's no big deal.

"Uthafucka!" yells Jase again as he pushes forward to attack Oliver. Craig is still standing next to him and pushes him back, saving Oliver from a fist to the jaw.

"Go calm down, man," he tells Jase, giving him a little shove toward the front of the bus. Jase walks away, muttering incoherently.

"This shit has got to stop," Damon warns again, pointing a menacing finger at Oliver. "I don't want any more practical jokes. Got it?"

"Jeez. You don't have to be such a pill," Oliver scoffs.

"I mean it, Oliver," Damon threatens. "Don't push me on this."

"Yeah, yeah, I got it," Oliver placates.

"I mean it." Damon brushes past me to talk with Jase. He sits down next to the frustrated singer and whispers a few things, pushing his hand forward in what looks like the universal sign for *calm down*. Jase shakes his head several times, but whatever Damon says settles him. He nods, puts on a pair of headphones, and closes his eyes. Brad looks at me with a tight smile and shakes his head. He turns to Oliver with a disappointed look, lowers his eyes to the ground, and walks away.

FORTY-SEVEN

It's been two weeks since my overnight camping trip with Marin. Two weeks since we laughed and joked and bonded. Two weeks since I tasted her sweet lips. Two weeks since I held her in my arms and felt her body tremble with need and lust and release.

We've spoken half a dozen times since our fight at the concert venue, but always about upcoming interviews and schedules and such. She's been polite and professional, and I hate it.

I miss her. I miss our playful banter. I miss her scent. And her smile. I miss how smart and hot she sounds when she talks about her work. I miss funny stories about her and Grace's adventures in college. There's no one else around right now who gets me the way she does.

I don't want to cause problems with her job. That's the last thing I would ever do. She's so smart and ambitious and hardworking. She deserves everything she's earned, but damn if I don't want her kind heart and warm body back in my life and my bed.

There's nothing from the band's standpoint to prevent us from being together. Craig and Phoebe have been together since the band started and no one has a problem with it. Who knows how Sasha would feel, but who cares? Sasha's company works for me—or I should say us—not the other way around.

We've wrapped up our sound check and are heading out. Marin is talking and laughing with Karine. She tilts her head back and her body shakes. I love her laugh, which can elicit a smile, unclench my worried belly, or make my shaft hard in seconds. I miss knowing that laugh was usually shared with me, directed at me, caused by me.

"Hey, C.O.," I call out to my brother. "Wait up," I say, jogging over to him and Oliver.

"What up, B.O.?"

"Listen, I was hoping to do a little something different tonight . . ."

FORTY-EIGHT

M A R I N

The crowd here in Albuquerque, New Mexico, is going wild. The guys have pretty much stuck to their standard set list but these fans don't know it and despite hearing these songs in this order at every concert for the last few weeks—along with their "impromptu" interplay and "ad libs" (which have been scripted in advance)—I'm still riveted. They are quite charismatic.

The two winners of tickets and backstage passes from this morning's radio interview and giveaway are practically jumping out of their skin with excitement. I snap a few photos and plan to post one tomorrow morning. I'm awaiting the band's cover of Led Zeppelin's "Whole Lotta Love" when Jase goes off script.

"We've got a special treat for you tonight. Our own Brad Osterhauser, guitar guru and Grammy-nominated songwriter, has a new song he is debuting tonight." Jase has to wait a few minutes for the cheering to die down before continuing.

"I know our lawyers are going to shit bricks with what I'm about to say, but fuck 'em. I want you all to take out your cell phones and get ready to record. If you're going to bootleg anything tonight and post it on YouTube, this should be it." He steps back and Brad comes over to the microphone. He looks beyond sexy in a pair of tight khaki pants, a snug black t-shirt, worn-out suede sneakers, and a denim vest.

"Thanks for the introduction, man, and thanks for being a great crowd tonight." He pauses while the audience whoops and hollers. "This is a new song and as Jase said, this is the first time I'll be playing it for anyone. It's called 'One Night is Never Enough.'"

He takes a quick glance to the side of the stage where I'm sure my jaw is on the floor. I look around at the crew, my stomach flip-flopping, hoping no one recognizes he's turning my words from our camping trip back on me.

When you walked in the room
My heart went boom
My emotions went zoom
I knew one night wouldn't be enough

So I took a chance
I stole a glance
I made an advance
To try romance
But you took a stance
You maintained your distance
Made it clear
Love's not in abundance

See, you had goals and dreams
Ambitions you held in high esteem
Your work ethic wasn't a scheme
But not everything is what it seems

Because that perfect moment
Your perfect touch
I'd give up anything

I miss it so much
One night is never enough

I know you're scared about what it could mean
I know my life is not really your scene
I know you deserve so much better than me
I hope you'll see past all that to what we can be

So don't put up a shield
I want you to yield
Our hearts can be healed
Because one night will never, ever be enough

Because that perfect moment
Your perfect touch
I'd give up anything
I miss it so much
One night is never enough

As I listen to the beautiful words, tears threaten. I widen my eyes and take a few deep breaths to keep them at bay, reminding myself any relationship between us jeopardizes my job, my future. I'm taken by the melody—the same one he played for me when we were in Ojai—and the case he's making for why we should be together.

When he finishes, the crowd screams and applauds. I'm quite certain there are many women in the audience right now who would love for that song to be written for them.

I can no longer resist what's been building between us these past few months. He's amazing. Funny. Smart. Creative. Passionate. He's quite honestly, aside from my dad, the best guy I've ever known. In this moment, I know the song is beautiful but inaccurate. *I'm* the one who doesn't deserve *him*.

*

The concert continues as usual, with the guys sticking to the set list including their two encores. After the lights are turned on and the audience starts to file out of the concert hall, I head over to the green room with our two contest winners. I introduce them to the band and take photos for both our publicity purposes and the radio station. After security escorts them out, Damon announces the bus is ready to take everyone back to the hotel. I board last, hoping Brad is sitting alone so we can talk.

When I get on board, he's sitting with Craig and Phoebe. He doesn't even look up when I walk past. By the time I get off the bus at the hotel, he's already gone and I'm guessing he's returned to his room. No doubt there's a plate of bacon in his near future. I want to share that bacon with him. I want to share so much more with him.

So this is it. The moment of truth. Do I go to him? Do I tell him how much I loved his song? How much I love him? Or do I hide behind my job?

I get in the elevator and push the button for the fourth floor where all our rooms are located. I know Brad is in room 4153. I'm always aware of which room is his. I walk up to his door and breathe deep, like in yoga. I'm not sure what I'm going to say but I knock anyway. He opens the door and before I can speak, his lips crash down against mine. My fingers tangle in his hair and he grabs my ass and lifts me up so I am cradled against his pelvis. I wrap my legs around him and he backs me against the wall, one hand holding me up, the other stroking my jaw as his lips and tongue continue to explore mine.

"Thank God you're here," he rasps against my mouth, cradling me against him.

"I loved your song," I moan as his erection presses into my most intimate spot. I wouldn't be surprised if he could feel my wet heat through my clothes.

"Naked. Now," he growls, sending tingles across my body. He lowers me to the floor and guides me to the bed, slamming the door behind us. We're a hurried tangle of arms, legs, lips, and tongues, tearing off each other's clothes like animals.

I lie down on the bed, naked, and Brad grabs my legs, pulling me to the edge. Within moments he's sheathed himself in a condom, nudged my legs apart, and wrapped my legs around his waist.

"I'm going to take you hard, Marin, and then I'm going to take you slow. I'm going to take you in this bed, in the shower, and up against the wall, and on that chair. Then maybe, just maybe, I'll think about letting you leave the room."

"Yes, B. Yes, yes."

As he pushes inside of me, I rock myself against him to prolong the ecstasy.

"Jesus. You're killing me, Marin," he moans before kissing me silly. I roll us over so I'm on top of him, lying in his arms while he trails gentle fingers up my arm and across my back, those callouses prickling my skin, eliciting goosebumps. I've never felt so content, so cherished . . . and yet so scared.

"God, I missed you," he breathes into my hair, his lips skimming the top of my head as I rest on his chest.

"I missed you too. I can't fight these feeling anymore," I tell him, lifting up off his chest to look him in the eyes.

"REO Speedwagon," he says with a smile.

"What?"

"REO Speedwagon. It's a band from the seventies and they had a big hit called 'Can't Fight This Feeling.'" After a pause he adds, "Please don't leave me again." I can hear the pain in his voice.

"I won't. I'm so sorry, B," I whisper, grasping onto him tighter.

"Shh," he soothes. "It's okay. You're here now."

"I'm just so scared. I need this job and I need to make sure nothing interferes with that, but I can't deny the feelings I have for you," I add, rising up on my elbow to look in his eyes while I stroke his jaw with my hand.

"It will all be okay, Marin. I promise," he assures me.

"For now, can we keep this between us? I don't want it getting out that I'm sleeping with a client." He turns to face me and places his lips on mine, so tender and gentle.

"That's not gonna work for me, Marin. I don't want to hide our relationship. I want all our friends on the tour to know we are together. That we're a couple." I open my mouth to protest but he brushes his finger across my lips. "I get that you're scared, but I promise you, it will be okay."

"Okay," I acquiesce. I can't fight it anymore. He takes my hand in his and brings it to his lips, brushing my knuckles against his mouth the way he has done a dozen times before.

"Don't forget how good this is. How right it feels." His eyes shine with warmth and sincerity. "I know I won't." He rolls me onto my back, raises my hands above my head, and links our fingers together before kissing me again.

"Aren't you tired?" I ask him with a laugh.

"Exhausted. You've worn me out, woman. Honestly, I'm afraid if I fall asleep and wake up, this will have been a dream. I don't want to say it's just a dream."

"Don't want to say it's just a dream," I repeat. "That's not a bad name for a song."

"Hmm, not bad at all," he says before kissing me again. "I think I need some more inspiration."

After he makes tender love to me, I lay my head on his chest. His beating heart is a lullaby that soon puts me to sleep.

*

The next day, we board the bus to take us to Denver, Colorado, the next stop on our tour. I walk ahead of Brad, his hand resting on the small of my back, but not in an overt way. I grab the handrail to move ahead when his hand snakes around my waist. He spins me around, dips me down, and plants a kiss on my lips in front of everyone. When he rights me, I'm met with the sounds of clapping and cheering.

"I am so proud to be with you, Marin. I want everyone to know we are together," he tells me.

I hear "finally" and "it's about time" called out over the cheers and applause. Not knowing what else to do, I blush and curtsy. Brad holds my hand and pulls me into his lap on a seat on the bus, kissing me again and again.

"I can't stop kissing you," he whispers to me in between planting sweet kisses on my cheeks and lips. Phoebe comes bounding over, reminding me of Grace.

"Oh my gosh. I'm so excited for you, Marin." I'm a little embarrassed and unsure of what to say. She sits down on the empty seat next to us. "If you could have seen some of the bimbos B.O. has hooked up with over the years . . ." she says, her voice trailing off as she rolls her eyes.

"Hey now," Brad shoots back. "Let's not get into that." He shakes his head at her and gives a death stare designed to shut her up. I look back at him in mock accusation.

"Really now?" I retort and start laughing.

"Oh, I didn't mean it that way, B.O.," she scoffs. "I mean I'm so happy you two are together because Marin is so awesome."

"Well, that's true," says Brad, before leaning down to kiss me again.

A few hours into our bus ride, we stop off at a little diner for lunch. My phone rings while we're sitting at the table eating greasy burgers and fries. It's from the agency. Shit! Brad flashes me a look of concern.

"Sasha," I tell him with my lips pulled into a grim line. I stand up from the table and slide my finger across the bar to answer the call. "Hello, this is Marin." I steady myself for what they are about to say on the other line. Harlot. Hussy. Jezebel. Slut. Whore. I'm waiting to be called one of those names. I called Mom all of those at one time or another.

"Marin, it's Sasha and Amy."

"Hi guys." I try to keep my voice light.

"Listen, do you have a minute where you can talk in private?" Sasha asks. Shit! This is it. I'm getting fired.

"Yeah, sure." I walk away from our table, out the restaurant door, and around the side of the diner. "I'm alone now. What can I do for you?"

"We've heard a rumor you are dating Brad. Is it true?" asks Sasha.

"Yes. Yes, it is," I say, bracing myself for whatever they have to say.

"I see. I'm surprised," says Sasha.

"We didn't give Brynn the Kings Quarters assignment because we were trying to avoid these potential . . . entanglements," explains Amy.

"I understand," I say, holding my breath.

"Well, don't let it get in the way of your work," advises Sasha.

"Okay . . ." I respond, dragging the word out as I wait for the other proverbial shoe to drop.

"Okay," repeats Sasha. "Talk with you later," and she hangs up.

My shoulders sag and I let out a loud exhale. I hadn't recognized how stressed out this decision had made me until I was wrapped in sweet relief. I go back inside the restaurant and walk back over to Brad, who puts his mouth to my ear.

"Everything okay?" he whispers.

"Yes. Everything is fine. They said it was fine."

"I knew it would be okay," he confirms. I pull back from him. Did he have his hand in this? Did they only say it was okay because they work for him?

"You didn't have anything to do with that, did you?" I ask.

"No. I haven't spoken with Sasha or Amy since we left on the tour. Damon handles everything. And everything has worked out," he adds, tapping me on the nose with his finger before following it with a soft kiss. He turns back to his burger and takes a big bite, giving me a grin and a wink.

FORTY-NINE

M A R I N

I should be working but I've spent the bus ride from Denver to our next stop fielding phone calls, texts, emails, and social media posts from my friends wishing me a happy birthday. It's so strange to be so far away from everyone I hold near and dear. If I were back in school right now, we'd be planning a night of cake and cocktails.

Brad and the guys have been huddled around the dining table, working on the harmony for the new song, "One Night Is Never Enough," that Brad wrote for me. I can't keep the smile from my face as I listen to the perfect blending of their voices together, knowing I'm the one who inspired the ballad.

The time and scenery fly by and before I know it, we're at the Grand Hyatt Hotel. As we disembark the bus, Deeana hands me my room key, a packet of information about the hotel, and more importantly, an oversized basket filled with frosted sprinkle cookies from my favorite bakery in Manhattan Beach. A hundred-to-one odds, this is from Grace. I yank the taped card off the basket.

HAPPY BIRTHDAY GIRLIE!!! I love you and miss you tons. Hope your day is filled with hot guys, cheap beers, and lots of cookies. XOXOXOXOXO!!!

God, I love her. Cookies—check. I glance over to find Brad talking with Damon. He looks back at me and smiles. Hot guy—check. A twelve-dollar Heineken from the hotel minibar will have to do in lieu of a cheap beer, but two out of three isn't bad.

Brad balks at the size of the basket and makes a joke about the ocean running out of shrimp, in reference to one of our favorite *Seinfeld* episodes.

"I know," I concur. "This cookie basket is enormous. Obscene."

"Grace?"

"Who else," I laugh as we walk through the hotel lobby to the elevators.

"When were you going to tell me it was your birthday?" he asks, pushing the elevator call button.

"Oh, it's not that big of a deal," I shrug. Brad takes the basket from me and lifts it up and down a few times, balking at how heavy it is.

"I would have been happy to make it a big deal."

"Oh yeah?" I ask. "What would you have done? Hired a clown for me?"

"Oh now, that's just cruel," he shudders as we walk down the corridor to our rooms.

"I'm teasing." I run my hand through his hair before wrapping my arms around him. "I already have what I want for my birthday."

"I want to give you more. I want to give you everything," he tells me, and I fall a little more in love with him. We walk into his hotel room when he pulls away from me and sits us down on the bed. I watch as he reaches his hand into his backpack and pulls out a blue Tiffany box with a white bow.

"What's this?" I breathe out.

"A little something for your birthday," he grins.

"How did you know?" I'm so confused.

"Really?" he responds with a raised eyebrow. It dawns on me.

"Oh, Grace, of course," I concede, shaking my head. "I didn't realize the two of you had become so chummy."

"We only talk a few times a day," he says in an offhanded manner, "and sometimes before bed."

"What?" I exclaim on a half laugh, half choke.

"I'm kidding."

"I would hope so."

"She did text me it was your birthday today and asked me to do my best to make it special since she couldn't celebrate with you."

"You think jewelry from a fancy store is going to do that?" I challenge.

"I certainly hope so," he responds. "Although I can take this back," he teases.

"Oh, I wouldn't want to inconvenience you." I'm hoping he can tell from my playful tone that I'm not going to say no to a gift from him. To *anything* from him or with him.

"Probably better this way," he adds. My hands shake as I take the box and open it. Inside, cushioned between sheets of crisp white tissue paper, sits a gold starfish on a chain. I lift it out of the box, overcome with emotion.

"It's a starfish," I exhale.

"It is. You're my starfish."

"It's . . . stunning." I've never received anything this beautiful before. I don't count the diamond pendant Mom and Charles gave me for my college graduation. Guilt gifts don't count. This isn't guilt, though. This is—dare I say it?—love.

"I hope you know how special you are to me, Marin."

Tears prick the back of my eyes. "You're special to me too." Even though we haven't said the L-word yet, I feel it in my heart, I see it in his eyes, and I feel it in his kiss. I'm not ready to say the words myself—to say them first—but I do my best to communicate back to him everything I feel.

FIFTY

The bus ride to Cheyenne, Wyoming, is lulling me to sleep. My head slumps on to Marin's shoulder before I jerk it back up.

"Sorry," I mumble. She runs her fingers through the hair at the back of my head and on my neck.

"That's okay," she soothes. "You didn't get much sleep last night."

"No," I yawn.

"I slept like a baby," she purrs while continuing to stroke my neck, "after you wore me out."

"Mmm," I groan. "Best part of my day," I say leaning into her ear. "Can't wait to wear you out again."

"I need to up my game because I wasn't able to put you to sleep," she whines and pouts. Damn! I love her playfulness. Our banter makes these moments on the tour bearable.

"Oh, your game is top-notch," I assure her. "If you improve your game any more, you might kill me," I chuckle.

"Good to know," she winks. "Then why were you up all night?" she asks, tilting her head to the side.

"I was trying to find a coding error causing a glitch," I explain on another yawn. I reach under my glasses and rub my fingers over my tired—and no doubt bloodshot—eyes.

"Did you find it?"

"I did, but at a cost," I say putting my head back on her shoulder.

"You're so talented. Your game idea is amazing, and I know you can make it happen." She runs her fingers through my hair. "You're burning the candle at both ends, though. Will you be able to focus on the game development when the tour wraps?"

"I'll have a few months in LA before we leave for the European tour," I explain and if I'm not mistaken, I can feel Marin tense up next to me. Is she worried about what that means for us or is she sympathizing with me because she knows this isn't where my heart is?

"How long is the European tour?" Her fingers slow down and rest on my neck.

"Six months," I exhale, lifting my head from her shoulder and running my own fingers through my hair.

"Oh." She bites her lip.

"I've got four months in LA though," I say, hoping to communicate to her things with us don't have to change. She sits up a little taller and smiles, but it doesn't quite reach her eyes.

"That will give you a lot of time to get your game to the next level," she responds. Huh. Maybe she doesn't want anything beyond these next few weeks. Maybe this is just a fling for her and once we are back, she'll forget all about me. Nah. Not possible. Before I can assure her that I intend for this relationship between us to continue, I notice Damon sitting across the aisle from us, listening to our conversation.

"Everything good, Damon?" I ask. He jerks back, pretending to look surprised I'm talking to him, but I see through the charade. I know he was eavesdropping.

He pulls his thin lips into a grin and says, "Oh, hey Brad. Marin. Everything is great."

"Glad to hear it," I reply with an exaggerated head nod. He turns back to his laptop and I give Marin a kiss on the cheek before settling my head on her shoulder. I feel her shift and lean over to kiss me. I sigh with contentment knowing I'm here with her now and will talk with her in private about what I'm certain will be a great future for us together.

FIFTY-ONE

"I'm ready for round two." Brad raises his eyebrows up and down. We're in Cheyenne, scheduled to leave for Salt Lake City, Utah, tomorrow and I'm naked in his bed, watching *Seinfeld* reruns. He's finished toweling off from his shower when he jumps on the bed.

"You're insatiable," I smirk, rolling my eyes.

"Only when it comes to you and bacon." He prowls toward me, and as he's about to kiss me, my phone rings.

"Hold that thought." I hold up a hand in front of him. He falls back onto the pillow and I stand up.

"This is Marin," I say, swatting Brad's hands away from my ass as I walk away.

"Hi, Marin," the disembodied voice says. I'm shocked beyond belief by who is on the other end. It's my sister—my *half-*sister—Sydney.

"Oh, hey," I say, as Brad gets up and walks over to me with a concerned expression on his face. He must be able to tell from my change of tone this is someone I was neither expecting nor am happy to hear from.

"How are you?" Sydney asks, all chipper and sweet.

"I'm fine. Uh, is everything okay?" Now Brad is looking over and mouthing "who is it?" and "what's wrong?" at me.

"Everything is fine. I was calling because I know you are going to be in New York next week and I was hoping we could see each other," her voice rising toward the end, like she's asking a question and not stating she wants to see me.

"How did you know I was going to be in New York?"

"Mom told me." There's no hint of judgment in her tone.

"Oh, of course. Mom," I say, shaking my head. Of course my mother would be keeping tabs on me. Never mind the fact I haven't spoken to her in weeks—and that was only a brief text. Brad grabs my hand and mouths "your mom?" with raised eyebrows. I shake my head no and hold up a finger, indicating I need another moment.

"Yeah. Well, anyway, she told me you were working with a band and will be in New York for a few nights and I thought . . ." Her voice trails off.

"Well, I'm probably going to be pretty busy with work," I start. She sighs on the other end. "But let me see what I can do."

"Oh that would be awesome, Marin. I would really love to see you."

"Yeah, well, let me call you back tomorrow, okay?"

"Okay. Bye."

I turn and standing in front of me is a very naked Brad.

"What the hell is going on?" he asks with concern. He reaches his hand out to hold mine.

"That was my half-sister, Sydney."

"Ah, the sister from another mister," he responds. "That explains the attitude."

"You know I don't like that expression," I admonish.

He shrugs. "Okay, that was your sister, and . . . ?"

"*Half*-sister. She lives in New York and called because our mom told her I was going to be in town and she wants to meet up," I say, letting the words rush out and wash over me.

"How old is she?"

"Sydney is fifteen."

"When was the last time you saw her?"

"Two years ago, when I graduated from college. Mom and *Charles*," I sneer, "insisted on coming to the ceremony."

"Two years. That's a long time to go without seeing your sister," he suggests. I look into his sincere eyes and deep down I know he's trying to help, but at this moment, all I want to do is punch him in the face.

"She's my *half*-sister and we've never been close."

"Why's that?" He leads me over to sit down on the nearby bed before throwing on a pair of gym shorts and handing me a t-shirt.

"We just aren't, B," I snap. I'm taking out my foul mood on him and I know that's unfair. "I'm sorry," I say, putting my hand on his cheek. "I don't want to talk about it."

"Maybe it would help to talk about it," he suggests. I sigh and my shoulders lean in. "You can trust me, Marin."

"My dad and mom split up the summer I turned nine. She was the assistant to an investment banker in Sacramento. They had an affair, she got pregnant, and she left me and my dad to go have a new life. A year after Sydney was born, they all moved to New York for Charles's job." Did I really just tell him all this? The only other person I've confided in before was Grace and that's only because she got me drunk freshman year and forced me to reveal all my deepest, darkest secrets so we could be besties.

Brad doesn't say anything in response. Instead, he gives me a gentle squeeze. I drop down onto the bed and stare up at the ceiling. He lies down next to me and links his pinky with mine.

"That had to have been hard."

"When Mom left, Dad was devastated. He didn't get out of bed for weeks and almost lost his job. I took over the household duties from grocery shopping to managing the bank account."

"Jeez, you were only nine." I love how he remembers that detail. Like he's really listening to what I say.

"Yeah, but if I didn't do something, it wouldn't get done. It took everything he had just to get up and shuffle into work."

He pulls up onto his elbow to look down at me and places a kiss on my temple. "You've had to be brave and strong for so long. Too long, I think."

"What else was I going to do? He was my dad."

"Was?"

"He died my sophomore year of college," I whisper. He exhales loudly. I know I'm dumping a lot on him right now, but he asked, and I want him to understand this part of me.

"You miss him." And it's not a question.

"I do. I miss him on all the milestones like Father's Day, his birthday, Christmas. But more than that I miss him in the mundane, everyday ways, like how he used to leave half-empty glasses of water all over the house, abandoning them when they got too warm in favor of a colder one. Or the way he sliced bananas into my morning cereal."

"You and your mom never reconciled?"

"No. She was always more interested in her new family. She missed birthdays and recitals. Mother's Day was reserved for time with her new daughter. Not me."

"I get it. But what about your sister?"

"Half-sister," I correct him again. "We saw each other over major holiday breaks from school and I was forced to spend a week with her over the summer. But other than that, we're nothing to each other." When I say it out loud, I sound like an awful person. "I don't mean it like that," I clarify. "I just mean we don't have a relationship."

"Maybe this is a chance for you to reconnect."

"It's easy to see what an incredible bond you and Craig have. But I don't think that's in the cards for me and Sydney."

FIFTY-TWO

B R A D

The trust in her eyes right now is almost my undoing. As sad as I am to hear of her family troubles, I'm elated she feels comfortable enough confiding in me. When she first answered the phone, I thought it was her mom. While up until now she had never told me about her relationship with her mom, I knew something was up. Her reaction to the "sister from another mister" comment was my first clue.

The way she talks about her dad like he was the Second Coming was my next clue. I didn't realize he was gone, and she was effectively all alone. I'm surprised there are no signs of tears. My Marin has such a big heart, I'm sure this is killing her inside. She's being brave. Too brave.

"It's okay if you want a shoulder to cry on," I offer her, wrapping my arm around her and drawing her to me. She pulls back up and stands.

"I shed enough tears already. I'm over it now."

"If you're over it, why don't you meet up with Sydney?"

"Just because I've come to terms with my mom's choice doesn't mean I want to spend time with the girl who replaced me," she spits out. Clearly, she hasn't gotten over all this. I don't know how to respond.

My dad could be a real son of a bitch, especially when he was drinking, but it's not like he had another family on the side. We were the only ones who got both the good and bad aspects of his personality. Mom did the best she could, but it's hard to teach full time, deal with my dad, and raise two boys who showed no interest in school but wanted to play music in the garage all day.

In fact, my relationship with my brother Craig was the only thing that kept me going some of the time. It was amazing to have a friend, protector, and ally. Don't get me wrong. It wasn't all terrible. We had our family camping trips and visits to my grandparents for Thanksgiving. I spent some good times rebuilding computers with Dad and playing music with Mom. Craig was *always* there for me, helping me and making sure I was taken care of. I would do anything for him, and I know he feels the same way.

"I know I'm probably overstepping my bounds here, but I think you should meet up with her," I say. I stand up and walk over to her and rub my hand up and down her arm. "I get it, but at the same time, you seem to be punishing her—and yourself—over your mom's mistakes. It won't bring your dad back." I'm wary how she is going to respond. I'm preparing myself for her to pull away from me or punch me in the arm, but instead she sighs and sags into my chest. I can feel silent tears falling as I rub her back.

FIFTY-THREE

M A R I N

Brad and I are sitting in the front of the tour bus talking about whether or not bananas are an indecent food as we make our way from Salt Lake City to Reno, Nevada. It's been a long bus ride and there was only so much work I had to do to help pass the time.

"Let's make things interesting," he says, waggling his eyebrows.

"What did you have in mind?" I raise my eyebrows in response. He laughs and shakes his head.

"A bet. I win, you give me a blow job in the bathroom," he suggests with nonchalance. I choke on my own spit. The noise attracts the attention of others on the bus and I hold my hand up to let them know I'm okay.

"What?" I whisper to him, my eyes bugging out.

"You heard me. I know you did," he says with a smug grin.

"Is that something you've been missing out on these past few weeks—blow jobs on the bus?" I ask.

"I've never been blown on the bus before," he says. "It would be a first."

"Really?" I ask with skepticism. "I find it hard to believe you've never gotten a hummer on the road."

"I didn't say that," he clarifies. "I haven't gotten one on the *bus*."

"Oh."

"So what do you say? You game?" he asks tilting his head to the side.

"Well, what do I get if I win?" I ask.

"What do you want?" he shrugs.

"Hmm. If I win . . ." I pause for a moment, thinking. "If I win, I get a massage."

"Yeah you do," he says, smiling lasciviously.

"Not *that* kind of massage," I scoff, slugging his arm. I roll my eyes. "I want a *real* massage, like from a spa."

"Here I thought I was going to get to touch your soft body all over." He nuzzles his nose into my ear. "God, you smell good," he groans.

"The whole point is if I win, *I* win."

"You're saying that like you don't win when I put my hands on your body. That hurts, Marin." He pretends to be wounded and I can't help but laugh.

"Oh, did I hurt your fragile ego?" I mock.

"Woman, don't be starting something you can't end," he retorts.

I lay my hand on his chest, bat my eyelashes, and give him a little pout. "Do we have a deal?" I ask.

"You bet your ass." He grabs his phone from his back pocket and opens his Yahtzee app. He rolls first, and the game is moving along with each of us rolling respectable numbers on our turns. On my next turn, I roll three 4s. I roll again and two more 4s show up. Yahtzee! I try to act cool, but it doesn't work.

"Yes!" I call out. "Take that."

"You suck," Brad grumbles, grabbing the phone from my hand.

"No, those points mean I won't have to suck," I say, and break into a fit of laughter. Brad scowls at me before succumbing to laughter himself. I win the game and Brad promises to make an appointment for me to have a massage at the hotel in New York in a few days. I can't wait. All this time sitting on the bus, hunching over my laptop, and sleeping on hotel mattresses has wreaked havoc on my back. A massage is just what I need.

"Okay, rematch," he says.

"Bring it," I retort with confidence.

"New stakes. If I win, you call your sister back and make plans to meet her in New York."

"B . . ."

"Hear me out," he says. "Life is too short to let shit get you down."

"I . . ." I start, but I don't know how to respond. He's right. I don't need to let the relationship with my mom cloud my relationship with Sydney. "Okay," I acquiesce.

"Good," he says with a tight smile and a pat on my knee.

"If I win—"

"Facial?"

"No," I laugh. "I think you've raised the stakes a little bit higher."

"Oh?" he asks, a curious look on this face. "What did you have in mind?" His tone is challenging but playful.

"I win and you talk with Craig about your video game dreams."

He stiffens next to me. "Marin . . ."

"No, you hear *me* out. You just finished telling me life is too short to let shit get you down. If you're not happy with this"—I gesture around the bus—"this life, then you owe it to yourself to do something about it." He slumps forward in his seat a little bit. I grab his hand and use my free one to guide his face toward mine.

"I'm not saying you need to quit the band, but I do think you need to tell him you've got other hopes and dreams you want to pursue one day. Believe me, if he loves you half as much as you love him, he'd want you to be doing what makes you happy." He takes his free hand and rubs his thumb across the apple of my cheek. He lowers his head to mine and gives me a sweet, slow kiss.

"Okay."

"Okay," I repeat. We play a competitive round of Yahtzee, and when it comes down to the end, he's beaten me by fifteen points. We both let out relieved exhales. Part of me is glad to have been forced to give Sydney a call. Another part of me is thankful Brad won't be forced to confront a truth he's not ready to. He leans into my ear and nuzzles his nose against it.

"All this talk of blow jobs. I need to get you somewhere alone," he whispers.

"I am *not* having sex with you on this bus." My voice is firm and steady. There is *no* way that's going to happen.

"Let's go make out though." He grabs my hand and guides me toward the back to the bus. He pulls the curtain aside from one of the bunk beds, climbs in, and pats the space next to him. My eyes dart around, fearful someone is paying attention to us, but no one seems to notice. I climb in and close the curtain behind me.

It's a mad rush of lips and tongues, groping, and heavy petting. "I need to be inside you . . . like yesterday," he pants in my ear. The warmth of his breath causes ripples of pleasure to erupt across my neck. I'm so keyed up right now.

"We can't," I breathe, trying to keep my wits about me.

"Why not?" he asks as one hand squeezes my ass, while the other pinches my nipple. The dual sensations swamp me with lust.

"There are seven other people on this bus." I push him slightly off me while still keeping my hands on his body.

"Right." He lifts off me farther and scrubs his hand over his jaw. "I seem to forget everything when you're around," he says with a smile.

FIFTY-FOUR

A limousine is waiting outside the hotel for me, the band, Damon, and Phoebe. It's the morning after our Reno tour dates and now we are heading to New York for the band's outdoor performance for the *Today* show's summer concert series. Never in my wildest dreams did I imagine that, fresh out of graduate school, I would be accompanying a client to one of the most coveted publicity opportunities on the planet.

It's only a twenty-minute drive from the hotel to the Reno-Tahoe International airport. The limo pulls right up to a small jet waiting on the runway. We aren't flying commercial. No, this is a private plane to whisk us off to the Big Apple. I'm giddy. I spend the five-hour flight thinking about what's coming up.

We'll only be in New York for three days—one day for some interviews, one for an in-studio rehearsal at a sound stage in New Jersey, and one for the concert appearance on the morning talk show. We'll be relying on a local crew to help with equipment and sound checks. The rest of our normal team is getting a few days off to relax in Reno before they head out to San Francisco.

As for the rest of us, we'll have time to explore the city. I'm planning to cash in on the massage I won in Brad's Yahtzee challenge and meet my half-sister at the hotel for lunch.

Sasha will be meeting us in the Big Apple, as she's the one who secured this coveted opportunity for the band based on her amazing connections with the show producers. I'm hoping to get some one-on-one time with her to assess how I'm performing so far on the job. Considering we only have about two weeks left in the four-month stint, I'd love to get a sense whether she has a full-time position for me in her company or if she can place me with one of her clients. If not, I'll need to start sending out resumes.

Yet the thought of leaving the band makes my stomach tight. I know I'm feeling sad because whatever is going on with me and Brad will be over soon. It's not hard to recognize these emotions for what they are. I don't know how I'm going to say good-bye. I don't know if I *want* to say good-bye. We've never talked about whether there's a future for us. We've sort of been enjoying this little traveling bubble we're in. I don't want to bring up the topic of the future. I don't want to be the one to put myself out there first.

I'm also feeling stressed that Sasha maybe isn't all that happy with my job performance. The feedback I've received so far has been minimal, and getting sick and having to pawn off some of my duties to colleagues—and even the client—doesn't make the best impression. I also get the sense Damon doesn't like me. Without his endorsement, I don't know if Sasha will have a place for me when this assignment is over. Out of work and unable to make my rent is not a position I can afford to be in.

To make matters worse, I got my period. Damn!

I check into my room and head right over to Brad's. Despite the fact we are sleeping together, and everyone knows it, I still want to maintain some semblance of professionalism. The minute I walk in the door, he has his hands in my hair and his lips on mine. He trails kisses down my throat, which turn me on.

"Looks like we have until tomorrow morning until the car picks us up for the interview. What shall we do to pass the time?" he ponders aloud in between little nibbles on my neck.

"I'm sorry to spoil the impending mood, but I have my period," I inform him.

"Oh," he says with a mixture of surprise and disappointment.

"Yeah, so . . ."

"Well, there's stuff we can do that doesn't involve"—he motions toward my private parts with his hand—"you know."

"What kind of stuff?" I ask with a flirtatious wiggle of my eyebrows.

"I never did get that blow job on the bus." He sticks out his lower lip and ducks his head to show a set of sad, hangdog eyes. I don't know whether to laugh or roll my eyes, but I choose to play along.

"Oh no. Sounds like you've been so deprived." I give him a sympathetic nod of the head and my own version of sad eyes.

"Oh, believe me," he says, stroking my cheek and smiling, "my woman keeps me very satisfied."

"Good to hear," I laugh.

"But—"

"Of course there would be a 'but' in there," I interrupt.

He grabs my ass and gives it a good squeeze. "I do like your butt," he admits.

"I've noticed, B," I retort. "However, as mentioned, I'm out of commission for a few days. But that doesn't mean I can't find a way to bring you a bit of happiness."

He leans back and stretches his arms out wide. "I'm all yours, babe. Do what you will."

So I do, bringing him maximum pleasure given my limited resources. As Brad stretches out on the bed, trying to catch his breath, I lie down next to him and lay my head on his chest.

"This reminds me of how things started out between us. The innocent cuddling," I say, as I trace circles on his skin with the tip of my finger.

"I like how things are now much better," he counters, stroking my back.

"I'm sure you do," I chuckle.

*

After dinner, a message is waiting for me on my cell. Sasha wants me to call her when I'm back at the hotel so we can "catch up." Nervous knots fill my belly. When I call her back, she asks me to meet her in her room—a suite on the top floor.

I hesitate before rapping my knuckles against the door. It's been several months since I was blindsided by this assignment and back then, in her office, it was evident that I was reluctant to go on tour with a rock band. I'm not sure what she's going to say or do. I'm not sure what I want her to say or do.

If you asked me four months ago what I wanted, I would have said it was a job with a tech company in Seattle. That was before a certain beanie- and glasses-wearing guitar player needled his way into my life and my heart. Now maybe I want to stay in LA. Maybe there's a chance we could make something work. Maybe I should bring up the subject to him.

Before I can absorb these revelations, Sasha answers the door. She's dressed in cropped black pants, high-heeled black Louboutins, and a red silk blouse. So stylish.

"Come on in, Marin," she says, moving to the side so I can pass by. I walk into the room and lower myself to the couch where she's gestured for me to sit. "So, how are things going?" I'm not sure if she's asking about the band, the position I wasn't prepared to take, or with Brad.

"I think we're making some good headway in continuing to build the band's image online," I say, taking the professional fork in the road.

"Yes, we are gaining followers and driving engagement. I can't help but think there's more we can do, though," she responds.

"Okay." I plaster a fake grin on my face and nod. More we can do? What does she have in mind? Because I've been working my tail off posting, promoting, and engaging on behalf of Kings Quarters. I've literally worked myself sick on their behalf. I'm not sure how much more I can give her, or them.

"You're doing a fine job, Marin. You're thorough, conscientious, and creative," she begins. Pride surges through me at hearing an industry legend—this woman I admire so much—praise me. "However," she starts, and I can feel my shoulders slump in defeat, "we need to increase our social media followers. For a band of this magnitude, our number of followers, likes, and retweets should be higher."

"Let me give it some thought and come back to you with some ideas," I say with a nod.

"Good, Marin. I challenge you to find a way to really move the needle."

"I'm up to the task." I once again plaster a confident-yet-fake smile on my face.

"I trust you are feeling better?"

"Yes," I exhale. "That ear infection was a crazy fluke. I'm certain it won't happen again," I assure her.

"Being out on the road can be exhausting. I want to make sure you are taking care of yourself." She wants to make sure I'm okay? But she just finished telling me the nonstop effort I'm putting into my client work isn't cutting it and I need to give her more.

"I'm fine," I respond, trying to temper my growing frustration with her contradictions.

"What about things with Brad? Damon says you two have gotten particularly close."

And there it is. When she said there wasn't a problem with me dating him, she didn't mean it. She thinks I'm getting distracted by him and that's why my work is suffering. If anything, I want to succeed *for* him. And Damon thinks I'm a distraction for Brad. On more than one occasion, Brad has mentioned that Damon pressures him to write songs instead of spending time with me. You think he'd be happy with "One Night Is Never Enough." It's going to be a huge hit. I'm certain of it. Jeez. When did this all get so complicated?

"Things are fine. Very casual. Nothing to even mention," I say, trying to appear nonchalant and give the impression it's sort of a thing to pass the time. That, of course, couldn't be further from the truth. I'm fairly certain I'm in love with him. I ache for his touch. I warm from his smile. I float from his praise. I want and want and want all the time.

"Mmm hmm," she says with a nod and a grin. She's not buying my bullshit. A change of subject is in order.

"Going back to our efforts to drive online interaction with the band, what if we offer some sort of national giveaway to coincide with the appearance on the *Today* show?" I suggest. "Maybe people could post their favorite song from the outdoor concert and tag the band?"

"That's the kind of thinking I like," she says with a smile. "Unfortunately, for that type of giveaway, we would need time to get legal involved. But keep thinking along those lines."

"I will," I say, grateful we've gotten off the subject of Brad and back onto work.

"I've got some calls to make, so I'll see you tomorrow morning for our interviews."

"Thanks, Sasha." I grin and rise, give her a little nod, and walk out, relieved this meeting is over. I go down to the hotel bar to find Brad and the guys holding court. Two blondes are hanging on Jase, and a bevy of other attractive women surround the guys. It's like a scene from a movie.

I'm about to snap a photo when Brad turns around. His smile levels me. I feel a slow grin cross my face as a range of emotions cross my heart. What started as a lust-fueled dalliance has indeed become a distraction—a threat to what I thought I wanted. I don't know how to reconcile all this, and having my period isn't helping matters. If anything, I want to go back to my room, curl up in my bed, and try not to think about what the future holds.

FIFTY-FIVE

B R A D

When I turn and see Marin standing in the doorway of the bar, I give myself a mental high five. I'm a lucky bastard, that's for sure. "Night all," I say to the guys and the gaggle of women plotting how to score with a musician that surround them.

"Hey, B.O." Damon calls out. "Your two beers come out to $17.50." Is he serious? He wants me to kick in money for beers? Shouldn't the travel budget cover this petty stuff? I roll my eyes and toss a twenty-dollar bill on the table. I have more important things to consider, like the witty, warm, and loving woman standing in front of me.

"Hi pretty lady," I smile at Marin, taking her hand and guiding her to the bank of elevators. I hold onto her, rubbing my free hand on her back, while we travel to the twenty-eighth floor.

"I think I'm going to stay in my own room tonight," she says, using her key card to open the door.

"Why? Is everything okay?" I ask, more panic in my voice than I had expected. What the hell? Did I do something wrong? Is she breaking up with me? Did Sasha say something to her?

"I have cramps." She sighs a little and puts her hand on her belly. I place my hand over hers, rubbing my fingers back and forth.

"Is there anything I can do?"

"No," she says with a small grin and shake of her head, "but thanks. Sometimes I hate being a girl."

"I'm glad you're a girl," I say in reply. She gives a little chuckle. "C'mon," I steer her away from her door and toward my room. "Let me help you into bed and I'll order some pickles and ice cream from room service," I suggest. She laughs hard now.

"I'm not pregnant and this isn't a nineties sitcom," she replies with a raised brow.

"Okay, what? Chocolate?" I ask. "Ah-ha! I nailed it. With that look in your eyes I know I've said the magic words."

"Well, I wouldn't say the words are magic, but I wouldn't object to a chocolate milkshake," she says sheepishly.

"I can do that." I walk her into my room and go over to the phone. I order us both chocolate milkshakes while she uses the bathroom.

When Marin emerges, I walk to the bed, pull back the covers, and give a little pat, indicating for her to lie down. She grabs an extra pillow and curls up next to it, her belly pressed against the side.

"How old were you when you got your first period?"

"Really?" she says, grimacing. "You want to go there?"

"Sure. Why not?" I ask. "We have some time before the milkshakes arrive." She clutches the pillow closer to her chest and readjusts her head on the pillow at the headboard.

"I was sixteen, which is rather late. Lucky for me, all my friends had already gotten it so I knew what to expect and could ask them any questions. I never had to have 'the talk'"—she lifts off the bed to make air quotes—"with my dad, and as we've already established, my mom wasn't around."

"Well, that was good, right?"

"Yeah. My best friend, Stephanie, got it when she was thirteen. That's three whole years earlier than me. Three years of cramps and acne and bloating," she says with a shudder.

"Poor girl," I sympathize.

"You have no idea," Marin says, and takes a deep breath. "She also had three years of boobs I didn't."

"If you ask me, you made up for it just fine," I admit, giving her a lascivious look.

"Hardly," she scoffs. "I could have used a few extra years' worth of . . ." she starts, sitting up to stare at her chest, ". . . percolating."

"I think you're perfect," I tell her, kissing her forehead and sharing a grin.

"Thanks," she blushes.

"So you and your dad never had 'the talk' about your period. Did he ever talk to you about sex?"

"Oh God no," she rushes out.

"So you learned about that on the street too?" I nod, giving her faux mad props for being a badass. She can't help but laugh.

"Exactly. Got a good education out there on the streets."

"How good?"

"You mean, you want to know how many men I've been with?"

"Only if you want to tell me."

"I'm surprised you want to talk about this. In fact, I'm not even sure I want to know how many girls you've been with."

"I'm happy to share my number, but in general terms, it's more than Craig and less than Jase," I offer.

"That's a rather wide range, isn't it?"

"Probably," I say with a laugh. Not that I want to discuss Craig's private business but I'm pretty sure he's only been with Phoebe. Jase, on the other hand, defines the length of his relationships by how quickly he can learn the color of a girl's thong.

"Tell me about your first time," she requests.

"My first time, huh?" I reply. "It was in high school. Her name was—well, *is*, but was . . . you know what I mean. Her name was Ali Gibbs. She was a junior and I was a sophomore. She was really into the band and would come to all our shows. She'd had sex before and offered herself up to me after one of our gigs. Her parents were out of town and she said we could hang there. I wish I could say I was in love and it was special, but it wasn't. What about you?"

"I was nineteen and in college. His name is Logan Rogers. We were both sophomores and I was certain it was love. He was certain it was a one-time thing."

"Oh shit. That sucks."

"Yeah, I was pretty devastated at the time."

"I'm assuming he was your last until me?" It's hard to keep the humor out of my voice.

Marin laughs. "Uh, no," she says shaking her head.

"Yeah, you can't be that good at it and only have done it once," I tell her.

"I'm that good, huh?" she says, flashing me a flattered look.

"That good," I confirm.

"There have been a few others including Dan Daniels, who was my one and only long-term boyfriend from college. We dated for two and a half years. We met during our first week of junior year. He was a transfer student and lived in the same building as me and Grace. We dated all throughout college until he moved to Pennsylvania for business school and I ended up at USC. We tried the long-distance thing for a while but couldn't make it work." Thank goodness.

"What do you think would have happened to the two of you if he had gone to business school at USC?" Before she can answer, there's a knock on the door. Room service.

"Saved by the bell," she jokes, swiping her hand across her forehead in exaggerated relief.

FIFTY-SIX

MARIN

After the rehearsal, Damon offers to treat our group to lunch at a famous New York deli. Considering Brad has referred to him as "Dinosaur Arms" more than once—on account of his short arms that can never reach the check—I'm guessing Damon is downright giddy about tomorrow's performance. After lunch, I grab a cab to Nirvana spa, where Brad has booked my massage prize.

I enter the spa and take in a deep breath, hoping the soothing scents of lemons and cucumber will help me relax. I've got a lot on my mind right now and I'm not certain any amount of kneading, manipulation, or pressure is going to help. But I'm going to give it a try and smile all the way. I walk to the front desk and tell my name to the high cheekbones behind the counter.

"Welcome, Ms. Collins," she says with a cool smile. "I see you have a full-body massage, triple oxygen facial, and our trademark zucchini and sesame body buff scheduled for this afternoon—all prepaid." I'm shocked . . . and elated.

"If that's what it says," I respond, not wanting to argue. This is beyond generous.

"There are instructions for the digital lockers posted in the women's changing room. You'll find robes and sandals there too. Enjoy your afternoon."

"Thank you," I reply. I walk through a set of frosted glass doors and follow the crisp and clean hallway down to the women's room. After changing into a robe and sandals, I sit in a waiting area. I help myself to a glass of mint-flavored water and flip through a fashion magazine. A group of women are seated on an oversized couch, whispering and laughing with one another.

"Ms. Collins," a well-muscled man calls out. He has deep-set, dark eyes and equally dark hair. Rising, I walk over to him.

"I'm Marin," I say. He reaches his hand out to shake mine.

"I'm Edgar." He pronounces it with a rolled *r* at the end. "We are starting out with a seventy-five-minute full-body massage," he explains as I follow him down the hallway into a small room. There's a massage table in the middle, two small chairs, and a table with various massage oils and lotions. "Do you have any particular issues you want me to work on?"

"No. I'm looking for overall relaxation," I explain. "I have been spending a lot of time sitting on a bus or sleeping in hotel beds."

"Good. We'll pay particular attention to your back and shoulders. Why don't you disrobe and lie face down on the table? I'll be back in a moment." I do as he asks, slipping off the robe and slippers and climbing underneath the heavy blanket, being sure to pull it up over my body. A moment later there is a soft knock on the door and Edgar walks in.

He places his large hands on my shoulders and starts to work them into my muscles. At first, I have a hard time relaxing.

"You are very tense," he says. Don't I know it. I'm not sure it if is because of work and the uncertainty surrounding my job, or could it be because I'm having lunch with my half-sister tomorrow and I don't know if I'm ready to deal with the certain onslaught of confusing emotions? Is it Brad and all the unknowns we face as the tour ends? Or is it that I'm not used to having a strange man's hands on me, having grown both familiar with and sated by Brad's calloused fingers?

"Clear your mind, Miss Marin," he says. Clear my mind. Work. Sydney. Brad. "Focus on the sound of my voice." Focus on his voice. Clear my mind. "Focus on the sound of your breathing." Focus on his voice. Clear my mind. Focus on the sound of my breathing.

Ahh. All of a sudden, I've never felt more relaxed. My body feels like jelly as Edgar, my Peruvian masseuse, works his magic on my overworked muscles. What feels like only a moment later, Edgar wakes me with a gentle nudge.

"Miss Marin," he whispers. "We're all done." I can't believe I fell asleep. Well, I can *believe* it. Edgar's hands are miracle workers. I mean I can't believe I missed all the amazing feels I would have gotten if I had been able to stay awake. "Take a minute or two and be sure to get up slowly. I'll bring you a glass of water. He walks out and comes back a minute later with a glass of water with a cucumber floating in it.

After I manage to get off the massage table and put on my robe and slippers, Edgar returns again and guides me back to the waiting room. He explains that someone will be by to take me over to my body scrub in about ten minutes. I could get used to this kind of treatment.

One buffed body and a clogged-pore-free face later, I emerge from Nirvana feeling . . . well, like nirvana. It was an amazing afternoon and I'm relaxed and ready to take on all the challenges ahead. Of course, I need to be sure to thank Brad for being so thoughtful. I find him in his hotel room.

"I am relaxed, cleaned, and buffed beyond belief," I tell him as he opens the door. "Thank you for everything. It wasn't necessary. The massage would have been more than enough."

"You work hard, and I lost our Yahtzee game fair and square. It also doesn't hurt I maybe wanted to feel how soft they could get your skin," he says, raising his eyebrows up and down.

"You're welcome to check it out for yourself, but I should remind you I still have my period," I say with a disappointed sneer.

"I remember and it's okay. We can just cuddle," he says, pulling me into his arms on the bed and wrapping them around me. "Out of curiosity, how long does your period usually last?" I can't help but laugh and pat his chest.

FIFTY-SEVEN

After a successful morning outdoor concert at the *Today* show followed by a short nap, Brad and I are in the elevator at the hotel, heading to the Red Window where I'm meeting Sydney for lunch. She practically squealed when I told her I would be able to see her. I'm still not sure this is a good idea but having Brad here to act as a buffer makes things easier. Plus I'm still feeling real loosey-goosey from my massage yesterday. I'm not ready to let such a high level of relaxation go.

He gives my hand a squeeze as we walk into the restaurant, which is downstairs from our Times Square hotel. Light wood tables and dark wood chairs are lined up, and modern, black-and-white bar stools stand at attention at the stocked bar along one wall. I look around and notice a few groups seated at tables and a few individuals at the bar, but no sign of Sydney. I'm concentrating on the shelves of alcohol along the wall, thinking I may need a shot or two to get through this lunch.

While I ponder this, a beautiful blonde seated at the bar, her hair in a sleek high ponytail, turns around. Sydney. That's

Sydney? She looks so . . . grown up. She's grown about four inches since I last saw her. She's wearing a tight-fitting pair of jeans with some strategically placed slashes and holes, gold wedge sandals, and a colorful patterned tank top showing off ample breasts. She's also wearing more makeup than a magazine cover model. This is my fifteen-year-old little sister? Brad must think the same thing.

He whispers, "How old did you say Sydney is?"

"Fifteen," I whisper back as she bounds over and envelops me in a hug.

"It's so good to see you, Marin," she says.

"Wow," is all I can say in response. I pull back, keeping my hands on her shoulders, and glance down. "You look so grown up." She glances down her body as well.

"Yeah, well, that happens," she says with a shrug. She looks over and notices Brad.

"Sydney, this is Brad," I say. Sydney studies him.

"You look familiar," she says in a scrutinizing tone. "Lose the glasses and hat," she tells him. Brad swallows hard and glances around the restaurant before taking them off.

"Oh my God," she squeals and looks back at me. "That's . . ." she breathes, "Brad Osterhauser."

"Yes," I say.

"Oh my God, oh my God," she screams.

"Shh," I say, trying to calm her down while Brad puts his glasses and beanie back on.

"Nice to meet you Sydney." Brad reaches out his hand to shake hers. She grasps his hand and shakes it up and down, her mouth gaping open in shock.

"How did you know Kings Quarters is my favorite band?" She's still holding onto Brad's hand. I pull her hand off his and motion us over to a table to sit down.

"I didn't," I start. "Brad is . . ." and before I can finish, he grabs my hand, gives it a squeeze, and speaks.

"I'm Marin's boyfriend."

My boyfriend? We'd never talked about what was happening between us. I know we aren't dating other people. When would either of us have the time? We're pretty much together nonstop, but *boyfriend*? That sounds so . . . official. With the tour wrapping up soon, what does that mean for us moving forward? I don't have time to dwell on this because Sydney is drooling over my "boyfriend."

"Can I get a selfie with you?" she asks.

Brad chuckles. "Sure," he says. He removes his beanie and glasses, stands, and walks around to Sydney's side of the table. She stands too, and he holds her camera up and away from them so he can grab a shot.

"My friends are going to fuh-reak." She taps the screen on her phone, no doubt uploading the photo to Instagram.

"So, Sydney," I say, trying to get this reunion back on track. "What's been going on with you?"

"No way," she says. "My life is totes boring. You're dating Brad Osterhauser. You go first." As I'm about to speak, her phone chirps. She looks at her text. "That's my friend Rainn. She is so jealous. She loves you," she tells Brad.

"Aw, that's really sweet," he replies with a grin. Before Sydney can ask more questions about my private life, the waitress comes over and takes our lunch order.

"Mom said you were working with a band, but she didn't say who it was. It's Kings Quarters, right?" she asks in an eager tone. *Is she judging me?*

"Yes. That's the band I'm working with. At least for a few more weeks."

"That's how you two met?" she asks.

"Yes," I answer, working to keep the emotion out of my voice. Again, I question whether she's trying to make some sort of statement that I'm more like our mom than I want to admit. Brad, sensing where my mind is going, squeezes my hand under the table. "Speaking of Mom, how is she?" I ask, trying to keep the scorn out of my voice for Sydney's sake.

"Oh, she's the usual pain," she says rolling her eyes. She notices the shocked look on my face and continues, "She's just so . . ." Her voice trails off and she taps her head with her manicured hands, like she's trying to find the right words.

"Annoying? Controlling? Passive-aggressive?" I suggest with a raised brow.

"All of the above," she laughs.

"Some things never change." I shrug.

"Ugh. You are so lucky you didn't have to deal with her as much growing up," she huffs. I look at Brad who cringes. If Sydney recognizes her faux pas, she doesn't show it.

"Frankly, I'm surprised she let you come meet me alone," I confess.

"I told her I was going to a friend's house across town and she gave me cab fare," she confesses with a shrug. "To be honest, she's so busy with her friends and charity work," she says with obvious disdain, "I'd be surprised if she even noticed I was gone."

"What about Charles?" I ask, and I'm surprised when I don't shudder at the sound of his name on my lips.

"Dad works, all the time. He's never home for dinner anymore." There's a touch of sadness in her tone. I wouldn't be surprised if he was having an affair with his new secretary. Of course I don't say that out loud, though. It crossed my mind. It crossed Brad's mind too; he looks at me with his eyebrow raised.

Poor Sydney. She didn't ask for any of this. It wasn't her choice to be born into a totally dysfunctional family dynamic, and I warm up to her.

"So tell me about you," I say.

"Nothing really to tell," she says with a shrug. I'm about to ask her a question, to get her to start talking, when she continues, "I really love fashion, like clothes and jewelry and makeup and shoes and stuff like that, and I want to be a fashion designer when I'm older and I love fun patterns and colors. I want to follow in the footsteps of Trina Turk, if you know who she is. I love how she uses color and awesome fabrics. I want to be on *Project Runway*. They have a new show called *Project Runway: Junior*, which is for teenagers. You get to compete against other teenagers, just like on the regular show, and then if you make it to the finals you get to create your own fashion line and show it at New York Fashion Week and you get a full scholarship to FIDM—that's the Fashion Institute of Design and Merchandising," she says, with a clarifying nod to Brad, "and all sorts of other cool stuff like money and sewing machines. That would be so amazing." She looks up to the ceiling with stars in her eyes. "I don't think Mom would let me try out for it, though. She doesn't understand how important this is to me and she makes me go to a school where we have to wear these boring gray uniforms, but I would totally kill it. In fact, I made this shirt." She takes a breath to let us absorb all she's said and look at the adorable tank she's made.

"I really love my friends. They're my life, you know," she explains. "Except for Cami. She's become such a brat," she says rolling her eyes. "She's so self-absorbed. Plus she told Mason who told Emma she thought I was getting fat, so I kind of hate her right now. Oh, and I also hate my algebra teacher, Mr. Pfizer. He's *so* boring. If I could get into FIDM now, I wouldn't have to worry about passing algebra, which would be awesome." Sydney is talkative. Very talkative. To the point where Brad looks at me with wide eyes and a smirk.

"Will you ladies excuse me a minute?" asks Brad, as he rises. "Going to the restroom." He gives my shoulder a squeeze and flashes me a sweet grin. I grip his hand with mine and squeeze back. Sydney and I continue talking, but a moment after he leaves, our chat—or should I say, Sydney's soliloquy—is interrupted.

"Oh my God!" A skinny girl with jet-black hair, green eyes, and full lips races over to our table, teetering on too-high heels. She looks like a fourteen-year-old who raided her mother's makeup drawer. Sydney stands up, pulls the dark-haired girl into an embrace, and lets out a squeal.

"I know, right?" Sydney replies.

"Am I too late? Did he leave?" the girl asks, devastation crossing her face. "Please tell me I'm not too late," she pleads in desperation, putting her hands on Sydney's shoulders and shaking her. Sydney laughs as she pulls the girl's hands off.

"Rainn, this is my sister, Marin," she says, turning to me.

"Holy . . ." replies Rainn, her eyes widening in disbelief. It's obvious she has heard about me and considered I'm some sort of myth or old wives' tale. Like a yeti or bigfoot or some other mythical creature.

"Nice to meet you, Rainn," I tell her.

"Okay, wow," she says, pulling out a chair and sitting down. "This is major."

When Brad returns to the table, he and Rainn make eye contact. Her jaw drops to the floor and she lets out a scream. Not a silent scream or a mild squeal. No, she lets out a full-on bloody murder scream. Other people in the restaurant look around and murmur. I'm silent and dumbstruck, unsure how to respond to this crazy display of fandom. Brad, taking it all in stride, laughs.

Sydney manages to calm Rainn down, while Brad takes back his seat, right across from the awestruck teenager.

"Oh—my—God." She leans over and grabs his hands in hers. "Can I say, I am totally in love with you. You're my third favorite famous person," she says with a perma-smile on her face.

"Only your third favorite?" asks Brad with a playful pout. "Let's see if we can do something about that," he suggests. Rainn giggles and keeps looking back and forth between Sydney and Brad.

"Brad is Marin's boyfriend," explains Sydney.

"Shut up!" Rainn exclaims, looking over at me in surprise. I nod my head. "You are so lucky." Her shoulders hunch forward, her eyes widening, and her mouth hangs open. I wouldn't be surprised if she started drooling right there.

After forty-five minutes of being peppered with questions from Rainn and Sydney over lunch, it's time for us to say good-bye.

"Do you think we can we get a picture together?" Brad asks Rainn with a hopeful shrug.

"You want a picture with me?" she exclaims, pushing her hands up to her mouth in shock.

"Well, yeah. Gotta have a memento of lunch with my third favorite fan," he says, throwing her comment back to her. Brad puts his arm around the petite girl and draws her into his side. He grabs his phone and raises it above his head for a selfie. "Let's get one with your phone too," he suggests. Rainn unlocks her phone and hands it to him so he can snap a few photos.

On the last one, he leans down and gives her a chaste kiss on the cheek. That proves to be a huge mistake because Rainn screams again. The hostess walks over and glares at us, so I put an arm around Rainn and calm her down. At the same time, I hold up my hand to the hostess, letting her know I've got this covered.

I turn to Sydney and give her a genuine smile. I've enjoyed my time with her. She's growing into a smart and funny young lady. Despite my earlier reservations about having any type of relationship with her, I'm glad Brad encouraged me to give this a try. I'll be sure to tell him later. For now, I want to make sure Sydney knows how I'm feeling.

"I know you're super busy, but thanks for meeting with me," she says.

I pull her in for a hug and give her a good squeeze. "I'm really glad you called me." When I release her, I'm sure to look in her eyes so she knows I'm being sincere. "I'm sorry I haven't been around for you these past few years." I mean it too.

"You've been great," she says in confusion as if she doesn't understand how hard this dynamic has been for me—what her being born had meant for me and the life I had. I'm ready to let the hurt and frustration toward her go—to have a relationship with her outside of the feelings I have for my mom.

"Let's talk with Mom and maybe you can come out to visit me for a few days over the holidays," I say. I don't know where I'm going to be—LA, Seattle, or somewhere else. I'm pretty certain I'll have some time off though.

"Oh my God, that would be awesome." She lurches forward to embrace me again.

"Great to meet you Sydney," says Brad, who leans in to hug her as well.

"You too," she responds with a huge smile. As the girls leave the restaurant, they turn back and give us a wave.

"Thanks," I tell Brad, wrapping my arm around his waist. I look up at his gorgeous face smiling down at me.

"That was fun. Thanks for letting me come along."

"I'm glad I did this," I say to him. "Thank you for encouraging me to meet with her."

"Yeah?" he asks. "I'm glad."

"Yeah. She's pretty awesome. She's not at all what I expected and I kind of feel bad I've missed out on so much time with her."

"Well, you have a chance now to have a real relationship with her."

"I do. Thanks to you and your meddling," I say with sass. Brad laughs and guides us out of the restaurant, back up to the hotel room.

"Is that right?" he asks. "Maybe you'd prefer it if I stayed out of your business and your life."

"You can't get rid of me that easily." I slug his arm. But when the tour ends, who knows where we'll be?

"Thank God," he retorts, pulling me in for a soft but purposeful kiss.

FIFTY-EIGHT

MARIN

I'm staring out the bus window, one hand absentmindedly rubbing the pane. The other rubs my aching belly, stress manifesting in my gut. *What happens when the tour's over?* No. Not, *where am I going to work?* Or, *how am I going to pay my bills?* Those are the things I *should* be worrying about. Instead, I'm trying to figure out how I'll walk away from the incredible man I've fallen in love with.

I should be uploading my resume to job search websites and researching companies I want to target directly. I'm about to open my laptop when my cell rings.

"This is Marin."

"Marin, this is Dan Archer at the *Village Voice*. How are you today?"

"I'm fine, Dan. What can I do for you?" I figure he wants to set up an interview with the band.

"I was given your name from someone at the *Today* show who said you are the PR contact for Kings Quarters."

"Yes, I handle PR for the band. Were you interested in setting up an interview?"

"No, but I am interested in getting the band's comment on a story we are planning to run in our next issue."

I'm starting to get a bad feeling about this. "Okay. What is the story about?"

"We're running a story that Johnny Davidson was seen snorting cocaine in the green room before the *Today* show concert appearance last week."

Holy shit! This is bad. Really bad. I'm not embarrassed or ashamed to admit I am out of my depth here. I know through my PR training that saying "no comment" only makes you look guilty. Even in my panicked state, I remember that much from my studies. Otherwise, I don't know what to do. I get up and walk to one of the bunk beds.

"You were looking for what in particular?" I ask, trying to remain calm.

"Does he confirm or deny the allegations? I'd like to know if the band itself has any comment," Dan explains. Well, of course I already know what Johnny will do. Deny, deny, deny. That seems to be his M.O. He seems to be denying all around that there is even a problem. Everyone else here is okay letting the problem fester, because they are too afraid to speak up and get him the help he needs. Of course I would love to do something to help him, but I know it is not my place.

"What is your deadline for comment, Dan?" I ask, trying to figure out how much time I have to sort through this mess.

"We go to press with the story end of day tomorrow. I would need to hear back from you by three p.m. eastern standard time."

Looking to give myself an out, I have an idea. "Dan, do you think you can send me this request in writing? I am on tour and on the bus right now without access to pen and paper to write down all the details. That would be very helpful."

"Sure," he says. "No problem."

I give him my email address and he repeats it to ensure he has it right. I'm sure he knows I am trying to buy some time, but he doesn't let on. He promises to send me an email within the next ten to fifteen minutes and I assure him I will respond before his deadline. After we hang up, I run to the restroom. I'm feeling all sorts of nauseated right now, the bile rising in my throat. I take a few deep, calming breaths and return to the bunk. Brad, sensing something is wrong, comes over and sits down next to me.

"What's the matter?" he asks putting his hand over mine.

"Oh, a little work thing. Nothing for you to worry about," I respond with a fake cheerful smile. He gives my hand a squeeze and my cheek a kiss. "If you don't mind, I do need a few moments to make a phone call. Would you excuse me for a moment?'

"Of course. Do your kick-ass job." He returns to his laptop, and I keep refreshing the email app on my phone, waiting for Dan's email to arrive. When it does, I read it over twice:

From: DanielArcher@thevillagevoice.com
To: MarinC@sashavpr.com
Subject: Kings Quarters Commentary Requested

Marin:
Thanks for your time on the phone a few moments ago. As mentioned, a source has confirmed Johnny was seen snorting cocaine in the green room of the Today show prior to his appearance during a summer concert. Does he want to confirm or deny the allegations? Does the band have a comment? My story goes to print tomorrow. You have until 3:00 p.m. EST tomorrow to respond. You can call me at the number from which I called you or email me back here.
Regards, Dan

With shaky fingers, I forward the message to Sasha and Amy and dial the main number at Sasha V PR.

"Sasha V PR," says the upbeat receptionist.

"Is this Tammy?"

"Speaking. How may I help you?"

"Tammy, this is Marin. Is Sasha or Amy available?"

"I think they are both in a meeting right now. Can I put you through to voice mail?"

"No, I'm afraid this is a bit of an emergency. Would you be able to slip them a note and let them know I need to speak to them right away?"

"Sure, Marin. Hold on a sec." She places me on hold and the silence is deafening. The only sound over the rumble of the tour bus wheels is my heart beating.

"What's so important you had to pull me out of a meeting with Tesla, Marin?" Amy sounds annoyed.

"I'm so sorry to bother you and disrupt your meeting."

"I take it this is important, so why don't you tell me what's going on?"

"I forwarded an email to you. A reporter with the *Village Voice* called and—" I begin. I take a look around me to ensure no one is listening. I put my hand over the phone to muffle my voice as much as possible. "He's going to run a story about Johnny doing cocaine at the *Today* show." It all comes out in a rush.

"Shit," she breathes out. "Does Damon know?"

"No, I called you and Sasha first."

"Good thinking. Okay, stay by the phone. Let me talk with Sasha and I'll call you back in a few minutes." A few minutes stretches into thirty. When they call me back, Sasha asks me to rehash everything I told Amy and peppers me with questions about what I said to Dan, who was in the green room in New York, if Johnny was ever out of my sight, and if this has been an issue I've noticed before. I'm truthful with her about everything I know and everything I've seen, being mindful I'm not in a secure location and need to be careful what I say out loud. I also consider that *she*—Sasha—was at the *Today* show with us.

"I wouldn't be surprised if it's true. I've suspected for a while. Perhaps we should use this as an opportunity to get him some help," I offer.

"Marin, you didn't—" starts Amy.

"No!" I retort right away, adrenaline fueling my rapid response.

"Is the pressure getting to you?" questions Amy. "You wouldn't be the first person to manufacture a crisis to get ahead."

"I wouldn't," I say, not quite fathoming why I'm having to defend myself. "I didn't."

"I'm sure you didn't, Marin. You're doing a fine job," says Sasha. *Fine* job. Why not an amazing job? I'm working my ass off and am not moving the needle enough.

"Why would I create a problem only to admit I can't solve it? That makes no sense," I explain with clear frustration in my voice.

"Where are you now?" Sasha asks.

"About an hour away from the hotel," I respond.

"Okay. When you arrive, find a conference room at the hotel where we can have a private call with Damon."

"Should I go tell Damon what's going on?" I ask.

"No," says Sasha. "I will call him now. Once you check into the hotel, find Damon, find a room, and call us. We'll be here." Then she hangs up.

Nothing in school prepared me for the sheer panic or chaos of an impending crisis. Reading case studies and analyzing after-the-fact what did and didn't work doesn't compare. As scared as I was when Dan first called, the feeling has given way to excitement as I get a firsthand view of how these things should be handled by one of the finest minds in my industry.

I glance back, and Damon, steaming, gives me a nod. After we arrive at the hotel, I let Brad know something with work has come up. I secure a private conference room and Damon and I meet there to call Sasha and Amy.

Amy sounds stressed out, but Sasha is calm. I imagine this is why she's such an amazing public relations professional. No scandal, issue, or crisis can faze her. I'm leaning forward in my chair, eager to hear what pearls of wisdom come out of Sasha's mouth.

"I've given this some thought, and they don't have video surveillance in the green room at the *Today* show," she begins. "If they did, they would have already broken the story themselves."

Wait, what? Why aren't we talking about Johnny's drug problem? "I don't know who their eyewitness is, but if we can't get this to go away by ignoring it, we can hire a private investigator to figure out who this person is and find a way to discredit them," she continues.

This is her strategy? What about the classic crisis management rules I learned in school? Admit the mistake, make amends, promise to do better next time.

"I like it," says Damon, nodding. "I'll instruct the guys to let me know if a reporter contacts them about a story, and that they should refer all inquiries to you. I'll also remind everyone they've signed NDAs and that any requests for comment are to be directed to me."

"Pardon me, but shouldn't we address the elephant in the room?" I ask.

"What is that, Marin?" questions Sasha.

"Johnny has a drug problem."

"Did you see him doing cocaine in the green room? Maybe you're the eyewitness," accuses Damon. First Amy and now Damon?

"Damon, let's not go there," says Sasha. "Marin is a professional and her loyalties are with my company and you as a client." What about my loyalty to Johnny? What about getting him the help he needs?

"Keeping the band together is my priority," says Damon. "I'll do what it takes to protect their interests." I lift an eyebrow at that. "That includes making sure Johnny is okay," he says, looking at me with a grin—a big, fat, fake, vomit-inducing grin.

Yeah, right. Brad said he and Craig have spoken with Damon before and he's said he would get Johnny some help. That doesn't seem to have happened, and by the way he's acting now, he doesn't have a lot of concern about Johnny's welfare.

"Alright," says Sasha. "We're in agreement. Hold on and we'll call Dan." While we wait to be connected to the conference call, Damon stares at me, like he's challenging me to say something against the group. I look away and swallow hard. After a few beeps on the phone, Dan comes on the line.

"This is Dan."

"Dan, this is Sasha from Sasha V. Marin forwarded your message to me."

"Thanks for calling me back. I am eager to hear if Johnny or the band will comment on my story."

"Well, before we get to that, Dan," she starts, "these are serious allegations. I imagine you have something to back them up?"

"Yes, someone came forward and said she saw him snorting cocaine in the green room."

"Hmm. So an eyewitness," Sasha says thoughtfully. I picture her nodding her head, her thumb and forefinger poised on her chin.

"Yes," he hesitates. "Does he have a comment?"

"I suggest you make sure your witness is reliable, Dan. I would hate for you to open yourself and the paper up to a libel suit." She's threatening him? She's threatening him. I'm disgusted. I would have expected this type of behavior from Damon—he's always come across like a real sleaze—but I've admired Sasha for a long time, at least up until today.

"I appreciate the advice, Sasha," Dan says, and you can hear him exhale loudly from his nose. He's unnerved by her comment. "So, I take it you don't have an official response?"

"No, I don't think we want to comment at this time," she says as a challenge.

"Okay. Good-bye." That's it? They aren't going to say anything else?

"We'll call you right back," says Amy before she hangs up. Is this how they do things? I'm grossed out and want to go take a shower and wash all this off me. Sasha and Amy call us back right away.

"Had to call you back. We had a reporter pretend to hang up once and stay on the line to listen to our internal discussion.

Don't want to make that mistake again, not with this issue," explains Amy.

"So, that's it?" I can't contain my confusion.

"That's it," confirms Sasha. "Now we wait and do damage control if the story breaks."

"I'll monitor things from here," says Amy. "If you hear any more from Dan, Marin, refer him to Sasha or me."

"Sure thing," I reply with a grim smile.

"That's it for now," says Sasha. "Damon, let's connect tomorrow about what's next."

"Sounds good. Thanks for your always wise counsel," Damon replies.

Yep, I'm gonna need a long shower.

FIFTY-NINE

"I can't wait any longer," Craig begins. He, Phoebe, Brad, and I are sitting in a little Las Vegas diner called the Salt Shaker, which Craig and Brad discovered a few years ago when they were starting out. According to the guys, they serve a great breakfast, especially for the money. They were right. We've finished stuffing ourselves full of eggs and hashed browns at prices even I can afford.

Breakfast has been a welcome break from monitoring the *Village Voice* website to determine if the Johnny-cocaine-*Today* show story will break. It doesn't. Sasha's veiled threats must have done their job. As disgusted as I am, I'm also feeling relieved I don't have to endure any more of her slimy tactics to make this thing go away. I'm not able to focus on this further because, out of nowhere, Craig drops the mother of all bombshells.

"What do you say about getting married?" Craig says to Phoebe. I look over at Brad and he's staring at Phoebe with a huge grin on his face. He doesn't look surprised, so he must have known about this.

"What?" she exclaims. "Are you serious?"

"Yeah, I am." Craig pulls out a red jewelry box labeled with an obscenely expensive designer name and opens it up to show an impressive diamond ring. It's a simple setting with one large, round stone in the middle and two smaller round stones flanking each side. Despite its size—which is huge, by the way—it's unpretentious and exactly Phoebe's style.

"Yes," she says, tears streaming down her face. "Yes, I will marry you," she repeats before flinging her arms around Craig's neck and kissing him all over his face. She pulls back and looks embarrassed by her reaction, but there's no need for apologies. Her response is what it should be when you're absolutely in love with someone.

"I'm so happy for you," I say to her, with tears welling in my own eyes. I give her a warm hug and get up and go around the other side of the booth to give Craig a hug too.

"So, do you want to get married here?" she asks, lifting her shoulder up.

"You want to get married here? In Las Vegas?" he asks with skepticism.

"Well, we're here and B.O. is here and I'm sure Marin would be happy to be a witness, or my maid of honor," she says, looking at me.

"It would be my honor," I tell her.

"I thought you would want to wait until we finished the tour so we could have something big back home," Craig responds.

"I don't need anything big. Only you."

"God, I love you." He puts his hands on her face and kisses her silly. It's raw and real and so absolutely lovely.

"I love you too." She laughs and kisses him back. "So what do you say? Ready to get married?"

"Right now?" he asks with a laugh.

"Yeah, today," she says smiling.

"Hell yeah, I'm ready."

Brad gets out his cell phone and starts tapping on the screen. "Do you guys want a regular priest or justice of the peace or an Elvis?" Brad asks them.

"Oh, definitely an Elvis," says Phoebe with a laugh, looking at Craig and nodding her head up and down.

"Really?" he questions.

"If we're going to get married in a quickie ceremony in Vegas, it's got to be by an Elvis." Her tone is playful but firm.

"If my girl wants a Vegas wedding, she gets a Vegas wedding," Craig says with a shrug.

"Okay," confirms Brad who continues to punch into his phone. "Alright. The King Wedding Chapel it is." He holds the phone up to his ear and we all watch him. "Yes, hi," he says into the phone. "We are interested in getting married today and I was wondering if you have any availability." Brad nods as he listens to the inaudible voice on the other end.

He pulls the phone away from his mouth and turns to Craig and Phoebe. "What do you guys think of an indoor chapel with a one-song serenade?" They look at one another with goofy grins on their faces and nod. "Yeah, that will work," he says into the phone. "The name's Osterhauser—O-S-T-E-R-H-A-U-S-E-R . . . Sounds good . . . Yeah, that's no problem. I'll pay cash when we arrive," he says into the phone again after a moment. "Okay. We'll see you soon."

Brad turns to the group. "Okay, so you're set for the Hound Dog Package which includes the chapel, Elvis to marry you, flowers, and a stuffed animal hound dog keepsake," he says shaking his head with a laugh. "The wedding ceremony is my gift to you. Congratulations."

"I love it," replies Phoebe, who reaches over to grab Brad's hand and gives it a squeeze. "Thank you."

"What time?" I ask.

"Two thirty," says Brad. I glance down at my watch.

"That's only two hours from now!" I say in surprise. "As your maid of honor, I'm sure there are some things we need to do to get ready. We've got to think about a dress and flowers and something old, something new, something borrowed—" I start.

"Yeah, yeah, and something blue," says Brad. "I'm not sure Phoebe wants all that."

"What do you want Phoebe?" I ask her.

"I could go back to the hotel and put a nice dress on. That's all I need," she says.

"Are you sure, babe? We can hold off until you can get a pretty dress or something," says Craig.

"Are you trying to get out of this already?" she asks with humor.

"No way. I only want you to be happy. I don't want you to look back on this in ten or twenty years and regret how we did this."

"I'm not going to regret anything. I just want to marry you. So why don't we go back to the hotel and change so we can go to the chapel."

"If that's what you want," he says, staring into her eyes, his love evident and intense.

"That's what I want," she replies, looking back at him with the same amount of love and intensity. It's almost too much to watch.

"Jeez," says Brad, breaking the mood. "I feel like we're intruding on a private moment here." Phoebe and Craig both turn to him and laugh.

"Do you want me to try and find a veil at least?" I ask Phoebe.

"That would be great if you can find one in time," she says.

"No problem. It's Vegas. I'm sure we can find anything."

Brad signals for the check. When the waitress brings it by, Brad takes a few bills out of his wallet and leaves them on the table. We all stand up and head out of the restaurant, back to the hotel to prepare for the wedding.

SIXTY

Wow! That's all I can say. The King Wedding Chapel is beyond my expectations. We're met at the front desk by a woman in her seventies wearing a too-tight outfit from the sixties. I gesture for Marin, Phoebe, and Craig to sit down while I get us checked in.

"Welcome to the King Wedding Chapel," she drones, "where you can't help falling in love."

"Good one," I respond in admiration of the pun. "I'm here to check in for a wedding. We have a Hound Dog scheduled at two thirty."

"Osterhauser?" she asks.

"That's us," I reply.

"Are you the groom?"

"No. Best man."

"Okay, well, the package includes the chapel, flowers, and a keepsake stuffed hound dog. There's an additional sixty-dollar officiant fee. Your total is $310." I pull out some cash from my wallet and put it down on the counter.

"If it doesn't work out and they end up in Heartbreak Hotel, call us. We have a sister company that handles annulments and divorces." She hands me a business card. I pull it up to my forehead and hold it in my hand giving a mock salute. "We'll call you in a few minutes."

True to her word, Ms. Too-Tight calls our name after a few minutes and we are led into a small chapel. I don't know much about decorations and weddings, but I do know this place is tacky as can be. There's a small fountain with some chubby angels on it in the front and two large, black candleholders on either side. A few artificial plants are around the stage too including some chrysanthemums, which is weird because it's nowhere near Christmastime.

Craig and Phoebe take their places in front of the fountain and Marin and I stand on either side. Ms. Too-Tight comes back into the room with a bouquet of red roses for Phoebe to hold.

"It's extra if you want to keep the flowers," she says.

Phoebe giggles. "I wouldn't expect it any other way," she replies. I'm so happy for my brother. He couldn't have chosen a better girl. She's down-to-earth and loves him for him, not for all the fame surrounding him. The only girl I think is even more impressive than Phoebe is standing right next to her. Marin has a huge smile plastered on her face as she watches Phoebe and Craig exchange vows.

"Place the ring, and then I'll sing," says Elvis. I hand him the two wedding bands Craig and I picked up at a jewelry store inside the Bellagio Hotel while the girls took care of the something-old-something-new shit. Craig slips the platinum band, which matches the engagement ring he gave Phoebe earlier, on her finger and Elvis's hips swivel while he croons about being nothing but a hound dog. Craig grabs Phoebe and starts doing the twist with her. Marin watches them, laughing.

"Now, by the power vested in me by the King, the Lord, and the state of Nevada, I now pronounce you husband and wife. You may now kiss the bride." Craig grabs Phoebe by the waist, dips her back and plants a big ass kiss on her. She winds her arms around his neck and kisses him back. Again, Marin smiles through the whole thing and I can't take my eyes off of her. Elvis notices and turns to me.

"What about you two? Want to get married? We're having a buy-one-get-one-half-off special," he offers. Married? Me? I've never given it much thought, but now that I think of it, and think of it with Marin, it doesn't scare me. In fact, it sounds kind of nice. It's been a long while—come to think of it, I don't think it's *ever* happened—since my shaft and my brain and my heart have all agreed on the same girl. Until now. I give Marin a look like, *What do you say?* She rolls her eyes.

"No, thank you," she says to Elvis with a laugh. "I would love to grab a few photos, if I can, though." Craig and Phoebe pose together, showing off their wedding rings, and pose along with Elvis, giving their best King sneer. I jump in for a third photo and Elvis takes one of the four of us.

We say good-bye to Elvis and Ms. Too-Tight and head back to the hotel to change clothes before we go over for a sound check at the Colosseum at Caesars Palace, where we're playing shows for the next three nights. We get backstage and it's business as usual with equipment being set up, people rushing around, and Jase, Johnny, and Oliver huddling with Damon.

"Hey everyone!" calls out Craig. "Can I get everyone's attention, please?" The guys turn around to find out what's going on. "Hey. Everyone. Can I get your attention!" Craig calls again. Everyone settles down and turns toward him. "I have an announcement to make." He grabs Phoebe by the hand and says, "*We* have announcement to make." People murmur and whisper. "I wanted to let you know this beautiful woman standing next to me . . ." he starts. Phoebe blushes and glances down at the ground. "This beautiful woman has agreed to be my wife." Everyone starts to shout and cheer. "Quiet. Quiet down. That's not all," he says, trying to garner everyone's continued attention. "We got married this afternoon." He lifts their joined hands in the air.

There is a rush of people making their way over to congratulate the happy couple.

"No way," shouts Jody.

"Yep. By an Elvis impersonator," Phoebe replies, "and Marin's got the photos to prove it." She giggles. Everyone looks at Marin who smiles and nods. Jase, never one to be out of the spotlight, starts to sing "I Can't Help Falling in Love with You." I walk over and grab my acoustic guitar, deciding to accompany him and join in on the song.

By the time we get to the bridge, everyone but Marin has joined in. She's holding her phone up, walking around and recording the whole thing. Even Damon is singing. He's also rubbing his finger across his lip while he stares at Marin. It's kind of creepy. I don't have time to think about it because I look over to my brother and he's never looked happier.

"What do you think Elvis would be doing right now if he were still alive?" Marin asks me as she returns to my side.

"Clawing at the inside of his coffin, trying to get out."

"You're awful," she laughs, reaching over to tap my arm. "No, he'd be outside, 'cause he's always leaving the building," she tells me with a big smile and head nod. Damn it if I don't love her sense of humor. I tease her and give her a look of mock horror. "Sorry," she cringes. "That was super corny," she adds, tilting her head down and shaking it in embarrassment.

"Okay, okay," I tell her. "I'll marry you and listen to your terrible jokes for the rest of our lives." She scowls at me.

"Ha ha," she sneers, at which I let out a hearty laugh. I tuck her into my side and kiss the top of her head. Little does she know, I'm not certain I was joking and the fact that it doesn't scare the shit out of me is very telling.

SIXTY-ONE

Tonight the band is filming one of the shows at a hotel concert venue in Las Vegas for a pay-per-view TV special. I'm guessing they are going to go a little off script and do a few things to make this a special event. I'm not disappointed when it comes time for them to play one of their most popular songs—"Late Night Revolt."

Johnny kicks off the song with a drum intro and Craig and Brad join in with their guitars. Keyboards by Oliver are next. Jase steps up to the mic but misses his cue. The guys keep playing but look around at each other, questioning what is going on. Jase turns to face the band and crosses his arms back and forth in front of him, waving at them to stop playing. He turns back to the crowd, which has grown silent in uncertainty.

"Hold up. Hold up," he says.

"What's wrong?" asks Oliver dramatically.

"I can't remember the words," Jase says with a shrug.

"What?" asks Craig, leaning into his microphone.

"I forgot the words. Maybe someone can come up here and help me." The crowd goes wild. Girls throughout the stadium jump up and down. Most of them were already standing and dancing along to the music, but now it feels as though the venue is shaking with all the fevered movement from women who want to come up on stage and meet the band.

I don't know whose idea this was but it's social media gold. This may be what we need to increase the band's online following.

"Is there anyone out there who knows the words to 'Late Night Revolt'?" asks Jase. "Who would be willing to come join me on the stage and help me out?" He puts his hand up to his forehead to shield his eyes from the bright venue lights. He looks into the first few rows and my eyes follow his sight line to a statuesque brunette wearing a red halter top and tight jeans. She looks like she's about to knock herself out with her oversized breasts bouncing up and down. He leans down to point her out to one of the five security guards poised at the front of the stage.

The security guard points to her and beckons her forward with a crook of his finger. Her friends are going crazy, pulling out their cell phones to get ready and record this for posterity. She climbs up the staircase on the side of the stage and walks to where Jase is standing.

"Hi there, darling," he says, wrapping his arm around her. "What's your name?"

"Amanda," she breathes out, trembling, while staring at him.

"Thanks for coming to help me, Amanda."

"My pleasure," she replies, finding her confidence. She wraps her arm around him and puts her hands on the mic. "I'll help you out anytime, anywhere," she adds. Jase raises his eyebrow at her and gives the same look to the crowd.

"Now, do you know the words to 'Late Night Revolt'?"

"I know all the words to all your songs," she purrs.

"Alright." He gives the mic over to her. He turns to the band and gives them a signal to start playing. Johnny starts his drum intro again and the rest of the guys follow suit. Amanda enters at the right point and her voice is quite good. Jase is looking at her and nodding his head up and down. He glances over to the other guys and they are all nodding back and smiling. Amanda is doing her absolute best to work the stage and the crowd. When she gets to the second chorus, Jase walks over to her, puts his hand on the mic, and the two of them sing it together.

The crowd eats it up. I snap a few photos with my phone, using the zoom feature to make sure I get in nice and tight on Jase and Amanda. When the song is over, the entire crowd is on their feet cheering and clapping. Jase pulls Amanda into a hug and gives her a kiss on the cheek. Amanda, not content with that, grabs onto his face and gives him a large smack on the lips. He whispers something into her ear and she nods. She hands him the mic and lifts her arm to wave to the crowd, turning from one side to the other so she can see and be seen by everyone. The security guard escorts her off the stage and helps return her to her seat.

"Wow! That was incredible. Let's hear it again for Amanda," Jase says, letting the crowd provide some more applause. The concert continues as usual and before I know it, the guys are backstage, guzzling bottles of water and signing autographs for the few fans who managed to score backstage access.

SIXTY-TWO

B R A D

After the show and our brief walk through the casino, I wrap my arms around Marin in the elevator as we ride to our rooms. "Pretty great day, huh?" It's a rhetorical question, no doubt about it. Today was incredible. "I can't believe Craig and Phoebe are married," I continue. I'm sure I have a goofy smile on my face, but I can't help it. Craig is more than a brother to me. He's my best friend and I couldn't be happier for him.

"It was," says Marin. "Before I forget," she pulls away from me and grabs her cell phone from her bag, "I want to email you the pictures and videos from today." She taps her phone screen over and over before saying, "Done."

We walk arm in arm down the hall to our block of rooms. We get to my room and I push her back against the door and grab her face in my hands. I lower my mouth to hers and kiss her with all the feeling and emotion I can. Without saying a word, I want to tell her how I feel. How I'm in love with her—completely gone. I have no problem saying the words to her. I've never said it to anyone before, but I've never met anyone like her before.

I know if I say it, it will freak her out though, especially with the tour ending in another week or so. Knowing her, she's agonizing and stressing about what comes next for her career and for us. I don't want to add any fuel to the frustration fire, but I do want to communicate to her I want to be around.

She pushes me back and, panting, says, "I need to do a few things in my room before I'm done for the night." She runs her hands up and down my arms.

"How much time do you need?"

"Give me twenty minutes. I'll make it worth your while," she adds, placing her hand on my chest.

"How do I argue with that?"

She reaches up and kisses me on the lips, the cheek, and the nose. I watch her sexy, curvy ass as she walks down the three doors to her room. When she goes inside, I open my door and head inside, deciding to order some room service while I wait for her. When she returns, as promised, she rocks my world—in all the ways that matter.

SIXTY-THREE

MARIN

It's about eight the next morning and my cell phone is buzzing. I reach over Brad and grab it. It's a number from the Sasha V offices, so I slide my finger to turn it on.

"Hello, this is Marin." My voice is rough with sleep.

"Marin. It's Sasha."

I sit up in the bed and pull the covers over my breasts. I know Sasha can't see me, but somehow, I sense she can tell I'm naked in Brad's bed.

"Good morning, Sasha. What's going on?"

"What's going on?" she asks in exasperation. "Why don't you tell me what the hell is going on?" I've never heard this sharp tone from her before and I have no idea what she's talking about. I get out of the bed and find my clothes on the floor to put on while I hold the phone between my ear and shoulder.

"I don't know what you're talking about, Sasha." I try to remain calm. By this time, Brad is awake and looking at me with concern.

"Don't play coy with me, Marin. I just got off the phone with Damon and he's beyond pissed."

"Damon's pissed? At me?" *What did I do?* I rack my brain trying to think of what I did wrong. Oh no. I didn't get a signed release form for Amanda last night and posted her picture onto the band's social media accounts.

"Oh my God, Sasha. I'm so sorry," I begin. Brad reaches over for his cell phone. He scrolls through and gets a horrified look on his face. I take a deep, shuddering breath and continue talking with Sasha. "I didn't think I needed that girl's permission to use her photo after she got called up to the stage last night. I thought since all the attendees at the show tacitly agreed to be filmed when they entered the venue it was okay. There were signs all around saying filming was in progress," I explain in a panic.

I turn back and Brad is getting dressed in a hurry and pacing around the room, running his fingers through his hair, and talking in a hushed way on the phone. I look over to him and he shakes his head in disbelief. What is going on? Why is everyone having a conniption over this? Did the girl threaten to sue?

"This isn't about some girl on social media, Marin. Photos from Craig's wedding were leaked to the tabloids and are all over the internet, from Perez Hilton's blog to *People* magazine. Craig and Phoebe are livid, as is Damon."

"I . . . I don't know how those photos got leaked, Sasha. I don't," I say in response.

"You're the one who took the photos and they were sent to media from your email address," she states with conviction.

"I don't know anything about this, Sasha. I did take pictures at the wedding, but I only sent them to Brad. I promise you, I didn't leak any photos."

"You're fired, Marin."

"What?" I breathe out in disbelief.

"You're fired. Go pack your things and head to the Las Vegas airport. There is an American Airlines flight leaving for Los Angeles at 10:40. A ticket has been emailed to you."

"Sasha, you're making a huge mistake. Can we—" I start but she hangs up.

I've been fired? I've been fired. I'm beyond devastated. How could this have happened? Brad is standing in front of me rubbing his fingers around his temples.

"Sasha said you leaked the photos?" he questions, shaking his head in confusion.

"As you heard me tell Sasha, I *didn't* leak any photos. You're the only person I sent them to," I repeat in a pleading tone.

"Well, *I* didn't leak them. So if it wasn't me, there's only you." He scratches the back of his neck and stares down at the floor. As I walk toward him, he starts pacing. "You're always talking about your job and how important it is to you. How ambitious you are," he says, his voice rising with each word.

"Just because you aren't doing what you want to be doing doesn't mean I'm doing anything wrong by thinking of what I want to be when I grow up," I rush out defensively.

"Shit, Marin." He rakes his hands through his hair again. "Last night, you went back to your room all secretively, so you could send those photos out," he huffs in both disbelief and accusation, like the wheels in his head are spinning this thing out of control.

"I didn't go back to my room secretively. I went back to order a photo frame from Tiffany's as a wedding gift for Craig and Phoebe, you jackass."

"Did they offer you a big check for the photos? To pay off your student loans? Is that why you did it? Or was it to win points with Sasha?"

"Are you kidding me?" I spit out in disbelief. "I took a chance on us. I risked that oh-so-important job for *us*! All the courage *you* can muster is being judge, jury, and executioner right now without believing in me. In us!" I yell.

"He's my brother!" he fires back.

"And I'm your girlfriend! It's clear where your loyalties lie. Funny thing is, you didn't have to choose because I didn't do it.

You're so loyal to your brother you're willing to forgo your own happiness for his. That's real healthy."

"Don't try to deflect from your mistakes by attacking me and my shitty circumstances."

"Oh, poor baby. How hard it must be to be young and rich and beautiful, with everything you want thrown at your feet, living a dream most people would kill to have."

"Yeah, well, as we've established, this is not my dream."

"Well, don't blame me. If you don't want to be doing this, speak up. It's your life and your choice. Don't make me the scapegoat for all your aggression and frustration because you don't have the balls to tell your brother you don't want to be a musician anymore," I say, on a roll. "Why don't you grow a set?" I lash out.

"You talk to your boss like that?" he retorts.

"I thought you said you weren't my boss," I sneer, "and it doesn't matter anyway. I've been fired."

"She fired you?" he asks, a bit more sympathy in his voice than I expected.

"Yes. That's what happens in the real world when people think you screwed up your job. I need to go pack, because there's a plane I've got to catch back to LA."

"Wait. Let's talk—"

I grab my purse and cell phone, ripping the charger out of the wall, and stomp off, slamming the door behind me in the process.

I slam my hotel room door behind me after I get inside. I grab my suitcases, and without rhyme or reason, throw all my belongings inside, not giving a crap that Jody and Theo were awakened by the noise and are watching me in disbelief. I toss in everything except a Kings Quarters band t-shirt Cal gave me a few weeks ago. I don't ever want to see that piece of shit again. Not Cal, of course. The shirt. I won't ever see Cal again. Or Jody. Or Craig. Or Phoebe.

Or Brad.

Oh my God. I'm never going to see Brad again. That's when it hits me, and the waterworks start. We're over. Couples fight and couples get back together, but we're *clearly* through. He thinks I would do something heinous to him and his family for the sake of my career. He'll never be able to forgive something like that. Even if he could forgive me—which he doesn't even have to, because I didn't do it—could I forgive him for so easily doubting me?

I throw my toiletries from the bathroom into my bag and storm out of the room, being sure to give the door another good slam on my way out. I catch a cab outside the hotel and spend the ride over scrolling through every entertainment news site I can find. Indeed, photos are plastered over every single one—the photos I took and sent to Brad—and only Brad—along with headlines like "New Kings Quarters Queen on the Rock Scene" and "Bassist and Best Man Rock Vegas." How could this have happened? Meanwhile, Brad has called a dozen times. Well, forget him.

Sitting here in the Las Vegas airport, waiting for my flight to board, I've managed to tune out the blaring sounds of slot machines as people get in their last gambling fix before leaving Sin City. I can't really hear anything else except the sound of my own heart beating in anger, confusion, and frustration. I pull out my phone and text Phoebe. I can't imagine what she must think.

ME: *I hope you won't immediately delete this message. I can't even imagine what you must be going through right now. I want you to know, I had nothing to do with leaking those photos. I would never, NEVER do that to you. Not only do I respect your right to privacy, but I consider you a friend. I'm sorry for everything you are dealing with and I hope you are able to manage it okay.*

A few minutes later, my cell phone alerts me to an incoming text.

PHOEBE: *It's pretty much a clusterfuck right now. Damon and Sasha are doing damage control. They think we should just come forward and offer someone an exclusive interview to control the story. We'll figure it out.*

I read and reread her text. That sounds like the best course of action. Once their story is told, reporters and fans will move on to the next scandal or revelation. Knowing Phoebe and Craig, they'll weather this storm. A moment later, another text pops up.

PHOEBE: *And I know it wasn't you.* ☺

She believes me. *She* believes me, but Brad doesn't. His lack of faith is my undoing. My shoulders shake as I sob. The phone rings again. Brad. I can't deal with him right now, so I power down my phone and place it in my bag. No one in the gateway gives me a second glance. They probably think I'm some girl who lost all her money at the tables, or got married and divorced in some quickie ceremony, or regret all the things which should most definitely stay in Vegas.

These people, sitting around the waiting area, have no idea how my life has unraveled in a matter of minutes. Losing my job sucks beyond belief. I don't care about the job though. I'll find a new one. Or contact Sallie Mae to defer my student loans. Hell, I'll ask Mom and Charles for help if I have to. How could Brad not trust me? That's what I can't get out of my mind. How could he assume I would do something like that? It's like he doesn't even know me.

My body is on autopilot, and I don't recall getting on the plane, flying to LA, disembarking, grabbing my bags from baggage claim, and catching an Uber home. I toss my bags into the bedroom and throw myself down on the couch. I take a deep breath and try to think about what I'm going to do next.

I glance around the apartment and my eyes land on the starfish sitting inside the wooden bowl on our coffee table. I bury my head in my hands and cry. After I've lost about ten pounds of water weight in tears, I grab my phone from my bag, turn it back on, and send a text to Grace.

ME: *I'm home.*

GRACE: SQUEE!!!!! *Love you, girlie! See you tonight around 8!*

Hours pass before Grace gets home and I'm still rooted to the same spot on the couch, only by now I have had a few beers. The door bursts open and Grace screams "yay!" as she bounds forward and tackles me on the couch.

"You're back early. I missed you!" she squeals. Sensing something is not as it should be, she pulls back. "Shit! What's wrong?"

"I got fired and Brad dumped me," I say on a sniff.

"What?" she exclaims in shock and anger. "You . . . you need to start from the beginning."

I do, telling her all about the wedding and the photos and the accusations and the denials.

"Well, maybe it was just a shock. Why don't you call him? Explain again that you didn't do it. You guys can get past this. I mean the guy was gaga for you."

"Why should I have to fight for us? I'm supposed to look past the fact he thought I was a liar and betrayed his trust?" I question, my voice rising in anger.

"When you put it that way . . ." she considers.

"*He* put it that way," I lash out.

"When you keep score, no one ever wins," she advises. I glare at her. She places her hands in front of her in surrender mode. "Okay. What do you need me to do?" Before I can answer, my phone rings. Grace looks at it and back at me with a quirked brow.

"You going to get that?"

It's probably Brad calling . . . again. What could he have to say that he hasn't already said? Maybe he's calling to apologize.

Am I willing to forgive and forget? Of course I am. I'm in love with him. But I can't bear the thought of dealing with that possibility right now, so I shake my head. Grace grabs the phone and shows me the caller ID. It's someone from Sasha V. Maybe they figured out that I'm not the culprit. Maybe they'll offer me my job back. I grab the phone and hit the green button.

"This is Marin." I try to keep my voice steady.

"Marin, it's Judy at Sasha V." I pull the phone away and mouth "HR" to Grace, who nods in acknowledgment.

"Yes, Judy."

"We need to arrange for you to return the laptop and cell phone that were issued to you from the agency," she explains, no hint of judgment in her voice, but no friendliness either. My shoulders sag.

"Oh, sure," I say, nodding my head.

"You can bring them by tomorrow or I can send a messenger over."

"Send a messenger," I respond. "I'll be here all day."

"Okay. He'll be by around ten in the morning."

"I'll have them ready for him."

"Do you have any questions for me?" I've never been fired from a job before, but I'm pretty sure there's nothing I need to know. It's not like they're going to give me a severance package or write a letter of recommendation for me.

"No. I'm set."

"Okay," she says and hangs up. I turn to Grace and explain a messenger is coming over tomorrow to get my laptop and cell phone.

"Do you have anything personal on them you want me to wipe off or save somewhere else for you?" she asks.

"If you have a flash drive, that would be great," I reply. "I'll go through my files and transfer what I need onto my laptop here. I'll need to charge my old cell phone, since I won't have this one anymore." I get up off the couch and head into the kitchen to find my old phone and charger. I plug it in and feel Grace's arms wrap around me.

"It's going to be okay, you know."

"Is it?"

"Of course. When you feel like you can't go on, like there's nothing there for you . . ."

"Yeah?" Eager for Grace's words of wisdom, I glance up with hopeful eyes.

"Just remember: laundry. Laundry is always there."

I burst out in a laugh. It's a Gracism that I needed at that moment while Grace envelops me in her caring arms.

SIXTY-FOUR

BRAD

Something's missing and it's not just the ache I feel in my heart every time Marin walks out of a room. I *know* her. I *know* she wouldn't do this. I *know* I reacted poorly and I'm ready to apologize and sort this mess out. She's pissed, so I give her a few minutes to cool down. Meanwhile, I text Deeana to find out Marin's room number. Twenty minutes later, when Jody answers the door, she tells me Marin blazed in, grabbed her things, and tore out of there. I try Marin's cell but she doesn't pick up.

Marin said something about the airport, so I grab a cab outside of the hotel and offer the driver an extra hundred if he can get me to McCarran in ten minutes. Meanwhile, I try calling again but she doesn't answer.

"What terminal?" the cabbie asks. Shit! I have no clue.

"I don't know."

"What airline?"

I run my fingers through my hair and expel a loud breath. I try Damon's cell, hoping he'll know what flight Marin is on, but he doesn't answer either. I'm guessing he's busy handling this mess with Craig and Phoebe. I scrub my hand over my jaw as the cabbie weaves in and out of traffic hoping to get his big tip.

"What airline are you flying?" he repeats.

"Take me to Southwest."

He pulls up to the curb and I hand him the fare and promised bonus. He pulls away and I'm left standing there contemplating my next step. I rush into the terminal and look for a sales kiosk. I know security won't let me through without a ticket, so I purchase one for the upcoming shuttle to LAX, which runs every hour.

The wait through security feels interminable as I continue to call Marin's cell. No answer. Shit! She probably thinks I'm such an asshole. And right now, I feel like one. Stupid knee-jerk reaction. When I reach the front of the line, I hand my ticket and ID to the TSA guard.

"No way!" he exclaims. I don't have time for fanboys right now. I push my hand down in front of me a few times in an attempt to squash his enthusiasm. I look behind me and people in line stare curiously and whisper to each other. The last thing I want is to be recognized.

"Listen, Anthony," I begin, looking at his name badge. "I need a favor," I explain in a hushed tone.

"Dude. Anything."

"I need to get through this line without anyone recognizing me."

"So, no selfie?" He sounds disappointed.

"Tell you what. You give me your email address and I promise to send you a bunch of signed swag, tickets to a show, anything you want." He looks behind me, at the strangers watching.

"Cool." He scribbles something on my ticket and hands it back to me with a scrap paper containing his email address. He gestures for another agent to come over and explains that I need to get through screening right away or I'll miss my flight.

"You rock, man." We share a fist bump and the other agent gets me through the metal detector right away. From there, I haul ass to my gate. I look around, but there's no sign of Marin. For the next few hours, I race from gate to gate across terminals, checking all LA-bound flights for her. I even try sweet-talking the gate agent to look up her name on a flight manifest but am told privacy laws prevent the airline from sharing that information. Around one thirty, Craig calls.

"What the hell, man? You missed the sound check."

"Shit! I'm sorry." My shoulders sag forward. I'm disappointing everyone today, including myself. A gate agent announces boarding instructions for an upcoming flight.

"Are you at the airport? You're not bailing on me. I need you. The band needs you," he stresses. *What about what I need?* I need Marin. If there's any chance of me surviving another leg of this tour, I won't be able to do it without Marin by my side.

"Something came up, but I'm on my way back now," I explain raking my fingers through my hair as I look for the signs pointing toward baggage claim and the exits. I can't tell him I'm tracking down Marin. He's probably furious with her and I'm not in a place—both location and state of mind—to explain she would never betray us. That conversation will have to wait. It *will* happen. Just not now.

"It's a clusterfuck, dude. Could use you here." *It's a clusterfuck for me too,* I want to scream.

"Yeah. On my way." I've got to find Damon. For all his shortcomings, he'll be able to sniff out the truth.

"Yeah, that was genius, Brynn," Damon says into his cell phone. I'm just about to walk into the otherwise empty conference room that we've been using as staging for wardrobe and makeup back at the hotel. "I shouldn't have underestimated you when we first met in Sasha's office." Brynn? Sasha's office? Why do I get the feeling this has something with do with Marin? I lean closer to listen, being sure to hide my body behind the doorjamb.

"That shouldn't be a problem. Now that the band has gotten increased exposure, there is going to be even more need to manage press and their social media presence. Based on your brilliance, we finally got rid of that annoying Marin. I'll recommend to Sasha we bring you on full time."

"What the hell is going on?" I shout, crossing over to him. Damon looks at me and exhales loudly.

"Listen, I'll have to call you back," he says with little emotion into the phone. He pauses for a moment. "No. Everything is fine." He ends his call, turns to me, and plasters a fake smile on his face.

"Brad. Where have you been?"

"Never mind that, Damon. I heard you on the phone with Brynn. What the fuck is going on?"

"Nothing's going on. Brynn has been working with Sasha and the team to increase exposure for the band and she's done a great job, so we're going to bring her on full time once the US tour is over next week," he explains.

I'm not buying it. "So Brynn leaked the photo of Craig and Phoebe?" I half ask, half state in anger.

"No, that was Marin," he says. "Brynn's been doing damage control."

"Why don't I believe you?" I fire back. "You want to know what I think happened? I think you told Brynn to leak the photos and you promised her a job if she did. You never liked Marin."

"She wasn't right for you. She kept filling your head with ideas of leaving the band. You don't need someone hanging around who wants to keep you from your dreams," he snaps.

"This band isn't my dream. It never has been. Marin was the only one who encouraged me to follow my true dream," I huff. "She's the only one who cares about me," I say, taking in a deep breath.

Damon comes over and puts a consoling arm on my shoulder. "I care about you Brad," he says with fake sincerity. I want to punch those crooked yellow teeth out of his fucking mouth.

"Get the fuck off me!" I shout, shrugging him off. "You don't care about anyone but yourself."

"How can you say that?" He clutches his hand over his chest, like he's wounded. He'd have to have a goddamn heart to have it damaged. I should know. My heart has been aching these past few hours, ever since Marin left. Or ever since I let her leave, I should say. Who the hell am I kidding? Ever since I drove her away. I was such an asshole.

"How can I say that?" I repeat back in horror. "All you care about is making more money off us," I sneer, shaking my head.

"That's not true," he scoffs. "I've always been about you and the music. I've worked my ass of for you."

"You've worked your ass off for yourself. For the big payout."

"How can you say that?"

"We've been telling you for months that Johnny needs help, but you keep pushing the tour."

"He needs the music."

"No, he needs help. But you're so focused on the money, you're blinded to anything else and you threw Marin under the bus to get it. But you know what? The gravy train is over. You're fired."

"You can't fire me," he shoots back.

"Watch me!" I say, storming out. I know I should go find Craig and Oliver—explain to them what really happened. Tell them we need to fire Damon. Tell them I want out. All I can think about right now is how I screwed up this situation with Marin. I run my fingers through my hair. Shit! I was such an asshole to her. I know she only wanted me to be happy. Before I know it, I'm back in my room.

I pull my cell phone out of my pocket and dial her number for the thirtieth time. It goes straight to voice mail again. Of course it does. Why would she pick up after the horrible things I said to her? I hang up, unsure of what I should say. How do you tell the woman you love you totally fucked up? That you should have had more faith in her. That you should have had more faith in the two of you. Argh! I throw my phone against the wall and it smashes in pieces. Great. Just great.

SIXTY-FIVE

BRAD

It's been more than a week since I accused Marin of betraying me, and I've been begging for her forgiveness ever since. I've called and texted, but she won't speak to me.

The tour is over and the band is back in LA, and I've been staking out her apartment, hoping to see her. She hasn't left the house at all. In fact, I don't even know if she's in town. Maybe she's taken a job in Seattle, like she talked about. Or was desperate enough to visit her mom. Shit! What if she's gone? What if I can't fix this? There's only one real way to find out.

"Tempest Vallone's office." Grace sounds happy and hopeful.

"Grace, it's Brad Osterhauser." She's silent on the other end. I take that as a bad sign. In the limited time I've been friends with Grace, I haven't known her to be quiet. Ever. "Grace? Are you there?"

"I'm here and I'm at work." She sounds much less enthusiastic than before.

"I don't mean to bother you at your job, but I really need to talk to you. Can I meet you somewhere? Lunch? Coffee? Drink?"

She exhales loudly.

"Please," I add.

"Okay. Coffee. Meet me at the Coffee Bean on Beverwil in an hour."

"Thanks, Grace."

"Don't thank me yet," she says in warning. The hour wait to talk with Grace is agonizing. I don't know if she's going to help me win Marin back, but at least she's going to listen to what I have to say. I can't help but smile when she walks in the door. I lean over to hug her, but she pulls back and gives the kind of look my mother would give me and Craig when we played our music too loud and the neighbors called the cops.

"Coffee?" I ask.

"God, yes," she says and I'm starting to witness a little bit of the fun Grace I know—and love—coming out. "A house blend, two sugars. Your treat," she adds with a smug grin.

"Of course." I get in line while Grace grabs a table. When I have her coffee and a large dark roast for myself, I make my way over. She puts her cell phone down and looks at me pointedly.

"You really screwed up big time."

"I know," I say, my shoulders slumping forward. "I know," I repeat because I don't know what else to say.

"She would never," she starts, pointing a finger at me, "*never* do that to you."

"I know."

"She's loyal and honest."

"I know," I say, trying to reassure her I understand how amazing Marin is.

"Marin is a special girl but for reasons you know and understand, she's cautious. She didn't let you in because she needed you. She let you in because she *wanted* you."

I scrub my hands over my face. "I know," I say on a sigh.

"You're saying 'I know' a lot, but your actions don't match." I sit there, silent, and she adds, "Now's where you're supposed to say, 'I know.'" I give a small chuckle and she smirks at me. "She's the very best person I know, and you really hurt her." She shakes her head as if pained and looks down at her coffee.

"She says the same about you, you know. That you're the best person she knows."

"I'm not surprised. I'm awesome," she shrugs but throws me a smug look. "It would be weird if I say *I'm* the best person I know," she snorts.

"I've called and texted, but she won't respond to me."

"That was her work phone and the agency took it back when they fired her." Jeez. I feel like such an ass. "All this time, she thought you didn't care," she adds, shaking her head in frustration.

"I'm completely in love with her, Grace, and I'll do anything to make this right. I need to get her back," I say with urgency.

"Well, what do you want *me* to do about it?" she asks in an accusatory tone, hand cocked on her hip, before giving me a wink.

SIXTY-SIX

MARIN

"C'mon," says Grace. "I promise it's going to be fun."

Grace is dragging me away from my self-imposed prison for the past three weeks—our couch. It's been three weeks of resumes and only two Skype interviews. Three weeks fearing I won't be able to make ends meet. Three weeks since Brad thought I would betray him and his trust for the sake of my career. Three weeks since I had my heart broken. Three weeks without a word from him.

What we had wasn't enough for him to fight for us. It being over, knowing it was due to some trumped up BS is hard. Knowing he didn't believe me is beyond hard. If I'm being honest with myself, I know I could look past that initial reaction. I'm sure it looked bad, and no doubt he had Craig and Damon squawking in his ear. But knowing he didn't *feel* enough for me— to love me enough to fight for us—to think it through and recognize I would never do that to him . . . that's devastating.

Now I'm in the bathroom, wrapped in a towel after a shower Grace said was long overdue. She even insisted I do a deep conditioning of my hair and shave my legs and complete any other beauty rituals that will make me feel good on the outside, even though I'm feeling lousy on the inside. She's not trying to gloss over my sadness though. If anything, Grace has encouraged me to process it all. But for some reason, she thinks a little exterior sprucing up will do me some interior good.

As I wipe the steam off the mirror, Grace walks in to grab her makeup bag. "You doin' okay, girlie?" She gives my shoulders a squeeze.

"Yeah, I'm okay." I try putting on a brave face. Honestly, though, how could I be okay? In a matter of moments, I lost everything important to me and everything I'd worked so hard for, and it wasn't even my fault.

"Good. Because you can't be in a sour mood at a Bruno Mars concert. It's not allowed," she says with a smile. Grace's company got backstage passes to the show tonight and she's taking me to cheer me up.

We arrive at the STAPLES Center and, using our VIP passes, head backstage. Having spent more than three months on tour with a rock band, I'm used to what *backstage* means. There's nowhere to sit, it's filled with pulleys and cables, and there are a myriad of people rushing around to handle everything from set changes to wardrobe malfunctions. Bottom line, it's not as glamorous as it sounds. Yet, there is something exciting about being right there where all the action is.

Being this up close and personal with Bruno Mars is about as exciting as it gets. Grace was right, but I won't tell her that. It's impossible to be in a foul mood when Bruno Mars is shimmying on stage and belting out tunes in front of a ten-piece brass band. Behind the scenes, I can feel the vibration through the floor from the intensity of the music as it reverberates through my body.

"We're going to slow things down for a moment," Bruno says. The lights dim and a lone spotlight shines on him. "Now y'all know I've got a song called 'When I Was Your Man.'" You can't hear anything he says next because the crowd goes crazy. He struggles to get them to quiet down. "Now, now. Shh. Now that song is all about how a man should have done a better job of treating his woman right. Well, I have a friend who's in that exact situation, and he's here tonight to make apologies and grovel." The crowd whistles and cheers. "How many of you have heard of a little band called Kings Quarters?" The crowd goes wild, but the only sound I can hear is the rushing of blood in my body, like I'm underwater and everything else is muted and distorted. Grace squeezes my hand, shrugs, and smiles.

"Don't be mad at me. Just hear him out," she says. Here I thought Grace had gotten tickets through work. The traitor has been conspiring with Brad all along. Before I can process her betrayal, I look back onto the stage and Brad is adjusting the microphone and his guitar strap. He looks to the wings and gives me a grin. I close my eyes tight, the tears already falling. As much as I want to run away and not deal with the pain, I'm rooted to this spot. Grace looks over at me and squeezes my hand again. "It's going to be okay."

"Hi everyone. Thanks for letting me interrupt your fun with Bruno tonight." The crowd claps and cheers. "He was kind enough to let me come here tonight to share a new song with you. It's called 'Starfish.'"

I bury my head in my hands and sob. Grace rubs my back with gentle circles. "C'mon, girlie. Pick your head up and listen to the boy." I lift my head and Brad is looking over at me. He turns back to the crowd.

"I wrote it to tell the woman I love how sorry I am for not believing in her and in us. I screwed up about as badly as a man can. I need her back in my life. I need her to know how important she is to me, and I hope she'll forgive me." He gives another glance over to the wings to make sure I'm still here and listening. He strums a few strings and adjusts his guitar before starting to play a slow and achingly sweet ballad.

The bed is cold
The loneliness gets old
I know I'm being bold

But please, be my starfish

My loyalty was off-key
I screwed up royally
Please, be my starfish

All the risks were yours to take
It was a choice I forced you to make
There were warning signs I didn't heed
I abandoned you in your time of need

It's okay to complain
I'll take all the blame
I did act insane
I'm so sorry my starfish

I miss your body
I miss your touch
I miss your humor
I miss so much

You completely devastated me with one kiss
It's one of the things I truly miss
You are so much more than I ever wanted
Lonely nights and empty dreams leave me haunted

Don't mean to rush
But I know I must
Gain back your trust
Please, be my starfish

I did you wrong
So I wrote this song
Don't make me wait long
Please, be my starfish

I miss your body
I miss your touch
I miss your humor
I miss so much

Can't you see
What you mean to me
You're like the air I breathe
Please, be my starfish

You don't need to apologize
For the betrayal in your eyes
It was my faith that was in disguise
But I've had time to philosophize

I miss your body
I miss your touch
I miss your humor
I miss so much

I ain't too proud to beg just like the Temptations
I hope my sincerity creates a revelation
You and I should be the two in an equation
Because I love you, my starfish

I'm a sobbing mess when Brad walks off stage, sets down his guitar, and wraps his arms around me.

"I'm so sorry, Marin. I'm so sorry," he says, soothing me with his touch and words.

"I thought you didn't care," I eke out.

"Oh, baby, you're all I could think about."

"I'm sorry too. I'm sorry I didn't fight harder for us," I tell him back. His lips crash down on me and I wind my arms around his neck and draw him closer. When he pulls away, Grace is standing off to the side, smiling like a loon and clapping her hands together like a small child.

"I told Craig—that I wanted out of the band." He rubs his thumbs across the apples of my cheeks, brushing the tears away.

"I'm glad you said something to him," I say, nodding my head. "I know that must not have been easy."

"Second hardest thing I've ever done," he says with a pained grin.

"What's the first?"

"Watching you walk away." He tilts his head to the side and shakes it, his eyes wet with unshed tears. I run my fingers through his hair.

"You didn't need to do that for me," I tell him. I mean it. Knowing he's sorry, knowing he regrets not believing in me and in us—that's all I need.

"I didn't do it for you. I did it for me," he explains. "If it helps us, that's a bonus."

"I'm so happy for you," Grace squeals, as she bounds over to us.

"Thank you for forgiving me, Marin. I love you."

"I love you too," I respond before falling into a fit of tears again.

"Shh. Stop crying," he says. He wraps his arms around me and sways while whispering lyrics from his song in my ear.

I missed your body
I missed your touch
I missed your humor
I missed so much

I need you in my life
Please be my wife
Please be my only starfish

I pull back from his embrace. "What?" I gasp, drawing my hand to my mouth.

"Marry me," he says.

"Marry you?" I ask in shocked disbelief. *Is he for real?* "We've only known each other for a few months."

"If anything, these past few weeks have shown me I don't like my life without you in it." My heart is caught in my throat. "Before you tell me all the reasons it won't work, let me ask: do you love me?"

"Yes, B, I do. You own my heart."

"Then say you'll marry me," he responds with a casual shrug. "It doesn't have to be today. It doesn't have to be tomorrow, but someday. Just tell me we can be together. We'll work the rest out."

"Yes," I breathe and thrust myself back into his arms. "Yes, yes."

SIXTY-SEVEN

EPILOGUE
MARIN

True to Brad's word, it did work out. After Sasha found out Damon leaked the photo with Brynn's help, she told me she wanted me to come work for her in LA. But after the whole incident with the *Village Voice*, I lost a lot of respect for her. The thought of working for her no longer held any appeal. I did take her up on her offer to write me a letter of recommendation, though, because I had *earned* it.

I landed a job with a tech start up in San Francisco. I am challenged every day and I love being around the smart, driven people who work there.

After Brad left the band, the whole group kind of imploded. With them no longer together, Damon took Jase out on his own and he's enjoying great success as a solo artist. Not surprising, Damon didn't hire Brynn to work with them on Jase's publicity. It was a near tie for who loathed Brynn most with Grace edging me and Brad out slightly. Grace even vowed to put a hex that she learned from Cujo's dog groomer on Brynn. I don't know what happened to her, but whatever it is, I hope she's miserable.

Craig and Phoebe stayed in Hollywood. She's doing some freelance work on television shows and he is collaborating and producing with some other musicians and bands on their projects.

The collapse of Kings Quarters was pretty hard on Johnny. After a couple of benders, he hit rock bottom and got himself into rehab. I hope he's able to get the help he needs and shake his demons.

Oliver, being the stellar keyboardist he is, was picked up by another band who needed to fill in their roster and he's already on tour with them. I just hope they can survive all his practical jokes.

Grace is still toiling away at the agency but now she's an assistant agent, as opposed to assistant *to* an agent. The new job comes with more responsibility, more money, and a whole lot less aggravation, as her crazy boss can now torture her *new* assistant. With the raise, Grace was able to afford the rent on our beach apartment on her own. She is staying there and—in her words—crying herself to sleep each night over missing me so much.

As for B, he's following his own path and pursuing his video game. He's in development with a tech firm and already has angel investing from a top company. He's in San Francisco too and we live together in an old restored Victorian near Union Square. We are engaged, although we haven't set a wedding date yet. I'm still his starfish . . . I still take up two-thirds of the bed and all the covers, and he says he wouldn't want it any other way.

STARFISH:
After the Music

A ROCK STAR BONUS

Classic rock tunes flood my ears as I chop a cucumber for tonight's salad. I must have the volume cranked up pretty high, because I don't hear her arrive home. I do smell her vanilla scent before I feel her arms wrapping around me from behind and her soft lips leaving a trail of kisses across my shoulder.

"Mmm," I groan. "We better make it quick. Marin should be home soon." Marin's teeth sink into my flesh and her fingers tweak my nipple, which she's got easy access to since I'm cooking shirtless. I turn around and crash my lips down against hers.

Fuuuuck. There's nothing better than kissing Marin. Not even a plate of crisp bacon, straight from the pan, comes close to this. The taste of her lips. The slide of her tongue against mine. The way she yanks my hair.

I lift her up onto the counter and run my nose along her neck, breathing her in. How she manages to always smell so fresh and clean and uniquely Marin, I'll never understand. I undo the silky red bow at her neck (my sexy little executive) allowing me access to the tiny red buttons of her blouse. As I pop each one open, I plant a small kiss on the creamy skin I'm revealing, eliciting a sultry moan every time.

"How was your day Mrs. Osterhauser?" She tilts her neck to the side allowing me better access.

"It was good, but I missed you," she sighs. "And how was your day Mr. Osterhauser?" I stop fiddling with her buttons and gently stroke her cheek.

"Terrible. I want to be back in a hut in Fiji with you."

"Me too." She runs her fingers through my hair down to the nape of my neck. I let my head fall forward and relish her massaging touch. As I feel myself grow hard, I know I need her . . . now. I lift my head so it's eye level with her chest in order to work the remaining buttons open and as I do, I reveal a lacy purple bra. I love it.

"Lavender today," I whisper as I trace my tongue along the lacey edge over the swell of her breast.

"Mmm hmm. You can thank Jase for the $1,000 Victoria's Secret gift card he gave us as a wedding present," she chuckles. Not what I want to hear right now as I flick open the button of her black pants.

"Yeah, let's not bring up another dude when I'm about to ravish you on the counter," I tease.

"Point taken." She tugs the belt loops on my low-slung jeans.

"You're gonna be taken soon," I warn with a wiggle of my eyebrows. I drag down the zipper on her pants and I can tell I've rubbed against a sensitive spot when her head falls back, and she lets out a slow "Oooooohhhhh." Just as I'm about to drag them down her legs, the oven timer goes off. Damn!

"Something beeped," she advises. I scrub my hand over my jaw.

"That would be the lasagna."

"You got lasagna for dinner?" Her reaction to my choice of entrées must be well received, as she doesn't seem disappointed I've moved away from her to open the oven.

"No. I made lasagna for dinner."

"You made it? Like from scratch?"

"I did." She hops off the counter and grabs ahold of my arm while I remove the casserole dish from the oven so that she can check it out for herself. Smells damn good.

"Wow. How did I get so lucky Mr. Osterhauser?" I put the hot dish on the stovetop, whip off the oven mitt and turn until I'm flush against her. I push my forehead to hers and inhale.

"I'm the lucky one," I breathe while she uses those magic fingers to stroke my hair from root to tip. "We better let this cool off." She pushes back from me, glances down at my tented jeans and raises a brow. Next, she points to the painful bulge in my pants and then to the lasagna. She shrugs up her shoulders and holds her hands, palms up, in front of her as if she's questioning which one needs to simmer down. "You're awfully cheeky this evening. I think you might need to be punished," I joke. As I'm about to tickle her, she takes off toward the living room. I grab her by the waist as she squirms in my arms and laughs. Damn. Her laugh. It just guts me every time.

I toss her onto the couch, her back facing me. She twists around, breathing hard. I stay where I am so I can admire her. She licks her lips and brushes the hair away from her face. As I step forward, she reaches up and wraps her arms around my neck, pulling me down on top of her. Without hesitation or finesse, Marin rips open the button fly of my jeans and pulls them down.

"No underwear," she groans.

"Only get in the way," I grunt in response as her fingernails dig into my hips. She wraps her fingers around my shaft and gives a solid tug. My eyes roll to the back of my head at the pleasure. "Turn around." Marin does as I've asked. Looking over her shoulder, I undo the last button of her blouse and pull it away. Next I remove her bra, kissing each shoulder as the straps fall. I let my hands stroke down her arms until I reach her waist, and then ease her out of her pants to find a scrap of lavender lace passing as a pair of panties. When my mind isn't occupied with the look, the feel, the smell of Marin's amazing body, I'll have to remember to thank Jase for his thoughtful wedding gift.

I gently press Marin forward and pull her hips back so I can enter her from behind. Feeling her wrapped around me—without a condom—is indescribable. One of the many perks of monogamy. Having no barrier between us feels better for her too, judging by her guttural groan.

"Oh, B. Oh. You feel amazing," she hisses with pleasure, grasping the back of the couch, her hands white knuckling the fabric. I place my hands over hers and kiss her neck while I pound into her with gusto. God. I don't know what I love seeing more— my ring on her finger or my cock buried in her.

Her release is quick. Really quick. As she clamps around me, I chalk it up to my sexual prowess. Leaving her satisfied is just about the best part of my day. And while I know I could last a lot longer than this, she continues to pulse and throb around me. The raw need I have to let go is too strong, so I rupture. I lean my sweaty, heaving body against her, and in between ragged breaths, plant sweet kisses along the back of her neck. Her skin must be uber-sensitized, because she shivers.

I ease out of her and grab my pants from the floor. She follows suit, scooping up her clothes. She glides past me on her way to the staircase toward our bedroom, shaking her curvy ass as she goes. Before she reaches the stairs, she glances over her shoulder at me. Of course, I'm staring. Impossible to look away. She tosses me a wink and tells me she'll be right down.

*

Marin returns in a pair of yoga pants and a tank top. Her hair is piled on top of her head and her feet are bare, except for some lavender nail polish. Lavender. Like her bra and panties. Thinking about that sexy lingerie causes a swell in my pants again. This woman makes me feel insatiable.

"I'm starving," she tells me, plopping herself down on a chair at the kitchen table. "This lasagna you made better be good. I've worked up quite an appetite," she sasses.

"Oh believe me, I know how hard you worked," I sass back. "And this lasagna is going to rock your world." I cut a piece for each of us and add a healthy portion of salad to each plate. I place it in front of her and watch as she takes the first bite. Her mouth curls into a smile.

"Well done, Mr. Osterhauser," she praises. I would make a thousand lasagnas to have her looking at me like I'm her world.

"So, tell me about your first day back."

"It was busy, but good. While I was away, Tamika finished up coordination on that story with Wired magazine and it's running next week."

"Good. I know you were worried about going to Fiji with that loose end."

"You did a good job of keeping me relaxed."

"Best part of my day. And morning. And night." She grasps my hand and squeezes—the feeling mimicked in my rib cage. She releases my hand but the tightness in my chest thankfully doesn't ease. She moans again over the lasagna and chuckles to herself when she sees my pupils dilate. If I don't change the subject, I'm going to skip the rest of dinner and feast on her. "Don't forget. Grace gets in tomorrow at seven o'clock."

"Why would I forget. She's my best friend." She's looking at me like I've sprung a second head.

"Is she?"

"Yes!" she exclaims. When she notices I've tilted my head to the side—questioning her—she adds, "What are you getting at?" I raise an eyebrow. "That you're my best friend or Grace is yours?"

"That Grace and I are besties of course." She balls her napkin up and throws it at me, hitting me square in the face. I pick it up from the floor, smooth it out and hand it back to her while she grins smugly. "I still can't believe she's moving here."

"I know. Who knew she'd land an entertainment job in San Francisco?"

"With so many technology service providers starting up their own original productions, they need people who know how to deal with those Hollywood types."

"If anyone knows that, it's Grace," she affirms. "Thank you for offering her a place to stay until she gets settled."

"Of course."

"I know it might put a damper on the couch sex," she says, referring to the vigorous and sexy exchange we shared before dinner.

"Not to worry, sweetheart. There are a lot of other places we can have sex." She fans herself with her hand and lets out a shaky breath. "And anyway, she's going to be slammed at work. I'm confident it won't cramp our style."

"Slammed?" she repeats with seduction.

"Yep. Just don't think it will be in the same way you will be later," I respond with equal amounts of seduction.

"Something to look forward to," she winks.

"Indeed. So what do we have to look forward to when Grace gets in tomorrow?" I'd wager whatever they have planned includes something sweet.

"She wants to get a Ghirardelli ice cream sundae," BINGO! "and then go to karaoke." Karaoke? With Marin? A shudder runs through me. "What?"

"What what?" I aim for nonchalance.

"What's that look for?"

"I don't know what you're talking about," I shrug. She's not buying it.

"We've been married for twenty-three days and you're already lying to me," she mock huffs.

"Baby, you know I love you but I'm not sure karaoke is a good idea." Marin has a terrible voice. And I'm not just saying that because I was a professional musician and have unrealistic standards. She's awful and she knows it.

"I'll just lip sync," she advises with a nod. I try to maintain a blank face. "What?"

"What what?" I toss out again. I look down at my plate and shovel in a mouthful of salad to avoid both eye contact and having to say more.

"Come on. Out with it."

"With all due respect, love, and admiration, that's just not gonna cut it."

"What are you talking about?"

"With your voice, even lip-synching is painful to those of us around you." Her mouth gapes open in shock.

"But you won't even hear me," she whines.

"Doesn't matter." I shake my head. "We all know what you sound like and can hear it in our heads." She smirks at me.

"I think you're only saying that so we can have our first fight and then have make up sex."

"Yeah. Sure. That's it," I roll my eyes to let her know I'm humoring her.

"Why did I marry you again?"

"Because I rock your world in and out of the bedroom."

"Damn it. You got me there." Her eyes twinkle with humor. "I do."

"Speaking of 'I do', how do you want to celebrate our twenty-three-day anniversary?"

"Hot sex with my hot wife."

"So, like every other anniversary we've had so far?"

"What can I say?" I shrug. "I'm a creature of habit."

"Indeed you are," she smiles. She gets up from the table and grabs my empty plate, walking everything to the sink.

"I can do that. You worked hard today."

"That's okay. You cooked. I can clean." While she rinses dishes and loads the dishwasher, I put the remaining lasagna in a Tupperware and store it in the fridge. When did I get so domesticated? I glance over at Marin, my heart bursting with love for her. And damn it, why didn't I do it earlier? "Besides, you worked today, too. Tell me about your day."

"I had a few conference calls with the investment team and the development company." I lean against the counter while I watch her sponge off a glob of tomato sauce.

"That's great. I know it was hard to give over the development to a team, but I think you've put the concept in good hands."

"Agreed." On both counts. Yes, it was difficult to turn over my baby—something that had given me so much comfort when I was miserable on the road with the band. But the video game development company is the best in the business. They have the financial backing, developer talent and overall intellectual capital to make it happen. I'm still involved as a consultant and investor, so it's really the best of both worlds. "Plus, it gives me time to go on three-week honeymoons and bake lasagnas."

"What about making dessert? Did you have time to make dessert?" she asks hopefully.

"I didn't." My lips are pulled into a grim line as I shake my head no.

"What?" She jokingly huffs. "Okay, this just may be the start of our first fight." I pull her into me. She laughs into my chest before looking up with her bright brown eyes.

"Already fighting, huh? We're like an old married couple already?" I tease.

"Speaking of old married couples, have you heard from Phoebe? She said they might be able to find out today whether it's a boy or girl." She leans away from me, grasps my hands and leads me into the living room where we sit down on the couch.

"I'm surprised she didn't call you from the doctor's office. You two are like—"

"Sisters from another mister?" she questions with a raised brow.

"No. Most definitely not." Yep! That's what I was going to say. Now of course I remember she hates that expression. "If I recall correctly, you chastised me for using that expression once."

"I recall," she nods. "So what were you going to say about me and Phoebe?"

"You two are like . . . peas in a pod."

"Peas in a pod? Really?"

"Okay, fine. You got me. I was going to say sisters from another mister," I confess.

"I knew it." She wags a finger at me in jest. I respond with puppy dog eyes earning a pillow to the face and a laugh.

"Craig called me today, but Phoebe wanted to tell you."

"So you know?"

"I do . . . but I've been sworn to secrecy."

"I'm fairly confident I could use my considerable interrogation skills to get it out of you," she challenges. Oh boy. Knowing what "weapons" she has in her arsenal, I know I'm a goner. I'd be the worst spy, unable to resist her temptation.

"Why don't you just give her a quick call right now, so I don't have to be persuaded to divulge their secret.

"You don't think you would enjoy the grilling?" she poses, wiggling her eyebrows up and down while trailing a finger seductively down my chest.

"Oh, I know I would. But I can't do that to Craig."

"Okay," she pouts, getting off the couch to grab her cell phone.

∗

After a twenty-minute call for a gender reveal—it's a girl—and a lot of shrieking, Marin and I are back on the couch dreaming about how we are going to spoil our little niece.

"I can't believe I'm going to be an auntie," she squeals. I love her enthusiasm for my family. Well now, our family.

"And it's all thanks to me," I crow proudly.

"Is that so?" she scoffs. "I do believe Craig and Phoebe had a bit more to do with it than you did. Unless there's something you're not telling me." I shudder and she laughs. Phoebe is most definitely like a sister to me.

"What I mean is that if you hadn't married me, you wouldn't have Craig and Phoebe as your brother and sister. Hey, look at that. Phoebe really is your sister from another mister now." I gesture my hand forward and she playfully slaps it away.

"That totally reminds me. I never asked you how Jase responded when you told him my sister Sydney was only seventeen." I love that Marin no longer refers to Sydney as her half-sister. I scrub my hand over my jaw and chuckle. Honestly, when I saw Jase hitting on Sydney at the wedding, I saw red. I've grown to think of her as my little sister over the past two years. Not only is she underage—despite looking twenty-five years old—but she deserves a lot better than an arrogant womanizer like Jase. Don't get me wrong. I love him like a brother and despite his successful solo career these past few years, we've remained close. But she's not the bridesmaid he should have been looking to hook up with at the wedding.

"At first, he didn't believe me."

"Not surprised." I'm not sure if Marin agrees that Sydney doesn't look her age or whether Jase just thinks I would be a cock blocker.

"I think he might have thought I was in cahoots with Oliver on a practical joke."

"Oh my god," she groans before shaking her head and snickering. "I can't believe Oliver found out where Jase was staying while on tour in London last month and had his entire room filled with balloons."

"Those weren't balloons. They were blown-up condoms." Marin's chuckle morphs into a full-blown laugh and I join her.

"Those two," she shakes her head. "Well, Sydney's age is most definitely not a practical joke. She's grown into quite a lovely young lady. But she's still a child."

"Sydney didn't seem all that thrilled with me after I convinced him she was underage."

"She'll get over it. And he's lucky I was busy being the bride and didn't have time to address the issue. Any other time I would have caught him looking at my little sister like that . . . I would have chopped off his balls." I wince and instinctively cover my junk. Marin playfully swats my arm.

"No need to feel sorry for Jase. If I recall, he went home with not one but two of your girlfriends from college."

"Of course he did," she retorts with a roll of her eyes. Jases's sexual exploits are quite legendary. My blood still boils that she knows first-hand. I honestly wasn't sure how to respond when Marin confessed she once saw him getting a blow job. I know it wasn't his fault she walked in on him, but it didn't stop me from wanting to connect a fist to his jaw. As I stew on this, we sit in silence for a beat for two.

"I'm really glad they could all come to the wedding," she sighs. She must not have been thinking about Jase and his blow job, which is certainly a relief. And regarding her happiness at the band being able to make the wedding, all I think is me too. Despite all my complaints about band life, touring and the behind the scenes shenanigans, those really were some great years. They also led me to the amazing woman in front of me.

"Me too."

"Johnny looked good," she offers. She's right. He did look good. After a few unsuccessful stints in rehab, he finally found solace, health and a solution for substance dependency at an ashram in India of all places. A year of stress elimination and self-development, complete with meditation and yoga, did the trick.

"It took some doing, but he figured out what works for him."

"I know it wasn't easy, but he's on a good path. I'm proud of him."

"Yep. A year of self-imposed celibacy most certainly couldn't have been easy," I joke. She eyes me up and down, dragging in a deep breath.

"No. I can't imagine that was easy." She bites her lip while she eye fucks me.

"Don't think you could go a year with getting some of this," I challenge, holding my hands out to the side and swiveling my hips. I'm quite certain I look ridiculous.

"Ugh," she groans. "And just like that, the moment has passed," she jokes. I lean over to tickle her, and her fingers jump right to my hair.

"I knew it," I respond in triumph. "You're powerless to resist me."

"Whatever." She rolls her eyes.

"Say it," I prod her.

"Say what?"

"Say you're powerless to resist me."

"No," she brushes me off.

"Say it," I command.

"No." Her response is more forceful than before.

"Say . . . it!" I demand with humor, digging my fingers into her ribs, which elicits a giggle.

"Never," she responds defiantly. I pin her arms above her head and stare down at her. She's breathing hard—both from evading my tickling fingers and from being completely turned on. I move her slightly so I'm holding both of her hands with one of mine, and use the other to stroke her cheek.

"Say it," I whisper.

"I'm powerless to resist you," she whispers back. I lean down and kiss her. I release her hands and I am rewarded with a gentle tug of my hair. As much as I want her now—really, I can't imagine not ever wanting her—I need to have her in our bed. Our bed. That's never going to get old.

"Why don't you go up to the bedroom and wait for me in nothing but those tortoise shell frames. I'll just lock up down here and be right up," I suggest. She nods and I'm transfixed watching her move up the staircase. Just before she disappears from sight, she bends down and catches my eye.

"You may no longer be in a band, B., but you're still a rock star in all the ways that count." And just like that, my world is complete.

The End

Keep reading for a teaser of

The Subway Girl

A new, standalone contemporary romance from Lisa Becker

Coming 2020

(This is an uncorrected copy and may differ from the final published novel.)

PROLOGUE

Those catlike, green eyes. That long, flowing brown hair wrapped around her right shoulder, tucked underneath the collar of a pink trench coat. A radiant smile of straight, gleaming white teeth, lined up perfectly, sinking into a juicy magenta lip.

Ryan Carlson looked up briefly from the tablet perched on his lap and knew his life had changed forever. Leaning against a pole several feet ahead of him on the crowded One train to Times Square stood the most exquisite woman he had ever seen.

In a moment, as quick and powerful as a strike of lightening, he knew he *had* to meet her. *Yeah, right, approach a total stranger on the subway.* He had no doubt he'd come off looking like a weirdo or a stalker, as there was certainly no shortage of those in New York City. He knew he was neither. Just a regular guy—a decent guy—looking for the right girl.

He took a moment to examine her further. There was no engagement ring or wedding band on her hand, although she did wear a wide silver thumb ring. She was dressed in a pair of black workout pants and that pink coat.

She probably has a boyfriend. One look at her, and it was hard for him to imagine someone wasn't already lucky enough to be with her. He'd been on the receiving end of betrayal and wouldn't put someone else through that kind of hell. *Maybe she's single. Maybe it's my fate to meet her. Yes. It's fate.* He was convinced of it.

Men probably approach her all time. His mouth went dry as he tried to think of what he would say. He honestly didn't know. It wasn't like this situation had come up before. All he knew was he was determined to meet her.

His heart raced as he took a deep, calming breath. With sweaty palms, he grabbed ahold of the pole next to him and lifted out of the seat while he considered his next move. As he got closer to the woman, he could hear her mumbling to herself, and her charming accent caused his stomach to clench in the most amazing way.

"Fifty-Ninth Street–Columbus Circle," the conductor droned over the loudspeaker as the subway car rattled and whistled. The lights flickered, and when they came back on, the woman was no longer clinging to the pole. With a rising panic, Ryan's eyes quickly surveyed the subway car. She had managed to move toward the door just as the train pulled into the station. Ryan tried to maintain an eye on the pink coat as passengers pushed to get off the train.

A large man with a bad comb-over, dressed in a brown, tattered, two-hundred-dollar suit and scuffed shoes blocked his way. Not wanting to be rude, Ryan gently shifted the shabby businessman aside and muttered, "Excuse me, getting off."

Ryan stepped off the train and stood on the subway platform, two exits before his intended stop, stretching onto his toes looking both left and right, seeking out the pink coat. He jumped up a few times trying to see over the hordes of people exiting and entering the train.

"Watch it, asshole," a woman carrying two reusable shopping bags cautioned as she pushed her way past him. With each passing second, his mystery girl was getting farther and farther away. Knowing he had a fifty-fifty chance, Ryan turned left and traversed in and out of the packed underground tunnel, seeking her out. He walked back and forth, peering up and down staircases and escalators to no avail.

She was gone.

A hopeless romantic. A cynical web show producer. An unscrupulous camera operator. A sleazy businessman. An aspiring actress. A scheming ex-girlfriend. Find out how these characters' lives intersect and fate intervenes with a chance at love when an average guy is awed by a gorgeous mystery woman on a New York subway and vows to meet her.

The Subway Girl, coming Spring 2020.

Keep reading for a sample of

Links

A second chance romance from Lisa Becker

Now Available

PROLOGUE

1 9 9 9

Charlotte Windham did a quick check of her teeth in the small compact mirror hanging from her key ring before knocking on the oversized wooden door. She undoubtedly had some remnants from lunch trapped within the metal wires of her braces. She pulled out a piece of apple peel from her right incisor and patted down her dark brown hair which, despite seeming an impossibility, was both simultaneously stringy and frizzy. She let out a loud exhale and knocked on the door.

A housekeeper, wearing a grey uniform, opened the door and welcomed her in. She led her past a formal entry and proper living room into the kitchen –a large, modern space with granite countertops, light wooden cabinets and enough kitchen gadgets to stock an upscale home goods store. Despite coming here twice a week for the past three months to tutor the Stephens brothers, Charlotte always stared in awe at the amazing home which was such a far contrast from the small two bedroom apartment she shared with her mom.

"The boys will be right down," said Norma kindly, gesturing to the kitchen counter which housed an array of soft drinks and snacks. Charlotte fidgeted with the silver locket around her neck -a gift from her father who died in Somalia when she was a young girl while serving in the Marines. Before she could dwell on it further, Garrett and Marcus bounded down the stairs and into the kitchen.

"You're such a wuss." Garrett punched Marcus in the arm.

"Dude!" Marcus countered, reaching out to swat his twin brother, but finding him already out of reach. "Oh, hey Charlotte."

"Hi, Marcus." Walking up, Charlotte gave him a little wave. "Hi Garrett," she breathed, looking at him for a nanosecond, before shifting her eyes to the floor.

"Oh hey, Glasses," Garrett casually tossed out. Charlotte instinctively adjusted the oversized black frames perched atop her nose. The glasses were a necessity since she was eight. While she would have loved to get contact lenses, they were a luxury her mother couldn't afford. She looked through the slightly smudged lenses and took in the image before her.

Marcus and Garrett Stephens were identical twins but couldn't have been more different in Charlotte's eyes.

At age sixteen, both Stephens brothers were already five foot nine and if their growth patterns and genetics were on track, they were well on their way to being more than six feet tall. Hazel eyes were offset by dark eyelashes, the kind women yearn for. Straight white teeth were the centerpiece of a dazzling smile punctuated by a large dimple on the left cheek.

To the untrained eye, it was difficult to tell them apart save for the small cleft in Garrett's chin, which she mused must be a mark left by the gods to name him as one of their own. To Charlotte, he was a god of perfection (unless you counted his lackluster academic performance.)

The personality differences between the twins were a bit starker than the physical ones. Both boys were exceptionally ambitious about their future goals. Garrett was determined to be a professional golfer. As a junior, he was already the star player of his high school team. The intense schedule of practice, private lessons, matches and rigorous weight training sessions coupled with his disinterest in school left him teetering precariously between a pass and fail in several classes, most notably, English. Without keeping his grade to at least a C, he would be forced off the team, on the bench and out of the sightline of those who could make his dreams of playing college and, one day, professional golf, a reality. Hence his need for a tutor –Charlotte.

Mr. and Mrs. Stephens had originally hired a local teacher to assist Garrett, but found the attractive young woman to be too much of a distraction. When Lindsay, their daughter, brought Charlotte over to work on a school newspaper project, they quickly realized the mousy teenager would pose no distraction to Garrett and would serve as the perfect tutor because the two were in the same English class.

Marcus, on the other hand, was determined to go to a top college and medical school. Though he earned high marks in all his classes, he wouldn't be guaranteed acceptance without a higher score on the reading and writing portion of the SATs. Charlotte would serve a dual purpose in helping both brothers, as she had earned one of the top scores in the state on her SATs and was recently honored at a school assembly.

So twice a week, Charlotte would spend an hour helping Garrett with class assignments and an hour with Marcus working on SAT prep.

"Dude. Just ask her to prom. What's the worst that can happen?" Garrett grabbed a handful of chips from a bowl and shoved them in his mouth.

"Uh, she could say no and humiliate me in front of everyone," Marcus replied. "Enough about me. You going to take Gabriella?"

"Nah. Already tapped that."

"One and done, huh?" Marcus smiled wryly.

"Yeah. You know me. Love the chase; hate the commitment."

Charlotte cleared her throat, reminding them she was indeed neither invisible nor deaf. They both looked at her and she grinned at them, gesturing with her head to the table.

"You go first. I got a call to make," said Garrett. "Let me show you how it's done." Marcus sat at the table and pulled out his SAT prep workbook. Charlotte sat next to him and smiled.

"Let's get started with page sixty-two today," she began as Norma continued to tidy up the kitchen. Marcus looked at the question and studied the multiple choice responses. Meanwhile, Charlotte glanced at Garrett, who pulled out his cell phone while cracking open a diet soda.

"Hey Christy. It's Garrett." Marcus turned the page to Charlotte, who nodded in acknowledgment as he selected the correct answer.

"Nothing. Just hanging out. What about you?" continued Garrett.

"Remember the root words we talked about last week," Charlotte advised Marcus, while maintaining an ear to Garrett's conversation. Marcus continued to go through the options.

"Listen, I really liked the way your hair looked, all pulled up in a bun today. I was wondering if you'd wear it like that when we go to the prom together. Whadaya say? Wanna go with me?" Garrett crooned smoothly into the phone. Charlotte sighed and looked at Garrett longingly, not wishing he would notice her hair as it was a mess most of the time, but that he would at least notice *her*.

"Yeah? Cool," said Garrett. Marcus tilted his head to the side in a few quick bursts, ushering Garrett out of the room

"Perfunctory. Is that the right answer?" Marcus said to Charlotte, whose eyes had followed Garrett to the living room. His question snapped her back to the task at hand.

"Yes. That's correct," she said, faking a smile. The hour dragged on as Charlotte wrapped her head around the fact there was no chance -ever -she would go to the prom with Garrett, let alone have him notice her. Once her time with Marcus was done, he shut his practice book and grabbed his soda from the table.

"Thanks, Charlotte. See you at school tomorrow," he said before walking out of the kitchen and shouting, "You're up, loser!"

"No, no, no. Watch your language, Mr. Marcus," chastised Norma, who was in the kitchen preparing stir fry vegetables for dinner. She had started working as a nanny for the Stephens when Garrett and Marcus were babies and stayed on as a housekeeper as they grew. Marcus rolled his eyes, but with his back turned to Norma so she didn't see.

Garrett came into the kitchen a few minutes later –late as usual. Charlotte straightened herself up and pushed her hair back off her face and her glasses up higher on her nose. She smiled at him. He reluctantly sat down and took out a spiral notebook and his copy of *A Tree Grows in Brooklyn*.

"Can we only do a half hour today? I've got plans to meet the guys at the gym." Before she could answer, Norma chimed in.

"No, no, Mr. Garrett. You know the rules. One hour." Norma shook her head. Garrett scowled at her as he was now on the receiving end of a finger wag from Norma. "You know your parents say school is very important."

"Yeah, yeah." He turned to Charlotte. "So, where do we start, Glasses?"

"Well, what Norma just said is a perfect segue into talking about the themes of the book, one of which is the important role education plays in Francie's life."

"Uh huh," he said, walking over to the bowl of chips and bringing it to the table.

"Why don't you find three places in the book illustrating why or how education is important to Francie."

Garrett exhaled loudly, stuck his pencil in his mouth, and flopped open his notebook, noisily shuffling the papers until finding a blank sheet.

While he poured through the text, slightly huffing with annoyance, Lindsay walked into the kitchen. In strong contrast to her brothers, Lindsay was a petite and bubbly girl who favored her mother's looks –a perfect blonde bob and bright green eyes.

"Hi Charlotte," she said, making eyes at her like she knew Charlotte was enjoying her proximity to Garrett. Charlotte's eyes bugged out and she shook her head, warning Lindsay from saying anything. Lindsay just grinned at her and giggled. "Come up to my room when you're done."

"Okay," replied Charlotte as Lindsay walked away. Garrett continued to write on his paper and let out a loud huff, realizing he had made an error. He grabbed for an eraser and grazed Charlotte's hand as he did.

Every stringy and frizzy hair on the back of Charlotte's neck stood up on end. She let out a shaky exhale and tried to calm her emotions. Just his slightest touch –accidental though it was –set her heart afire. If only he would see her as anything but a brain in oversized black frames.

One

Damn! I'm late...again. You'd think with nothing to do, I'd get my act together enough to be on time for a family lunch. I fell asleep on the couch after my rigorous night's activities with Dani, spelled with a heart over the "i."

She's a Laker girl. It took me three weeks, and a dinner reservation at Genevieve, to convince her to go out with me, but it was worth the effort. She was insatiable in bed and her flexibility was a total turn on. Without much sleep last night, it's no wonder I passed out on the couch after my morning workout.

I rush past the valet and glance at the incoming call on my cell phone thinking it's Mom checking on my arrival status. It's not Mom. It's only been a few hours since I slipped out of Dani's bed before she woke up this morning and she's already calling me for the second time today. I let it go to voicemail again and figure she'll get the hint. Then again, she likely won't. Dani with a heart over the "i" isn't the brightest bulb in the marquee.

As I race to the restaurant, I scowl knowing Mom's going to have my head. Actually, she's probably used to it by now. I'm surprised they don't give me fake arrival times knowing I'm always ten minutes behind.

I rush through the revolving door of the restaurant, through the bar, and smack into a woman. She brushes against my bum shoulder and the pain burns right through me. Minding the manners Mom hammered into me from a young age, I mutter, "Sorry," when I'm honestly not. I look down and notice something familiar about her.

"Hi, Garrett," she says, sharing a small smile. "It's been a long time. How are you?"

"Um. I'm fine." My brows furrow as I wrack my brain trying to figure out who the hell this woman is. She's short, about five two and roughly my age. I glance down and notice full, round breasts, slightly wide hips and thick thighs. Not my usual type, so I'm pretty sure I haven't slept with her. At least I don't have to worry about that embarrassing scene. She's got chocolate brown eyes, looking at me with warmth. "And...how are you?" Shaking my head I am still trying to place her.

"I'm doing well," she replies, her smile growing.

"I'm glad to hear that," I say, trying to be polite and end this awkward reunion that clearly has me clueless.

"Well...I guess I should go." She turns back and waves to a woman sitting in a far booth of the restaurant. On further inspection, she's waved to Lindsay, my sister, who of course made it to our family lunch on time. Seated with her are my parents, with Mom frowning at me and shaking her head. Like she didn't expect I would be late. Marcus isn't here yet either. Guess the twin thing really does run deep.

"You know Lindsay?" I ask her.

"Uh, yeah," she says, with a small chuckle and a noticeable hint of sarcasm.

"My parents?"

"Of course." She shakes her head slightly like it's hitting her I have no damn clue who she is. Then she confirms my suspicions and just lays it on the line. "You don't know who I am, do you?" Her eyes are alight with humor.

"Umm. I'm afraid you have me at a disadvantage," I splutter, rubbing my hand behind my neck –my tell –before flashing her my most charming, dimpled smile. Before she can respond, a lady in her mid-sixties with salt and pepper hair wearing an outfit appropriate for someone twenty years younger –but this is LA after all –walks over.

"Pardon the interruption," she begins. "I would just be kicking myself if I got home and didn't take advantage of telling you what a big fan I am."

"Oh, thank you," I say, turning on the faux charm I reserve for situations such as this.

"My husband and I loved your book." The lady turns fully toward this mystery woman. "I wish I had it with me for you to sign. Maybe I could get your autograph on something else?" I cock my head to the side and watch Mystery Woman. She turns back toward the elderly lady and smiles sincerely.

"Sure. I'd be happy to sign something."

The lady reaches into her oversized zebra-print bag and produces a pen and small notepad. She hands them to Mystery Woman and turns to me, smiling.

"Who should I make this out to?" asks Mystery Woman.

"Donna and Frank. Your *dear friends*, Donna and Frank."

"My... dear... friends... Donna... and... Frank," Mystery Woman murmurs aloud as she writes a note. Watching her autograph the note, I can't help the grin spreading across my face. Once she finishes, Donna reads through the note, her eyes widening with delight.

"Thank you, Charley," she says.

"My pleasure," replies Charley –Charley? –who looks tickled.

"Charley?" I rack my brain to no avail.

"Yes," replies Donna with pride. "You are standing with the brilliant novelist Charley Windham." She turns back to Charley before walking away. "Thank you again, dear."

"Charley Windham?"

"Uh-huh," responds Charley, giving me a look like I should piece it together.

"Charley Windham. Why does that name sound so familiar?" I rub my hand on the back of my neck while Charley looks at me with amusement. "Wait, you're Charley Windham. Who wrote *The Crossing Guard*?" Charley shakes her head and laughs.

"That's me." Charley giggles, unable to control the wide smile spreading across her face.

"Yes. Now I know. I read your book. In fact, everyone on the tour read it. You couldn't walk around a locker room or airport terminal without seeing someone with it in their hands."

"That's nice to hear." She grins at me with her head tilted and nodding her head slightly up and down, giving me the impression she's waiting for me to say more.

"That explains who you are, and I get you would know who I am, but how do you know my family?"

"That is the question of the moment, isn't it?" She smiles smugly.

"You're enjoying this, aren't you?"

"Immensely." She is grinning unabashedly.

I look back over at my parents and sister and see my brother Marcus walk in through the restaurant's back entrance. After a quick exchange, Lindsay points to where Charley and I are standing. Marcus waves to Charley and she waves back.

"Oh, you know my ugly as shit brother too?"

"Ugly as shit? You're identical twins," she laughs.

"Nah." I shake my head with a playful sneer. "I got the looks. He got the brains."

"You got the looks?" She watches me with a raised brow.

"Yep. All of 'em."

"I suppose you got all of the humility too?" I can hear the humor in her voice.

"Seems more like humiliation these days." I rub the back of my neck and look down at my shoes. I really messed things up and now I don't know if my career is over.

"Hey, don't knock yourself. Not your fault you have shoulder issues." She places a hand on my arm and her slight touch causes all my blood to rush south.

"You follow my career?" I ask, my spirits surprisingly improving. There's something about this woman that's got me intrigued and I don't just mean 'cause I can't place how I know her.

"I've been known to glance at the sports page now and then," she says with smiling eyes.

"So, how did you say you know my brother again?" Marcus, his wife Abbey, and Lindsay start to walk over to us.

"I didn't."

"You're not going to tell me."

"I'm finding it quite entertaining you don't know who I am," she says again.

"Of course I know who you are," I scoff.

"You do?"

"Yes. You're the charming and talented writer having dinner with me on Saturday night." Charley lets out a nervous giggle and glances down at the floor and damn, if that's not the cutest thing I've ever seen.

"You want to have dinner with me on Saturday?" she says on a breath and I wonder how she would breathe my name as she's coming undone beneath me. Before I can respond, Marcus places his hand on her shoulder.

"Well aren't you a sight for sore eyes." Charley turns toward him and Marcus scoops her up into a big hug.

"Good to see you, Marcus. This must be your wife." She turns to the short red head with wide green eyes and a full smile standing between Marcus and Lindsay.

"Yeah, this is Abbey," says Marcus, turning to the side, allowing the small woman to shake Charley's hand.

"Wow. I'm a huge fan," she begins, grasping Charley's hand and pumping it furiously. "The *Crossing Guard* was my favorite book of last year. My book club spent hours discussing it."

"Oh, thank you," says Charley, with the same genuine appreciation she showed to Donna a few minutes ago.

"I didn't realize Marcus knew you. I probably would have begged him to ask you to come meet with us," Abbey continues, still holding onto Charley's hand.

"Oh, believe me, she doesn't owe me any favors. It's the other way around. If it weren't for Charlotte here, I probably wouldn't have gotten into a good college," he says to Abbey.

"Charlotte?" I repeat.

"Of course. Charlotte Windham. You know, our high school English tutor," he says, looking at me like I'm a dumbass.

Charlotte Windham. Charlotte Windham. Then it hits me. "Oh, Glasses. You're Glasses." I smile widely, proud of myself for finally putting it together.

"Yep. I'm *Glasses*," Charlotte sighs loudly. "Well, I need to get going. Great catching up with you all again and nice to meet you Abbey."

"I'm sorry, Charlotte," says Lindsay, shooting daggers at me with her eyes. *What is that death stare for*, I wonder.

"It's okay. Um...give me a call if you want to grab lunch. I'm waiting for a manuscript back from my editor, so I've got a ton of free time." With that, she turns and walks away.

"You're an idiot." Lindsay shakes her head and scowls at me.

"What? What did I do?" I'm flummoxed.